PRAISE FOR KEVIN J. ANDERSON

"Kevin J. Anderson has become the literary equivalent of Quentin Tarantino."
—The Daily Rotation

"Kevin J. Anderson is the hottest writer on (or off) the planet."
—Fort Worth Star-Telegram

"The scope and breadth of Kevin J. Anderson's work is simply astonishing."
—Terry Goodkind

"Kevin J. Anderson is one of the best plotters in the business."
—Brandon Sanderson

"One of the greatest talents writing today, Kevin J. Anderson is a master of adventures that are filled with dynamic, unforgettable characters."
—Sherrilyn Kenyon

SELECTED STORIES

FANTASY

KEVIN J. ANDERSON

WFP
WORDFIRE PRESS

Selected Stories: Fantasy

Kevin J. Anderson

Trade Paperback Edition – 2018
WordFire Press
www.wordfirepress.com
Copyright © 2018 WordFire, Inc.

Hardcover edition ISBN: 978-1-61475-695-8
Trade Paperback edition ISBN: 978-1-61475-689-7
Cover design by Janet MacDonald
Cover image by adobe stock
Kevin J. Anderson, art director
Kevin J. Anderson & Rebecca Moesta, Publishers
Published by
WordFire Press, an imprint of
WordFire, LLC
PO Box 1840
Monument, CO 80132
Join our WordFire Press Readers Group and get free books, sneak previews, updates on new projects, and other giveaways.
Sign up for free at wordfirepress.com

❀ Created with Vellum

CONTENTS

INTRODUCTION

Tell me a story.

It's a game all writers play, an improv act. Some writers are structured; they plan thoroughly, choose carefully, write only what most inspires them, while others can be loose and nimble, reacting quickly and running with an idea, meeting the challenge at hand.

When J.M. Barrie put the Llewellen Davies boys to bed and they pleaded for a story, he made up tales to order about Peter Pan and his adventures. A.A. Milne entertained his son Christopher Robin by telling stories of Winnie-the-Pooh, Rabbit, Owl, and the Hundred Acre Wood. When I was younger, I used to babysit often. Playing with rambunctious kids and trying to get them down to bed, faced with the incessant "Oh, please, can't we stay up just a little longer?" I learned that the only way to trick them was to offer a story. "What do you want to hear?" I would ask. They wanted me to make up Star Trek stories because we had watched *Star Trek* before going to bed, or one time in particular I had to spinoff from a *Space: 1999* episode, continuing the adventure. Other times they wanted stories about dragons or magic bicycles.

Any good babysitter—any good *writer*—had to fill the bill. This was good training, learning how to write a story inspired by a prompt.

In my short story career, I often thought of intriguing concepts to explore, tales that needed to be told. Then other times I would be contacted by anthology editors who, just like those demanding kids in my babysitting years, would say, "Tell me a story about ..." They were putting together a book on sea monsters, time travel, metaphorical unicorns, dragons, even enchanted garments. Enchanted garments? All right, I'll take the challenge. For the anthology *Pandora's Closet*, I wrote one of my funniest and most beloved short stories, "Loincloth," about a spell-cursed ape man's loincloth found by a shy and mousy nerd in a Hollywood prop department.

It's what a writer does. You have an idea and you write the story. If you don't have the idea, you go out and find one. If you have a well-oiled imagination, which you exercise regularly, the ideas will come and you always make the best of it.

One of the lessons I teach in my many master-class writing workshops is to always do your best work. There's no such thing as phoning it in. If you are asked to do a story about a magical garment, don't roll your eyes and write a slapdash story just to meet the deadline and pick up the paycheck. Even if it's just a story for an anthology about purple unicorns, whether or not you can take the theme seriously. Do the best damn purple unicorn story in the volume, or don't accept the job.

No matter what story it is, whatever you write will be some reader's first introduction to your work. So, make a good impression. Besides, the people who buy an anthology about purple unicorns really want to read about purple unicorns.

I have told this story so many times that it actually did result in an anthology of purple unicorn stories, at first as a joke, but then as a full-blown professional anthology, *One Horn to Rule Them All*, which we put together as a charity effort to raise money for the Don Hodge Memorial Scholarship. That proved so successful we did a red unicorn anthology, *A Game of Horns*, and then a dragon anthology, *Dragon Writers*, and a sea monster anthology, *Undercurrents*. Together, the profits from those books have funded dozens of high-end scholarships for the Superstars Writing Seminar.

It's a challenge and it's a game. What am I going to write today? What story will I play with? What idea needs to be explored? Sometimes it will be fantasy, sometimes science fiction, other times edgy horror. The tales in this volume all fall under the general umbrella of fantasy, and it's a big umbrella—from knights and dragons to subtly inhuman shape shifters in the modern world, or even superstitions and beliefs of ancient sea monsters that might or might not be real.

Tell me a story, you ask.

Turn the page.

—Kevin J. Anderson

In college, while I was a determined, aspiring writer, I took a Japanese history class and became very interested in the myths, legends, culture. It seemed a very fertile ground for fantasy tales. I read a lot of the short fiction of Lafcadio Hearn, whose Japanese-inspired fairy tales and ghost stories were rich, clever, and inspirational. I came home one day from my classes, sat down at my electric typewriter (yes, that's how long ago it was), and wrote this story in one sitting.

I sold it to a nice, well-respected small press magazine, Grue, *and was very surprised some months later when I received a notice that "The Old Man and the Cherry Tree" had been selected for* The Year's Best Fantasy Stories *anthology published by DAW Books.*

THE OLD MAN AND THE
CHERRY TREE

H e had lived almost his entire life within the walls of the Buddhist monastery. The priests there told him the Shogun would cut off his head if he ventured outside ever again.

Many years before, his father had been a powerful lord, a *daimyo*. But the Shogun had gone to war with the *daimyo*, ordering that all the lord's family be executed. On the final night, while the father sat bemoaning his imminent loss of his life, the boy's mother had managed to steal away to the nearby monastery with her dearest son. She begged the head priest to save him, to secretly give her some other boy to be executed in her son's stead. The man told her it would be improper for a priest to undertake such a task; but after she offered large sums of money, the priest admitted that the monastery was sorely in need of a second golden image of Amida for the altar. Besides, the boy he had in mind for the exchange was a mere foundling anyway, given over to the care of the monastery however the priests saw fit.

They struck the bargain. The mother kissed her son, then gave him to the priest as he emerged from the monastery with a second boy who somewhat resembled the *daimyo's* son.

Before the priest could take her son into the monastery walls forever, she reached into her robes and carefully withdrew a package wrapped in fine silk. Upon seeing the silk, the priest's eyes opened eagerly. "This is for my son," she said, handing it to the child. "Your father's blade—the sword of a great *daimyo*." She unwrapped the silk to reveal a lovely jewel-encrusted short sword. Gold covered the grip, and fine characters danced on the blade. "You must keep it always by you because it will bring you good luck. When all else has been forgotten, still it will tell you the name of your father—see, it is engraved on the blade. You will learn to read it after the good priest has taught you the characters." The priest's eyes reflected the gold of the sword, and he fervently promised to care for the boy. The mother bowed and disappeared with her false son into the night shadows from which she had come.

The boy grew up in the monastery. The priests soon stopped trying to take his father's sword from him when they realized they would never be able to sell it, not with the name of the rebellious *daimyo* engraved on the blade. And they never made the effort to teach him to read, considering themselves safer if the boy was not constantly reminded of his true identity.

The boy took his pleasure in gardening, caring for the plants and trees in the monastery's beautiful garden. He was especially captivated by a single cherry tree which had been planted by three novices the very morning the Shogun had cut the heads off the rest of the boy's family. The small cherry tree had stood so frail and frightened in the garden, reminding the boy of how he must appear to the other monks.

As the boy grew older, he never shaved his head, or took the vows, nor studied the sutras as did the other novices. He planted and tended his flowers and trees and shrubs in the garden, until the monastery became known for the beauty harbored within its walls. But above all, the boy—now a young man, actually—tended the single cherry tree with all the love he possessed, until it became the glory of the entire garden. In spring the cherry tree would explode with pure white flowers, as if a sweet-scented winter had dropped gently into the monastery garden. At the time, it was said that the blossoms lingered longer on this cherry tree than on any other in all of Japan, and people traveled great distances to gather up some of the fallen petals, which they used for curing the sick and for making love potions.

Sometimes, in secret, the *daimyo's* son would climb up into the tree and look out over the monastery walls which kept him imprisoned. None of the priests had bothered to tell him that the old Shogun had died, nor that the new one did not care about the young man's family name. Instead, he sat up in the boughs under the silver moonlight and looked out to see the wide world he would never be able to explore, listening to the wind in the leaves of his tree and the faint sounds of snoring from the monks' sleeping quarters.

In time, he came to consider the cherry tree his closest and dearest friend. He talked to it as he tended the rest of his garden, and the other novices began to snicker and laugh among themselves about the strange gardener who talked to trees.

So, the years passed. The tree continued to grow, and the gardener continued to grow older. Year after year the white blossoms came, and the *daimyo's* son—now an old man—took no greater joy than in watching the petals drift in the wind. He wept for those that caught like kites on an updraft and escaped, floating down on the other side of the monastery wall.

Each spring many people came to see the blossoms, some even making grand processions all the way from Kyoto. The pilgrims talked among themselves about the exquisite beauty of the delicate white flowers, and of the glowing, honest satisfaction in the face of the old gardener who stood so proudly beside his tree.

And then one year the tree did not blossom.

The other plants in the old man's garden launched forth their leaves and flowers as always, but day after day the cherry tree remained barren, as motionless as a stillborn babe. The people who came to see the tree departed in disappointment—it had once been magnificent, they said sadly, but the old cherry tree had died, and they would have to go elsewhere from now on.

The monks began to talk that they would soon cut down the marvelous tree and burn its wood in the fire.

The old man could not bear to hear this and, recalling the days of his youth, he somehow managed to climb into the tree, searching the branches for buds, any small flickering of life. But the branches were as dry and as barren as the paper on which the monks copied their sutras. The old man saw other cherry trees in the distance, gleaming with their white flowers and scattering petals into the wind. Then his heart knew for certain that the old cherry tree had died, and he threw his arms around the lifeless bole of his only friend, weeping until the curious monks came out and called for him to come down. His legs were weak, but he managed to descend the tree and stood shaking. The monks left him, whispering among themselves, and went back to their work.

As he looked long and hard at the lifeless branches of the cherry tree, the old man decided what he must do. That night, when all the monks slept, he crept out into the darkness of the garden and lifted up one of the flat rocks he had long ago placed around the cherry tree. Under the rock rested his father's jeweled sword, glinting in the light of the dying moon—the colorful silk wrappings had rotted, but the sword was untarnished and as sharp as ever. The old man looked grimly at the blade.

There was one way to show one's utmost devotion, to remove grief and end this life of confinement and pain. Brave warriors followed their lords to death, committing *seppuku* to show their absolute loyalty no matter how their lord had died. And if the warriors could slit their bellies in an ecstasy of pain and honor, couldn't the old man do the same at the death of his dearest companion, his cherry tree? His father's sword was a special sword, the sword of a great *daimyo*, perhaps even containing a little magic. This act would be his final gift to the tree he had loved for so many years.

The old man loosened his robe and squatted down as near as he could to the dead cherry tree. He held the sharp point of the *daimyo's* sword against his stomach, looking down at the engraved characters signifying his father's name—but he still could not read them. The night was cold and crisp, probably the last such night in spring. The noise of the rustling barren branches above sounded to him like a death rattle.

Done properly, *seppuku* would have been a grand occasion—with many priests and faithful companions. But the old man did not have even so much as a white cloth to sit upon. Tradition required that once he had slit his belly, once he had proven his devotion and bravery, his closest friend was then permitted to strike off his head to end the pain. But the old man had no best friend, and so, after he made the deep thrust and long sideways cut, he was forced to bear the pain as best he could, until he could bear it no longer ... and then it made no difference. His blood spilled onto the earth.

~

THE NEXT MORNING the monks came out into the garden for their tea and found him there. They shook their heads, muttering at how the lonely old man had finally ended his life, but that he had not even done *seppuku* properly. The old gardener had become well-known and many people—bringing their donations—would have come to see the death ceremony. The old man had been very inconsiderate not to let them know of his intentions. Some of the monks came to carry him away and marveled at the beautiful sword they found upon him. No one knew where he had gotten it, and none of them recognized the name of the long-forgotten *daimyo* written on the blade. The monks cleaned the sword and placed it in their treasury.

But that morning, when the sun rose high enough that its rays struck the old cherry tree, something wondrous happened. The wind picked up. A shiver ran through the ground as a silence descended on the garden. Some of the monks dropped their tea, burning their fingers, scowling at each other. They all looked at the dead cherry tree.

The barren branches trembled, as if the old tree were straining with all its might ... and suddenly every branch, even the smallest twigs, brought forth a deep red flower, as scarlet as fresh blood. As the monks watched, gaping in amazement, the tree covered itself with flowers, more than it had ever borne before.

One brash novice crept up to the new flowers in wonder and touched them. He cried that the petals felt wet, then yelped in pain. "It burns! My fingers!" He tried to wipe the moisture off on his robe, then ran to hide inside the monastery.

Word spread quickly throughout the land, and people flocked to see the Blood Tree, as it had been named. The Shogun himself came to see the miracle, and when the monks told the story of the old man who had tended the tree, and of the mysterious sword he had used to commit *seppuku*, another old man from the vicinity recalled the name of the rebellious *daimyo* and how a previous Shogun had executed the entire family. The others remembered how at the same time the monastery had received a generous donation from the wife of the *daimyo* ... and although they could not be certain, many guessed the identity of the gardener.

The Shogun commanded that the monks bring him the ashes of the old man, and they carried out a simple clay urn, bowing their heads in embarrassment that they had not given the ashes a more ornate resting place. The Shogun spoke in his most respectful voice so that all could hear. "If this old man was truly the son of a rebellious *daimyo*, trapped for all his life in the sanctuary of the monastery walls for his own protection, long after it was necessary, I ... I, the Shogun, now pardon him. I set him free so that he need no longer remain inside these walls."

So saying, the Shogun reached into the urn and flung the ashes high in the air, watching as they drifted out to explore the world on their own.

The Blood Tree shuddered, and, with a cracking sound, collapsed into a heap of charred splinters, burned from the inside out. The people gasped, and even the Shogun was amazed.

MANY YEARS LATER, wandering peddlers could sometimes be seen at night, keeping to the shadows, and entering houses where the seeds of dissent had already been sown, secretly offering to sell splinters of the Blood Tree which would cause almost-instant bad fortune and possibly even death to one's enemies.

The Shogun caught several of these peddlers and executed them.

Jules Verne was one of the many classic writers who influenced me when I was young, eager, and dedicated to becoming a writer. Even at only eight or nine years old I would curl up in a chair and struggle through big, leather-bound volumes of A Journey to the Centre of the Earth, The Mysterious Island, *and* 20,000 Leagues Under the Sea. *This fascination is reflected not only in several of my short stories, but in my novel* Captain Nemo, *an exploration of the lives of Jules Verne and his character Nemo.*

When I was asked to write a story based on H.P. Lovecraft's chilling Cthulhu Mythos, I simply couldn't resist folding Captain Nemo into the story. What if the Nautilus encountered some ancient, cursed ruins, deep under the sea?

20,000 YEARS UNDER THE SEA

H e dreamed of tentacles again. The battered *Nautilus* cruised listlessly through uncharted waters, its engine struggling, pumps and pistons wheezing like an injured man trying to catch his breath. The hull seams showed the strain of the recent battle, and some rivets leaked water, preventing the armored sub-marine boat from diving deep.

But the dreams of her captain were darker and more restless than the seas around them.

In his stateroom, Nemo's bunk was padded with fine cushions, and he tossed under silken sheets that were fit for a caliph—*stolen* from the corrupt caliph, as was the *Nautilus* and everything else.

In the nightmare, he fought alongside his loyal crewmen against the slimy, thrashing tentacles. Though Nemo's true war was against evil men and their unquenchable thirst for slaughter, the giant squid was a mindless beast of nature. The squid had tried to crush the armored hull in its suckered embrace, and Nemo and his men fought it with cutlasses, harpoons, and daggers, covering the deck with foul-smelling slime and a gushing of black ink like a shadow made out of acid. A well-placed harpoon blinded the monster's eye and penetrated its rudimentary brain, then the wounded creature released its death grip, slipping away from the sub-marine boat and into the sea, taking four crewmen with it.

Captain Nemo and his surviving sailors tended their injuries.

The men already had many scars from years of engineering slavery at Caliph Robur's prison camp of Rurapente. After escaping in fire and blood, Nemo had declared his own war on war; nature, however, didn't care about their battle or their pain—the giant squid proved that.

Nemo would not be deterred by storms or by attacking monsters. He tried to rest while Mr. Harding and his engineers repaired the motors. Others caulked and welded hull breaches, reinforcing the seams on the wounded vessel. The navigator steered through the night, looking for some sheltered place where they could put in and complete repairs.

Exhausted and sore, Nemo tried to rest, if only for a few hours, but nightmares of that soulless tentacled creature granted him no peace. Even in sleep, Captain Nemo continued his battle....

Thus, it was a relief when Mr. Harding tapped on his cabin door. "Sorry to disturb you, sir, but we found an island. Looks uninhabited."

Nemo climbed from his bunk, disentangling himself from the silken sheets that reminded him too much of tentacles. "I'm on my way."

∾

NEMO WAS AMAZED his navigator had been able to find this bleak and rugged island. With its crescent-shaped cove bounded by black walls that plunged down to the waterline, it reminded Nemo of a claw.

When they encountered the giant squid, the *Nautilus* had been stalking naval battleships in the southern seas, eager to eliminate the bloodthirsty soldiers before they could prey upon innocents. Nemo left any merchant vessel unmolested, but French, British, or Spanish warships were sunk to the bottom of the sea. No mercy. The sailors aboard would have shown no mercy to those they preyed upon: innocent women and children who became pawns in political power plays, like Nemo's own wife and son, like the families of the other engineering prisoners from Rurapente.

Because the seas were so rough south of Terra del Fuego, few sailing vessels wandered far afield for the pleasure of exploring.

Now, damaged and limping along, the *Nautilus* had blundered upon a bleak no-man's-land not far from the untouched shores of the Antarctic continent. This isolated, never-inhabited island was surrounded by mist and freezing drizzle.

The sun was only a pale, gray fuzz swathed in mist when Nemo emerged from the hatch with Mr. Harding and engineers named Louart and Fallon. He inspected the glistening hull for traces of slime or pools of blood, but the spray of rough waters had washed the *Nautilus* clean.

Nemo inhaled the salty, mist-laden air, but there was a sour, rotten taint to it. Louart asked, "What's that smell, Captain?"

"This is a sheltered cove," Harding suggested. "Maybe a school of fish ..."

Fallon said, "I remember each year when the alewives would die off and wash ashore. Made the whole port stink."

Nemo did see numerous fish floating belly up on the surface of the cove. "But these are all different species. They wouldn't have died off at once."

Harding got down to business. "No matter, Captain. We're here to make repairs and be on our way."

Nemo gazed up at the sheer cliffs. Seabirds wheeled about, not the usual gulls but black ones that looked like bats. As they hunted in the shadowy mist, their screeches were haunting.

In some trick of the warming dawn, the mist thinned, and hazy light dappled the surrounding cliffs and the mountains inland. Nemo saw more than just boulders and outcroppings: the cliffs were scattered with blocky geometrical shapes, graceful pillars, magnificent but crumbling towers. Even from this distance, with details blurred by fog, the structures looked unspeakably ancient.

"They're ruins, Cap'n!" Fallon cried.

Nemo frowned. "We're off the coast of Antarctica. No civilization ever existed this far south. Even the savages in Terra del Fuego have nothing more than huts."

Louart pointed toward the mysterious city inland. "And yet, Monsieur Capitaine—they exist."

Nemo turned to his second-in-command. "Mr. Harding, I'll let you continue the repairs. I intend to see that city."

Harding never argued. "Suit yourself, Captain. We have plenty of work to do." His bearded face was smeared with grease and his hands were dirty. "I spent hours in the engine room. We'll have to take the motors apart, replace one of the screws. That squid did us a lot of harm."

"Can you fix it?" Nemo asked.

The other man raised his eyebrows. "Of course, we can fix it— we built the boat in the first place. It's just a matter of time."

"Time to explore, then."

Joined by five companions, Nemo took a boat to shore, searching for a safe landing spot against the cliffs. At last, they encountered a cleverly hidden road cut at an angle down the rock, all but invisible except when approached face-on. The wide path was paved with moss-slick flagstones cut from black obsidian. The carved steps were at the wrong height for human legs.

Inland, the strange, bleak island was littered with ruins, white stone structures with trapezoidal doorways that were too low and too wide for an average person. The streets spread out in unsettling angles, and the walls were constructed with a disorienting oblique- ness that made Nemo feel as if he were falling when he faced them.

Temples or observatories crowned outcroppings, and huge columns rose high, but many were broken, strewn about like the bones of prehistoric animals. Boulevards led across a high plateau and then plunged over a cliff edge. Rounded arenas had once hosted some kind of unknown sport or spectacle.

On the lintels of collapsed buildings and an altar of what must have been a temple of worship, or sacrifice, Nemo saw a repeated dot pattern that seemed familiar to him, but he couldn't place it.

Standing tall, dark stone obelisks were covered with strange glyphs unlike any alphabet Nemo had ever seen—a mixture of runes, hieroglyphics, and squiggles. He had learned many languages in his life, and after years of oppression at Rurapente, he was fluent in reading and writing Arabic. His engineers understood the language of mathematics. The language of the ancient engravings seemed an amalgam of all those things.

Even in the gray cold mist Nemo smelled brimstone, and a pall of old smoke seemed hung in the air. These ruins reminded him far too much of Rurapente....

He had been selectively captured in the Crimean War along

with other scientists, engineers, and visionaries. The evil Caliph Robur forced them to work in his isolated prison. As the ambitious French engineer de Lesseps carved a channel across the Suez Isthmus that would connect the Mediterranean to the Red Sea, the caliph had commanded Nemo and his fellow workers to build him a warship unlike any the world had seen: an armored vessel to prey upon trade ships that came through the new Suez Canal. He could become the world's most accomplished pirate, the greatest leader, the master of the world.

For years Nemo and his comrades had toiled in slavery. They were rewarded with wives whom they learned to love, even families that gave them a spark of solace in their captivity. Caliph Robur had made the *Nautilus* his fortress, until Nemo and his men overthrew and assassinated him during a test voyage, stole the armored sub-marine boat, and raced to Rurapente to save their families. But they were too late. The caliph's political rivals had already marched upon the secret base and slaughtered everyone....

Nemo could never burn away the images of his return to Rurapente. The foundations of buildings stood like blackened stumps of teeth. The smelting refineries had been caved in, windows smashed, bricks crumbled. The living quarters had been burned to ash and slag. Everything ... destroyed.

The oppressive silence had been broken only by a faint whistle of wind. As he stood there, Nemo had thought he heard the shouts of raiders, the crackle of flames, the clang of scimitars against makeshift weapons, or against soft flesh, hard bone. Screams of pain and pleas for mercy from the desperate slaves, the women, the children—everyone who had endured life at Rurapente. All dead.

And was this place any different?

He and his companions found weathered statues hewn from lava rock, details blurred by time and something more. Together, two crewmen pried loose a stone figure that had toppled face-first into the crumbling gravel and frozen mud. When they lifted it up, Nemo saw not the figure of any man, but a creature with a face that was a hideous mass of tentacles, and eyes that even in the pitted and eroded stone looked as empty and unimaginable as the universe.

Louart paled and made the sign of the Cross, though he had not previously demonstrated any penchant for religion. "It must be one of their gods," said Fallon.

"Or one of their demons," Nemo said.

They continued to explore, studying friezes that depicted the daily life of a civilization inconceivable even to the most fevered opium dream, populated by barrel-like creatures with starfish heads. None of the men spoke, uneasy, awed, and intimidated.

The sour smell of rot was more pronounced as he led the way to the steep path down to the cove. The sun ducked behind the mist again, and gray shrouds thickened around them.

Mr. Harding was on the upper deck of the *Nautilus* waiting for the captain. "Those are ruins even greater than the city of Pompeii," Nemo told him.

The gruff second-in-command scratched his bearded chin. "Then you'll be even more interested in what we found in the cove, Captain. There's an even larger ancient city submerged under the water." His lips quirked in a small smile, "And this one's intact."

$\sim$

WHEN THE *NAUTILUS* had fought its way to the shelter of the natural harbor at night, no one had been looking deep below. As Nemo peered into the deep cove, he could see the shimmering fever-dream architecture of the sunken city. "That city down there has waited a long time for us. It might have been submerged for twenty thousand years or more."

"I don't intend on staying here anywhere near that long, Captain," Harding said. "We'll get to work."

Nemo picked Louart and three other men to don exploration suits and join him. The Rurapente engineers had designed the suits for Caliph Robur, after he lied that he wanted to explore the bottom of the sea; in truth, Robur had needed those suits so his underwater army could augur holes in the hulls of helpless ships.

Nemo gathered the waterproof leather suit, the weights, the buckles, the helmet, and the wrappings that sealed all the seams. As he and his team fastened their helmets and attached the breathing hoses to tanks so they could inhale the stale compressed air, he thought again of his war against war.

The *Nautilus* could have been an unprecedented means of exploration, a boon for science. Before being captured in the Crimea, Nemo had seen much of the world, dared many adventures, but thanks to the smoke and the misery of Rurapente his spirit of curiosity had been snuffed out like a bright ember under a bootheel. Now, though, this ancient and mysterious underwater city intrigued him.

He sank slowly and gracefully toward the bottom. The pressure of the water closed around him like a squeezing fist, but the reinforced suit protected him. His weights pulled him down until the *Nautilus* was only a strange angular shape that eclipsed the rippling daylight. The other men spread out as they drifted down and landed with slow gracefulness. Together, they turned on their galvanic lights, shining yellow into the gloom.

The buildings of the sunken city were similar to the ruins up above, but here they were better preserved. The walls stood upright and arches gracefully framed entryways into ominous temples.

Taking the lead, Nemo walked with his armored boots on the silty floor, sending up puffs of murk to expose broad flat flagstones. They passed titanic facades, statues, obelisks covered with markings, friezes that depicted the creatures with the barrel-bodies and starfish heads, and another species that were formless conglomerations of bubbles or masses of pseudopods that seemed to be servants or guardians to the starfish-headed creatures. And more images of the tentacle-faced creature from the toppled statue. The arches and rune-encrusted pillars again bore that familiar dot pattern. Perhaps it was something from a book Caliph Robur kept inside the *Nautilus* library.

They spread out to explore, and their galvanic lights bobbed along. The sunken metropolis carried a weight of ancientness, a weariness of years that extended far beyond the twenty thousand years he had suggested. Perhaps these buildings had been erected long before humans had ever populated this planet.

A golden glow flared and then died down, but the suit made Nemo sluggish, and the hazy glow had faded by the time he turned. He felt a chill. He had encountered many predators under the sea, had fought off sharks and a giant squid, but this fear was different and inexplicable.

Louart approached him, signaling with a gloved hand. The two men pressed their face plates together so that when Louart's voice echoed through the thick glass. "Notice, mon Capitaine. No coral, no seaweed, no rubble."

Nemo indicated a cluster of perfectly placed sea anemones and a large fan of corral, but Louart shook his head inside the helmet. They touched panes of glass again. "Those are intentional—decorations. Something is *tending* this city."

Nemo realized the other man was right. Always when he ventured to the sea bottom, the marine flora was scattered and lush: sponges, shellfish, anchored kelp, and waving fronds of seaweed. Here, though, the cove appeared sterile. He realized that he hadn't seen any fish.

The group spread out again, wary. Nemo shone his light around, found a line of imposing arches that seemed to guide him on. He walked under the first span, and the second, until he saw a domed and thick-walled structure ahead, sealed and armored like a bunker ... or a crypt.

Nemo felt drawn to it, as if compelled. The vault door was barricaded with a complex stone mechanism ... clean, smooth stone. Any normal ruins would have been encrusted with marine growth and cemented shut by coral, but the lines here were razor sharp and clear of debris.

He shone the yellow galvanic beam to illuminate the door. It was covered by a stylized bas-relief that showed a creature with the smooth dome of a skull and baleful red eyes that glowed with inset phosphorescent jewels. The lower half of the creature's face was covered with twisting, curling tentacles.

Though the thing was frightening, Nemo felt a tantalizing tug on his heart that ignited his anger. This thing with the tentacled face symbolized Nemo's own hatred toward those who wrought violence, and it seemed to possess a power to eradicate war. This was something far more deadly than the *Nautilus*, if only he would set it free....

With great difficulty, he pulled himself away and withdrew beneath the looming arches. He could hear his breathing in the helmet, and his heart was pounding like drums. He looked around for his companions.

One figure, Louart, stood close to a tall, ethereal spire of rock carved into delicately balanced segments. The man studied the carvings, then pulled himself to a higher section to see.

Although the sunken ruins were perfectly preserved, they were still fragile with unspeakable age. As Louart placed weight against the joints, the segmented spire wobbled and bent. He pushed himself backward and out of the way as the stone sections collapsed.

The galvanic lights flashed in random directions as the other men backed away from the tumbling stone. Suddenly, the golden glow appeared at the edge of Nemo's vision, brightening and rushing forward. He caught only a glimpse out of the curved helmet.

A swarm of light and bubbles erupted along the corridors of the ancient city. It was a mass of living spheres, like gelatinous blind eyes clumped into a sentient form. All the spheres turned forward, as if targeting the intruder who had knocked down the spire.

Louart saw the thing coming and flailed away. The bubble mass moved so swiftly that it reached the man before the last spire block had tumbled to the ocean floor. The shapeless amoeboid swarmed over Louart. He fought with his arms and legs, but the bubble creature surrounded him and *squeezed*.

Nemo and his companions hurried to Louart's defense, but they were too slow underwater. The ocean was so incredibly silent. Nemo and one other man had spears; the others carried scimitars. The bubble thing continued to contract around its victim, and a sudden splash of red exploded in Louart's helmet, filming the faceplate.

Nemo hurled his harpoon, and it glided through the water, sizzling into the amoeboid thing, puncturing several of the spheres before it disappeared into the mass. But the formless creature rearranged itself, extending pseudopods in other directions. By now Louart was surely dead, perhaps even half digested. The other crewman threw his spear, to no effect.

The bubble thing squirmed along and retreated among the empty buildings of the sunken city. Nemo knew that it could have killed the rest of them, but the creature had retaliated only against the one man who had caused damage.

The other men were panicked, and Nemo pointed upward. His three comrades tore off their weights and floated upward to the waiting *Nautilus*.

Nemo remained in the ancient city, warily looking around. He glanced back toward the tantalizing, armored tomb that he hadn't had the nerve to explore, then he, too, released his weight belt and swam up to daylight.

～

EVEN WITHOUT LOUART'S BODY, the *Nautilus* crew held a solemn funeral for him. Afterward, Harding came to stand in the doorway of the captain's quarters. "We've lost too many crew already, Captain."

Nemo sat at his small desk but did not nod. "We would all be dead if we'd stayed at Rurapente. This way, at least we can keep fighting."

"Fight against what, Captain? A giant squid? Some primordial monster in an ancient city?"

"The world is not a safe place, Mr. Harding, and there are other kinds of wars besides the one we chose. We can either give up, or we can continue our fight. This is a setback, but it is not a defeat."

Nemo stared at the books on the shelves, ancient Arabic tomes that Caliph Robur had considered essential—military strategy reports and treatises about the use of bladed weapons, instructional manuals on methods of torture (some of which masqueraded as medical texts). But he thought he remembered seeing something ...

"When will the repairs be completed?"

His second in command stood in cold silence for a moment before answering, "Tomorrow, sir."

"Then let me read tonight."

After hours of paging through documents, he found the volume that contained the familiar dot pattern he'd seen on so many of the ruins. It was a thick handwritten book bound in a curious pale leather. The text inside had been penned in a dark brown ink; all the words were scribed in a trembling hand, as if the author were afraid to put into words the nightmarish thoughts that consumed his brain. *Necronomicon*.

After years as the caliph's prisoner, Nemo was fluent in Arabic, but this writing seemed to be an odd archaic dialect, written by a man named Abdul al-Hazred. Pages and pages of speculations seemed utter gibberish, something concocted in the hashish houses of Cairo or scrawled by a man dying from a madness plague.

According to the mad Arab, the dot pattern was a sign of the Old Ones, creatures from beyond time and space that had settled Earth soon after its formation, long before any natural life had emerged from the ooze. He saw drawings of the starfish-headed things depicted in statues in both the above-ground ruins and the sunken city. The *Necronomicon*'s ravings told how the Old Ones had found a way to traverse the airless chasms of open space, how they had created and enslaved a race of shapeless sentient clusters of protoplasm called Shoggoths that were their servants, their guardians, their caretakers.

The preposterous imagined history laid out a march of epochal events, how a race of tentacle-faced beings—immense and powerful strangers from beyond the stars—had engaged in a great war against the Old Ones, nearly wiping them out, but the Shoggoths and the Old Ones fought back, defeating the octopoid creatures, at least for a time. And the Old Ones had retreated into their cities beneath the sea.

Nemo thought the ruined city on this mysterious island might have been one of those ancient and impressive dwellings of the Old Ones. And the shapeless bubble thing that had attacked Louart—was that a Shoggoth?

The bas-relief carved in the doorway of the armored crypt was much like the octopoid race. The *Necronomicon* named the beings in a word written in blocky letters, as if al-Hazred had dared himself to write the word: CTHULHU.

He closed the book. Rationally speaking, Nemo didn't believe any of it. And yet in a primitive and easily frightened corner of his mind, he thought he knew the answers.

~

MR. HARDING DELIVERED the welcome news that repairs were nearly completed and the *Nautilus* could be under way by nightfall.

The crew let out a ragged cheer. After the death of Louart, the oppressive anxiety that hung over the abandoned island and the ruined city had begun to seep into their psyche like mildew in a dank tomb.

Nemo, however, heard the report from his second-in-command as if it were distant background noise. He wasn't yet finished with this ancient sunken city. The tales from the *Necronomicon* had inflamed his imagination, caught hold of him like an incurable fever.

If he had read the ravings of the mad Arab in the camp of Rurapente, he would have discounted it all, but after what he had seen, not just the statues and cyclopean buildings, but the appearance of the murderous—protective?—Shoggoth that had killed Louart, he knew it had to be real. And that thing sealed in the armored tomb pulled on him like the inescapable current of the fabled maelstrom off the coast of Norway.

"I'm going back down there, Mr. Harding." He raised his voice and glanced at his crewmen at their stations on the bridge. "I'd like three volunteers to accompany me—but I won't require it." He didn't speak further, because he didn't want to be challenged to explain what he was doing or why.

Harding looked skeptical, but he held his tongue. The crew were terrified, knowing what had happened to their comrade, but they were Nemo's men and they would do anything for him. In the end, he had more volunteers than he needed.

As he suited up, Nemo felt preoccupied, his thoughts focused on what he knew was down there. In his life he had fought pirates, been shipwrecked, crossed Africa in a balloon, fought in the Crimean War, and suffered years of imprisonment under a murderous caliph who wanted to be the master of the world. But he doubted he would ever face anything as nerve-wracking as this. His obsession went beyond fear.

In their weighted underwater suits, the four explorers plunged to the bottom of the cove, shining their galvanic lanterns into the murk. They were all more wary now, seeing movement in every shadow, alert for the golden glow of the lurking Shoggoth. The men each carried a spear in one hand and a cutlass in the other, although the previous day's encounter had shown that such primitive defenses were ineffective against the Shoggoth.

This time, Nemo was pulled by an invisible force, like a questing tongue drawn to a broken tooth. He felt a call of that other being whose very image and name exuded awe. *Cthulhu.* The crypt seemed to contain more power than Nemo would need to win his war against war.

The four galvanic beams shone out, illuminating the arches that led to the squat armored building. The circular walls were like low battlements surrounding the sealed temple—or was it a tomb?—of an Elder God.

The other men spread out, holding their spears and cutlasses, on guard for the swarming mass of one of the Old Ones' guardians. But Nemo faced the graven image of the cosmic creature. This being was different from the builders of the ancient sunken city; it might have caused the destruction of the starfish-headed Old Ones. But if so, why would they build a temple to it here? Why honor Cthulhu with such an impressive and elaborate tomb?

He ran his gloved hands along the complex locking mechanism that sealed the crypt door. The stone components were carefully carved and arranged like a puzzle, a mystic trigger built by minds immeasurably superior to his own.

This mechanism was a problem unlike other engineering challenges he had faced in Rurapente, but his hands had their instincts. He applied his mind to the problem, sliding the components sideways, then down, then back into a different interlocking configuration. Something seemed to be guiding him. He felt the stone door thrum beneath his fingertips, as if an energy inside were building, awakening.

Next to him, the men scrambled backward, and Nemo turned to see if the Shoggoth was coming, but his companions were staring at him, at the temple ... at the door cracking open. What seeped out was not a golden glow, but the opposite—an emptiness of light, a shadow that sucked at the beams of their galvanic lamps.

The water grew suddenly colder, penetrating even his thick undersea suit. The stone door spread wider, and darkness boiled out, along with an ominous emerging figure—a titanic looming shape that seemed much too large to have been contained within the structure.

A current blew Nemo backward like a howling storm wind as the crypt burst open, and the enormous thing with baleful eyes and facial tentacles emerged. The statues had conveyed only a hint of the overwhelming cosmic *presence* of what Abdul al-Hazred had named Cthulhu.

Then Nemo realized what he should have known from the start —that this was not a temple or a tomb ... but a *prison*.

One of his men thrashed in a frantic effort to swim away, but the reawakened Cthulhu turned a horrible, maddening gaze upon him—and the man's struggles immediately ceased. He drifted motionless, struck dead by the mere sight.

The galvanic lamps flashed wildly in all directions as the other two fled. Nemo was stunned and tumbling, trying to reorient himself in the water. He slammed into one of the stone walls and held on for balance. Nemo's mind couldn't contain the immensity of the emerging Cthulhu, a being that had been locked away for twenty thousand years or more beneath the sea.

What have I unleashed?

The water around him suddenly glowed, frothing golden as if illuminated by an unknown and insane source of light. Through his faceplate, he saw a roiling blob of bubbles, a conglomeration of translucent spheres that might or might not have been eyes—it was the Shoggoth returned to continue its attack.

But the formless thing did not pursue Nemo or his companions; instead, it confronted the horrific Elder God. The light in the water continued to grow, and another Shoggoth streaked in from a separate part of the city. Then a third—and four more!

The Old Ones may have been long extinct in this isolated city, but they had left these shapeless but somehow faithful creatures to maintain their cursed metropolis. The Shoggoths did more than just maintain the buildings, arches, and sunken gardens; they were also here to keep the Cthulhu thing imprisoned.

Nemo and his men tried to find shelter behind the enormous facades, unable to do anything but watch. In their scramble away, they had dropped their cutlasses and spears. Nemo's eyes were so blasted that he could barely see details in the glaring light, the masses of bubbles, the thrashing tentacles, and a defiant roar that vibrated through the fabric of the universe.

The Shoggoths swept in and surrounded the powerful, unspeakably evil creature that had emerged from its millennial prison. The formless creatures showed no vengeance toward the *Nautilus* men seeming to regard them as utterly beneath notice.

Nemo and his companions tore away their weighted belts and clawed their way upward, rising toward the distant surface while expecting to be struck dead at any moment.

Below, the battle continued with all the fury of an active undersea volcano. The emerging Cthulhu tore Shoggoths to pieces, ripping the masses of bubbles apart, but the spheres reconverged. The Shoggoths were many, and they had been placed there for the sole purpose of guarding this monster. In a hurricane of golden light and swirling pseudopods, they drove the Cthulhu thing back, unable to destroy it—how does one kill a godlike being that has existed since before time?—but at least the Shoggoths could contain it. They surrounded the ancient monster in a cocoonlike embrace and pushed it back toward the tomb chamber.

Nemo finally broke the surface of the water, and he detached his helmet, gasping. The muffled sounds suddenly grew louder; next to him, the men couldn't stop screaming. Nemo's own throat was raw, and he knew he must have been screaming as well.

Careless and terrified, they dropped their helmets into the water and climbed the rungs to fight their way aboard the imagined safety of the *Nautilus*.

Mr. Harding stood watching them, surprised and alarmed. "Engines are ready to go, Captain, but what—"

Below, the supernatural storm continued to unleash explosions of light and inky shadows. "We must depart immediately!" Nemo said. "Now!"

Harding didn't argue. Seeing the expressions of absolute terror, not just on the other sailors but on their brave captain as well, the sailors moved more swiftly than they ever had in their lives.

When he spoke, Nemo's voice was torn and hoarse. "Take us away from this island. Far, far away."

The repaired engines hummed, and the sub-marine boat lumbered forward, picking up speed. Beneath them, the cove's deep water looked like a storm of lights and fire, inconceivable colors in a simmering battle that Nemo himself may have triggered ... but one in which he could do nothing to fight on either side.

"What was down there, Captain?"

"Nothing I could understand, Mr. Harding."

The second-in-command gave a small nod, then focused on business, intent on more than cosmic monsters, Elder Gods, or vanished alien cities. "The *Nautilus* is in prime condition again, Captain. Engines at full power. Hull integrity, ramming blades, and reinforced bulkheads all check out. We can continue our mission."

Nemo stared ahead through the dragon's-eye portholes. The *Nautilus* left the mysterious island behind and cut across the water into dark and uncharted seas. His own war against human hatred and bloodshed was an all-consuming struggle, a war so big that he knew it could never be won ... still, the battle had to be fought.

Yet, the war he had just discovered between the Old Ones and Cthulhu was so much vaster, so much more ancient, so much more inconceivable that his own puny struggle against the evils of man seemed laughably trivial in comparison.

But it was his struggle, and it was all Nemo had left. "Yes, Mr. Harding, we will continue our war." He lowered his voice. "Even if it doesn't matter to the rest of the universe."

The *Nautilus* cruised away from the nightmarish island, toward the normal trade routes, continuing the hunt.

Another story unabashedly influenced by Jules Verne. After the publication of my novel Captain Nemo, *I was invited to contribute a new story to* The Mammoth Book of New Jules Verne Adventures. *I decided to try an interesting epistolary take on Inspector Fix, the villain from* Around the World in Eighty Days. *I worked with my friend and occasional coauthor, Sarah A. Hoyt. (She and I just published a new alternate history novel,* Uncharted: Lewis and Clark in Arcane America.)

EIGHTY LETTERS, PLUS ONE

(WRITTEN WITH SARAH A. HOYT)

Letter #1

September 30, 1872
London, England

My dearest Elizabeth,

I leave this note for you, as the house was empty when I came home to pack. Doubtless you're out enjoying a quaint diversion with your women friends. As for me, I am unexpectedly off to the Suez, my dear. I've been dispatched to intercept a notorious thief who stole fifty thousand pounds from the Bank of England.

The villain is sure to leave the country and use his ill-gotten fortune to live extravagantly abroad. Detectives have been dispatched, one to each major port, and I have been chosen to keep a sharp eye on all British travelers who come through the Suez. I have a clear description of the thief, a well-dressed man with fine manners. Should I find him, I will shadow him till a warrant can be dispatched.

I'm sorry to leave you with nothing more than a note on this, our first anniversary, particularly since you never had the proper wedding you deserved. I still feel a bit of remorse over our brash elopement to Gretna Green, but you know your parents would never have consented to our love match. I still remember how haughtily your mother said that, because I need to work for a living, I should come in through the tradesman's entrance.

I trust you will keep a stiff upper lip while I'm away. The bank has offered a substantial reward to the detective who captures the thief, and I am convinced I'll get him if he comes my way. All that's needed in law enforcement these days is flair. You have to know how to nose these vermin out. And I, of course, I have excellent flair. As I've told you many times, I have a veritable sixth sense for these things.

Two thousand pounds will allow us to buy a better home and to hire a servant to do the house work for you. I know you expect such things out of life. It will also prove to your parents that, though you disobeyed them, you were ultimately right to choose me as your husband.

Meanwhile, I will write to you every day I possibly can. I'm sure you'll hardly notice I'm gone.

Yours, with much love,

Herbert Fix
Inspector, First grade

Letter #9

October 9
Suez, Egypt, Africa

My dear Elizabeth,
Good news! After all these days of waiting, the thief has finally come to the Suez.

Today, when the steamer *Mongolia* docked at the quay in Suez, I spotted a passenger forcing his way through the clamoring and stinking crowd of locals. You would not believe the mob of natives and black Africans that press around every passenger, offering to sell monkeys, unguents, jewelry, and the most grotesque pagan idols. One wretch even had the temerity to offer me some ground mummy which, he said, would strengthen my virile parts! I shudder to think, my dear, of you having to witness such sights.

By great luck, the fellow who came out of the *Mongolia* was in search of a government official. He nosed his way directly to me and held out a passport, for which he wished to procure a visa from the British consul. He was a wiry, dark-haired Frenchman, but he carried an Englishman's passport—his master's. Of course, I immediately glanced at the passport, and the description was exactly that of our thief! I could do no less than try to stop the man.

I told my suspicions to the consul and begged him to delay this man until I could get my arrest warrant. To my great disappointment, however, the consul said that I had no proof the traveler—Phileas Fogg—was guilty of any crime, and that without such proof he could not be detained.

I must therefore follow this rogue to his next stop, which is Bombay. I have talked to his servant, Passepartout—a good sort of fellow, but French and therefore garrulous. The man is convinced his master means to circle the globe to win a preposterous bet. Apparently, the cunning devil made a wager with the gentlemen in his club that he could go completely around the world in a mere eighty days. With my keen intellect, I realized immediately that this outrageous boast is nothing more than cover for his escape with the stolen money.

Hoping to pry more information from the talkative Frenchman, I took him on a shopping expedition to the bazaar. There, merchants offer all types of goods, including a very expensive perfume called Attar of Roses, of which a single drop can be mixed with oil or water to make many concoctions prized by the local ladies. Since you are always in my thoughts, I meant to buy you a dram of it. I also saw a fly swatter made from an elephant's tail, which I thought might amuse you. But, as I'm sure you'll understand, I had scarcely any time for frivolous purchases

Passepartout wished to obtain new shirts and other accouterments for his master. Due to the haste with which they left London, they had brought no more luggage than a carpetbag! Tell me, what man—not a thief and not in possession of fifty thousand pounds—would thus abandon his home and everything in it?

The loquacious Frenchman continually bemoaned the fact that

he had left the gas burning in his room and that his master wouldn't allow him so much as a moment to run back to turn it off. This is not the natural behavior of a man who truly intends to return home.

I have applied for a warrant, which should catch up with us in Bombay. My dear Elizabeth, the reward money is as good as ours. I have not had the time to pick up any souvenirs for you just yet, but I am sure to buy you something in Bombay once the villain Fogg has been arrested.

Yours affectionately,
Herbert Fix

Letter #20

October 20th, 1872
Bombay, British India

My dear Elizabeth,

Here I am, once more, fulfilling my promise of writing a letter a day to you. I will also post at once the letters I wrote aboard the steamer.

Unfortunately, we have made such rapid progress—Fogg bribed the owner of the liner to have the engine stoked with extraordinary zeal—that my warrant is not yet with the police here. I am more certain than ever of my quarry's guilt. What man but a fleeing criminal would throw away money in such a way?

Only those who have not had to work for their income view it as of little importance. I know you do not like it when I speak of the extravagance of the lace on your sister's gowns, but were it not for your parents' private, she would surely weigh her expense more carefully and not burden herself with so much expensive frippery.

But worry not, my dear. Soon you'll be able to afford dresses as good or better than hers. In fact, time permitting, I might pick up some fabric in Bombay, which is a city of goodly size and filled with all manner of strange things.

The streets are extraordinarily crowded with dark people attired in cotton robes. On the way to the police station, I saw a man who lay completely at ease upon a bed of sharp nails. Imagine! I also saw a man hypnotize a deadly snake by playing his flute.

I'm rather upset at not having received the warrant yet, but you may be confident in my abilities, my dear. Rest assured—Phileas Fogg, who really has no intention of going around the world, will no doubt remain several days here, which will certainly be sufficient time for me to arrest him. Meanwhile, maybe I'll find you an appropriate gift ... perhaps some silk with which the native women wrap themselves, something called a sari.

Oh, I almost forgot to acknowledge that I received your letter, which had been forwarded from Suez to the consulate at Bombay and which, vexingly, made it to town when the warrant didn't.

It is extraordinarily kind of you to say that you'd gladly forego the two thousand pounds for the sake of having me near you again. Your female emotionalism is quite charming, in its own way, but I know you are not serious. If I obeyed you, I have no doubt you'd soon resent our poverty.

And, more importantly, I cannot let the villain Fogg go unpunished.

Bear my absence with fortitude, for I'm sure the arrest warrant will come soon, and I'll return to you in glory and bearing the reward money that will start your climb back to the sphere you abandoned in order to marry me.

With my regards,
Herbert Fix

Letter #21

October 21st, 1872

Dear Elizabeth,

The warrant is not yet here. I write in haste and frustration. It turns out that Phileas Fogg intended to leave Bombay for Calcutta via the Great Peninsular railway. I was at the point of stepping into another train carriage, when Fogg's servant Passepartout arrived breathless, hatless, barefoot, and bearing the marks of a scuffle.

Though I fear you'll reproach me for my rudeness, I confess that I eavesdropped on the conversation between him and his master. The Frenchman had lost his shoes and barely escaped after violating the sanctity of a heathen pagoda on Malabar Hill—which is forbidden to Christians (or, at any rate, to anyone wearing shoes).

I was, as I said, on the point of stepping into the train carriage when I realized that, rather than waiting for the warrant from England—which might not reach us in time—I could simply find the temple and give the heathen priests the name and destination of their transgressor. Then *they* could press charges.

You see, the British authorities are extraordinarily careful never to offend the native religions—it is part of keeping control over this great uncivilized mob—and therefore, what that fool Passepartout did was an offense before British law. I'll get a warrant for that crime, too, then meet them at Calcutta, and have both men properly arrested.

I will write to you soon and announce the date of my return home with the reward money.

Yours, in haste,
Herbert Fix

∿

Letter #25

October 25th, 1872
Calcutta, British India

Dear Elizabeth,

At last Fogg and his servant have arrived. I was in some anxiety that something had befallen them in the noisome, uncharted jungle as they crossed the subcontinent. As I waited, pacing, I could not stop thinking of the thief and all those bank notes rotting away in the verdant wildness of India like mere mulch, and my reward unclaimed! I was truly in despair—but now the two men arrived at last, and the magistrates had them arrested at the train. Everything was going so well.

Unfortunately, Fogg bought his way out of the situation by posting an exorbitant bail of two thousand pounds, as if it were nothing. *Two thousand pounds*—the same amount that could have made the two of us comfortable for so long, thrown out like so much rubbish!

As I've said before, money that one has not earned is easy to discard.

Sadly, it appears that the thief will escape once more, and I must continue my relentless pursuit, even if it takes me all the way around the world. He is boarding the *Rangoon*, which lays at anchor and is to depart in an hour for Hong Kong.

My duty is clear. I have no choice but to follow, despite your half dozen letters imploring me to come home, which I recently collected from the consulate. Again, your letters have safely made the passage, while the desperately needed warrant lingers somewhere on the way. How can such a discrepancy be explained? Bureaucracy can be truly exasperating.

My greatest worry now is that Fogg is flinging money about with such abandon that the reward—being a fixed percentage of the recovered money—is shrinking visibly before my eyes.

I'm sure it will still be enough to make you happy.

I shall get him in the British colony of Hong Kong. Fogg and Passepartout are now traveling with a beautiful and clearly genteel young lady they picked up somewhere in the jungles of India. I suspect an elopement, and though you might call it unworthy of me —considering that we also eloped—I should be able to arrest Fogg for *that*, too, because elopement, until sanctified by marriage, can be prosecuted as a crime. I will question Passepartout for details about this woman.

Yours,
Herbert Fix

Letter #37

November 6th, 1872
Hong Kong

Elizabeth,

We are arrived in Hong Kong after much adventure. In your letters you expressed the wish that you could join me in my pursuit. You must realize that this traveling abroad, though exhilarating for a man, would be much too demanding for a delicate woman such as yourself. You are much happier at home.

Just before we landed we met with a hurricane, the greatest storm I've ever seen. It was as if the heavens themselves were on my side, whipping the seas and the wind into a frenzy to delay us. And while I was gripped by the most horrible nausea, I hoped we'd have to turn and run before the squall, which would slow our journey to Hong Kong. This made it more likely the warrant would arrive, and it would also disrupt whatever plans this scoundrel has for escaping the law.

Alas, the vessel braved it, and we made landfall shortly after.

Meanwhile, I learned that the relatives of the mysterious woman are not likely to chase Fogg for besmirching her honor. Auda is a mere native, despite her pale skin—an Indian princess, whom Passepartout and Fogg supposedly rescued from being burned with her husband's body, a barbarous tradition of immolation. Now she is traveling with them.

They have already reserved berths on the *Carnatic*, which was scheduled to depart tomorrow for Yokohama. But I met Passepartout on his way from the quay to his master's hotel, and he told me the *Carnatic* has unexpectedly changed its departure time to this evening instead. The Frenchman was in a great hurry to tell Fogg about it, but I waylaid the simple-minded and naïve servant and got him intoxicated in an opium den, a very common establishment in these parts

The man will sleep for at least a day, till long after the *Carnatic* has sailed. I am sure Fogg will not leave without his man. If my plan succeeds in delaying them, I shall go to the embassy and see if there are any forwarded letters from you.

Yours,
Herbert Fix

∾

Letter #45

November 14th, 1872
Yokohama, Japan

Elizabeth,

Once more I write in haste. Fogg, having missed the *Carnatic,*
engaged a small sail boat, the *Tankedere*—and he allowed me to
travel with him. He does not even suspect that I am his nemesis!
And Passepartout refuses to believe his master might be a thief.
Either he is a wily accomplice, or a fool.

It is maddening to be so near him for so long and yet not to have
the warrant that would stop him in his tracks. But there is nothing
for it, as we're no longer in British territory. My only hope now is
that he'll indeed go around the world in such a fashion hoping to
confuse pursuers. I shall arrest him as soon as he lands in England
again. Fogg intends to pursue travel to America aboard the *General
Grant.*

I've already engaged a cabin in the *General Grant,* and I've now
read the latest batch of your letters which, if you'll forgive me, are
rather tiresome in your insistence that I return to you at once. I
have a job to do. Despite the rate at which this scoundrel is
spending the stolen money, think of the renown his capture will
bring me, and how much easier it will make my rise in the world.

Only minutes ago, I saw Passepartout being dragged into the
boat by Fogg. Passepartout wore a most extraordinarily fanciful
oriental uniform, with wings and a false nose which would have
sufficed for a family of twelve. People on deck say this is a costume
worn in theater for the glory of some god or other. Foolish native
habits and abominable idolatry, of course, and one wonders how
even a Frenchman could bear to mix himself in it.

While I take a moment to catch my breath, let me tell you

something about Yokohama. It is a city of good size, and the native quarter is lit by many-colored lanterns. There are astrologers everywhere using fine telescopes. Scientific instruments to enhance their superstition. Most ironic. For fun, I thought about having a horoscope cast for you—an unusual and exotic gift—but I had no time to delay. I must catch Fogg.

Sincerely,
Herbert Fix

∼

Letter #64

December 3rd, 1872
San Francisco, United States of America

Elizabeth,

We are in San Francisco, the wild city of 1849, with its bandits, incendiaries, and assassins who all came here in the Gold Rush. The city looks more civilized than you'd expect, with a lofty tower in the town hall and a whole network of streets and avenues. It also has a Chinese town, that you'd swear came from China itself.

We found ourselves caught in the middle of some incomprehensible political rally—a dispute for the post of Justice of the Peace involving two men—and soon it turned into a brawl. I could not make heads nor tails of it, nor why anyone would seek to harm anyone else over such a silly squabble. I think these Americans are just hot-tempered.

In the turmoil, I actually protected Fogg from what might have been a disabling blow. Don't worry. Other than my clothes, nothing was hurt. Fogg insisted on buying me new garments, which are of a quality and cut to which even your parents could not object.

In your latest letters you reproached me for my "despicable Opium plot." I must say that you simply don't understand the business of men. Some deeds, though unpleasant, are necessary. Don't concern yourself about the matter any further.

You'll be heartened to know I'm now wholeheartedly working to speed Fogg's travel. Indeed, now that the thief is heading back to England, I am more than glad to help him. The sooner he gets there, the sooner I can arrest him. (And be back home with you, of course.)

And now we are to catch a train on the Pacific Railroad, headed for New York, from where we shall sail for London. I must rush to the train, so I don't lose sight of Fogg.

Herbert Fix

~

Letter #70

December 11th, 1872
New York, United States

Elizabeth,

Sorry for not writing for two days. Ran out of paper. You'd never believe what we've done in our trip across the United States. We rushed over a bridge mere moments before it collapsed, and in the process we'd gotten up such a head of steam that we didn't even stop until we'd passed the station! Then there was a herd of animals so large that they impeded the movement of the train. We had to wait until the beasts moved before the train could pass. Only imagine! The Americans call them buffalo, though Fogg said that such a classification is absurd. Not sure why.

The wonders of this continent! This world!

At one point, Fogg nearly engaged in a gunfight duel with another passenger, but they were interrupted by an attack from the savage Sioux, who kidnaped three passengers, including Passepartout—which, naturally, necessitated a rescue. Afterward, we caught an express train at Omaha station. Fogg, apparently imagining the demons of justice after him, is not fond of sightseeing, only rushing onward and onward. All the better, for that means I'll collect my reward sooner.

Now we've reached New York at last—but alas the vessel in which we expected to cross the Atlantic sailed forty-five minutes before our arrival. Fogg will no doubt find some boat to purchase or coerce. I very much fear there's not much money left out of the fifty thousand pounds he stole, but I shall still reap fame for apprehending him. Wouldn't you like to be the wife of a hero?

Herbert Fix

~

Letter #80

December 21
Friday
Liverpool

Elizabeth,

We have made landfall, and I served Phileas Fogg with the warrant, but—how could misfortune befall me so? After all my labors, after pursuing him round the world, I am not to enjoy success. Despite every indication, it appears that Fogg is not the thief after all, for the man who actually stole the fifty thousand pounds was apprehended three days ago, whilst I was traveling!

Worse, that upstart Passepartout punched me when he learned my true purpose in accompanying them on their long journey. Now I am bruised and tired, humiliated, disappointed—but at least I'm home, where doubtless you'll be waiting for me.

Herbert Fix

~

[On embossed letterhead identifying it as belonging to the law firm of Everingham, Entwhistle and Brown—on the fireplace mantel of Fix's home.]

London
December 18th of 1872

Dear Mr. Herbert Fix,

This letter serves to notify you that your wife, the honorable Elizabeth Rose Merriweather Fix, has returned to her parents' home and is suing you for divorce on the grounds of abandonment.

Our client has further instructed us to inform you that she did not object to your poverty or even your low upbringing, but she cannot forgive your obsession with career at the expense of her peace of mind and felicity. She further instructs us to inform you that you married her under false pretenses, always having characterized your marriage as a love match, when it is clear you love nothing more than your reputation and the pursuit of your own ambitions.

Lord and Lady Merryweather advise you to pose no argument and seek no reconciliation with their daughter, as they have the means to see you dismissed from your employment.

Sincerely
Nigel Entwhistle, Esquire

I grew up in a small farming town in Wisconsin, a rural culture straight out of a Ray Bradbury short story which had both charms and horrors for an imaginative young boy who wanted to be a writer. I like to say my childhood was a combination of Norman Rockwell and Norman Bates.

Drawing on all those experiences, I wrote a series of short stories loosely connected to the fictional small town of Tucker's Grove, Wisconsin. I remember spending a lot of time walking along the railroad tracks, looking at discarded junk along the siding, letting my imagination wander. This story is about a demon-possessed train....

LOCO-MOTIVE

M y best buddy Alan got killed yesterday, demolished by a hit-and-run train. They found Alan's car smashed to pieces, scattered all up and down the embankment like wrapping paper on a Christmas morning.

The Locust Road intersection is well marked. I know that, drunk or not, Alan would never have driven into a goddamn freight train. According to the railroad company's schedules, no real train was even *close* to the crossing at that time of night.

Imagine, coming back from college to be pall bearer for a closed coffin—that's the part that really sucks. Goddamn it, Alan—you were supposed to be best man at my wedding if I ever got married.

But it gives me an excuse to come back home. To see for myself if that awful train has returned for one last run. How visible would an all-black locomotive be if it shut off its one-eyed headlight, slavering oil and grinding red-hot coal in its belly, waiting to pounce on Alan's car as he drove home?

Alan and I were kids together. We did all that stuff like running across the fields, hiding between the rows of corn, daring each other to climb just one rung closer to the top of old man Pickman's silo.

Alan collected wheat pennies; I collected silver Mercury dimes. I've still got my heavy ceramic mug half-full of those dimes, up in my room at home somewhere. We used to spend hours and hours each summer on our bikes, riding down the country roads to the bank in Tucker's Grove, where we'd exchange one roll of coins for another and then eagerly scavenge in the new rolls for our individual treasures: my dimes, his pennies.

We watched superhero cartoons together on Saturday mornings, usually at my house because we had a big color TV; my parents would get crabby when we'd wake them up so early in the morning. Then it was outside in the snow or the sun, talking about how much we preferred *Lost in Space* and "Voyage to See What's on the Bottom" to *Star Trek* because those shows had better monsters (though we both got *heavily* into *Star Trek* in high school).

There's usually one day every summer, somewhere in the middle, when you get so bored you *almost* wish it was time for school to start again. Of course, I never said anything like that to Alan because he probably would have punched me in the stomach even for *saying* such a stupid thing. That was when we decided to head off for the railroad tracks.

The tracks were about a mile away, but you could see them across the fields, riding high on their isolated embankment and cut off from the world by rickety barbed-wire fences. The fences didn't prove to be any obstacle at all for us, aside from the occasional sissy fear of getting lockjaw if you scratched yourself on one of the rusty barbs.

Out on the tracks we felt *away* from everything, kings of the mountain, just Alan and me. The twin steel tracks stretched away for the longest distance before they curved sharply toward Bartonville, which we couldn't even see on account of the low hills in between.

Aimlessly, I walked along, stretching my legs to step on one crosstie, then the next. Alan tried to balance on the thin steel rail, but he kept falling off after four steps or so. Once, we placed a couple of Alan's wheat pennies on the rails just before a train came, and afterward we had looked in awe at the shiny, squashed copper disk—you could barely see the ghost of Lincoln's face smeared long and flat from the thunderous passage of the train.

The spaces between the ties were filled with gravel, cinders, and other junk. Two tall, silver-painted towers stood on either side of the tracks, one facing each way down the line, with dead green and red lights that would shine a warning when trains came.

Off in the distance, in the opposite direction from Bartonville and the big curve of the tracks, we could see old man Pickman and his ancient tractor pulling the disks across the field and chewing up dirt. The firing of the tractor sounded like toy gunshots in the empty air; apart from that, we could only hear a couple of birds, and the wind. Pickman pulled his muddy tractor up on Locust Road, trying to cross from one field to the next, but the tractor sounded like it couldn't go on with life anymore. It popped and backfired before it gave up completely, right near where the tracks crossed the road. We could barely hear the sound of Pickman's shouts as he got off the tractor, jumped up and down, and kicked one of the machine's huge back tires. Alan and I both giggled and watched for a long time as he stomped off down the road to his big white farmhouse.

The old farmer got boring after a while, though, and Alan changed the subject. "Where do you suppose all this *junk* comes from?"

He indicated the embankment by the tracks, and I noticed all the debris scattered up and down the fence line. A refrigerator door, a broken and rusted plow, an automobile fender, some hubcaps, the top of a stove, and more—it was the oddest assortment of ruined things you could imagine. I had never really paid much attention before, thinking it as natural as the long grass and the wild roses along the fence line. But Alan was right—there wasn't a logical explanation for why that kind of junk would all be there, a mile away from the nearest farmhouse.

I shrugged, but Alan kept thinking aloud. "Do you suppose a *train* put it there?"

"You mean hobos? Why would they want to throw junk like that?"

"No, I mean a *train*! Like, a *live* train that comes out after dark and attacks cars and things. What if there's a big, black locomotive, you know, and it grabs stuff, tears it apart, and throws the pieces all up and down the tracks." Alan's eyes were glistening with his own imagination.

"That's dumb, Alan." It was one of the only times I made fun of his ideas. "Why would it do that?"

But he seemed emphatic, and I could see he really wasn't kidding. "Maybe it's angry, *really* angry because ... well, because it's a *train*—it's stuck on the rails, and it can't go anywhere else. It's trapped. A car can drive wherever it wants, you know, and so can a tractor. But not a train."

It made sense to me, and Alan didn't pull my leg often. I found my mind wandering, imagining, seriously considering the idea—and it was just exotic enough to capture my imagination. While lying in bed, trying to sleep at nights, I *did* hear trains all the time, some of them with odd whistles, and it seemed to me I heard too many crashing and rattling sounds to be explained by the clatter of a simple passing train.

On hot summer nights when the sheets were sticky from the humidity, I slept in my underwear and left my window open to listen to the crickets and the grasshoppers ... but just when I was finally dozing off, I could sometimes hear that one special train, the vengeful locomotive that was angry because it could never get off the tracks. It was a really spooky idea, just the type of thing we needed to improve a boring summer day. "But where does it come from?" I asked.

Solemnly, Alan turned to point at where the curve of the tracks swung behind the hills and vanished from our sight. "There."

"Where? In Bartonville?"

"No, stupid. See where the tracks disappear? It doesn't just go around the curve to Bartonville—*maybe* sometimes that curve is something else. Like a doorway into another dimension. You know, like the *Twilight Zone*." Alan said this with great seriousness, and to us—after years of watching fantastic TV shows—the idea was eminently reasonable.

I couldn't argue with that. Enchanted, I stared down the tracks, and then slowly, trying to appear nonchalant, I stepped off the crossties and onto the cinder bed at the edge of the embankment. I didn't want Alan to think I was chicken. But I saw that he was anxious to get away from the rails, too.

Of course, we had to see if it was all true. We double-promised to come back that night, sneaking out after dark and after our parents had gone to sleep. Since it was summer, it didn't get dark until late, so I set my alarm clock for 11:15 and put it under my pillow.

I didn't plan to go to sleep, but with two hours of lying there in the humid summer heat, I ended up having the most vivid nightmare: the giant black locomotive, murderous and wanting to destroy machines and people, waiting for me, burning not coal but human bones. Luckily, the muffled alarm brought me out of it before I could wake up yelling for my parents. I was shaking in the darkness, and I almost didn't dare to get up. I lay there looking up at the ceiling. The sluggish breeze moved the curtains so that they sounded like slithering ghosts against the windowsill. But I knew what Alan would think if I didn't show up, so I got dressed and sneaked out of the quiet house, being careful not to let the screen door slam shut.

Alan was waiting for me at the end of our driveway, and we walked down Locust Road without saying anything until we were out of earshot of the houses. The road stood out plain in the moonlight, but we didn't want to cut across the fields in the dark. Raccoons and skunks and possums come out into the fields at night, and other things you don't even want to imagine. The moon was full and high up in the sky, and we would get to the tracks around midnight—it was going to be so perfect.

"I dreamed of the train," I told Alan.

"So did I." We didn't say anything else until we reached the railroad crossing. Old man Pickman's tractor looked like a sick mechanical cow standing half in the ditch and half on the road where it had stalled.

"Let's walk down a-ways."

I followed Alan out onto the tracks, stepping from crosstie to crosstie, as we walked farther from the road. The bugs in the grass seemed very loud that night, and the noise hung in the air. We kept walking, oddly silent but neither of us willing to admit we were scared.

The insect buzzing stopped abruptly, as if someone had switched off a radio. We heard a distant grating sound as one of the tall signal towers swung its colored glass lens into place. A red light stabbed at us like a bloodshot eye. A train was coming! Then, a moment later, the *other* signal tower, the one facing the opposite direction, swung its light into place and shone the red light the other way.

I couldn't say anything. Alan gasped, "This is it! This is it!"

We heard a sound like a muffled roar, and then, emerging from around the Bartonville curve, crawling out of another dimension where it could sit and brood on its vengeance day after day, we both saw a gleaming yellow headlight. The light was like a spear pointing at us, charging down at us, and all we could do was stand there, hypnotized.

I jerked on Alan's arm. "Come on! Get off the tracks!"

We both tumbled down the embankment and scrambled for cover in the thick wild rose bushes. We would have a bad time explaining all our scratches to our moms the next day, but I was too scared to care right then. The black locomotive came on, relentlessly charging down the tracks that chained it to its never-changing route. Dark smoke belched from its smokestack and was swallowed up by the night and the stars. The locomotive's one-eyed headlight, a searchlight, poked ahead, looking for victims. The thing wasn't like a passenger train, or even a freight train, but like something out of a cowboy movie, an old coal-burning locomotive —just exactly the way I had pictured it. Two large wheels under the empty engineer's compartment clattered powerfully, heaving a gleaming brass piston back and forth, driving the entire train. The wide, triangular cowcatcher in the front of the locomotive looked like a guillotine blade. Seven cars, all black, trailed behind the locomotive—it reminded me of a giant metal caterpillar, with each black car one of its segments.

I wanted to blink my eyes and make it go away. It's not real! We just made it up! But how can you deny a couple million tons of hot, angry steel charging down the tracks in front of your very eyes?

The black train chugged and clattered past our hiding place, and we could feel the heat of its big coal-burning furnace. I wanted to cry then, even in front of Alan. But the big yellow eye of the locomotive didn't see us—instead it focused on new prey. It paused, hissing steam like a fighting cat, seemed to tense and coil its mechanical muscles, and then *lunged* forward—toward old man Pickman's stalled tractor.

The tractor didn't move, of course—it was just a tractor. But the locomotive reared up off the tracks, and it struck. Its shining pistons detached themselves and reached forward like steel mantis arms to grasp the heavy old tractor and pull it onto the tracks. The steam hissed and built up; black smoke poured out of the smokestack, and the wheels churned backward. The locomotive took its mechanical victim, dragging it along the tracks like a spider returning to its lair.

The locomotive stopped right in front of us and proceeded to *tear* Pickman's tractor apart. Wheel guards, the two small headlights, parts of the engine, the rusty and uncomfortable seat on its thick spring—all were shredded by invisible steel jaws under the locomotive itself. We could feel the heat, smell the oil and the hot steel of an overworked engine.

As it destroyed the tractor, the black train tossed the scrap metal along the embankment, like you would throw chicken bones after a barbecue. One of the huge black tractor tires crashed down right by us, almost smashing me, and I yelled out loud. In a second, I was up and running toward the barbed wire fence, not caring at all about skunks or possums or raccoons in the soybeans. Alan shouted at me to get down.

The locomotive let out the most horrible roaring explosion I've ever heard in my life, like it was *really* angry at us for having discovered it. I dove over the fence, bouncing on the wires, not thinking about scratches or cuts or even lockjaw. Alan was right on my heels. Behind me, the locomotive reared up off the tracks again, keeping its back seven cars firmly on the rails. It was like a snake, a big black cobra maybe, trying to strike, trying to smash us. It came down hard on the embankment, and the bladelike cowcatcher made a deep smoking impression in the dirt.

But it missed us, and we were out in Pickman's soybean field running like hell, not even trying to dodge the rows. The locomotive bellowed in anger, trapped on the rails but promising to get us both someday. We ran and ran, and after a while the locomotive turned back to destroying the poor old tractor.

∾

NEITHER ALAN nor I went back to the railroad tracks again all summer, no way. That autumn my dad had us pack up and move back into town, since he'd grown tired of the country life by then. Alan and I drifted apart, now that we weren't constantly in touch with each other; sure, we were still friends, but it wasn't the *same*.

Then in high school we rediscovered our friendship, falling back into the best-buddies bit. Since Alan was almost a year older than I, he got his driver's license first and took me all over the place, and because he turned eighteen first, he could get me all the beer I wanted. I remember spending many a weekend afternoon on his back porch, shootin' the breeze with the stereo turned up, and looking across the fields at the distant railroad tracks.

After graduation, I went off to college; Alan went instead to a local technical college where he picked up a something-or-other degree in electronics. He ended up working as a manager for a chain restaurant in Bartonville and partying a lot.

Meanwhile, I was doing the typical college stunt of waiting until Friday night to start a term paper that was due on the following Monday. Last week, I had planned on doing an all-nighter, but spent most of my time feeling stupid and miserable because the girl I'd been chasing all semester still wouldn't go out with me. I finally gave up on the term paper an hour or so past midnight and flopped on my unmade dorm bed, going to sleep with all my clothes on....

Even after so many years, I dreamed of the black locomotive again, slavering thick oil from its mechanical jaws, searching for us with its one yellow eye. It charged at me and I ran, but I couldn't get off the tracks—I was trapped, and the train was gaining on me, wanting to grind me to a pulp beneath its crushing wheels and scatter my limbs all up and down the embankment. I woke up drowning in sweat.

And that was the night Alan got killed in his car by the Locust Road crossing. Demolished—parts of his car thrown gleefully all along the tracks....

When I heard, and when I figured it out, I went into the bathroom for almost an hour, bent over the John, trying to be sick, sick at myself. I think it might have hardened me up inside, so I could face going back home.

Alan's funeral was like a regular class reunion. Everybody was there, all the people who ever knew him. Even the freaks and the jocks came, the ones who would never sign your yearbook or bother to talk to you in the halls. Now they couldn't even look Alan in the face because of the closed coffin. I think I held up pretty well, even though I was distracted. What kind of jerk gets *distracted* at the funeral of his best buddy?

Afterward, back home, I went alone to my old room and closed the door. Mom and Dad seemed willing to let me work it out for myself. I found the old ceramic mug half-filled with my silver Mercury dimes; it had been buried in the junk on one of my closet shelves. I sat down on the neatly made single bed that had been mine for so many years, but my bedroom became a guest room when I moved out. I looked out the window and waited for sunset to come.

I HAD to drive to the Locust Road tracks this time, telling my parents I wanted to go cruising for a little bit, to clear my head. Dad warned me not to drink too much—he spoke out of habit, I think, from all the times I had gone out cruising with Alan. But partying wasn't what I had in mind at all.

I pulled my car over on the shallow, rutted ditch next to the railroad crossing, shut off the headlights, and got out. I had some time yet before midnight, and the moon shone full again. I walked out into the brisk autumn night. I could see my breath, like the smoke coming out of a black locomotive.

I stared at the tracks a long while before I got up the courage to step between the iron rails. In the moonlight down the embankment I saw something glint, and when I looked closer, I realized it was the broken rearview mirror from Alan's car.

The vengeful black locomotive wasn't *real*—it was all made up, just a fantasy shared between us two kids. There's a certain power in naïveté, I think, and if you believe in something with all your heart, all your terror … well, who knows? Maybe there really *is* a Santa Claus or an Easter Bunny or a Boogey Man, from all the children in the world believing in it with pure unquestioning faith that only a kid can have. Alan and I had *believed* in the killer train, and we had challenged its reality by going to see, to prove it was only imaginary—and the nightmare had called our bluff.

Now, I had to *believe* I could destroy it. But I was a lot older and a lot more cynical this time.

I started to walk down the tracks again, all alone, listening to the coins jingle together in my pocket. I headed toward the Bartonville curve, away from the road and all hope of rescue.

The darkness made the ground hard to see, and I stumbled more than once on a broken crosstie. But I walked until I got between the two skeletal signal towers on either side of the tracks, then I put my hands on my hips, trying to look defiant, and shouted into the night.

"Come on, you son of a bitch! Come get me!" The words echoed out, and the insect noises paused a moment before starting up again; when nothing happened, I felt belittled and stupid. "What's the matter? Are you *chicken?*"

A loud, unearthly bellow exploded from the darkness far ahead. The furnace in the black locomotive was stoked up with a little bit of Hell itself, and a blast of heat forced the steam to surge upward and scream through its whistle. I thought everyone in all of Rutherford County must have heard that noise.

Then its eye suddenly appeared, a round yellow bullet coming straight at me from around the curve and out of its unreal dimension. I was flooded with light, transfixed. I heard the rattling rhythm of the locomotive's wheels, the clatter against the tracks, the chug of its pistons. Smoke spurted from its stack as the train charged toward me, thinking only of murder.

My hands were shaking as I dug around in my pockets. Trying to keep cool, I pulled out two of my special dimes, my silver Mercury dimes, and stooped down to lay them on the tracks, one on each steel rail. I stepped back, remaining between the tracks, not even thinking about trying to run. Silver dimes ... everyone knew that *silver* was deadly to supernatural things. What would the horror movies be without silver bullets, silver crosses, silvered mirrors? I tried not to think about it too much because I had to *believe* this game would work. And these silver dimes were special, cherished from childhood. I cursed myself over and over again for having majored in science, for insisting that things had to make *sense* before I could believe in them.

But this would work. I knew it would work. I *knew* it would work. How come you can remember all sorts of stupid things from your childhood, but you can't remember what it was like to *believe* in something? I crossed my fingers, and then I double-crossed them. That might help.

The locomotive's cowcatcher looked like a spearhead as it came at me. I could see the engine's brass pistons grabbing forward and back, reaching out to stab me. Its eye never blinked, but I could see the slavering oil dripping from its mechanical jaws, and I definitely felt the heat pouring off of it. The base of its smokestack had begun to turn a cherry red from its exertion. And in the engineer's compartment, I could see a figure. Alan. Riding the train, unable to get off. I knew he saw me waiting for him. The train blasted its steam whistle.

The black locomotive came down the tracks at me like a cannonball. I stood there petrified, looking at the pitifully small coins resting on the tracks as if they were really supposed to protect me. The train didn't pause—I knew it wouldn't; it didn't want to give me a chance to jump off the tracks. But I felt calm inside—at least I knew what was going to hit me; Alan hadn't even had that much warning. I had a terrible urge to shut my eyes, but I couldn't. The nightmare was real now, and I couldn't hide under the covers.

Then the black locomotive struck the little circles of silver, but it seemed to impact an invisible wall of concrete. The locomotive smashed together, splitting into ribbons of iron. The boiler burst, and orange flames erupted from splits in its iron-plated side. The wheels ground to a screaming halt as the other seven cars piled up; and then the whole train exploded again, blasting up into the silent starry sky in a rain of hot shreds of metal. I never saw what happened to the shadow of Alan on the train—maybe he was never there in the first place.

I felt the heat and the push of the shockwave. I stood unmoving, waiting for a big chunk of shrapnel to come down and kill me after all. But nothing did, and I stared at the wreckage for a few minutes, listening to the *patter* and *thunk* of broken iron falling to the ground.

After a pause, the insects started singing again.

I bent to pick up my dimes and found that both had been flattened by the locomotive's momentum, smeared out into gleaming silver ovals. I pocketed them with reverence, as if I were holding talismans, splinters of the cross—they would always be special, a part of unreality that would ruin my chances of a career in science.

I BARELY REMEMBERED WALKING BACK to my car, but as I drove back to town, I got the shakes really bad. Nobody noticed the difference later, though I found I could face Alan's death, now that I had done something about it. Later on, I realized how you selectively learn to forget the things you can't explain.

There's always junk scattered along the railroad tracks—discarded bits of twisted metal, rusted pieces of machinery—but nobody knows what it is or how it got there. Someday I'm probably going to come back to the Locust Road crossing, and I'll look for a piece of that black locomotive, to keep with my souvenirs of Alan.

Another story set in Tucker's Grove, with time travel, dinosaurs, and a lonely old farmer. This is a very vivid tale for me, and I can picture every scene perfectly, and the character is drawn from an ancient, widowed farmer who lived next door from us, Mr. Reindahl. As a boy, I would run across the hayfields and keep him company, climb the big box elder tree in his front yard, and listen to his stories. I spent a summer helping him bale hay (which was really hard work!). All that time, I didn't know I was collecting ingredients for stories. (Another story later in this collection, "Heroes Never Die," was also influenced by old Mr. Reindahl.)

DRILLING DEEP

"I can only stay a week, Dad." David sounded apologetic. "The other paleontologists are already out digging in Montana, and they can't survive very long without me."

"That's okay." Arne Christensen gave a nothing-bothers-me shrug. "I'm glad you came at all. It's been so long."

David opened the cupboard above the sink where Arne had kept the jelly jar glasses for the past twenty years. He removed a glass and turned on the faucet, but only a thin, murky trickle crept out.

Arne leaned forward in his worn overalls, making the kitchen chair creak. "The well's gone bad, Davey—and what does come out tastes like salty muck. I'm getting Harry Warner's rig out here to start drilling a new one."

David tasted a drop with a simultaneous smile and grimace. "It's called *connate water*, Dad—fairly unusual. It's the salt water from ancient seas, trapped underground when the rocks were formed a couple hundred million years ago."

"No wonder it tastes like dinosaur piss."

"You're off by a few years, Dad. But no matter." David always liked to explain things, and Arne listened with full attention, since he'd never had a chance to go to college—too much work to do on the farm. Nevertheless, he found the world endlessly interesting, with or without scientific explanations.

Arne smiled, and his single gold-rimmed tooth flashed in the early morning light. He had always (jokingly) watched the gold prices in the paper, threatening to sell his tooth if things got too bad on the farm. Fortunately, things looked good this year; he had rented out most of the usable farmland, keeping only about ten acres for himself, now that he was alone.

David set the glass back on the cracked contact paper in the cupboard, as if he hadn't actually wanted a drink but simply needed something to do. Arne ran a dirty fingernail along the edge of the gold-flecked Formica of the kitchen table. "What is it your team is doing out in Montana, again? More dinosaur bones?"

David knew the subject would fascinate his father. "We're looking into the K-T extinction event. Sixty-five million years ago the dinosaurs and a whole list of other animals just *died*, all at once, probably because of an asteroid impact. To find out more details, we have to dig down sixty-five million years and look at the rocks."

Arne frowned. "How do you dig down millions of years?"

David relaxed while talking about his work. "In geology, new rock layers are laid down on top of the old ones. Like a stack of bills—new ones on top, oldest ones on the bottom. The deeper down you dig, the further back in time you go."

Arne's old fatherly interest had never dimmed despite David's occasional intellectual coolness. He was proud that his son knew so many things that he himself had never figured out, although David couldn't help but feel superior to a "hick farmer" who had no real geology training.

"But because of upheavals and weathering," David continued, "the past is closer to the surface in some places—and it just so happens that sixty-five million years ago is close to the surface in Montana."

THOUGH THE RED-WINGED blackbird's song sounded like an unoiled hinge, Arne enjoyed the flavor it added to the early morning peace. Regretfully, he started the generator on the well-drilling rig, drowning out nature's noises with more civilized racket.

David had been away from the rise-at-dawn farm life for many years now, and he was still asleep inside the old house. The well-drilling rig made one hell of an alarm clock, though, hammering the bore pipe like a piledriver with percussive violence.

Thunnngg

The pipe bit into the dirt.

Thunnngg

The rig pounded it below the surface, like a disoriented mole tunneling toward the center of the Earth.

Arne mused to himself, "I'm drilling back in time." Though he didn't entirely understand it all, he was fascinated by David's geological analogy. "Digging down a million years." He would chew on the concept as if it were an old piece of tough jerky.

If you went back in time by digging down into the ground, then were all the people in those underground earth-homes literally "living in the past?" He grinned at his own joke; he would have to tell it to David as soon as he woke up.

Thunnngg

There, now the rig had sunk the pipe all the way into yesterday.

Thunnngg

And the day before.

Thunnngg

Picking up speed. Now David was still in college, and his mother had just died.

Thunnngg

David a little boy.

Thunnngg

David just born.

Thunnngg

Arne and Elizabeth first married.

Thunnngg

And that was World War II.

Thunnngg

World War I.

Thunnngg

The Civil War.

Thunnngg

The Revolutionary War.

Thunnngg

In 1492, Columbus sailed the ocean blue.

Thunnngg
King Arthur and the Knights of the Round Table.
Thunnngg
Jesus Christ.
Moses.
Thunnngg
The dinosaurs.
Adam and Eve.
Thunnngg
Even though morning coolness still clutched at the air, Arne discovered he was sweating.

DAY AFTER DAY, the rig hammered each section of pipe up to its neck in the dirt. Arne screwed together another section and set the rig in motion again, letting his thin probe bore through the ancient strata.

The work wasn't too hard, it wasn't too monotonous. The hose dumped water down the shaft, and the rig hammered it into muck, pounding the pipe sluggishly downward. Arne pumped up the gray sludge, spilling it across the sloping farmyard like a dead lake of wet cement.

Two hundred feet down.

Arne's eyes bounced up and down, watching the center pipe in the rig as it rhythmically rose and fell, like the pendulum on the biggest grandfather clock of all. He could easily run the rig himself, but David did his best to seem helpful (which mostly entailed standing around and talking a lot, keeping his father company). The summer stillness was broken only by his conversation and the cyclic *thunnngg* of the rig.

The insert pipe came up, spilling battered sludge, but now a glistening black stain swirled in the gray clayish ooze, like a shadow from the past. As the mud continued to spew from the shaft, the black became darker. David bent down in the mud and ran his fingers through the black ooze. "You just struck coal!"

Arne was both surprised and proud to see his son so willing to get his fingers dirty. "Coal? Like real coal?"

David sounded like a lecturing teacher again. "It's not too uncommon to hit coal when you dig a well, Dad. This is probably low-grade stuff, but I can take a sample to a friend of mine, so he can analyze it."

Arne was genuinely amazed. "So, how far back did I drill?" Seeing David's puzzled look, he added, "I mean how many years down did I go? To hit the coal?"

"Oh." David's face looked like a jumble of jigsaw puzzle pieces falling into place. "Of course. Let's see, coal would be about three hundred million years ago, during the Carboniferous period. Not too bad for six days work."

Arne beamed. David saw the expression, smiled, and described the picture for his father. "Lots of swamps covered the land. Towering fern-trees, giant insects, big lizards. Volcanoes. The air hot and steamy." He raised his eyebrows. "Do you know what the coal is, Dad? Why it burns?"

"No." He knew David wanted to explain it to him.

"Rocks don't burn. Anything that burns had to be living at one time. Wood burns because trees spend their lives soaking up sunlight, storing 'solar power' in their trunks. When you burn wood, you release that sun-energy again.

"Coal is from those big, steamy swamps of three-hundred million years ago, all the vegetation crushed under layers and layers of rock over time, squeezed and concentrated. When you burn a lump of coal you're releasing 300-million-year-old sunlight."

Arne let out a sigh. "Ah, Davey, you should have been a teacher."

Less than an hour later they struck water.

THE SUN NUDGED toward the southwestern horizon, and Arne stood in his mud-splattered overalls, hoe in hand, at the edge of the vast garden. He realized he looked like an old cover from *Reader's Digest*, the kind that were "Rural with a Vengeance" according to David.

Each spring Arne planted a garden six times larger than he needed for himself, but he enjoyed the work, and he enjoyed giving the vegetables away. And if he didn't feel like harvesting everything that ripened, he threw it all in the compost pit; the vegetables didn't care if they were harvested or not.

Inside the farmhouse, David had cooked a fancy farewell dinner for himself and his father. Arne usually cooked for one, and— thanks to the fouled well—he had become accustomed to not cooking at all in the past week. David had filled a few old milk jugs with water at the neighbor's to tide them over until the new well could be hooked up to the house's existing plumbing.

By himself outside, Arne waited in the expectant silence, looking out across everything he had known. It had changed very little since his own childhood. The unplanted half of the garden stood in black, hard chunks, just as the plow had piled them a month before. The garden seemed transformed in the reddening sunlight of the dying afternoon.

Arne stared at the lifeless earth, amazed at the lack of weeds. Although there had been no rain for two weeks, several viscid puddles lay in the dirt, covered with slimy green. He hadn't noticed them before. As he watched, the pools seemed ... alive, crawling, oozing, glittering with ancient secrets: algae groping for a foothold on the blasted, sterile landscape of a newborn Earth. When Arne pulled in a hitching breath, the air seemed oppressively damp and steamy.

Suddenly, something felt wrong. The sun hung motionless on the horizon, but as he watched, it picked up speed in the opposite direction and heaved itself above the edge of the world, like a fiery red behemoth whirling from west to east. The huge clock-hand of the sun moved backward, counterclockwise.

A thousand conflicting thoughts battered on his mind, terror yet awed fascination at the same time.

What if, in his thoughtless drilling, he had punctured a bubble of the past, a cyst buried three-hundred million years below the surface? Like the primordial water that had invaded his old well, causing it to dry up? What if that ancient past was even now seeping toward the surface?

Arne blinked, and the illusion of the sun's motion vanished, leaving it half-sunken on the horizon. When David called him to come in for supper, he almost ran to the house.

⁓

THAT NIGHT, Arne had no nightmares because he never slept at all.

He lay tossing on his creaky bed, smelling the taint of brimstone in the air. He and David had sat up and talked next to the fireplace, where Arne insisted on burning a few old lumps of coal he had found in the basement. His eyes sparkled with childlike fascination as the 300-million-year-old light spilled into the present.

David had to leave the next morning to catch a flight to Great Falls, Montana, and already Arne felt more lonely than he had been in years.

In the numbness of night, Arne could hear the echoing drip of the faucet in the kitchen. How could a faucet drip with no water pressure behind it? The dripping pounded deep into his consciousness, into his imagination.

Drip drip drip drip drik drik trik tik tik tick tick tick tick

Nature's own clock. Time was passing … but he couldn't tell which direction it moved.

From outside, through the window screen, came night sounds he had never heard before, awful and primeval. Eerie calls and haunting burbling noises as of something moving slowly through a swamp. The air in the bedroom felt hot and humid, intensifying all sounds.

A thrill of fascination traced Arne's spine, a thrill of fear. He had immersed himself in something strange, a true mystery of nature. He didn't know whether to be eager for morning, or to be terrified of it.

⁓

ARNE STOOD on the porch in the still-wakening dawn and stared out into the new universe of what had been his backyard. His jaw hung open in an unabashed expression of awe.

He took a step off the porch, compelled to walk toward the misty, primeval swamp that had appeared during the night, seeming to stretch beyond his distant fields. Ruddy sunlight shimmered and reflected in the steamy air, as if slowed down by plowing into the past.

The ground felt spongy and damp beneath his work boots. He could smell the bizarre vegetation and the sultry ooze lurking in the swamp. He paused, torn between his fascination and the urge to run and hide under the bed.

He thought about calling for David, but the sense of wonder clouded all his fear. Arne was experiencing something no one else had ever imagined. David would never believe this; in fact, Arne feared that his son might not be able to see it at all. This simply couldn't be real.

The air was hushed and brooding, as if noise-making creatures had not yet evolved. Far off, beyond where neighboring Tucker's farm would someday be, Arne could see the smoke-belching crown of an ancient volcano, but the rumble had been reduced to a low drone in the steamy air.

Giant rushes and wide-spreading ferns rose around him, dripping star-points of dew. Huge fern-trees towered overhead, some rising almost a hundred feet high. Primitive evergreens and trees with no flowers clustered in the wet undergrowth. When a sound like a chainsaw whizzed past, he gawked at an armored dragonfly with a wingspan of two feet. The dragonfly circled Arne's head and then sped deeper into the swamp, as if beckoning him to follow.

He walked along, hypnotized by the primeval beauty.

Billowing seed-ferns and giant, cactus-like club mosses shed green reflections into the heavy forest. A large beetle scuttled sluggishly down the fallen trunk of a fern-tree, picking its way across a wet mass of algae.

Arne pondered beside a quiet, glassy pool crowded with bored-looking fish. All around him was a pervasive, relaxing hum, like a cicada's song played backwards. A spider the size of an apple watched him from a scale-tree but did not seem interested in prey so large.

Arne felt a delicious lull in himself and enjoyed a moment of peace. He had always known there were mysteries in the world far greater than himself. This made the most profound religious experience seem like no more than a sneeze. He wished David were here with him. He decided to return to the house—at least to within shouting distance, so he could rouse his son. No one should miss this!

Arne didn't think he had stayed in the swamp for long, and the sun still hung low in the morning sky. He hadn't gone far, but when he turned back toward the farm house, the prehistoric swamp had swallowed everything, and stretched for miles and miles in all directions.

The past sprawled forever and ever before him, and he had to go three hundred million years to get home again.

And now for something a little lighter. I was invited to contribute a short story to an anthology called Pandora's Closet, *fantastic stories about magical garments. You never know what strange subject an anthology editor might pick, but any good writer fires up the imagination engine to see what might come to mind. Given all the possibilities, I decided that the most entertaining story would be about an enchanted loincloth....*

LOINCLOTH

(WRITTEN WITH REBECCA MOESTA)

All alone in the props warehouse on the back lot of Duro Studios, he made his case to Shirley in his mind, rehashing the argument they had had the night before. This time, though, he was bold and articulate, and he easily convinced her.

Walter Groves opened another one of the big crates and tore out the packing straw mixed with Styrofoam peanuts. "Not exciting enough for you, am I? You don't feel fireworks? I'm too sedate—not a man's man? Think about it, Shirley. Women say they want nice guys, the shy and sensitive type, men who are sweet and remember birthdays and anniversaries. Isn't that what you told me you needed—someone just like me? You've always despised hypocrites. But what do you do? You fall for a bad boy, someone with tattoos and a heavy smoking habit, someone who can't keep a job for more than a month, someone like that last jerk you dated, who treated you rough and left you out in the cold.

"But I loved you. I treated you with respect, drove you to visit your grandmother in the hospital, and fixed your computer when the hard drive crashed. I got out of bed when you called at three in the morning and came to your apartment just to hold you because you had a nightmare and couldn't sleep. I gave you flowers, dinners by candlelight, and love notes—not to mention the best six months of my life. 'Someday, you'll regret it. Maybe not today. Maybe not tomorrow, but soon'"—he pictured himself as Bogart in *Casablanca*—"you'll realize what you threw away. But I won't be waiting. I'm a good man, and I deserve a wonderful woman who values me for who I am, who appreciates my dedication, and wants a nice, normal life. Go ahead. Have your shallow, exciting fling with Mr. James Dean in *Rebel Without a Cause*. I'll find someone sincere who wants Jimmy Stewart in *It's a Wonderful Life*."

Scattering straw and packing material, he pulled a long plastic elephant tusk out of the prop box. The faux ivory was sharp at one end and painted with "native symbols." He glanced at the label on the box: Jungo's Revenge. After marking the name of the film on his clipboard, he listed the stored items beneath the title. He sighed.

If only he could have come up with just the right answers last night, maybe Shirley wouldn't have dumped him. If only he could have been tough like Mel Gibson in *Braveheart*, confident like Clark Gable in *Gone with the Wind*, or romantic like Dermot Mulroney in *The Wedding Date*. Instead he had squirmed, speechless with shock, his lower lip trembling as if he were Stan Laurel caught in an embarrassing failure. Walter had made no heartfelt appeals or snappy comebacks; those were as much fiction as a script for any Duro Studios production.

Shirley had grabbed her stuff—along with some of his, though he hadn't had the presence of mind to mention it—and stormed out of the apartment.

Sharon Stone in *Basic Instinct*. That's who she reminded him of.

The large, black walkie-talkie at his hip crackled, and even through the static of the poor-quality unit, he heard the lovely musical speech of Desiree Drea. Her voice never failed to make his heart skip a beat, then go back and skip it all over again. "Walter? Mr. Carmichael wants to know how you're coming with the props. He needs me to type up the inventory."

"I … um … I—" He looked down at the box, searching for words, and seized upon the letters stenciled to the crate. "I'm just now up to *Jungo's Revenge*. I've finished about half of the work."

As Desiree responded, he could hear the producer's voice bellowing in the background. "Jungo! It's all worthless crap. Trash it."

The secretary softened the message as she relayed it. "Mr.

Carmichael suggests that it's of no value, so please put it in the dumpster."

"And tell him he damn well better stay until he finishes," the voice in the background growled. "We need that building tomorrow to start shooting *Horror in the Prop Warehouse.*"

"Tell him I'll do what needs to be done," Walter said, then clicked off the walkie-talkie, though he would gladly have chatted with Desiree for hours. He didn't have anything better to do that evening than work, anyway. He was very conscientious and would finish the job.

Chris Carmichael—producer of low-budget knock-off movies. The Jungo ape-man series, a bad Tarzan knock-off, had skated just a little too close to Tarzan's copyright line. The threatened legal action had caused the films to flop, even though they were direct to video. Walter had seen one of them and thought that the movies were bad enough to have flopped all on their own, without any legal difficulties to help them along. If anything, the publicity had boosted the sales.

He pulled out the other plastic elephant tusk, then some ugly looking tribal masks, three rubber cobras, and a giant plastic insect as big as his palm that was labeled "Deadly Tsetse Fly." Walter shook his head. He had to agree about the worthlessness of these props. There wouldn't be any collector interested in even giving them shelf space. If there had been enough fans to generate a few collectors, the Jungo franchise might never have disappeared.

Near the bottom of the crate he found a rattle, a shrunken head, and another tribal mask, but these props were far superior to the others. They looked handmade, with real wood and bone. The shrunken head had an odd leathery feel that made him wonder if it was real. He shuddered as he took it out of the crate.

It seemed unlikely that Chris Carmichael, a tightwad with utter contempt for his audiences as well as his employees, would spend money on the genuine articles to use as props. Maybe a prop master had purchased them online or found them in a junk bin somewhere. Beneath the last of the witch doctor items, at the very bottom of the crate, he found a scrap of cloth that made him smile as he pulled it out and brushed off the bits of straw that clung to it.

A leopard-skin loincloth, the only garment Jungo the Ape Man had ever worn in the films—all the better to show off his well-developed physique, of course. Walter tried to remember. According to the story, Jungo had killed a leopard with his bare hands when he was only five years old and had made the loincloth out of its pelt. Apparently, the loincloth had grown along with the boy. Maybe the leopard had been part Spandex.... Jungo was probably the type of man Shirley would have fallen for—wild, tanned, brawny, and barely capable of stringing together three-word sentences. Walter groaned at the thought.

Now Desiree was another story entirely. Even on the big studio lot, they often crossed paths. He saw her in the commissary at lunch almost daily—because he timed his lunch hour to match hers. She was strikingly beautiful with her reddish-gold hair, her large blue eyes, her delicate chin, and when she smiled directly at him, as she had done three times now, it made him feel as if someone in the special effects shop had created the most spectacular sunrise ever.

But Walter still hadn't gotten up the nerve to ask if he could sit and eat with her. He was a nobody who did odd jobs around the lot for the various producers. Some of them were nice, and some of them were ... like Chris Carmichael. The man was Dabney Coleman in *9 to 5*, or Bill Murray before his transformation in *Scrooged*. Carmichael had put in a requisition and Walter had pulled the card: One man needed to clear prop warehouse. It was really a job for four men and four days, but Carmichael always slashed his budgets to leave more money in his own expense account. Carmichael didn't even know who Walter Groves was.

But Desiree did. That was all that mattered.

He gazed at the leopard-skin loincloth, hearing Shirley's words ring in his head. "You aren't a man's man. You don't let yourself go wild." He sniffed, trying to picture himself in the role she seemed to want him to play. What if Desiree felt the same way? What if all women thought they wanted a nice man but were only attracted to bad boys?

He picked up the witch doctor's rattle and gave it a playful shake, then put it down by the mask and the shrunken head. Even though she had hurt him, he wasn't the type either to put a curse on Shirley, or to transform himself for her into a muscular hunk of beefcake like Jungo. He would have needed an awfully large special effects budget to pull that off. Walter held up the leopard-skin loin-cloth to his waist and considered the fashion statement it would make. It looked ridiculous—even more so in contrast with his work pants and his conservative windowpane plaid shirt.

"If I wore this, what would Desiree think?" Would it convince her that he was a wild man, or would she just think him pale-skinned and scrawny? All alone in the prop warehouse, he had no particular need to hurry up. Carmichael, who never noticed anyone's hard work, had already said that the props were junk.

Before he could change his mind and think sensibly, Walter unbuttoned his shirt and peeled it off. Taking a deep breath, he slipped off his shoes and trousers and tied on the loincloth. He surveyed the effect, looking critically at his skinny chest, thin arms, white skin, and the leopard-skin loincloth. He cast a skeptical glance at the witch doctor mask. "Exactly how did I expect this to bring out the wild man in me?"

Then something happened.

His heart began to pound like drumbeats in his ears. His skin grew hot and his blood hotter. He felt dizzy and then very, *very* sure of himself. The worries and confusion of his life seemed to float away like soap bubbles on the wind. His attention focused down to a single pinprick. Everything was so clear, so simple. He had worried too much, *thought* too much, suppressed all of his natural desires. He drew a deep breath, kept inhaling until his chest swelled. Then on impulse, he pounded on his proudly expanded chest. It felt good and right.

He didn't have to worry about the prop inventory or about Shirley. She had made a bad choice, and she was gone. He no longer needed to think of her. Outside the sun was bright. He was a man, and Desiree was a woman. Everything else was extraneous, a distraction. He was a hunter and he knew his quarry. A real man relied on his instincts to tell him what to do.

He let out a warbling call, broadcasting a defiant challenge to anyone who might get in his way. Barefoot, he sprinted like a cheetah out of the prop warehouse and onto the lot. He had seen where Desiree worked. He knew where to find Chris Carmichael's trailer. His vision tunneled down to that one focus.

He streaked past the people working on various films. Someone made a catcall, but most of the crews ignored him. Employees at Duro Studios were accustomed to seeing axe murderers, Martians, barbarians, and monsters of all kinds.

Chris Carmichael's headquarters were in a dingy, gray-walled trailer on the far end of the east lot. The success of a producer's films earned him clout in the studios, and Carmichael's track record had earned him this unobtrusive trailer and one secretary.

Desiree.

Walter yanked open the door and leaped in. He hadn't decided what to say or do next, but an ape-man took matters one step at a time. He reacted to situations, without planning in excruciating detail beforehand. Instead of startling Desiree at her keyboard and the producer on the phone, he blundered into a shocking scene that would have made his hackles rise if he'd had any. Carmichael stood with both hands planted on his desk, crouched like a predator ready to spring. Desiree shielded herself on the other side of the desk, trying to keep it, with its empty coffee mugs, framed pictures, and jumbled stacks of scripts, between herself and Carmichael.

He leered at her, moved to the left, and she shifted to the right. She was flushed and nervous. "Please, Mr. Carmichael. I'm not that kind of girl."

"Of course, you are," he said. "If you didn't want to break into pictures, why would you work in a place like this? I can make you an extra in my next feature, *Horror in the Prop Warehouse*. Ten-seconds screen time minimum, but there's a price. You have to give me something." Now he circled to the right and she moved left.

"Please, don't do this. I don't want to file a complaint, but I'll call security if I have to."

"You do that, and you'll never work in this town again."

Before she could reply, Walter let out a bestial roar. He wasn't sure exactly what happened. Seeing red, he acted on instinct, and charged forward. He grabbed the producer by the back of his clean white collar, yanked him away from the desk, and spun him around. As he spluttered, Walter the ape-man landed a powerful roundhouse punch on Carmichael's chin and knocked him backward into the chair he reserved for visiting actors.

Startled, Desiree gasped, but Walter was already on the move. He bounded over the desk, slipped an arm around her waist, and crashed through the screen of the trailer's open window, carrying his woman with him. The rest was a blur.

When he could think straight again—after the witch doctor's spell, or whatever it was wore off—he found himself on the rooftop of one of the backlot sets, sitting next to Desiree, his lips pressed against hers. With a start, he drew back. Her hair was rumpled, her cheeks flushed, and she wore an expression of surprise and amusement. "That was a bit unorthodox, Walter," she said, "but you were amazing. You saved me when I needed it most."

"What have I done?" Walter glanced down at the loincloth, flexed his sore knuckles, and knew with absolute certainty that he would soon die from embarrassment. He was sitting half-naked on a roof at work and had just made a complete fool of himself in front of a woman he had a genuine crush on. "I'm sorry. I'm sorry!" He scuttled backward, stood to look for a ladder or stairs, and quickly found an exit. "I didn't mean to hurt you. Mr. Carmichael's going to get me fired, for sure."

"Who, Chris? He has no clue who you are," she said. "Anyway, I'm going to hand in my own resignation. I've had enough of that man."

"I … I need to put something decent on. I can't understand what got into me." He felt his cheeks burning. His legs wobbled, and his knees threatened to knock together. Some ape-man!

Before Desiree could say anything more, he bolted, cringing at the thought that someone else might see him this way—that Desiree *had* seen him. He was sure Jungo never had days like this.

By the time he got home, Walter was consumed with guilt. He felt flustered, exposed, and too embarrassed for words. He couldn't believe what he had done, prancing around the lot in nothing more than a loincloth, crashing into the producer's trailer offices. He had punched out Chris Carmichael! Then, after jumping through a window with Desiree, he had somehow whisked her off to a rooftop and *kissed her*! He was the very definition of the word "mortified." To make matters worse, Walter had gotten dressed again, called in a friend to finish clearing out the warehouse, then slunk off the lot, taking Jungo's loincloth with him. He could justify this, since Carmichael had made it clear that the props could be thrown into a dumpster.

He sat miserably in his empty apartment—without Shirley—and wondered how he could possibly make it up to Desiree. He didn't much care about Chris Carmichael. The man was a cad, but Walter himself had stolen a kiss from Desiree, practically ravished her! Considering the power the loincloth had worked on him, he could easily have gotten carried away. In the process of saving Desiree, he had proved that he was no better than that jerk of a producer.

And Walter had just left her stranded there, on the roof of the movie set. No, no, that wasn't Walter Groves. That wasn't who he really was. Though he wanted nothing more than to crawl under a rock, he knew what he had to do for the sake of honor. He had to go find Desiree and beg her forgiveness.

For a long time, he stood in the shower under a pounding stream of hot water, rehearsing what to say until he knew he couldn't put it off any longer. Every moment he avoided her was another moment she could think terrible things about him. He dried his hair, dabbed on some aftershave, and put on his best dress slacks, a clean shirt, and a striped blue necktie. This was going to be a formal apology, and he wanted to look his best. Pulling on his nicest, though rarely worn, sport jacket, he rolled up Jungo's loincloth and stuffed it into the pocket. Though it didn't make any sense, he would try to tell Desiree what had happened, explain how the magic had changed him somehow into a wild man, someone he wouldn't normally be.

After dialing information, then searching on the Internet, he tracked down a local street address for D. Drea. He knew it had to be her. Gathering his resolve, he marched out to go face her. He didn't need the crutch of a loincloth or some imaginary witch doctor's spells to give him courage to do the right thing. He would do this himself.

On the way to her apartment, he didn't let himself think, forcing himself onward before the shame could make him turn back. He had to be like Michael Douglas in *Romancing the Stone*, not Rick Moranis in *Little Shop of Horrors*. Nothing should disrupt the apology. Leaving his cell phone in the car, he walked to the door of her apartment, raised his hand to knock, then hesitated. He wasn't thinking clearly. He really should have brought flowers and a card. Why not go to a store now, buy them, and then come back?

He heard shouts coming from the other side of the door, followed by a scream—Desiree's scream!

He froze in terror. What should he do? Desiree was in trouble. Maybe he should run back outside, get his cell phone and call 911. He could bring the police here, or better yet, pound on her neighbors' doors and find someone who was big and strong. She screamed again, and Walter knew there could be only one solution. He tried the knob, found the door unlocked, and barged in. He found Chris Carmichael already there, reeking of cheap cologne and bourbon.

"Leave me alone," Desiree said. She held a lamp in one hand, brandishing it like a club.

Carmichael let out an evil chuckle. "Now that you no longer work for me, we can have any sort of relationship I want. There are no ethical problems."

She raised the lamp higher. Walter stepped forward, outraged but quailing at the idea of a fight. When Desiree saw him, her eyes lit up.

Carmichael turned.

Walter blurted, "Hey, What-what's going on here?" He wished he could hide or, at the very least, run back out of the apartment and return to do a second take of the scene. He needed to be a tough guy, like Dirty Harry in *Sudden Impact*—"Go ahead, make my day"—and the best he could come up with was a Don Knotts-worthy "Hey, what's going on here?" He groaned.

Carmichael recognized him, and his eyes grew stormy. Ignoring Desiree for the moment, the larger man lurched toward Walter, grabbed him by the shirt, yanked his tie, and drew Walter closer to him. "You're that little freak that sucker-punched me in my office, aren't you? Where's the spotted underwear?"

"I-I-I don't need it."

"You'll need an ambulance is what you'll need."

Indiana Jones would have done something different. He would have punched the villain, starting an all-out brawl, but as

Carmichael lifted him and twisted his tie, he could only make a small *meep* sound.

"You put him down," Desiree cried, and Walter's heart lurched. She was actually defending him!

Carmichael laughed again. "You can't even save yourself. How do you expect to help this mouse?" He pushed Walter up against the wall, clenched his fist, and drew back his arm, as if cocking a shotgun.

Walter was sure his head would go straight through the drywall. "Wait. Wait, please." He swallowed and drew a deep breath. "If you're going to do this, let me face it like a man. I ... I'd like to use the restroom, please."

Carmichael blinked, then gave him a knowing smile. "Oh, afraid you're going to wet yourself, eh?" He let Walter slump to the floor. "Sure. Why not? Desiree and I were just enjoying an intimate conversation. We can wait."

He glared at her and she sat down on the sofa, not sure what to do. Walter scurried into the bathroom and closed the door, his mind spinning. Maybe Desiree kept a gun in the bathroom, perhaps taped behind the toilet tank, like in *The Godfather*. But he found nothing there and a quick search of the drawers and the medicine cabinet revealed no other weapons he could use to save the day.

He stuck his hands in his jacket pockets and his fingers brushed a patch of sleek fur. The loincloth. It was his only chance.

Walter burst out of the bathroom wearing nothing but the scrap of leopard-skin. Barefoot and bare-chested, his mind filled with the thoughts of a hunter. Testosterone and adrenaline pumped through his veins and he let out a wild yell, pounding on his chest. His hair was a mess, his eyes on fire. Seeing his enemy, the producer, he lunged toward him like a hungry lion attacking a springbok. Walter felt total confidence and did not hesitate.

Chris Carmichael, who used his position of perceived power to intimidate people, faltered. When he saw Walter leap toward him, he suddenly reconsidered what he'd been about to do.

Walter let out another roar. His lungs seemed to have twice their normal capacity. "*My* woman!"

Carmichael had probably never been challenged before. A producer, even a bad producer of second-rate movies, could boss people around in Hollywood. But Walter the ape-man, wearing nothing but his loincloth in Desiree's apartment, had no doubt that he himself was king of the jungle. Carmichael turned, took several steps in retreat, then paused. Through his hunter-focused gaze, Walter watched his prey, preparing to throw himself on the man if he made a move in the wrong direction.

Desiree decided for both men, though. As Carmichael started to turn back, she lifted her lamp, and smashed it on his head. He crumpled to the carpet like King Kong falling off the Empire State Building. The rush in Walter's mind drained away, and he found himself standing naked in Desiree's apartment, except for the ape-man's loincloth. He shivered, and goose bumps appeared on his arms. "What did I do this time?" he said, looking down at the producer with dismay.

But Desiree was close to him. Very close and very beautiful. "You protected me, Walter. You saved me." She slid her arms around his waist and gave him a hug. "You're my hero."

It was not the magic of the loincloth that made his heart start pounding again. "You-you don't mind?" he asked in surprise.

"I'll show you how much I mind in just a minute." She stepped away and looked down at the unconscious Carmichael. "But first, help me take out the garbage. We'll put him in the hall and call the police." Walter and Desiree rolled the man like a skid row drunk into the apartment hallway.

Desiree closed the door, locked it, and turned to face him. Suddenly he felt as if he were the prey and she the hungry lioness.

He gulped. "I'm really a nice guy most of the time. But I can be bad, if I need to be."

"Walter, I *like* that you're a nice guy. It's the first thing I noticed about you, even from a distance. You may not have known I was watching, but I've seen you hold doors for other people, help them carry things when their arms were full, loan them lunch money, listen to what they say. Most of the time, that's exactly what women want. It's what *I* want. But women are … complex creatures. So once in a while we also like a bit of a wild man. You seem like the best of both worlds to me."

"You may never be safe," he pointed out. "What if Mr. Carmichael comes back? I don't think he'll leave you alone."

With a lovely smile she led him to the couch and sat him down. "In that case, maybe you'll just have to stay here to protect me."

There was a stirring in the loincloth, and he felt very self-conscious. "Maybe I should get dressed in real clothes."

"No, Walter. You stay just the way you are." Desiree leaned over to kiss him.

The seminal reason I wanted to become a science fiction writer is H.G. Wells's The War of the Worlds. *When I was only five or six years old, my parents let me watch the classic film of* The War of the Worlds *and it changed my life. That was what I wanted to write. I was so moved and inspired and fascinated by the story that I couldn't get it out of my head.*

And I've used that inspiration in much of my writing. This story is one of the most obvious, featuring a young H.G. Wells and his own (fictional) inspiration for the horrific Martian invasion.

SCIENTIFIC ROMANCE

Late after dark on a chill November night, young Wells followed T.H. Huxley up to the labyrinthine rooftop. The air felt damp, tinged with a clammy mist, yet the sky overhead was dark and clear and sparkling with stars.

The meteors would begin falling soon.

The minarets and gables of London's Normal School of Science provided nooks, crannies, gutters, and eaves where students could hold secret meetings, perhaps rendezvous with young girls from the poorer sections of South Kensington. Wells doubted, though, that any of his classmates would climb to the sprawling rooftop for the same purpose as his teacher and mentor led him now.

Huxley's creaking bones and aching limbs forced the old man to move slowly along the precarious shingles. Wells knew better than to offer the professor any assistance. Huxley finally found a spot against a gable and eased himself down. Leaning backward, he propped his head up and stared into the depths of the universe.

"Is this your first meteor shower, Herbert?" Huxley asked. "The Leonids are a good place to start. We should see about twenty per hour."

Wells, at only eighteen and much more limber, struggled to find his own comfortable observation place. "I've seen shooting stars before, sir," he said, "but I've never actually … studied them."

Huxley gave a wheezing laugh. His voice sounded strange to Wells, a private conversational tone instead of the forceful oratory for which he had become famous across England. "From what I can see, young man, you study every facet of life with those quick and darting eyes of yours."

Wells blushed, then ran a hand across his face to hide his embarrassment. His unkempt dark hair fell over his forehead, and his moustache showed gaps where the whiskers hadn't yet filled in enough.

He fidgeted, working himself into an awkward squat, holding onto a gutter for balance. Huxley intended to stay out here for hours, but the conversation interested Wells more than his personal comfort. Ideas made mankind superior to other creatures … and superior men had superior ideas.

The flash in his peripheral vision took him completely by surprise. "There!" he shouted, gesturing so rapidly that he nearly lost his precarious balance on the angled roof. A streak of brilliant, white light shot overhead then evaporated, so transient it seemed barely an afterimage on his eyes.

"The first meteor of the night," Huxley said with a smile, "and you spotted it, Wells. I'm proud of you. But of course, your eyesight is much better than mine."

"But your eyes have seen more things, sir," Wells said, then hated the reverential tone he had let slip.

"Don't flatter me," Huxley warned. The old man's wit and intellect were as bright as the sun, but his personality remained acerbic and abrasive. Wells would tolerate any number of rebukes, though, for the insights the professor had given him during his biology lectures.

Even now, Huxley fell comfortably into the role of teacher. "Make note of the meteorites we see this evening, and you will be able to envision their radiant point in the constellation Leo."

Wells settled back to continue watching. Bright in the western ecliptic, the ruddy point of Mars hung like a baleful eye, not twinkling, though the other stars around it glittered and flickered.

He shivered from the chill in the air, then tapped his foot, always moving, trying to get warm. Due to his severe financial situation, Wells was underweight and scrawny … even cadaverous, if one were to believe his roommate and friend, A.V. Jennings. On Tuesdays, the day before weekly pay for the scholars, Wells occasionally could not afford lunch, and Jennings would take him out to fill up on beefsteak and beer so that they could return replenished to the workbench in Huxley's laboratory.

Wells's wardrobe was meagre, consisting of grubby dark suits and worn celluloid shirt collars. His thin jacket was insufficient against the chill of the November evening, but he had no desire to go back inside the school building.

A second meteor appeared overhead like a line drawn with a pen of fire, eerie in its total silence. "Another!"

Around them the city of London made its own nighttime noises. Horse carts and black cabs clopped quietly by, while prostitutes flounced into dim alleys or waited under the gas streetlamps. Across the park, in the boarding house at Westbourne Grove where he and Jennings shared a room, Wells knew the other residents would be engaged in their nightly carousing, brawls, singing, and drinking. Here, high above it all, though, he enjoyed the peace.

Within moments a third meteor passed overhead, far from the trivial human concerns around him. This shooting star was larger and louder than the others, sputtering. Mentally tracing the fiery line back to its origin, Wells saw that the meteor radiated from a point in the sky not far from Mars itself, almost as if the red planet were launching them like sparks from a grinding wheel.

"Do you ever imagine, Professor Huxley, sir," he said as an intriguing idea formed in his mind, "that perhaps these flaming meteors are signals of a kind, even ships that have crossed the gulf of space?" Wells had had many outrageous ideas since the age of seven, and he often spoke his speculations aloud, sometimes to the entertainment of others, sometimes to their annoyance.

Huxley shifted position, looking over at his student with keen interest. "Ships?" His eyes held a bold challenge, as did his tone. "And from whence would they come, Wells?"

Wells rose to the occasion. "Why not ... Mars, for instance?" He indicated the orange-red pinpoint of the planet. "According to theory, as the solar system cooled, each planet became hospitable to life in relation to its distance from the Sun. On Mars, therefore, intelligent life could have begun to evolve long before any such spark occurred on Earth."

At the mention of evolution, Huxley perked up—just as Wells had known he would. The professor had spent his life as a proponent of Darwinism, had debated buffoons and ill-educated orators in so many forums that Huxley became infamous as "Darwin's Bulldog."

Another shooting star passed overhead, as if to emphasize Wells's point.

"Martians," Huxley said with a wry smile. "Interesting. And what do you suppose a Martian would look like?"

Wells folded one leg over the other, in spite of his precarious rooftop position, and restrained himself from answering instantly. Huxley did not suffer foolish or glib answers. "I would suppose that since the Martians are a much more ancient race, they would have minds immeasurably superior to our own. Their bodies would be composed almost entirely of brain."

Two more faint Leonid meteors danced overhead unnoticed. Wells uncrossed and recrossed his legs.

"And what would such beings look like?"

Wells frowned, letting his thoughts flow. "Natural selection would ultimately shape a superior being into a creature with a huge head and eyes. He would have delicate hands, tentacles perhaps, for manipulating tools—but his mentality would be his greatest tool."

"An interesting exercise, Wells. You have quite an imagination." Huxley leaned forward from his cramped position against the gable, scooting across the roof tiles so that he could speak in a low, hoarse voice to his protégé. "But why would Martians want to come to our green Earth? What is their motive?"

Wells was ready for that one. "Mars is a dry planet, cold and drained of resources. Our world is younger, fresher, more vibrant —filled with all the things they have lost over the course of their evolution. Perhaps even now the Martians are regarding this Earth with envious eyes. They might even be drawing up plans for invasion."

As a boy, Wells had studied military history, staging mock battles in the park, and observing the movements of one historical army against another. But an interplanetary war was beyond his comprehension.

"A war of the worlds?" Huxley actually chuckled at this. "And you believe that such superior minds as you propose would engage in an exercise as trivial as military conquest? You must not consider them so evolved after all."

Wells kept his thoughts to himself, for he had suddenly realized that perhaps Thomas H. Huxley was a bit naïve himself.

In his life, Wells had seen the gross divisions of the upper and lower classes and how each fought amongst the others for dominance. His sweet, hard-working mother had sent him off to be apprenticed to a draper, where he had labored as a virtual slave. After escaping that fate through his own calculated incompetence, Wells had lived with his mother where she was the head domestic servant in a large manor, and she had commanded the workers beneath her. His angry father had once been a gardener, but for years had found no better employment than occasional cricket playing....

The hierarchy remained, no matter what their social standing, powerful and powerless. It proved to Wells's satisfaction the Darwinian basis that all humans had been predators at some time in the past.

Wells answered his professor carefully. "If the Martians are a dying race," he said, "it would be survival of the fittest. The Martians would see Earth ripe for conquest, humans as inferior cattle."

"Survival of the fittest—I'll concede that point, Wells," Huxley said. "We must hope the Martians do not invade." He shifted back to his former position, where he watched for further Leonids.

The two sat in silence, looking into the clear sky. Wells shivered, partially from the cold, partially from his own thoughts.

They watched the stars fall as the red eye of Mars blinked balefully at them.

THE FOLLOWING DAY, in the bustling laboratory section of Huxley's biology course, Wells felt feverish. He wondered if he had caught a chill from the previous night's vigil.

Nevertheless, the sounds of clacking beakers, the smell of old chemical experiments, and the chatter of students engaged his mind. He soon became totally absorbed in the setting up of microscopes and experimental apparatus for the morning's exercise.

One of Huxley's assistants—a demonstrator who delivered occasional lectures when Huxley himself was too ill to speak—prepared the laboratory activity. As if he were a prize French chef, he presented a pot in which he had prepared an infusion of local weeds and pond water. The resulting murky concoction was infested with numerous fascinating microbes.

Wells's workbench partner, A.V. Jennings, was the son of a doctor. He received a small stipend, which allowed him much greater security than Wells, though they both lived in an unpleasant boarding house an intellectual world away from the high atmosphere of Huxley's lecture hall.

Now, while Jennings set up their shared microscope on a narrow table against the windows, Wells went forward with his microscope slide to receive a drop of the precious infusion, as if it were some scientific communion. He carefully slid a cover slip over the beer-colored droplet and returned to where his partner had finished preparing the apparatus.

Under watery light shining through a veil of gray clouds, Wells focused and refocused the microscope. Jennings had a sketchpad, as did Wells, to record their observations. Wells feverishly sketched the alien-looking creatures he observed: protozoans of all types, alien shapes with whipping flagella, hairlike cilia vibrating in a blur ... blobby amoebas, various strains of algae.

As Wells scrutinized the exotic creatures swarming and multiplying in the tiny universe of a drop of water, he felt like a titan. His looming presence stared through an eyepiece to observe the tiny struggles of pond microorganisms....

Wells realized that the other students had stopped their conversations and stood at attention, as if a royal presence had entered the room. Professor T.H. Huxley had deigned to visit his laboratory this morning.

The intimidating, acerbic old man strode around the various

workbenches where his students diligently studied the infinitesimal animals they found on their microscope slides. Huxley nodded approvingly, made quiet sounds but little conversation, and moved from station to station.

When the great man came to where Wells stood proudly beside his microscope, Huxley said in a gruff voice, "Morning, Wells." The professor bent over to study their slide, adjusted the focus ever so slightly as if it were his due. "Lovely euglena you have here under the light." He made another noncommittal sound, then moved on to the other students.

Wells stood looking after his mentor, disappointed. Huxley had made no mention of their shared experience with the meteor shower, their imaginative conversation. He had come here for no purpose other than to scrutinize his insignificant students … in the same way that Wells and Jennings had been studying the microbes.

His cheeks flushed, and the cool feverish sweat swept over him. He extended his imagination farther, wondering if other powerful beings might even now be scrutinizing Earth in the same manner, curious about the buzzing and swarming colony of London.

The hair on the back of his neck prickled, as if he could sense the probing eyes watching him from afar.

He was startled to find Jennings regarding him oddly. "You don't look at all well, Herbert," he said. Jennings reached over with practiced ease and touched Wells's forehead. "In fact, you're burning up." He frowned. "I think you should go home and rest before this grows more serious."

~

THE FEVER CAUGHT HOLD with nightmarish strength, and Wells fell into a labyrinth of delirium fostered by the powerful resources of his own imagination.

He saw meteors falling and falling, huge cylinders accompanied by green fire that blazed across the sky. The interplanetary ships crashed to Earth, pummeling England like quail shot.

In the great impact craters where they settled and cooled, the cylinders opened up to reveal that they were warships from the red planet, carrying hordes of invading Martians—hugely developed brains with tentacled limbs evolved under a lower gravity.

Their vast mentalities had turned toward the conquest of Earth. The most insignificant of these extraordinarily developed creatures had a military intellect far superior to the combined genius of Napoleon and Alexander the Great.

Using their whiplike appendages, the Martians built war machines, clanking metal things on tall stilt-like legs that surpassed even the imagination of Leonardo Da Vinci.

The clanking machines strode about the English landscape like the industrial contraptions he had seen among the dark factories of the dirty towns where he had worked as a draper's apprentice. But these machines were equipped with weapons, powerful heat rays that burned everything in sight.

Hot like Wells's fever.

And overhead the meteors continued falling, falling.…

WHEN THE FEVER FINALLY BROKE, Wells awoke in his narrow, lumpy bed to find Jennings tending him, laying a cool rag over his forehead. A patch of bright, hot sunlight spilled through the window, warming his skin.

Wells croaked, his voice uncooperative, but he spoke quickly, not wanting his roommate to get the best of him with a first witticism. "What now, Jennings?" he said. "Are you practicing to become a doctor like your father?"

Jennings smiled. His eyes were red-rimmed, as if he hadn't gotten much sleep. "You've had quite a time of it, Herbert. Been sick for days, feverish, haven't eaten a thing but a bit of broth I managed to acquire for you."

"Worst of all, you've missed three of my lectures," said another voice.

Weakly, Wells managed to prop himself up enough to see another man standing in the small, stuffy room. T.H. Huxley himself.

"Since you are one of only three students who has so far proved worthy of a first-class passing grade," the old professor said, "I wanted to see why you were so rude as to forsake my class." Huxley's voice was stern but subdued, as if he were restraining his normal booming tone only with great difficulty.

"Not to worry, sir," Wells said. "I'm sure Jennings took good notes."

It embarrassed him that Huxley had to see how lowly his student lived. The room in South Kensington had a crowded, squalid appearance, with too many brutish noises that carried through the walls as other boarders came in drunk at all hours. The air was cold—no one had brought up coal for some time—and smelled rank from unemptied chamber pots sitting out in the hall.

The professor maintained a mock stern expression. "I should have been quite disappointed had you died, Wells. Though you are only eighteen, I see great potential in you."

Huxley paced the room as if searching for something significant to say. Wells waited for him. "Quite humbling, isn't it?" the professor finally said. "A superior creature such as yourself, highly evolved and possessed of a grand intellect—laid low by something as crude and insignificant as an Earthly germ."

Wells gave a wan smile in response. "I'm sorry, sir. I shall try to prove my evolutionary superiority henceforth."

Huxley sighed reticently and paused at the door, ready to leave. "You may wish to know, Wells, that I have decided this will be my last semester teaching. I've spent far too many years trying to show everyone the obvious truth, and I shall give it up and retire out of sheer exhaustion."

Distraught, Wells cried, "But, sir, there's so much more we can learn from you!"

"I have wasted far too much time and energy in debates with fools over the correctness of Darwinism. I've earned myself a rest. But I will need someone to carry on, eventually."

Huxley opened the door, adjusted his hat, and frowned back at his sick student. "With your imagination, I think you can make something of yourself, Wells," he said. "Don't disappoint me."

Then Huxley left, heading out to far more pleasant surroundings on the other side of the park.

Wells leaned back into his bed while Jennings stared at him in awe. "That was quite a benediction, Herbert."

Wells lay back and closed his eyes, dizzy with residual weakness from the fever. But his mind was already whirling and spinning, filled with a thousand thoughts.

"I think I'll rest for a bit, Jennings," he said.

After all, he had to restore his health before he could begin his life's work.

Another story directly influenced by H.G. Wells and The War of the Worlds. *Wells published his novel in 1897, during the Mars craze inspired by astronomer Percival Lowell, who chronicled the canals he saw on Mars through his giant refractor telescope in Flagstaff, Arizona. I researched Lowell and visited the Flagstaff observatory. In one of the documents, I discovered a brief description of a plan Lowell developed, to dig giant canals in the Sahara, fill them with burning oil, to send a signal that would be seen by real Martians, far away. I thought this audacious plan would be a terrific foundation for a story, and when I added Wells's Martians ready to invade Earth, it became even more than that. This story, and the previous "Scientific Romance," are the core of my H.G. Wells novel,* The Martian War.

CANALS IN THE SAND

Under the sweltering heat of the Sahara, Percival Lowell stood beside his own tent at the center of the camp and reveled in the clamor of his vast construction site. The excavations extended beyond the vanishing point of the flat desert horizon. Thousands of sweating workers—who worked for mere pennies a day—moved like choreographed machinery as they dug monumental trenches according to Lowell's commands, scribing a long line in the sand.

Lowell had seen the same on Mars, long canals, straight lines extending thousands of miles across the rusted desert. His own observations had absolutely convinced him that such markings must be indicative of surface life on a dying world.

Other astronomers claimed not to see the network of canals, that the lines on the disk of Mars were not there. It reminded him of the trial of Galileo, when the high church officials and Pope Paul V had refused to see the moons of Jupiter through the astronomer's "optick glass," denying the evidence of their own eyes. Lowell couldn't decide if his own contemporaries were similarly bull-headed, or just plain blind.

He took a deep breath, ignoring the pounding sun. The fiery heat and dust and petroleum stench practically curled the hairs in his mustache. With recently washed hands, he fished inside the front pocket of his cream jacket and withdrew his special pair of pince-nez, with lenses made of red stained glass. Through the copper-oxide tint, he could look out at the blistering and dead Sahara, seeing instead the scarlet sands of Mars. *Mars.*

How could one stand out here in the desert and not intuitively understand why the Martians would need to construct an extravagant set of canals to transport precious water from the melting ice caps down to their ancient cities? Water covered sixty percent of the Earth's surface, while Mars remained one vast planetary wasteland. The Martians' magnificent canals had endured as their world grew parched and withered with age, as their civilization mummified. By this time, those once-glorious minds must be desperate, ready to grasp at any hope.

Lowell strolled out along the well-packed path from the encampment to the long ditch his army of workers had dug in the shifting sands. Compared to what the Martians had accomplished, it seemed a child's futile effort, and it certainly wouldn't endure long—but then Lowell's canal was not required to.

It must remain only long enough to send a signal.

If Ogilvy's calculations were correct, Lowell had little time. He prayed his Bedouin workers would be fast enough. But he vowed nothing would deter him. After all, he had built his great Arizona observatory in a mere six weeks from groundbreaking to first light. He could certainly handle digging a ditch, even if it was ten miles long out in the middle of the Sahara.

NIGHT ON MARS HILL in the Arizona Territory, at an elevation of 7,000 feet, with clear skies far from the smoke of men. The big refractor and the observatory dome had been completed just in time to allow observations of the 1894 opposition of Mars.

Lowell spent his every free moment at the telescope.

His fellow Bostonian William H. Pickering, an astronomer for Harvard, and his assistant Andrew Ellicott Douglass, both stood inside the chill, echoing dome of the Flagstaff Observatory, waiting for Lowell to relinquish the eyepiece. The wooden-plank walls of the observatory dome exuded a resinous scent. From where he sat in the uncomfortable chair, porkpie hat turned backward on his head and sketchpad in his lap, Lowell could sense their impatience.

"It is *my* telescope, gentlemen, and *I* will do the observing," Lowell said, not removing his eye from the wavering disk of the ruddy world, where fine lines appeared and disappeared as the seeing shifted in the Earth's atmosphere.

"Mister Lowell, sir," Pickering said, clearing his throat, "I understand your eagerness to use the refractor, but *we* are your professional astronomers, with the proper qualifications—"

Lowell finally turned, feeling annoyance heat his skin. "Qualifications, Mr. Pickering? I have exceptionally keen eyesight—and an exceptionally large fortune, which has built this telescope and pays your stipend. Therefore, I am fully qualified."

He snorted, looking down from his seat on the padded ladder and adjusting the porkpie hat on his head. "Perhaps if your Harvard had agreed to engage in a joint venture with me, Pickering, rather than calling me 'egoistic and unreasonable,' I would be more inclined to share. But instead, my own alma mater could not be convinced to do more than give you two gentlemen leave to work here, and then lease—*lease!*—me one of their small telescopes."

Douglass took a step back and looked to Pickering for his cue. Pickering, as always, cleared his throat and searched in vain for words.

Lowell's nostrils flared over his mustache. "You gentlemen are welcome to devote your nights to the study of the heavens at any other time, but this is *Mars* and it is at opposition. Please indulge this unworthy amateur." He turned back to the telescope, while the others shuffled their feet uncomfortably, and continued to wait. Within moments, Lowell had become totally engrossed in the view, his universe shrunk down to the tiny circle visible through the eyepiece.

Tact was a commodity that served little purpose when time was short. Lowell had selected Pickering, in part, because of his successful studies of Mars in 1892 at Arequipa in Peru. Pickering, a decent though somewhat stuffy administrator, had spent the winter of '93 in Boston supervising the design and construction of this observatory, which had been shipped out piece by piece to Flagstaff the following spring. Every bit of the project was a rush because Lowell demanded that the telescope absolutely must be functional by the time of the planetary opposition. Such a close encounter with Mars would not come again for many years.

Lowell drew a deep breath, shifted himself in his seat high above the observatory floor, and craned his neck. He fiddled with the eyepiece, and Mars stared back at him. He had the strangest sensation of being on the opposite end of a microscope, as if some immense being from across the cosmos were watching *him*, as someone with a microscope studied creatures that swarmed and multiplied in a drop of water.

His hands working independently, guided by the information channeled through the refractor tube, Lowell deftly sketched Mars, copying the lines he saw on the face of the planet. He had never been an armchair astronomer and would go blind before he ever allowed himself to be considered one. He and his staff had already recorded some four hundred canals on Mars—canals that other observers preposterously refused to see!

Lowell's outspoken beliefs had earned him much scorn, but no descendant of the great Boston family could remain quiet about deep convictions. In this case, and in many others, Percival Lowell knew he was right and the rest of the world was wrong—and he had proved it.

Well after midnight, his eyes burned. He flipped over the page in his sketchpad to where he had already scribed another perfect circle for a new map. Daylight hours were best used to prepare for the next clear night's observing.

Lowell noted that Douglass and Pickering had left unobtrusively, and he hoped they were at least doing work at the other telescopes, since the seeing was so extraordinary this evening. He blinked, oriented his hand and a newly sharpened pencil on the map pad, then pressed against the eyepiece again.

A brilliant green flash leaped from the surface of Mars.

Lowell barely restrained himself from crying out. The flame had been a vivid emerald, a jet of fire as of a great explosion or some kind of immense cannon shot, a huge mass of luminous gas, trailing a green mist behind it.

Once previously, Lowell had seen the glint of sunlight on the Martian ice caps, which had fooled him into seeing a dazzling message—but it had not been like this. Not so green, so violent, so prominent.

Before long he witnessed another green flash, and quickly noted the exact time on the pad in his lap. His excitement grew as he formulated his own explanation for the phenomenon....

Several days later he received a telegram from Ogilvy, a prominent London astronomer, confirming the green flashes from Mars. Ogilvy himself had counted flashes on ten nights, while Lowell himself had recorded several others, which had occurred during the daylight hours in England.

Lowell knew exactly what the flashes must be, and he exhibited no reluctance whatsoever in telling others about his theories. Obviously, these brilliant flares were indications of stupendous launches, a fleet of ships exploding away from Martian gravity into space.

There could be no other explanation. The Martians were coming!

~

WORK CREWS TOILED day and night to move the sand, some complaining, some happy for the meager pay, some shaking their sweat-dripping heads at the insanity of this loud American and his incomprehensible obsession.

The Bedouins thought he was mad, as did many of Lowell's colleagues. But the superstitious Bedouins understood nothing of the universe ... nor, for that matter, did most other astronomers.

He allowed no slacking in the construction for any reason. Shovels tossed sand up over the walls of the ditches; half naked boys ran with ladles and buckets, while camels strained to drag barrels of warm water along the length of the dry canal. Lowell supervised here, and he could only hope that the other two trenches would be completed in time to intersect with this one.

When the teams grew too tired to continue, he hired more. Lowell had spread his funds as far as Cairo and Alexandria. He had bribed port officials, paid for the construction of a new railroad out into the desert, leading nowhere, so that a private train could deliver supplies and workers to Lowell's canals.

The sand hissed in the breeze, glittering in the sun. A drummer pounded a cadence to keep the workers in a steady rhythm, like galley slaves. But they were being paid for this labor, and they had volunteered, so Lowell felt no sympathy for them.

Smoke curled into the air, carrying an acrid, sulfurous stench as brown-skinned men dumped wagonloads of hot bitumen into the newly dug trench. The sticky black mass would hold the sands in place, bind them into a thick, flammable mass. Still, the walls shifted, and the bitumen ran black and sticky in the heat of the day.

Grumbling, Lowell doubted the sloping walls of sand would hold if one of the great dust storms of the Sahara swept across the dunes. With one mighty breath, God could erase all of Lowell's handiwork, the fruits of years of labor and a squandered family fortune.

If only luck could hold until he sent his signal....

The great Suez Canal had been completed three decades earlier. For years the United States had discussed excavating a canal across Central America as soon as the government found some way to grab the necessary land. Lowell's own project was not impossible. It could not be impossible.

He strutted up and down the edge of the ditch, a dusty bandanna wrapped over his mouth, nose, and mustache. He recalled the ancient Hebrew slaves, erecting immense monuments for the pharaohs. But the pharaohs had had decades, even generations, to complete their enormous projects. Lowell had no such luxury.

The line in the sand stretched into a shimmer of mirage in the wavering air. Just a ditch, many miles long, extending to meet two other ditches in what his surveyors guaranteed would be a perfect equilateral triangle.

Back home in Boston, leaving the Flagstaff Observatory in the hands of Pickering and Douglass for the autumn, Lowell had calculated the absolute limit of his financial resources, determining the largest excavation he could complete, since the governments of the world refused to help in what they called his "crackpot scheme."

And still Percival Lowell had accomplished little more than a gnat, compared to Martian accomplishments, even allowing for the fact that their task would have been simpler, given that Martian gravity was only a third of Earth's. He had postulated Martian beings, therefore, three times the size of a human; in their reduced gravity, such Martians could be 21 times as efficient and have 81 times the effective strength of an Earthbound man. For such a species, the project of planetary canals seemed not unlikely.

Lowell's notebooks lay in the tent, but he had done the mathematics himself, letting the engineers double-check his work. Three trenches, each ten miles long, five yards wide, filled with liquid to a depth of an inch or so, equaled thousands and thousands of gallons of petroleum distillate, naphtha, kerosene. The convoys traveled endlessly across the Sahara: an impossible task, made possible—just barely—through the use of his great fortune.

It was a huge investment, but what better way could Lowell spend his money?

Douglass and Pickering had squawked when he had cut his generous allowance of funding for the Flagstaff Observatory down to a maintenance stipend. "How are we to continue our research?" their plaintive telegram had wailed.

"Come to the Sahara," he had replied, "and I will show you."

If Lowell succeeded in signaling the Martians, here and now, astronomical observatories around the world would never again lack for funding.

But they had to hurry. Hurry.

A BLUSTERY MAN, not intimidated by challenge, Lowell nevertheless found himself stuttering in awe when he met in Milan with the great Giovanni Schiaparelli—discoverer of asteroids and the original cartographer of the canals of Mars.

After spotting the green flashes, then laying plans for his great project to signal back to the Martians, Lowell had allotted himself half a year to travel to Europe and generate support. He had taken a first-class cabin on a steamer bound for England. Reaching London, he had sought out Ogilvy and immediately enlisted his aid.

The other astronomer had at first been skeptical that there could be any living thing on that remote, forbidding planet. Lowell, however, had been very persuasive.

Obtaining leave from his observatory, Ogilvy accompanied Lowell on his travels. Ogilvy's friend, a journalist named Wells, also asked to travel with them in hopes of getting a good story for his newspaper, but Lowell would have none of it. The newspapers had resoundingly ridiculed Lowell's theories about the Martian canals, and he wanted nothing further to do with reporters, not in the initial stages of a project of such importance.

The two men proceeded across the Channel and thence to Paris for an excellent dinner and conversation with the well-known French writer and astronomer, Camille Flammarion, who gave Lowell's idea a favorable reception. He beamed with pleasure to hear the Frenchman proclaim that Lowell's own theories about the canals and life on Mars had been "ascertained indubitably."

By train and private carriage, Lowell, and a wide-eyed Ogilvy—who had never previously visited the Continent—traveled to Italy to meet with Schiaparelli in his small villa.

Schiaparelli had been director of the Milan Observatory since 1862, where he had discovered the asteroid Hesperia, written a brilliant treatise on comets and meteors, and created his original maps of the Martian *canali* in 1877, only a year after Lowell himself had graduated with honors from Harvard. During that same opposition, the American astronomer Asaph Hall had discovered the two tiny moons of Mars, Phobos and Deimos—Fear and Dread. But using only an eight-inch telescope, Schiaparelli had exposed a more profound cosmic secret.

"When I originally drew my maps," the old astronomer said, struggling with his English, "I meant to represent the lines merely as channels or cracks in the surface. I understand that *canali* implies a different thing to non-Italian ears, suggesting man-made canals—"

"Not *man*-made," Lowell interrupted, extracting his pipe from its case and tamping a load of sweet tobacco from his pouch, "but made by intelligent beings, whose minds may be immeasurably superior to ours. Extraterrestrial life does not mean extraterrestrial human life. Under changed conditions, life itself must take on other forms."

"Yes, yes," Schiaparelli nodded, took a sip of his deep red wine, then a bigger gulp. He blinked his rheumy eyes. "But your subsequent observations have convinced even me, my friend."

Lowell leaned forward intently, lacing his fingers together over his knees. "I wish you could see what I have seen on the red disk of the Great God of War, Schiaparelli. Such wonders."

The old astronomer sighed. His rooms were filled with books, oil lamps, and melted lumps of candles in terra cotta dishes. A pair of spectacles lay on an open tome, while an enormous magnifying glass rested in easy reach on another stack of books.

"I can only imagine them. My own eyesight has grown so poor that I must now occupy my mind and my time with the study of history. Though I can no longer study comets or meteors or planets, even an old man with dim vision can make astute observations of history."

"Tell him about Mars, Lowell, my good man," Ogilvy said, searching for something else to eat, and finally settling on some water crackers and old cheese left out on the sideboard in the Italian's dim rooms.

Lowell opened his mind's eye wide as he spoke in an oddly quiet and reverent voice, totally distinct from his usual booming, commanding tone. Thoughts of Mars still made him breathless with astonishment.

"You drew the canals yourself, Schiaparelli—narrow dark lines of uniform width and intensity, perfectly straight. Some even compose portions of great circles across the globe. As I view them from Flagstaff in my best refractor, they look to be gossamer filaments, cobwebs on the face of the Martian disk, threads to draw your mind after them, across millions of miles of intervening void."

Schiaparelli rubbed his eyes. "In my youth I, myself, never conceived them to be more than blemishes."

Lowell raised his eyebrows dubiously. "Geometrical precision on a planetary scale? What else can it be but the mark of an intelligent race? If we could respond in kind, would we not be morally obligated to do so, in the name of humanity?"

Ogilvy coughed on his cracker and looked about for something to drink, finally settling on a wicker-wrapped bottle of Chianti that Schiaparelli had opened for them. He poured sloppily into a glass on the sideboard, then took a quick swallow, only to renew his coughing fit. Lowell scowled at the British astronomer for shattering his spell of imagination.

He puffed on his pipe and settled back in the fine leather-bound chair. Outside on the open balcony, pigeons fluttered in the sunlight. Schiaparelli still watched him with an intent stare. Ogilvy began to page through one of the open history books.

"Imagine it, Schiaparelli," Lowell continued. "Think of a parched, dying world inhabited by a once-marvelous civilization, beings with the science and ingenuity to keep themselves alive at all costs. Why, the very existence of a planetwide system of canals implies a world order that knows no national boundaries, a society that long ago forgot its political disputes and racial animosity, uniting the populace in a desperate quest for water. Water ..."

"And the dark spots, Lowell?" Ogilvy asked, turning back to the conversation. Schiaparelli drank more of his Chianti, amused and fascinated by the description. "Tell him about the oases."

Lowell stood up to stretch, placed his hands behind his back, and turned to the balcony to watch the pigeons. "Pumping stations, obviously."

The old Italian astronomer stared at where the walls of his villa met the ceiling, but he seemed to see nothing, perhaps only a blur with his used-up eyes. Lowell felt a rare flash of sympathy—losing one's eyesight must be the greatest hell a dedicated astronomer could imagine.

"But if Mars is so arid, Lowell, surely all the water would evaporate from these open canals long before it reaches its destination ... if the temperature is much above freezing, that is—and it *must* be above freezing in order for the water to be in its liquid state." Schiaparelli's forehead creased in a frown.

Ogilvy piped up, pacing the room. "And don't forget, my good man, the astronomical distances involved. If these canals were simple waterways or aqueducts, we would never be able to see them from Earth. They would be much too narrow. How do you account for that?"

Annoyed, Lowell turned to the Englishman. He and Ogilvy had already had this discussion in earnest several times, and again on the train ride to Milan. But he saw Ogilvy's raised eyebrow and understood that the other man had raised the question just to give Lowell a chance to explain.

"Ah, there is a simple answer for both questions," Lowell said, then paused to draw deeply from his pipe. "Almost certainly the lines we see are aqueducts with lush vegetation growing in irrigated croplands along the borders. The only remaining forests on Mars, towering high in the low gravity, sipping precious water from the fertile soil—much as the Egyptians grow their crops in the plains around the Nile. I estimate the darkened fringes of the aqueducts to be about thirty miles wide. This vegetation would not only emphasize the lines of the canals but would also shield the open water from rapid evaporation. Simple, you see? It is quite clear."

Ogilvy nodded, and Schiaparelli gave a distant smile. The old astronomer seemed more amused than impassioned by the concepts. Lowell came closer to his host, barely controlling his own enthusiasm. "My proposed plan follows a similar principle, Schiaparelli. The project I have conceived will take place on a much smaller scale, naturally, since I am but one man and, alas, our own Earthly civilization has no stomach for such dreams.

"I have already dispatched surveyors and work teams to the Sahara, in the flat desert in western Egypt. I will excavate three canals of my own, each ten miles long, across an otherwise featureless basin, to form a perfect equilateral triangle. A geometrical symbol impossible to explain with random natural processes, and therefore a clear message that intelligent life inhabits this world. To make them more visible, I must emphasize my puny canals with lines of fire, by filling the trenches with petroleum products and igniting them. It will be a brief but dramatic message, blazing into the night." His eyes sparkled, his voice rose in volume.

"But why this tremendous effort, my friend?" Schiaparelli asked. "Why now?"

Promptly, he and Ogilvy described the repeated green flashes, the launches of enormous vehicles, ships sent to Earth. Based on Ogilvy's observations and calculations derived from a careful scrutiny of celestial mechanics, Lowell believed he knew the travel time the Martians required to reach Earth.

Lowell's voice became husky. "As you can see, the Martians are on their way. We must show them where to land, where they will meet with an open-hearted welcome from Earthbound admirers of their past triumphs and their current travails."

Lowell took a deep breath and spoke with absolute confidence. "Gentlemen, *I* intend to lead that party. I will be the first man to shake hands with a Martian."

~

FINALLY.

Finally. Lowell had never been a man of extraordinary patience, but the last week of waiting for the three trenches to join at precise corners had been the most interminable time of his life.

Now, under the starlight and the residual heat that wafted off the baked sands, Lowell stood with his torch in hand, feeling like a tribal shaman, ready to ignite his weapon against the darkness, his symbol of welcome to aliens from another world.

The stench of petroleum distillates stung his eyes and nostrils. The chemical smell had driven off the camels and most of the workers, save those few foremen—mostly Europeans—who intended to watch the spectacle. On high dunes in the distance, the curious Bedouins had gathered by their own tents to observe. This would be an event for their storytellers to repeat for generations.

Working with his reluctant assistants Pickering and Douglass, Lowell had gone to a great deal of trouble to calculate the best time when the Sahara night would face Mars, so that his transient shout into the universe had the best chance of being seen—if not from the inbound Martian emissary ships, then from those survivors who had remained on the red planet.

Lowell turned to the telegraph operator beside him. Miles of overland cable had been run to the other vertices of the great triangle in the sand, so that the teams could communicate with each other. "Signal Pickering and Douglass at the other two inter-sections. Tell them to light their channels."

The telegraph operator pecked away at his key, sending a brief message. When the clicks fell into silence, Lowell stepped to the brink of his canal in the sand. He stared down into the bitumen-lined trench, the foul-smelling black mass that was now pooled with kerosene and gasoline dumped from enormous tanks that had been hauled across the desert by his private railroad.

Lowell tossed his torch into the fuel, then watched the fire spread like a hungry demon, rushing down the channel. The inferno devoured the dumped petroleum, hot enough to ignite the sticky bitumen liner so that the triangular symbol would burn for a long time.

Across the desert into the night, rifle shots rang out, signaling to other torchbearers stationed along the ten miles of each canal, who also tossed their burning brands into the ditch, so that the fire could engulf the entire triangle. Martians and fire, Lowell thought —what a strange combination.

Lowell's family had already made its mark on the world. Towns had been named after the Lowells and the Lawrences; his maternal grandfather was Abbott Lawrence, minister to Britain. His father, Augustus Lowell, was descended from the early Massachusetts colonists. His family had amassed its fortune in textiles, in land-holdings, in finance. But Percival himself would make the greatest mark—on *two* worlds instead of one.

An unbroken wall of flame roared up into the night. He prayed the Martians were watching. He had so much to say to them.

LOWELL FOUND it difficult to sleep even long after the inferno had died down. He lay on his cot in his tent, smelling the dying smoke and harsh fumes, listening to the whisper of settling sand sloughing into the bottom of the trench from the burned walls. Far off in the Bedouin camp a pair of camels belched at each other.

In only a year or two, the shifting desert would erase most of his line in the sand, leaving only a dark scar. But if his intended audience received the message, Earth would be a dramatically changed place in that time, and his effort would not be in vain.

Lowell found his situation incredibly strange: he, a wealthy Boston Brahmin, now resting fitfully in an austere tent in the middle of a vast desert that had been made even more unpleasant by his own construction work.

Summoning images of beauty to his mind, he recalled his experiences in Japan, as much an alien world as this Sahara, perhaps even as alien as Mars. He thought of colors bright as enamel and lacquer, gold filigree and cloisonné, the heady perfumes of peonies and burning incense. He remembered being escorted along narrow avenues of carefully tended trees where an explosion of white petals drifted on the winds for the annual cherry blossom festival. He recalled the delicate ritual of a tea ceremony, or the thin atonal melody plucked out on a *biwa* as spiced morsels sizzled on a small hibachi.

During those years as ambassador to Japan, Lowell had lugged his six-inch refractor with him, staring, staring, seeing the Earth but watching the stars....

He had graduated from Harvard with distinction in mathematics at the age of twenty-one, and he had received the Bowdoin Prize for his essay on "The Rank of England as a European Power Between the Death of Elizabeth and the Death of Anne." He had traveled the world, studied the classics, experienced numerous foreign cultures, proved his facility in languages, even tried to join the fighting in the Serbo-Turkish War. What did he care that mere astronomers scorned his ideas?

Lowell had sailed for Japan in 1883, where he was asked to serve as Foreign Secretary for a special diplomatic mission from Korea to the United States—though at the time he had never even seen Korea. Returning to Tokyo, he had later been asked to help write Japan's new constitution.

Lying sleepless on his cot, he spoke aloud to the apex of his tent, where the canvas rippled in a faint breeze. "I have experience as an ambassador to foreign cultures. I have diplomatic credentials. How could the Martians be stranger than what I have already seen?"

~

THE CYLINDER SCREAMED through the air with the wailing of a thousand lost souls, trailing behind it a tongue of fire from atmospheric friction and a bright green mist from outgassing extraterrestrial substances.

Lowell burst out of his shaded tent to see the commotion under the midday sun. A burnt smudge of smoke smoldered like a scar across the ceramic-blue sky. Booms of sound thundered in waves as the gigantic ship/projectile crossed overhead.

"It's the emissaries from Mars!" Lowell shouted, raising his hands in the air. "The Martians!"

Like an exploding warship, the cylinder crashed into the desert with a spewed plume of sand and dust. Lowell felt the tremor of impact in his knees, despite the cushioning desert. He laughed aloud, yelling for Douglass and Pickering to join him.

After the burning of the enormous triangle, most of the workers had returned to their widely scattered lands, leaving only a few team bosses to tidy up the loose ends of the construction. Lowell had sold his now-useless railroad for scrap steel, giving the salvagers a decent percentage of the profits. The place rapidly turned into a ghost town, which some of the European bosses had quietly begun calling "Lowell's Folly." Pickering and Douglass had returned from the other two base camps to join him here. To wait …

Now, as the dust settled in the distance, the other two astronomers ran up, their faces ruddy with sunburn and excitement. "We are vindicated!" Lowell cried. He clapped them each on the shoulder. "The Martians are here!"

The remaining Bedouin helpers fled the camp in panic, thrashing their camels to an awkward gallop across the dunes. *Idiots*, he thought. *Fools.* They did not realize the honor that had been bestowed here.

"The world as we know it is about to change. Come, let us put together an expedition. We must welcome our visitors from space."

THE HEAT from the pit rose up in a tremendous wave, overwhelming even the blistering daytime pounding of the Sahara. Pickering dropped back, coughing, but Lowell plodded forward, hunched over, shielding his watering eyes. On an impulse, he reached into the pocket of his cream-colored suit jacket and withdrew his bright red spectacles, placing them over his eyes, seeing the world as a Martian would, the better to understand them.

Because of the residual heat, he could not get close to the crash site, and he felt a terrible dread that the Martian ship had exploded when it struck the ground, that all the interplanetary ambassadors had been obliterated by fire.

But then he heard faint pounding sounds within the metal-walled cylinder, mechanical noises, a soft unscrewing.... Finally, Douglass dragged him back. "It's too hot, Mister Lowell! We must wait."

With savage disappointment, Lowell stumbled away, keeping his head turned to stare at the smoldering crater through his red-lensed spectacles. "I have waited years for this moment. I can tolerate a few more hours—but not much longer than that."

His eyes stinging from tears not entirely caused by the blistering heat, he followed the other two men back to the main camp.

DOUGLASS FETCHED SOME WATER, toiletries, and fresh clothes after sweaty hours spent in the dim shelter of their tents. He and Pickering ate ravenously of a quickly prepared meal, though Lowell himself felt no hunger. His stomach tied itself in knots as he felt his life's work coming to its climax.

Lowell used some of the tepid water to shave, leaning over a small mirror. Then he changed into a fine new suit, and straightened his collar, keeping his gaze intent on the still-glowing pit visible through the propped-open tent flap. Finally, in the cool of the desert night, he told his two companions to wait behind.

"You can't go alone, man," Pickering said, after clearing his throat again.

"Nonsense." Lowell brushed the other astronomer's grasp from his arm. "It was my money that brought the Martians to this landing site, and I claim the right."

"That's the same argument you used with your damned telescope," Pickering muttered, but did not pursue the discussion. Douglass hunkered down, looking forlorn.

Lowell strode across the surrounding dunes in his black leather shoes, mulling over an appropriate speech, wondering if by some miracle the Martians might speak English. No matter, he thought.

He had a knack for languages and would manage to communicate somehow.

Looking dapper, he approached the edge of the pit. He noted with fascination that the heat of the impact had been great enough to fuse some of the sand grains into lumps of glass. If the Martians could survive that, they must be prime specimens indeed.

He stood on the brink, looking down into the glow that lit up the crater as if it were day. A long, shiny lid had been unscrewed from the large pitted cylinder and lay on the blasted sands. Below, he saw clanking machines stirring, odd tentacled creatures moving about, exhibiting an industriousness no doubt born by their dire circumstances on Mars. Most remarkable, he saw, was a tall, newly assembled construction rising up on stiltlike, tripod legs. The heat was still incredible.

Magnificent! Lowell felt proud and overwhelmed to be mankind's emissary. Now that they had reached Earth, though, the poor Martians could be saved.

Lowell hurried forward to greet the Martians. The wonders of the universe awaited him.

Percy Bysshe Shelley's poem "Ozymandias" always resonated with me, a great and powerful tyrant from an ancient empire, whose fame and power are lost in history with nothing left but crumbling ruins out in the desert. In a much more modern inspiration, the Dream Theater song "Lost—Not Forgotten" from their album A Dramatic Turn of Events *is also about a horrific tyrant who may not deserve the fame he claims. I had this story on my mental back burner for several years until Jonathan Maberry asked me if I'd write a sword-and-sorcery story for an anthology he put together, and that was the trigger I needed. The anthology never saw the light of day, and I sold this piece elsewhere, but I love how it turned out, rich and colorful, and different from much of my other work.*

THE REIGN TO COME

E mperor Shaksus the Incomparable was dead, throwing his entire empire into turmoil. He had reigned for forty years, but his death was unexpected at the age of only 61. He died not from secret poison in his food or from a knife slipped into his back; Emperor Shaksus the Incomparable, a healthy bull of a man, had died of a failing heart as he relaxed for an evening in a steaming bath.

Unfortunately, even given his supposed prowess in bed with the beautiful concubines in his harem—all of whom he serviced quite regularly and vigorously, according to snickered whispers around the court—Shaksus had no heir, no children whatsoever. And although he insisted the fault must lie with the women, lest anyone dare question his virility, the obvious evidence suggested that the emperor's seed simply refused to take hold in any womb. Thus, the prosperous empire that stretched from the ocher mountains in the east, the white desert to the south, and the fertile lands of rival kingdoms to the north and west, was left without a leader.

The powerful court wizards knew what had to be done.

A spectacular funeral pyre raged for three days on the apex of the Temple of the Sun God, sending a banner of greasy, black smoke into the sky to signal a time of mourning. The body of Shaksus had long been consumed, but the temple priests had kept adding fuel to the flames along with the occasional body of a slave just to keep the fires bright. Messengers rode to the corners of the empire commanding one full moon cycle of respectful grief. But the court wizards knew they could not distract the people for long, and so they put out the call far and wide.

A new emperor had to be found.

Dressed in rags, but his very best rags, Aykin stood in the long line that stretched across the square leading to the dark and ominous arched openings of the Emperor's palace. The ornate, imposing structure towered over the capital city, but now stood mostly empty, the functionaries and concubines evicted, the windows covered with black cloths. Crows circled the tallest pointed towers.

Aykin stretched up on his thin legs, brushed dark, unruly hair from his brown eyes, and tried to peer around the shoulders of the burly, but dumb as a barrel, candidate who waited stoically in front of him. "I wish the court wizards would hurry," he muttered. There must be at least a hundred people ahead of him. "They haven't seen the best yet. I'll surprise them, I will." His bravado and confidence elicited no response whatsoever from Dumb As A Barrel. Aykin turned and flashed a grin at the well-dressed merchant behind him in line. "You'd best go home and see to your business. Once the court wizards interview me, they'll know who to choose as the next emperor."

The merchant gave him a withering sneer. "I don't believe the court wizards ever suggested that arrogance was a valued quality for leadership."

"Arrogance?" Aykin laughed. "I call it ambition, confidence, a clarity of vision. I know in my heart I'd be a good emperor. I'd make our land strong and wealthy."

The merchant assessed his rags, his frayed sandals, his unkempt hair. "It doesn't appear that you've put any of your skills to practice."

"I need the resources," Aykin replied. "I know I can do it."

When the court wizards had sent out a call for candidates, requesting to interview any person of any station who believed he could serve as the best new emperor, Aykin had made up his mind. What did he have to lose?

His mother had died on the streets when he was young, and he had never known his father. Who was to say he didn't have royal blood? Pampered nobles didn't know anything about real life, about survival, about making do. Aykin did. For several years he had led a band of street thieves, and they survived by their wits and their quick fingers. They had never been caught, although eventually—petty thieves being inherently unreliable—they had each drifted off on their own.

With the throne of Shaksus now vacant, Aykin saw his chance. Since he was unschooled, he only knew the muddled oral history of the empire, but he was aware that imperial dynasties had changed again and again over the centuries, often through wars, conquests, and assassinations, but other times exactly like this—the one fittest to serve, as chosen by the court wizards. Using inexplicable magic, they could pick the most suitable new emperor for the good of the land—and they were rarely wrong. Aykin knew they would not make the wrong choice once they spoke with him.

Rushing to offer himself for the position, the young man had taken the time to wash the grime off his face using the scummy water from a horse trough, and he had combed his shaggy hair with his fingers. He possessed a knife to defend himself, but the blade was so dull it had only made a mess when he tried to cut his hair. Thus, rather than looking noble and presentable, Aykin would have to make himself wild and wily, unpredictable, someone the armies and the citizens could cheer.

First, he had to convince the court wizards. He had to make his case.

"I wish these people would move faster," he muttered, again trying to peer around Dumb As A Barrel. The line of hopefuls shuffled forward, and Aykin saw one of the rejected candidates emerge, head down, from the dark archway of the emperor's palace. It was an older man, a wise scholar who held a bandaged hand close to his chest. He scurried away, paying no attention to the jeers of the crowd. Most of the people filling the plaza outside the palace had no interest in becoming the next emperor, but they were happy to mock those who failed.

Aykin drew a deep breath, reminding himself that he wasn't going to fail.

That very morning, after the court wizards issued their call, he had rushed to the middle of the capital, wanting to be the first in line. If he had made it, that would certainly have saved time and trouble for the empire, because then the wizards wouldn't need to interview so many other people. But he had found more than fifty people already there, all of whom fancied themselves of imperial quality.

So, he had to wait. All day. But showing patience was a good example of his abilities as a great leader. Patience. Yes, he would counsel himself for patience.

Another timid-looking candidate entered through the palace archways to meet the wizards. The rest of the people stood under the baking sun waiting and shifting. Aykin looked around him at the city, the tiled roofs, the whitewashed walls, the colorful pennants showing the eagle symbol of Emperor Shaksus. Black crepe and mourning fabrics still dangled in front of many windows.

Before long, the next candidate failed, left in disappointment, and then another entered past the two muscular guards. The line crawled forward. Aykin waited, and waited. Still fifteen more people in front of him.

A wine-seller with a brass cup and a skin full of a sour vintage walked down the line, offering drinks for two coppers. Although Aykin was sorely tempted, he didn't have the coins; he reminded himself that soon enough, when he was emperor, he would drink the finest wines. Soon enough.

The merchant behind him bought a cup from the wine-seller, sipped, then grimaced and dumped the red liquid on the flagstones.

Across the plaza the crowds swelled, then dwindled throughout the day. The people were ready to cheer their new emperor as soon as he was crowned, but they were not, in fact, enamored with the long and tedious process. Neither was Aykin.

His stomach growled; he had not eaten in two days. He was hot and sweaty. As the court wizards rejected candidate after candidate, he moved closer and closer to the marble steps and the arched palace doorway above. Finally, late in the afternoon, he reached the shade of the moving shadow from the high towers, but the temperature had already begun to drop. Aykin was determined to stay there all night long.

The door loomed closer as each person entered and left. Some never even departed, perhaps exiting through a different doorway, or maybe being kept on as staff members for the new administration, but the next volunteers were called in to state their case. Aykin knew the new emperor had not yet been selected, and his hope remained bright.

Vendors walked by with meat pies, tempting them with savory aromas. If he was free and running through the streets Aykin would have snatched one, but he restrained himself. That wasn't fitting behavior for a future emperor.

At sunset, when the evening bells tolled from the apex of the Temple of the Sun God , the silent burly man in front of him, Dumb As A Barrel, turned and simply left the line, walking away without a word. Though surprised, Aykin hurried up to take his place in the line. Only five more people stood ahead of him before the two guards who blocked entry with their braced spears and grim expressions. He was close. His heart began to beat faster.

When he finally climbed the steps and stood above the plaza, he turned to look back, astonished to see the hopeful applicants who had gathered throughout the day. The line stretched all the way across the vast square, and beyond into the main promenade street where Emperor Shaksus had hosted great parades, then continued into the winding streets of the city. All those people would be so disappointed as soon as he was crowned the new emperor.

When his turn was called, a portly man dressed in purple silk robes entered the palace, marching past the guards with his head held high and a grin on his face as if he meant to charm the court wizards. Half an hour later, he scuttled out, his head down holding a cloth-wrapped hand, and vanished into the gathering night shadows.

Aykin stepped forward. Only two more ahead of him! As the night gathered, the chill set in, but he knew that tonight he would sleep in imperial beds, surrounded with silks, perhaps even beautiful women. He would have a feast. He would never again feel hungry. He wouldn't have to cheat or steal to survive. But he had proved he was willing to do what must be done, and often emperors needed to make difficult decisions. Even his shady past might be something worth noting.

The next two candidates were found wanting, just as Aykin expected. Torches and lanterns began to glow throughout the city, and thousands of sparkling bright eyes shone in the gathering darkness. And when it was his turn, Aykin stepped up to the two stony-faced guards with their crossed spears. He was accustomed to guards sneering at him, calling him a street urchin, a beggar, or a thief (all of which were true)—he was used to it. Now they showed no disgust when they looked at his rags or his unkempt hair. Aykin was another qualified applicant, and they had seen many things since the death of Emperor Shaksus.

He raised his chin and waited, knowing he would be called next. The reign of Emperor Shaksus had been long and stable, different from the fire and bloodshed of other emperors. The history scrolls would not record many accomplishments from the mostly placid and unremarkable reign of Shaksus, and Aykin already began to think of how he would want his own name written for posterity. Aykin the Magnificent? Aykin the Undefeated? There were so many adjectives.

Finally, the guards separated their spears and stood apart to let the young man enter the great gallery of the huge palace. He swallowed hard and strode into the giant echoing chamber, reminding himself how long he had waited for this. His tattered sandals made whispering noises across the polished tiles. Torches surrounded the walls of the great reception area. Ahead, under the vaulted ceiling, shimmering braziers lit the empty throne where Emperor Shaksus had sat.

Robed in crimson and emerald green, the three court wizards faced him. The three wizards had shaved heads and voluminous beards. They wore heavy amulets, golden chains, and multiple rings with large polished stones. They looked weary, even bored. No wonder, Aykin thought, since they had already dispensed with so many applicants today.

With a spring in his step, he spread his hands to greet them. "I am Aykin, and I am your next emperor."

The three wizards stood in front of a beaten copper basin on a tripod erected between the shimmering braziers. They did not react to his boastful claim. Without waiting for them to ask questions, Aykin continued, "I am clever, I am ambitious, and I understand the people because of my common upbringing. This gives me advantages that—"

The central court wizard raised a hand like an executioner's axe. He spoke in a deep, gravelly voice, "Silence! We've not yet begun."

Aykin quieted himself and shifted from one sandal to the other. "I will be the greatest leader. I promise. Ask your questions."

The wizard on the right, the gauntest of the three, drew a jeweled dagger in his left hand. The blade was slightly curved, its edge polished so sharp that it was a silver whisper of steel. The gems in its hilt glinted in the light of the brazier.

"We don't need to ask questions," said the wizard. "Your blood will tell us all we need to know."

Aykin's heart skipped a beat. Was it some kind of test to see if he would show fear, or did they truly mean to attack him? He stood his ground. The opposite wizard took a step closer. "We don't need to ask you questions, because people lie, and we need the truth."

"I would never lie!" he lied, but then caught himself. He lowered his voice. "What is it you need to know?"

"We must see the reign that is to come before we can make our decision. What will you do as the next emperor? How will you lead the land? How will you make us prosper? Under your leadership, will this empire thrive or diminish?"

"It will thrive," Aykin said.

"We shall see." The wizard with the knife stepped forward and grasped Aykin's hand. The young man instinctively jerked it away, but the wizard held firm. "If you can't pass even the simplest of tests, young man, then you are dismissed."

With a huff, Aykin shoved his hand, fingers outstretched, toward the bald, bearded man. "I will do anything to become emperor. I'll show you. What do you need?"

"Your blood." With a quick sharp slash, he drew the blade across Aykin's palm. The young man yelped with the bright sting of pain, and the wizard pulled his hand over the empty beaten-copper basin. The blood spilled down into the bowl. Aykin felt the throbbing hurt, the pulse of his heartbeat, as the blood flowed out to cover the bottom of the basin, dripping and dripping until it had reached a level that was smooth and still.

Fascinated, Aykin stared down into the dark red emptiness in the shallow bowl. "What did you do that for?"

The wizards gathered shoulder to shoulder. "We must see the reign to come. We will see the kind of emperor you are."

They began to hum, and the light from the braziers crackled and brightened. Aykin felt a tingling of magic in the air. He couldn't take his eyes away as he looked down into the blood-filled basin. The dark surface shimmered, rippled, and he blinked, seeing shadows there, movement. Then images formed, and Aykin recognized himself—not himself as a street urchin, but himself as an *emperor.*

"Behold your reign," said one of the court wizards. They all watched intently. Aykin stared while as-yet-unwritten history played out before his eyes.

～

AFTER AYKIN the Magnificent took his throne as emperor of the land, he wore fine clothes, slept in an expansive bed with numerous enthusiastic and talented women. He was far too young to worry about finding a princess to marry.

He thrived on being the new ruler. Aykin got his feet under him for the first year of his reign, and he began to understand just how much unquestioned power he wielded. This was everything the young man had dreamed of.

For months, Emperor Aykin traveled from city to city, exploring his empire, learning whom he ruled, assessing which parts were weak and which were strong, which lords were sycophants and which might be problematic. Even though he had no shortage of advisors and counselors, Aykin had learned from his time on the streets—with all the friends who had helped him, then disappointed him—not to trust anyone.

He even found a few of his street-scamp friends, elevated them to positions in his government. His long-lost companions were giddy with the unexpected opportunity, but sadly proved to be inappropriate for their roles. One young friend was a particular embarrassment, caught stealing from the treasury and smuggling gold coins out to secret hiding places. Aykin couldn't understand the foolishness: the man had everything he could need, why should he bother to steal?

When his legal advisors instructed him that any thief must have his hands chopped off, Aykin accepted the punishment since he was, after all, the emperor and must be bound by laws. Even though his former friend pleaded for mercy, Aykin insisted the sentence be carried out, and the young man's hands were laid out on the chopping block, then severed with an axe and a scream. Wailing, his handless friend howled curses and insults at Aykin, and then the court advisors pointed out that the penalty for insulting the emperor was death. Since the muscular executioner was still standing there with his bloody axe ready, Aykin had the boy's head chopped off, too.

That night, the rest of his elevated friends ran away in fear, many of them taking coins and jewels as they fled. So Aykin put out a warrant for their arrest, and they were subsequently hunted down and executed, not just for the thievery but because they must certainly have cursed his name as well.

After his first year, Emperor Aykin had explored the boundaries of his empire, inspected his lands from the white powder deserts and the rugged mountains to the borders with the fat and fertile kingdoms to the north and west. He felt discouraged and saddened to see the limits of his empire, knowing there was so much more to the world.

Tutors had instructed him on the history of the empire, the conquests and defeats of the previous leaders. Emperor Shaksus had not expanded their lands at all during the forty years of his reign—in fact, he hadn't even tried. Shaksus showed almost no ambition, content with the empire as it was. Aykin decided to make his mark now that he was in command of the imperial treasury as well as the large standing army. He funded the military, trained his cavalry, increased recruitment, enlarged the armories, and six months later, in the warmest summer months, Emperor Aykin launched an exploratory sortie over the border of the weak neighboring kingdom of Daraka.

The Darakans were mainly farmers and shepherds. They had no fortresses along the border and they had grown soft after decades of peace. When Aykin's initial sortie proved successful, conquering villages and expanding his territory into rich farming lands, the emperor was so pleased that he called his generals and expanded his army by promising lands and riches to the new recruits.

His massive army marched forward with no warning. Previously, Emperor Aykin had withdrawn all diplomatic ties with Daraka, so their attack was swift, relentless, and unexpected. Before the autumn leaves had even finished falling from the trees, Aykin ruled all of Daraka. He had killed the king, taken over the castle in the capital city, and dispersed his own troops at strategic points throughout Daraka.

By now he decided it was time for him to get married, and because his advisors told him that the best way to consolidate the rule of two great kingdoms was through marriage, he took the hand of the princess of Daraka—a spindly yet pretty young woman named Cereline, who was red eyed and wild with grief after the defeat and execution of her father, the Darakan king. Aykin was sure she would come around, so he married her anyway. When she threatened to resist, he had her drugged so that she was in a stupor throughout the entire wedding, but cooperative enough during the ceremony and in bed that night.

The alliance between Aykin's empire and the kingdom of Daraka was now cemented, and his wealth and power had grown.

To the north of the newly conquered kingdom, there were rich gold and silver mines, which Aykin commandeered. In a clever and wise decision, he exploited the mines by drawing new workers from the commanders of the defeated Darakan army, sending them underground to dig gold and silver ore, which further enriched the treasury of his ever-growing kingdom.

After conscripting the Darakan soldiers as well as sending out a wider call to arms among his own people, Aykin kept making plans. And after winter was over he launched another offensive during the mud and rain of spring, which stretched the boundaries even farther. His troops swept across the lands beyond the Darakan border; they pillaged the countryside, burning villages, conquering one district after another, demanding fealty from the town lords and petty princes.

Once, when he came back to his imperial bedchamber drunk from celebrating yet another victory, Princess Cereline tried to kill him. He easily drove her off and afterward kept her locked in a guarded room by herself. Later, she tried to take her own life, since she could not take his, and she failed in that as well. Aykin grew impatient with her, but he needed an heir and, rather than letting her kill herself so he could simply take another, more cooperative wife, he fell back on drugging her in the evenings before having her brought to his bedchamber. Even so, it still took him three months to get her pregnant.

After another neighboring kingdom fell—mostly because they surrendered in terror—Emperor Aykin faced the defeated king. He realized that the easy conquest had come about because these people feared him, and fear, he decided, was a sharper weapon than a sword.

So, he reached a decision. When the defeated king bowed before him, Emperor Aykin took a curved scimitar from one of his loyal guards and personally struck off his head. The shock spread rapidly to surrounding kingdoms. Some forged alliances to build up their own armies, but the wise ones rushed emissaries back to Aykin's palace with sworn statements of surrender and loyalty.

Aykin absorbed land after land without spilling a drop of blood (except for the necessary pillaging his guards and soldiers caused, but that was to be expected). As his armies swelled with all the new recruits pressed into service, Emperor Aykin marched on the lands that had pulled together to resist him. His unstoppable wave crushed all those who stood against him, and in only a few years he doubled and then tripled the size of his empire. He built garrisons throughout the newly conquered lands, as well as his original empire, simply to maintain the peace, because many were jealous of his success and made halfhearted attempts to overthrow him. But they all failed.

He led a bloodbath across the continent, building immense fortresses, erecting giant monuments so that history would remember Emperor Aykin the Magnificent, the Undefeated. He built a pile of skulls plated in gold, from each enemy who had stood against him and failed. Under his leadership, his vision, and his strength Aykin's empire became the richest, most powerful, most feared empire in all the world and in all of history.

~

THE IMAGES in the beaten-copper basin faded as the blood blackened and congealed. Young Aykin stood giddy and astonished by what he had seen. "That is my reign," he asked in a whisper. "I will accomplish all that? I will make history. I will make our empire incomparably strong."

Grinning, he blinked and looked up in amazement. He knew he was the correct successor to the weak and unambitious Emperor Shaksus. The court wizards would crown him then and there, and he would begin his reign now that he knew what to do.

Instead, he was surprised to see all three wizards staring at him with eyes wide, their lips curled downward in revulsion. "We have seen your reign to come."

Their reaction annoyed him. Drunk with the immensity of all he had just seen, Aykin lashed out. "You will obey me! You have witnessed my power."

The court wizard raised the curved silver blade. "After so many years of peace and prosperity, we certainly don't need another ruler like that!"

Before Aykin could retreat, the wizard plunged the long sacrificial dagger into his chest, then stabbed twice more just to make sure. The young man reached up with weak and watery fingers, clasping at his wounds as he fell to the floor. He knocked over the tripod and spilled the beaten-copper basin, but his own blood made a much larger puddle on the polished stones in front of the empty throne.

Shaking with alarm and disgust the three court wizards called for guards to take the body away and clean the mess. "He has no place in our history."

Together, the three wizards cleansed the basin and propped up the tripod. They washed their bloody hands with perfumed water while the guards removed all signs of the street urchin. Finally, they gathered their courage and called out to the arched doorway of the palace. "Send in the next one."

As a new writer, I once attended a small writing workshop led by science fiction legend Damon Knight. I submitted a short story about a medieval con man making fake Splinters of the True Cross to prey upon the beliefs of villagers. Damon announced, in front of all the other writers, "This story is totally screwed up, but you do show some talent as a writer." I never rewrote it, but years later Rebecca and I were asked to do a story for an anthology centered around Renaissance Faires. I thought it might be an opportunity to use the Splinters of the True Cross idea again, and Rebecca ran with the concept, and we worked out the following story.

SPLINTER

(WRITTEN WITH REBECCA MOESTA)

Something about the Renaissance Faire beckoned to him like the sound of a hundred sirens luring a lonely sailor from the sea. In spite of the nearly hundred-degree heat of a California summer, he never tired of the beauty of it all—the jostling crowds in brightly colored clothing, the noisy parades of "royalty" and minstrels, the jugglers, the candlemakers, the serenity of a young mother with ample breasts exposed suckling a newborn child as if it were the most natural thing in the world. He loved the spectacle of a hundred different kinds of entertainers and artisans and food vendors, all putting on Elizabethan micro-performances minute by minute, doing their utmost to lure money from the cash-fat pockets of the faire-goers.

And it was those cash-fat pockets that brought Wil to these open-air festivals year after year. He never tired of the magic of thousands of bodies jostling together, muttering loudly, kicking up dust ... never noticing the slender young man with the wispy beard and peasant clothing who expertly and discreetly relieved them of their excess valuables. Pickpocket, thief, rogue, highwayman—after all, that was a legitimate part of the time period, too. Certainly, more authentic than either the churro or cappuccino seller.

It wasn't long before the first opportunity presented itself. Wil had learned to recognize those opportunities while he was still in high school, furtively watching for an unguarded purse or backpack; by now his instincts were so well tuned he hardly had to think about it. He had just passed the booth from which he'd shoplifted his own costume two years earlier, when he came upon a couple in casually elegant street clothes. They were having a heated discussion just outside a palm reader's tent.

"Why not?" the young woman said. "Are you afraid she'll tell us we should get married, after all?"

The young man scoffed. "Come on, they only say what they think you want to hear, anyway."

Quickly assessing the situation—it was important to be a good judge of character—Wil deduced from shoes, hair, makeup, and demeanor that the young woman would be carrying the money. *I'm even doing them a favor,* Wil thought. *A few arguments about money will give them a more accurate sense of their marriage compatibility than any palm reader could.*

He conveniently joined a cluster of people passing by, allowing himself to be crowded into the arguing couple. It took only one brief bump and a mumbled "Excuse me" to liberate an expensive Tumi wallet from the young woman's equally expensive Dooney & Bourke leather purse.

A little farther on, Wil ducked between two booths to determine the value of his acquisition. He was immediately impressed with himself: $281 in cash, and the wallet itself would fetch a good price at the local flea market. Wil tucked his prize into an interior pocket of his billowy brown knee breeches and moved on with a spring in his step. He would dispose of the credit cards, of course. Too easy to get caught using stolen cards.

And he didn't plan to get caught. Ever.

The next two hours proved considerably less satisfying. Discouraged, Wil bought a roasted turkey leg, then removed the pewter tankard he wore at his belt and had it filled with chilled ale. He sat down to eat on a bench in a small amphitheater where two jugglers were throwing knives at each other while making witty banter.

After polishing off his lunch, Wil tossed the turkey leg bone to the ground, not even bothering to look for a trash can. If someone scolded him about it, he could argue that his gesture was certainly truer to the Renaissance spirit than using a trash can was. If it really bothered some do-gooder, let *him* dispose of it. Wil had never believed in much except himself … and he'd gotten over himself long ago.

Wil headed up a rocky, hay-strewn path, his eyes beginning their automatic sweep. His vigilance was quickly rewarded when he spied a middle-aged man with a chest-length salt-and-pepper beard counting out bills from a leather pouch at his waist. One of the bills fell to the ground and was caught by a hot breeze and blown a few feet behind him onto the path. Noting that the foot traffic was light and no one else was watching, Wil bent smoothly for the merest second, plucked the bill from the ground and continued up the path before the bearded man even had a chance to turn and look for the fallen money.

Wil passed a tarot card reader and a cluster of college students singing madrigals beside a fake wishing well. At the glassblower's tent, he spotted a man in his mid-thirties making a purchase. He wore safari shorts, a golf shirt, designer sunglasses, and sockless leather loafers. A grade-school-aged boy and girl pranced impatiently beside him. A quick glimpse told the pickpocket that the man's wallet contained enough cash to pay Wil's expenses for weeks.

"Come on, Dad! You promised we could see the storyteller."

"And that's just what we're going to do." The man slid his wallet into the front pocket of his shorts and accepted a wrapped package from the glassblower. Wil hung back and decided this man might be worth following.

The man began herding his children up the path. "Why'd we have to buy Mom another glass unicorn?" the boy said.

"We get her one every year, Evan, whether she can come or not. It's not her fault Grandma broke her hip," the girl answered. "What a stupid question."

"Now, Orli, don't call your brother stupid."

Wil gritted his teeth as he watched Perfect Family Guy, more determined than ever to interject a little bit of gritty reality into the pampered PFG's perfect life. Wil was an old hand at rationalizing to himself. He had been making up excuses and explanations for so long that he had almost come to believe them. Almost.

They came to a small pavilion, where half the floor was littered with hassocks and colorful overstuffed cushions on which children sat or reclined. A man with a leathery face and white shoulder-length hair walked among them, telling stories. Wooden tables running along one side of the breezy tent held books bound in hand-tooled leather. The sign over the pavilion said, "Tales of Glorye."

Wil watched as Orli, Evan, and Perfect Family Guy seated themselves on cushions. Pretending a casual interest, Wil entered the pavilion and began browsing the books. The storyteller spoke in a rich, expressive voice. Wil let the words wash over him, but his concentration was focused on PFG.

When the tale ended about ten minutes later, many of the listeners came up to drop money into a hat beside the old story-teller. Most of the audience left, but Wil's three marks lingered to ask questions. He suppressed an impatient sigh, picked up another leather-bound book and leafed through it, pretending to admire the meticulous hand lettering.

The storyteller plopped the hat full of money onto a table not far from Wil.

"So, what happened next?" Orli asked the old man. "I mean, after the knight went back and told the King."

"Ah, now that's a much longer story."

"Do you have a book that has the story in it?" PFG asked.

"Over here on the table." The storyteller moved closer to Wil and selected a thick tome with a burgundy leather binding.

Perfect Family Guy showed it to his daughter. "Say, aren't you worried about leaving all that money just lying on the table?"

Finding the comment particularly ironic, Wil glanced over to see the old man smile. "I find that when you take care of the really valuable things, everything else takes care of itself. That's why I keep everything that's truly valuable to me right here in this pock-et," he said, patting the left side of his leather breeches.

"I can admire that philosophy," PFG said.

"Look," Evan said, pointing at the pages of the book. "There's the story he told today."

"And two stories that come before, and three that come after it," Orli said. "Daddy, can we get this?"

PFG stroked his daughter's hair. "It would be the perfect souvenir."

Wil gritted his teeth again. *Perfect.* The very perfection of this family was driving him insane.

"Let me wrap that for you." The storyteller moved to Wil's right, reached under the table, and came up with two sheets of heavy paper that looked handmade.

The children began looking at the books on another table. PFG got out his wallet and began counting out the money. When the storyteller laid the sheets of paper on the table and began wrapping the book, Wil saw his chance. The pocket that held the old man's "true valuables" was within a foot of Wil's hand, so he clumsily dropped the book he had been looking at. Pretending to reach for it, Wil awkwardly bumped the old man with his hip, at the same time slipping his right hand into the pocket and apologetically steadying the storyteller with his left hand.

The whole maneuver took less than a second. Wil felt an uneven lump in the pocket, something strange—but just as his hand closed around it, a searing pain shot up his arm. It was like nothing he had felt since the age of ten when he'd lost control of his bicycle going down the driveway, veered into the neighbor's yard, fallen, and ripped his leg open on a sprinkler head.

With another jostle, Wil snatched his hand back and bent to retrieve the fallen book. He fumbled around, momentarily blinded by the pain and sucked in a sharp breath.

The old man put a hand on his back. "You all right, lad?"

For a panicked second, Wil wondered if the old man knew he'd been pickpocketed, but when his eyes focused on the kindly face, he saw no suspicion. "No, I, uh ... sudden migraine." He put a hand to his head. "Probably the heat."

He handed the book back to the storyteller. As quickly as it had come, the scorching pain subsided, but Wil's hand still throbbed as if he had slammed it in a door.

Perfect Family Guy was beside him. "My wife gets migraines. They can get pretty nasty. Maybe you should lie down somewhere in the shade."

"There's plenty of room on the cushions," the old man offered.

"No," Wil said a little too quickly. "Thank you. I, uh, probably should take some medication for this. It's out in my car." Damn. Now that both men were so solicitous of him, Wil stood little chance of slipping in under their radar.

The storyteller regarded him with solemn eyes. "I hope you feel better really soon. Sometimes there's a trick to it."

"Do you need help out to your car?" PFG asked.

"Thanks. I'll manage." He left the pavilion, cursing himself for attracting so much attention from two potential marks. Surely, he could have toughed out just a little bit of pain when he stood to profit so much. Already the searing stab had receded to a mere pinprick in his mind. It had been foolish weakness, but he would not call attention to himself again.

Once he was out of sight of the pavilion, Wil hurried to put as much distance between him and the two annoyingly helpful men as possible. Safely on the other side of the faire, he scanned the crowds once more for opportunities. *This is easy.* He struggled to focus. *You're a natural.* But nothing felt natural right now.

He was filled with a sensation that was simultaneously pleasant and unpleasant, a fizzy alertness of the mind not unlike the way he felt when, after an all-nighter, his body replaced sleep with pure adrenaline. Wil forced himself to move into the flow of shoppers and sightseers.

There. Wil saw his opportunity. A young woman with hot-pink polish on the nails of her manicured fingers and pedicured toes was pushing a baby carriage. The mother stopped and bent to comfort the child as it continued to wail. Her attention was fully focused on the brat and not on the purse dangling from the stroller's handle.

He moved in. This was almost too easy. A simple swoop would do it.

His hand dipped into her purse, but the moment he touched the wallet, a lightning bolt struck the index finger of his right hand, shot through his wrist, traveled up his arm, and spiked into his brain. He simultaneously jerked his hand away and fell to his knees. The young mother looked up in alarm, her concentration startled away from her child who, also startled, stopped crying for a moment.

"Sorry," Wil gasped. "I tripped."

"You okay?" She moved around to the back of the stroller, darting a cautious glance down at her purse.

"Yeah, I'll be fine." Wil forced himself back to his feet and dusted off his breeches. "Good as new."

He backed away and lost himself in the crowd. That had been close. Damnedest thing about his hand, too. In a patch of bright sunlight, he examined his finger. It still stung, as if something small and sharp was embedded in it, but he could see no burn or blister, no cut, no sliver, *nothing*. Yet the pain—the pain in his hand, his arm, his head—had been real. He frowned. Maybe it was a pinched nerve, or maybe he really was having a migraine.

Wil always kept a bottle of ibuprofen stashed in his glove compartment, so he headed out the front entrance, remembering to get his hand stamped for re-entry. The parking lot offered no shade at all, and Wil considered waiting for the "shuttle," a wide, canvas-covered horse-drawn wagon that ferried attendees to and from their cars for tips. But the wagon was at the far end of the lot, and Wil didn't want to wait.

By the time he got to his battered '83 Dodge, he had worked up a substantial sweat. He got the bottle of extra strength pain reliever, took twice the suggested number, and washed them down with a grimace and a swallow of the flat, and by now hot, soda he'd left open in his car.

He rolled down the windows and took a short nap in the front seat to give the analgesic time to work. By the time he woke up it was late afternoon. The faire would be closing in a couple of hours, and parts of the parking lot had already begun to empty out. Wil felt greatly refreshed, in spite of the heat, and decided to get back to work.

He got out of his car and strode through the lot in the general direction of the entrance. As he walked, he glanced through car windows, looking for wallets, merchandise, purses left behind by faire-goers in the "safety" of their locked cars. For the most part, he ignored the older cars, like his, which usually weren't worth the trouble. He also avoided anything too new and too likely to have an alarm. Within ten minutes he had found one with a purse on the floor of the passenger side, "hidden" underneath the morning paper.

He grinned. "Haven't lost your touch, Wil."

All the doors were locked, of course, but he easily found a substantial rock that would remedy the situation. After a quick glance to make sure no one was around, he hefted the rock and swung it toward the window.

Several seconds later, Wil opened his eyes to escape the blinding white explosion in his head. He found himself flat on his back in the dirt, still grasping the rock. The slicing, stabbing, burning pain that grated up his arm was less intense now, but still impossible to endure.

When he dropped the rock, the pain finally began to subside. He hauled himself back to his feet, looked at the car window, and blinked in surprise. The window was not broken. Not even a crack. But he couldn't have missed—not with the force he'd used, not at such short range, and yet ...

Carefully, afraid of triggering the terrible pain again, he picked up the rock, this time with his left hand. He swung with all his might at the window—

Bam! Flat in the dirt again. Wil's head pounded as if a grenade had gone off in his right ear, and his right arm felt as if an elephant had walked across it. He whimpered—something no one had ever heard him do. He wondered if he might be having a heart attack. Wouldn't that be the left arm? It was hard to think.

His fingers let loose of the rock, and he lay on the tire-flattened grass until the pain had subsided to a mere pricking in his right index finger. He brought it up to his face and studied it again, but still found nothing.

Something was very wrong with him. Wil didn't have medical insurance, but there was a first-aid tent inside the faire. He could describe his symptoms, maybe have them examine him. At least it would be free.

He got up slowly, not even bothering to brush the dirt off. It might add an air of authenticity when he explained his symptoms, make the first-aid workers take him more seriously. On his way to the entrance, much to his chagrin Wil passed the Perfect Family waiting to take the wagon shuttle back to the parking lot. The wagon was coming, the horses clomping forward, the people pushing closer to get a seat aboard.

Wil hoped to walk past the annoying family unnoticed, but Perfect Family Guy saw him right away and managed to look genuinely concerned. "Hey, how's that migraine doing?"

Wil's first instinct was to lie, but what was the point? "I thought it was gone, but it seems to keep coming back."

The little girl, Orli, trotted out in front of the wagon, grinning. "Look—what pretty horses! Where's the video camera, Daddy? Can you take a picture of me with them?"

Two rowdy young boys began to clatter against each other with wooden swords they had purchased as souvenirs.

PFG nodded his sympathy toward Wil. "Could be one of those cluster headaches, I suppose. They come and go, and they can be as bad as migraines." Wil made a noncommittal response and stepped around the crowd, wanting to be away.

A younger boy, frustrated at being left out of his brothers' sword fight, pulled out his "Renaissance souvenir" pop gun and pointed it at them. "I'll get you both!" He fired the pop gun, augmenting the sound with his own yell, "BLAM!"

The hot and tired horses responded to the noise. Startled, they flinched in their harness, snorted, and lurched forward. Orli was standing right in their path, still waiting for PFG to film her with the video camera. The wagon driver wrenched at his reins, the horses lifted their hooves, and the girl shrieked.

Because he had been trying to get around the crowd, Wil was closest to where the girl stood. He jumped forward, knocked Orli out of the way, smashed into the nearest horse, and fell to the ground. Before he could roll away, he felt a hammer strike his chest. The girl had fallen backward to sprawl in the dirt and had already begun to sob, but the weeping came more from startlement and confusion than from severe pain. Wil, on the other hand, thought he might have cracked a rib or two.

The wagon driver backed the wagon up several feet and jumped down from the buckboard, and other people hurried forward to Wil and the girl. The horses snorted, as if embarrassed by the incident. Orli continued to cry softly, and her father quickly checked to make sure she was uninjured before moving to take a look at Wil. "Wow, that could've been bad! I don't know how to thank you. Are you all right?"

Surprised was the first thing that came to Wil's mind. He had acted completely without thinking, with no regard for his own safety. Stranger yet, he felt very little pain. "Fine." And he found it was true. His entire body was suffused with a pleasant tingling sensation. "Better than fine. I'm great."

Perfect Family Guy still looked concerned. "Could just be endorphins and adrenaline talking. You'd better have a doctor check you out."

A distant part of his mind seemed aware that his body was hurt. He pulled open the loose neck of his muslin peasant shirt and looked inside. A red flush of bruising was already beginning to appear beneath the skin. How odd. After the inexplicable agony he had experienced several times today—each time while trying to ply his trade—now he felt euphoria when he should *really* be hurt. And he'd only been trying to help someone, after all. There was definite irony in that: invisible pain after trying to steal, and a feeling of well-being when trying to help, despite a visible injury.

Wil's eyes narrowed as the thoughts flashed through his mind. *Was* it irony, or was this something more sinister? It had all begun after he'd tried to pick the storyteller's pocket. Had the old man done something to him, administered some sort of drug or hypnotized him?

He smiled up at the PFG. "You're probably right. I'll head back inside to the first-aid tent."

Perfect Family Guy still looked concerned. "They won't be able to do much in there. You might need an x-ray. Do you have insurance?"

Wil shook his head. PFG pulled out his wallet and removed a business card. "Here's my card. If you end up needing to see a real doctor, I'll make sure that your expenses get covered."

"Thanks." Wil glanced down at the little rectangle of paper, then put it in his pocket. *Bentley Watson-Taylor III, Attorney at Law.* "I hope I won't need it. I'm just glad Orli's okay." A tingling rush of good feeling started in Wil's hand and swept up his arm and through his body.

"Thank you, mister," Orli said, and gave him a hug. "I hope you're going to be okay."

Wil knew the hug against his sore ribs should have hurt, but he didn't even wince. "I'll be fine. You just stay out of trouble."

Back at the entrance he showed his hand stamp, went through, and headed toward the storyteller's pavilion.

On the way, he tested his theory. He tried to pick a pocket and received a fresh jolt of pain. Then, after helping an older woman push her husband's wheelchair up an uneven slope and position the man where he could watch a troupe of players perform humorously abbreviated Shakespeare plays, Wil felt the rush of euphoria again.

The old storyteller had definitely done something to him.

When Wil reached the pavilion, the old man had just finished spinning a tale and the few late-afternoon audience members left quickly. Wil walked straight toward the storyteller, stepping over the scattered cushions. The leathery face registered recognition and concern, but no surprise.

"What did you do to me?" Wil demanded. His voice was rough with mixed emotion.

The old man considered the question. "I shared something with you, as I do with all who listen to me. How is your headache? Are you feeling better now?"

Wil felt an acid spurt of frustration burn in his stomach. "You know it wasn't a headache, and no, I'm not feeling better. You tricked me."

The old man's expressive eyebrows climbed a millimeter up his forehead. "How so?"

Wil cast about for an answer. He wasn't sure how he'd been tricked or what had been done to him, but he traced the strangeness back to *here*, in this tent with gauzy walls and cooling breezes, and this enigmatic man from whom he had tried to steal something of "true value."

"You … you tricked me by saying you had something valuable in your pocket."

The old man nodded soberly. "You heard that, did you? That is true. I carry what I value most in my pocket. But how is that a trick?"

Wil seethed inside. Wasn't the answer obvious? "Because you

knew I'd hear you, and that I'd try to find out what was in your pocket."

"Ah." The storyteller's voice was barely a whisper. "And …?"

"*And?* When I touched whatever was in your pocket, it gave me a jolt of some sort. It hurt so much I let go and fell to the ground. That's how you tricked me. What was it? Some kind of trap?"

"I admit, I did speak the truth in your hearing, yet no one can choose what another person will do with the truth once they hear it. I did not make that choice for you."

Wil couldn't believe his ears. Was the storyteller actually implying that this was all his own fault? "Oh, no you don't, old man. You still did something to my hand, and I'm betting you know how to undo it. Every time I try to practice my … business, my hand, my arm, my body, my brain, *everything* hurts like hell. Well, fine. You made your point. Picking pockets is bad. Stealing is bad. I get it." He raised a fist. "Now make it stop or I'll—"

An excruciating pain sizzled up Wil's arm and blinded him for a moment. As soon as he lowered his arm and forced his fist to relax, the agony began to fade. "For God's sake, just make it stop."

"Make it stop? For God's sake …" The storyteller looked troubled. "Let me tell you a story—it's what I do. Please, sit down."

Wil wasn't sure why, but he sat. And listened.

"In the time of the Third Crusade, the Year of Our Lord 1190, many brave knights, greedy lordlings, and hapless soldiers traveled across Europe by boat or by foot, in order to secure the Holy Land from the evil Turks. Some crusaders truly felt a calling from God, but the real reason for most of the lords and commanders—third and fourth sons without lands to inherit—was to capture new domains to rule. Other knights simply came for the chance to fight, to kill the infidel, to find glory on the battlefield.

"One such knight—let us call him Roderick the Brash—led his soldiers into battle, cutting his way through Turkish lines to establish a foothold in Jerusalem. There, while attempting to occupy the ancient holy city, Roderick came upon a kindly old leather worker, who went by the name of Julius. The leather worker did good deeds for his neighbors in Jerusalem, without giving thought to whether they were Christians, Moslems, or Jews. He claimed to have been a centurion in the Roman army in the time of Jesus Christ."

Wil scoffed. "That would have made him over a thousand years old."

The storyteller simply looked at him. "It's a story. Would you like to hear more?"

"As long as there's a point."

"Julius himself was present at the crucifixion and had come into possession of a fragment of the True Cross, and a Splinter from this remarkable artifact had kept him alive for so long. Though he wasn't wealthy, the leather worker had sufficient means to meet his needs and was content. No doubt he experienced the same euphoria you did when you performed a selfless deed."

"That's a stretch. Are you telling me—"

The old man calmly went on. "When he learned that Julius the leather worker had such a treasure, this holy relic, Roderick the Brash came at night into his shop and demanded to see the fragment. Julius told him the story I just told you. And then Roderick struck him down with his sword and took the fragment for himself."

The old man's gaze was distant, and his voice hitched. After a brief pause, he reached into the pocket where he kept his treasure, where Wil had felt the first sharp sting. He withdrew an oddly shaped and unimpressive lump of very old wood, less than two inches long. "When the fragment encounters someone who needs its ... assistance, it shares a part of itself. A Splinter.

"Roderick the Brash had great need of it. After touching the fragment, Roderick attempted to ignore the message of the Splinter. He continued to fight and kill until the pain became so overwhelming it rendered him unconscious, and his men left him for dead on the battlefield. After that, Roderick had no choice but to change his ways. He performed his penance for many centuries, made his way through the world, and found his own contentment. And, over the years, the fragment grew smaller, bit by bit, as it found others who needed it."

Wil's impatience mixed with wonder, annoyance, and indignation. "So, I'm supposed to believe that you're a knight named Roderick the Brash, who lived during the Third Crusade? And that I've got a Splinter of the True Cross stuck in my hand?"

"I simply told the story." The old man gave him a noncommittal look. "Believe what you wish."

Wil blew out an angry breath, looking at the lump of wood. It wasn't the least bit impressive. "If I believe that's a real holy relic with magical powers, and an invisibly small Splinter is embedded in my finger, then I'd also have to believe that I no longer have free will. I'm just a rat in a maze, and God is some sort of cosmic experimental researcher dispensing either treats or electric shocks, depending on whether or not I do what He wants."

The storyteller did not answer the accusation directly. His pensive gaze seemed to look through Wil. His eyes seemed very, very old. "There are many possible interpretations—some harsher than others. Some say that the Splinter is a sort of … conscience for anyone who has discarded the conscience that God gave them. But I don't believe that.

"Others believe that because the cross is a symbol of sacrifice, a Splinter of the True Cross might bestow peace and happiness for every deed that is selfless or sacrificial, while selfish acts are rewarded only with pain."

The storyteller paused. "But I don't believe that either. All of my experience and knowledge have led me to conclude one thing, that a Splinter is distilled truth. No more, no less."

Wil wanted to object, to interrupt and call the man's words bullshit. He didn't believe in Biblical morality or in miracles and had never felt a need to go to church. He had certainly never let himself be bound by superstition. But something kept him silent.

"Each Splinter senses the good or bad potential of a person's actions, then gathers those effects, concentrates them into the *now*, and transmits the truth back to its owner. If a thief takes a wallet, he causes financial injury to the person he steals from. He also steals some of that person's time and robs him of his feeling of safety. Like a pebble dropped into a pond, there are ripple effects."

Wil rubbed his forefinger but felt no twinge of pain. "Now you're getting pretty esoteric."

"It is concrete enough. Perhaps the thief's victims would not have enough money to buy necessities for themselves or their families. Imagine that a person needed to fix the brakes on his car. If there wasn't enough money to fix the brakes, and the brakes failed, then a terrible accident could result. All these things factor together and are condensed by the Splinter into a single manifestation of pain, great or small. In the same way, a kind or unselfish deed helps both the giver and receiver. The Splinter concentrates consequences, intensifies truth."

"But ... but, if I believe you, then you've just taken away my livelihood!" Wil squawked. "That's how I survive. You don't have any right."

The storyteller smiled. "Imagine what the ruthless warrior Roderick the Brash must have experienced. How difficult it was to give up hatred, pillaging, and violence, stranded in a hostile foreign land, suddenly prevented from looting and killing.... Still, he learned to get by. So can you."

Wil squirmed. Something about the old man's interpretation rang uncomfortably true. "So, is there anything I could do to get rid of it? Short of amputation? I mean, if I did a lot of good deeds would it go away ... and leave me in peace?"

"I have met a few people who tried amputation. Strange, no matter how much they cut off—finger, hand, arm—the Splinter stayed inside them, as if it were in their blood. Perhaps you stand a better chance of finding peace if the Splinter remains in your finger."

The old man began to stack up his fine tooled-leather books. With a callused finger, he rubbed the intricate designs and workings, smiling at the craftsmanship. "It's not so hard to learn a new trade, given a little incentive, although you might find it comforting to revisit ... familiar surroundings from time to time."

Outside the tent, criers were announcing the closing of the Renaissance Faire for another day.

Wil just stood, unsettled, staring at the storyteller, not knowing what to do. "This is impossible. You don't really expect me to change who I am and what I do for a living just overnight, do you?"

"No, my friend. But you will have plenty of time. After all these centuries, who would know better than I?" He paused for a moment, holding up one of his ornate books. "You might discover talents you never knew you possessed. You already have quick hands, sharp eyes. Think about what you could become."

The old man's words were too much to absorb all at once. Wil had to let the implications sink in, and questions piled up in his mind. "I have plenty of time …?" Then, as he began to consider the possibilities, a familiar pleasurable sensation tingled in his hand. "You mean I could be a fine artist, a poet, a rock guitarist, even a surgeon? How would I choose?"

A small smile flickered at the corner of the storyteller's mouth. "Why choose? You could do them all. But use your abilities to help people, and you will find contentment."

The pleasant warmth seemed to be growing stronger. "Well, I guess I've always wanted to see other countries. Maybe I could join a service organization and travel while I learn some job skills—new ones, I mean—and some foreign languages."

Now the tingle seeped from Wil's hand into his entire body and, for the first time in memory, he felt a true sense of wonder.

The first story I ever sold (for a whopping $12.50) was to the small-press magazine Space & Time, *edited by Gordon Linzner. I was a senior in high school. "Luck of the Draw" was about a group of itinerant knights drawing straws to see who would slay the dragon and win the hand of the princess. I liked the idea enough that when I was asked to contribute to an anthology,* The Ultimate Dragon, *I rewrote the old story from scratch.*

Years later, Amazon asked me to write a serial novel for a new program they were launching, and I needed something fast-paced, a story that could be told in installments, week after week, and I kept coming back to this lovable group of rogues, medieval con men selling their services as dragonslayers. I pulled in part of the story from "Short Straws" and some other ideas to write my full novel, The Dragon Business.

SHORT STRAWS

Yes, a dragon was terrorizing the land, so the king had offered his daughter in marriage to any brave knight who slew the foul beast. Same old story. I was new to the band of warriors, but the others had heard it all before. This time, though, the logistics caused a problem.

"We could split a *cash* reward," said Oldahn, the battle-scarred old veteran who served as our leader. "But who gets the princess?"

The four of us sat around the fire, procrastinating. Though I was still wide-eyed to be part of the group—they had needed a new cook and errand runner—I'd already noticed that the adventurers liked to talk about peril a lot more than actually doing something about it. I was their apprentice, and I wanted for us to go out and fight, a team of mercenaries, warriors—but that didn't seem to be the way of going about it.

We knew where the dragon's lair was, having investigated every foul-smelling, bone-cluttered cave in the kingdom. But we still hadn't figured out what to do with the princess, assuming we succeeded in slaying the dragon. It didn't seem a practical sort of reward.

Reegas looked up with a half-cocked grin. "We could just take turns with her!"

Oldahn sighed. "One does not treat a princess the way you treat one of your hussies, Reegas."

Reegas scowled, scratching the stubble on his chin. "She's no different from Sarna at the inn—except I'll wager Sarna's better than your rustin' princess at all the important things!"

"She is the daughter of our sovereign, Reegas. Now show some respect."

"Yeah, sure, she's sacred and pure ... Bloodrust, Oldahn, now you're sounding like *him*." Reegas shot a disgusted glance at Alsaf, the puritan.

Alsaf plainly took no offense at the insult. He rolled up the king's written decree, torn from the meeting post in the town square, and stuffed it under his belt, since he was the only one of us who could read. Alsaf methodically began polishing the end of his staff on the fabric of his black cloak. He preferred to fight with his staff and his faith in God, but he also kept a sword at hand in case both the others failed. Firelight splashed across the silver crucifix at his throat.

Reegas spat something unrecognizable into the dark forest behind him. Gray-bearded Oldahn chewed his meat slowly, swallowing even the fat and gristle without a word, mindful of worse rations he had lived through. He wore an elaborately studded leather jerkin that had protected him in scores of battles; his sword was notched, but clean and free of rust.

I sat closest to the campfire, nursing a battered pot containing the last of the stew, letting my own meat cook long enough to resemble something edible. "Uh," I said, desperately wanting to show them I could be a useful member of their band. "Why don't we just draw straws to see who goes to kill the dragon?"

Alsaf, Oldahn, and Reegas all stared as if the newcomer wasn't supposed to come up with a feasible suggestion.

"Rustin' good idea, Kendell," Reegas said. Alsaf nodded.

Oldahn looked at all three of us. "Agreed, then. Luck of the draw."

I scrabbled over to my bedding and searched through it to find suitable lots. I still preferred to sleep on a pile of straw rather than the forest floor. The straw was prickly and infested with vermin, but it reminded me of the warm bed I had left behind when running away from my home. The straw was preferable to the cold, hard dirt—at least until I got hardened to the mercenary life.

I took four straws, broke one in half so that all could see, then handed them to Oldahn. The big veteran covered them in a scarred hand to hide the short straw and motioned for me to draw first.

Tentatively, I reached out, unable to decide whether I wanted the honor of battling the dragon. Sure, being wed to a princess would be nice, but I had barely begun my sword fighting lessons, and according to stories I had heard, dragons were vicious opponents. But I wanted to be a warrior instead of a shepherd's son, and a warrior faced whatever challenges they encountered.

I snatched a straw from Oldahn's grasp and could tell from the others' expressions even before I glanced downward that I had drawn a long one.

Alsaf came forward, holding his staff in his right hand as he reached out to Oldahn's fist. He paused for a long moment, then pulled a straw forth. His black cloak blocked my view, but he turned with a strangled expression on his face, looking as if his faith had deserted him. The short straw fell to the ground as he gripped his silver crucifix. "But, my faith—I must remain chaste! I cannot marry a princess."

Reegas clapped the puritan on the back. "I'm sure you can work something out."

Alsaf was pale as he shifted his weight to rest heavily on his staff. He nodded as if trying to convince himself. "Yes, my purpose is to destroy evil in all its manifestations. A divine hand has guided my selection, and I will serve His purpose." Alsaf's eyes glinted with a fanatical fury as he strode to the edge of the camp.

"Take care, and good luck," said Oldahn.

Alsaf whirled to face the three of us, holding his staff in a battle-ready stance. "I shall be protected by my unquenchable faith. My staff will send the demon back to the fires of Hell!" He looked at the skeptical expressions on our faces, then changed the tone of his voice. "I shall return."

"Is that a promise?" Reegas asked, and for once his sarcasm was weak.

"I give you my word." The puritan turned to stride into the deep stillness of the forest night, crunching through the underbrush.

~

IT WAS the only promise Alsaf ever broke.

~

"FOR OUR HONOR, WE MUST CONTINUE." Oldahn held three straws in his hand, thrusting them forward. "Come, Reegas. Draw first."

Reegas cursed under his breath and reached out to grab a straw without even pausing for thought. A broad grin split his face. He held a long straw.

I came forward, looking intently at the two straws, two chances. One would pit me against a scaly, fire-breathing demon, and the other would give me a reprieve. Knowing that the dragon had already defeated one warrior, I decided the princess wasn't so desirable after all. Alsaf had seemed so strong, so confident, so determined. I hesitated, hoping the puritan would return at the last possible moment....

But he didn't, and I picked a straw. It was long.

Oldahn stared at the short straw remaining in his hand. Cold battle-lust boiled in his eyes. "Very well, I have a dragon to slay, a death to avenge, and a princess to win. I had thought it too late in my life to settle down in marriage—but I will adapt. My brave exploits should be sung by minstrels all across the kingdom."

"Our kingdom doesn't have any minstrels, Oldahn," I pointed out.

The old warrior sighed. "I should have volunteered to go first anyway. I am the leader of our band."

"Our band?" Reegas said, sulking in his crusty old chain mail shirt. "Rust, Oldahn—with you gone we aren't much of a band anymore."

Oldahn patted his heavy broadsword and walked stiffly across the camp. It was a beautiful day, and the sun broke through in scattered patches of green light. Oldahn looked around as if for one last time. He turned to walk away, calling back to us just before he vanished into the tangled distance, "Don't be so sure I won't be coming back."

~

By nightfall, we were sure.

∼

The campfire was lonely with only Reegas and me sitting by it. Oldahn had fallen, and the fact that he was the best warrior in our group (old mercenaries are, by definition, good warriors) didn't improve our confidence. I could hardly believe the great fighter I had revered so much had been *slain*. It wasn't supposed to be this way.

I looked at Reegas, fidgeting in his battered chain mail. "Well, Reegas, do you want to wait until morning, or draw straws now?"

"Rust! Let's get it over with," he said. His eyes were bloodshot. "This better be one hell of a princess."

I picked up two straws, one long, the other short. I held them out to Reegas, and he spat into the fire before looking at me. I masked my expression with some effort. Reegas reached forward and pulled the short straw.

"Bloodrust and battlerot!" he howled, jerking at the ends of the straw as if trying to stretch it longer. He crumpled it in his grip and threw it into the fire, then sank into a squat by my cookpots. "Aww, Kendell—now I can't teach you some things! I meant to take you over to the inn one night where you would—"

I looked at him with a half-smile, raising an eyebrow. "Reegas, do you think Sarna takes no other customers besides yourself?"

Wonder and shock lit up his craggy face. "You? ... Rust!" Reegas laughed loudly, a nervous blustering laugh. He clapped me on the back with perverse pride. "I won't feel sorry for you anymore, Kendell." He drew his sword and leaped into the air, slashing at a branch overhead. "But I'm gonna get that rustin' princess for myself. Maybe royalty knows a few tricks the common hussies don't."

He turned with a new excitement, dancing out of camp, waving farewell.

Alone by the campfire, I waited the long hours as the dusk collapsed into darkness. The forest filled with the noisy silence of a wild night. As the stars began to shine, I lay on the cold ground with my head propped against the rough bark of an old oak. I gave up sleeping on straw in fear that I would have dreams of dark scales and death.

The branches above me looked like the black framework of a broken lattice supporting the stars. The mockingly pleasant fire and the empty campsite made me feel intensely lonely; and for the first time I felt the true pain of my friends' losses. I had wanted to be one of them, and now they were all gone.

I remembered some of the stories they had told me, but I hadn't quite fit in with the rest of the band yet. I was a novice, I hadn't yet fought battles with them, hadn't helped them in any way. And now Alsaf and Oldahn were gone, and Reegas had a good chance of joining them....

Since I had talked my way into accompanying the band, nothing much had happened. Until the dragon came, that is.

Of course, if I had known my first adventure might involve a battle with a large reptilian terror, I might have put up with my dull old life a little longer. My father was a shepherd, spending so much time out with his flocks that he had begun to look like one of his sheep. Imagine watching thirty animals eat grass hour after hour! My mother was a weaver, spending every day hunched over her loom, hurling her shuttle back and forth, watching the threads line themselves up one at a time. She even walked with a jerky back and forth motion, as if bouncing to the beat of a flying shuttle.

Me, I'd just as soon be out fighting bandits, dispatching trouble-some wolves, or chasing the odd sorcerer away under the grave risk of having an indelible curse hurled at me. That's excitement—but slaying a dragon is going a bit too far!

I couldn't sleep and lay waiting, listening to the night sounds. At every rustle of leaves I jumped, peering in to the shadows, hoping it might be Reegas returning, or Oldahn, or even Alsaf.

But no one came.

Finally, at dawn, I threw the last long straw on the dirt and ground it under my heel. I had only ever used my sword to cut up meat for the cook fires. I was alone. No one watched me, or pres-sured me, or insisted that I too go out and challenge the dragon. I could have just crept back home, helped my father tend sheep, helped my mother with her weaving. But somehow that kind of life seemed worse than facing a dragon.

I stared at the blade of my sword, thinking of my comrades. Alsaf and Oldahn and Reegas had been my friends, and I was the only one who could avenge them. Only I remained of the entire mercenary band. I had been with Oldahn long enough, heard his tales of glory, seen how the group worked together as a team. I couldn't just let the dragon have its victory.

Muttering a few curses I had picked up from Reegas, I left the dead campfire behind and set off through the forest.

The forest floor was impervious to the sunshine that dribbled through the woven leaves. A loud breeze rushed through the topmost branches but left me untouched. I knew the boulder-strewn wilderness well, and my woodlore had grown more skillful since my initiation into the band. While we had no serious adventures to occupy ourselves, there was still hunting to be done.

My anxiety tripled as I crested a final hill and started down into a rocky dell that sheltered the dragon's den, a broken shadow in the rock surrounded on all sides by shattered boulders and dead foliage. The lump in my throat felt larger than any dragon could ever be. The wind had disappeared, and even the birds were silent. A terrible stench wafted up, smelling faintly like something Reegas might have cooked.

I crept forward, drawing my sword, wondering why the ground was shaking and then I saw that it was only my knees. Panic flooded my senses—or had my senses left me? Me? Against a dragon? A big scaly thing with bad breath and an awful prejudice against armed warriors?

The boulders offered some protection as I danced from one to another, moving closer to the dragon's lair. Fumes snaked out of the cave, stinging my eyes and clogging my throat, tempting me to choke and give away my presence. I could hear sounds of muffled breathing like the belching of a blacksmith's furnace.

I slid around a slime-slick rock to the threshold of the cave. I froze, an outcry trapped in my throat as I found the shattered ends of Alsaf's staff, splintered and tossed aside among torn shreds of black fabric. I swallowed and went on.

A few steps deeper into the den I tripped on the bloody

remnants of Oldahn's studded leather jerkin. His bent and blackened sword lay discarded among bloody fragments of crunched bone.

On the very boundary of where sunlight dared to go, I found Reegas's rusty chain mail, chewed to a new luster and spat out. A scream welled up as fast as my guts did, but terror can do amazing things for self-control. If I screamed, the dragon would know I had come, the latest in a series of tender victims.

But now, upon seeing with utmost certainty the fates of my comrades, my fellow warriors, anger and lust for vengeance poured forth, almost, *almost*, overwhelming my terror. The end result was an angered persistence tempered with extreme caution.

Leg muscles tense to the point of snapping, I tiptoed into the cave where I stood silhouetted against the frightened wall of daylight. The suffocating darkness of the dragon's lair folded around me. I didn't think I would ever see the sun again.

The air was thick and damp, polluted with a sickening stench. Piles of yellowed skulls lay stacked against one wall like ivory trophies. I didn't see any of the expected mounds of gold and jewels from the dragon's hoard. Pickings must have been slim in the kingdom.

I went ahead until the patch of sunlight seemed beyond running distance. My jerkin felt clammy, sticking to my cold sweat. I found it hard to breathe. I had gone in too far. My sword felt like a heavy, ineffective toy in my hand.

I could sense the lurking presence of the dragon, watching me from the shadows. I could hear its breathing like the wind of an angry storm but could not pinpoint its location. I turned in slow circles, losing all orientation in the dimness. I thought I saw two lamplike eyes, but the stench filled my nostrils, my throat. It gagged me, forcing me to gasp for air, but that only made me gulp down more of the smell. I sneezed.

—and the dragon attacked!

Suddenly I found myself confronted with a battering-ram of fury, blackish green scales draped over a bloated mass of flesh lurching forward. Acid saliva drooled off fangs like spears, spattering in sizzling pools on the floor.

I struck blindly at the eyes, the rending claws, the reptilian armor. The monster let out a hideous cry, seething forward, fat and sluggish, to corner me against a lichen-covered wall. My stomach turned to ice, and I knew how Alsaf, Oldahn, and Reegas must have felt as they faced their death—

~

LET ME DIGRESS A MOMENT.

Dragons are not exactly the best-fed of all creatures living in the wild. Despite their size and power, and the riches they hoard (but who can eat gold?), these creatures find very little to devour, especially in a relatively small kingdom like our own, where most people live protected within the city walls. Barely once a week does a typical dragon manage to steal a squalling baby from its crib or strike down an old crone gathering herbs in the woods. Rarer still does a dragon come across a flaxen-haired virgin (a favorite) wandering through the forest.

Hard times had come upon this particular dragon. Only impending starvation had driven it to increase its attacks on the peasantry, forcing the king to offer his daughter as a reward to rid the land of the beast. The future must have looked bleak for the dragon.

But then, unexpectedly, a feast beyond its wildest dreams! This dragon had greedily devoured three full-grown warriors in half as many days, swallowing whole the bodies of Alsaf, Oldahn, and Reegas.

And so, when the dragon lunged at me in the cave, it was so *bloated* and overstuffed that it could barely drag its bulk forward, like a snake which has gorged itself on a whole rabbit. Its bleary, yellow eyes blinked sleepily, and it seemed to have lost heart in battling warriors. But it snarled forward out of old habit, barely able to stagger toward me....

I won't, by any stretch of the imagination, claim that killing the brute was easy. The scales were tougher than any chain mail I could imagine, and the dragon didn't particularly want its head cut off— but I was bent on avenging my friends and winning myself a princess. If I could just accomplish this one thing, I could call myself a warrior. I would never have to prove myself again.

Alsaf, Oldahn, and Reegas had already done much of the work for me, dealing vicious blows to the reptilian hide. But I still can't begin to express my exhaustion when the dragon's head finally rolled among the cracked bones in its lair. I slumped to the floor of the cave, panting, without the energy to drag myself back out to fresh air.

After I had rested a long time, I stood up stiffly and looked down at the dead monster, sighing. I had won myself a princess. I had avenged my comrades.

But perhaps the best reward was that I could now call myself a real warrior, a dragon-slayer. I imagined I could think of a few ways to make the story more impressive by the time I actually met my bride-to-be.

The monster's head was heavy, and it was a long walk to the castle.

Even though I've lived far from the ocean most of my life, I've always had a fascination with seafaring stories, adventures on sailing ships with sea monsters and mysterious islands. When I was in high school, the wonderful rock album Point of Know Return *by the rock group Kansas fired my imagination, especially with its cover illustration of a sailing ship plunging over the edge of the world into a mysterious void filled with sea monsters. This story, which has been through many different incarnations, was originally an attempt to fictionalize the title track of that album. It remains one of my favorites.*

SEA WIND

The man held everyone's attention as he shouted into the milling, familiar chaos of the harbor, forcefully waving the stump of his right hand. For reasons I would always regret later, I stopped to listen.

"I have been sent here by the captain of the *Sea Wind*, a three-masted lateener lying at anchor in your beautiful harbor of Lisbon!" His voice was hoarse and gravelly, as if from too much shouting in his life. He stood tall on an old wooden crate, flanked by two burly seamen in fine sailing clothes, canvas trousers, striped shirts. The smell of salt breezes and fish stalls hung heavy around us. Many merchants and dock workers flowed around the obstacle, wrapped in their own business, but others paused to hear what the man had to say.

"The captain bids me to tell you that the *Sea Wind* is now taking on crewmembers for a voyage of discovery. We need twenty brave young men, and we will pay well."

Francis, my older brother, pulled me with him as he pushed through the loose crowd, weaving our way closer to the man on the crate, our own task forgotten. I held two mended iron hoops in my hand, fresh from the blacksmith, which our father needed for a barrel he was making. I knew we were expected back at the cooper shop promptly, and I tried to tell Francis, but he impatiently made me hold my words. Only a few people were actually listening to the man.

"Where are you sailing?" an unkempt man called out, lounging against an empty cart with a broken wheel.

The man with the stump turned toward the question. "We shall sail westward to the newly discovered island of Madeira, a paradise with jungles, flowers, and fruits, and birds the colors of jewels! Then we sail southward along the coast of Africa to rich ports and lands unknown, perhaps even the kingdom of Prester John himself!" He wobbled on the old crate. "Our own Prince Henry commanded us to discover the world—"

"*Prince Henry* himself commissioned your ship?" Francis scoffed.

The man smiled uncomfortably, turning to gaze down at my brother. The two burly sailors did not seem amused by the challenge. "The prince gave *all* men the task of exploring the seas, boy. Not two years ago, his own Squire Eannes successfully rounded Cape Bojador in Africa—what was once thought to be Hell itself, where men are black as charcoal because they stand so close to the sun, and the ground is a burning lake of sand! Eannes brought back tales of vast lands farther south—and the *Sea Wind* will go *beyond*, mark my words! To lands of untold riches—pearls as big as your fist, more gold than our ship can carry!"

He looked directly at Francis, pointing with the raw pink end of his stump. "Do you remember the stories of Marco Polo? Of the exotic places he visited, the adventures he had? Would you like to see lands never before beheld by the eyes of Christian men?" He paused and lowered his voice, adding an intense fever to his words. "Would you like to sail with us on the *Sea Wind*?"

The man made me uncomfortable, but Francis's eyes were glittering. He had caught the fever. I tugged on my brother's sleeve, but he stammered out, "How long ... how long do I have to decide?"

"The *Sea Wind* will set sail in four days; but we intend to gather the crew today. Are you interested, boy? Can you write your name?"

"Of course!"

I don't know which question my brother was answering. I was afraid for him, but Francis looked so sure of himself. One of the burly sailors handed him a stained piece of paper and a quill.

Francis refused to meet my gaze and carefully wrote his name. Grandfather had shown him how to write it—Grandfather's name was Francis, too—but the old man couldn't show me how to write my name, since he had never seen what "Stefan" looked like.

The man from the *Sea Wind* smiled congratulations at my brother and rested his stump on his hip as if to say he would have shaken Francis's hand had he been able.

The iron barrel hoops in my hand had grown very heavy.

～

IN THE COOPER SHOP, Father turned back to his work, away from Francis, struggling to quell his anger. His voice was gruff. "You can't go. You are my oldest son. I need you here." He began to arrange the staves for the barrel.

Francis wouldn't let his dreams be broken so easily. He gestured to me, even though I wanted no part of this. "Stefan knows how to do the work as well as I do—he can carry on! I *am* going, Father. This is what I want to do, to sail the seas and see the world. I'm old enough now." He paused, still waiting for Father to look at him, to face him. "Don't make me run away from home."

With a tired, defeated sigh, Father let the curved staves fall together with a flat clatter and stood up, abandoning the work. "How long?" He drew a deep breath, looking down at the barrel and then at me as if I were part of a conspiracy. "How long will you be gone?"

Francis seemed to fight back a smile, knowing he had won. "Maybe a year, no more. We'll sail down the coast of Africa, maybe even find a passage to India. I'll bring back more riches than we've ever had!"

Father wasn't as angry as I had thought he would be. Instead, he seemed resigned to the fact, as if he had been expecting this to come any day now, knowing his son's restlessness as well as anyone.

"If you're going to be gone for a year, then you'd better at least help me finish this barrel."

～

FRANCIS BREATHED in awe as he stared at the *Sea Wind* lying at anchor in the harbor. "Look at her! Oh, just look at her." We sat on the wharf as the late afternoon sun turned golden heading toward the distant watery horizon. The waves brushed against the docks. The air was heavy with screaming gulls and the salty scent of the sea.

The masts of all the ships were like a forest on the water. The city of Lisbon stumbled downward from the surrounding hills like a staircase into the Tagus River where it met the ocean, forming a calm, sheltered harbor at its mouth. The *Sea Wind* rocked gently in the sleepy water, giving us a peek at the line of scum and barnacles crusted below the waterline. She was a magnificent ship, one of the largest in port—seventy feet from bow to stern—and could comfortably hold thirty men on a long voyage.

She had three raked masts, fitted with wide triangular lateen sails rippling in the wind, brushing against the spiderweb of rigging that entwined the ship. The *Sea Wind*'s hull was also finely decorated as an exploring ship should be to bear the pride of Portugal and Prince Henry the Navigator throughout the oceans. Her railing was painted gold, as was the stem, embellished with ornate feathers and curls.

Francis wrapped his arms around his knees as he sat, marveling at the ship he would call home for the next year, but I could see that wonder blinded his eyes. From looking at his expression, I knew my brother didn't notice that the gold paint on the railing was peeling and scarred by the graffiti carved there by other sailors. The ship creaked more than it should have in the gentle wash of waves, and the hull looked as if it might have shipworm. I squinted against the sun, and I could make out that the sails had been patched several times. The thick layers of barnacles at the waterline showed that the *Sea Wind* had been in the water a long time.

The wind picked up, and the ship creaked. "Francis ... what if you don't come back?"

"I'll come back."

"But you'll be out on the ocean, alone! Everyone knows about the sea monsters just waiting to prey on sailing ships! And you might sail off the edge of the world! You're going where no other vessel has sailed before."

Francis turned away from the ship, looking at me with scorn, but I could see the fear behind his eyes. "Stefan, somebody has to go. Somebody has to show the way, somebody has to dream. I talked to other sailors—the *Sea Wind* has voyaged south once before, but they thought they could never make it past Cape Bojador. They told me terrible stories of the bleak desert that pokes its finger into the sea, making the water dirty brown with sand and so shallow that the keel scrapes the bottom even twenty miles offshore. And they told me of barren cliffs of sandstone without so much as a weed growing on them. That was the edge of the world."

He blinked, swallowed hard to drive away his anxiety. "Or so they thought. So *we* thought! Until Squire Eannes rounded the Cape and came back to say there was more of Africa beyond … and more, and more! It wasn't the edge of the world—instead, it might be a gateway to India! Somebody's got to go—you know that."

I saw a strange expression on my brother's face, not just a sadness, but an actual pity for me. "You wouldn't understand. You were always content with the excitement of Lisbon, with helping Father make his barrels, but you know I've always wanted to go to sea, how I've stared at the ships, heard the sailors' stories. I *have* to go. I don't have any choice."

Even though less than a year separated us in age, he seemed infinitely older than me. "I'll miss you, Francis."

"I'll miss you, too."

ONE CANDLE in the corner guttered badly, flashing shadows like moths around the room, randomly switching the patches of light and darkness, but it was getting late and we would extinguish the candle soon anyway. Francis wanted to be in bed early, for the next morning he would go to board the *Sea Wind*—but I don't see how he could sleep this night of all nights. I would be lying awake myself.

Mother had already tucked our little brother Matthew into his basket of straw, supposedly to sleep, but the toddler could sense the tension in the air and his bright eyes watched as our family sat together in uncomfortable silence.

Father brooded by himself, not looking at Francis—I honestly didn't know if he approved or disapproved, if he were angry or sad.

Mother stared at Francis, as if she needed to say something but found it impossible to speak. Her fingers played nervously with a loose thread in her faded dress. Her dark hair was drawn back into a braid that was becoming undone, rampant hairs protruding wildly to shine in the uncertain candlelight.

"Francis …" Her voice sounded uncertain. "We love you."

My brother obviously didn't know how to reply. On the other side of the room, little Matthew began bouncing up and down, shouting in his tiny voice.

"How long until I'm old enough? I want to go on a ship, too! I want to go with Francis!" When Mother ran to the child, she was crying.

After a long uncertain moment, Francis met the gaze of Grandfather, his namesake. The old man sat in his chair, the one he rarely left except when he helped Father in the cooper shop. He was not yet too old to work. Grandfather spoke softly, which forced Francis to sit beside him in order to hear his words. I followed my brother, wanting to stay by him for every minute we had left together.

"Francis … you have talked with the other sailors?" the old man said in a raspy voice. "You know what awaits you … out there? In the unknown?"

Everyone in our family knew the story. As a boy, Grandfather had wanted to embark on a similar voyage, but before the ship had even left Lisbon harbor, he had tangled his hand in one of the winch ropes, crushing it, so that he was forced to return home without seeing the sea as he had hoped. Perhaps the old man now looked at Francis with envy, because he had a chance to complete the voyage his older namesake had never been able to do.

Francis had gotten good at his show of bravery. "I've heard stories of the abyss at the edge of the world where horrible creatures wait to devour unfortunate sailors. Of the great sea serpents and sirens and—"

"And the kraken? Have you been warned of the kraken?" The

fearful look on Grandfather's face said that he would refuse to tell the story, whether or not my brother had heard it.

Francis looked up into the shadows where the walls met the ceiling, lost in his own imagining. "They say that when you are out there, and the sea turns dark, and the sky turns darker—you'll know. You'll know when the kraken has come, veiled in storms. And when the wind whistles through your rigging and tears at the sails, when the water foams and seethes—you'll know."

Grandfather pushed his face closer to Francis's. "And when black tentacles thick as a mainmast rise out of the water to wrap around your ship and *crush* it as if it were straw—and when the kraken drags you under, *screaming*, to feed his children—you'll know. And you won't ever return, Francis, but your bones will keep him company far beneath the sea, alone forever—for the kraken can never die."

Francis looked nervously around the room.

Grandfather sounded forlorn. "And we will wait for you here, a year, maybe two, and we will know what has become of you, Francis ..."

"Oh, Francis!" I gasped, drawing a breath which was cold with shadows. The candlelight seemed to be dimmer than before.

A different light came into Grandfather's eyes. "But I know that no stories can change your mind. When that sea wind blows—you must follow it, you must go to the sea, answer your dreams. I know. There is no other way."

Francis smiled, undeterred. "You understand." He turned to look at Father, then back at the old man. "You understand."

∼

LIFE WAS LONELY WITHOUT FRANCIS.

He had left the morning before, looking both excited and afraid, waving from the side rails as the *Sea Wind* set sail away from Lisbon and out to sea. My older brother had been by me ever since I could remember, to talk with, to dream with.

And now I was alone.

Our small bedroom was dark, and the air was humid and filled with the raw scent of the wood slats Father soaked for his barrels.

Light rain trickled against the whitewashed walls of our house overlooking the harbor. Faint echoes of thunder rumbled in the distance.

Francis was gone, in distant waters.

Baby Matthew cried in the corner, frightened by the storm. I heard Mother comforting him, whispering into his tiny ear. "It's just rain, little Matthew. The storm won't hurt you—it's far away. The storm is far, far out at sea."

The storm was out at sea.

I lay on my straw tick mattress, damp with sweat and rain mist, and I knew I would waste my time trying to sleep for a while yet. Silently, I crept to the window and moved aside the canvas curtain, cut from an old sail, so I could peer into the night. Ricocheting raindrops glistened on my face.

The cobblestoned streets were wet, reflecting distant flashes of lightning. The other buildings, every one of them a white box with narrow windows decked with flowers, perched on the steep levels of the city. I could barely make out the dark water of the harbor, and I certainly couldn't see the ocean. But the storm was out there, and so was Francis.

Is the sea dark now, Francis? And the sky filled with storm clouds even darker? Does the wind sing through the rigging and tear at the sails? Does the white foam boil against the side of the ship and crash on the deck? Is that roar of thunder your cry for help?

I could picture him standing at the rail, his knuckles white and his fingers gripping the peeling gold carvings scarred by graffiti, trying to hold himself steady against the screaming wind and crashing waves, peering down into the dark sea, pale with terror and waiting for the black tentacles of the kraken to reach up and smash the *Sea Wind*.

Francis!

Will you ever return to us?

DAYS later I found myself walking alone on the beach, far from the harbor. As if the storm had never been, the sun beat down to strike away my sweat. I wandered down the shore, looking for shells, for flotsam, for treasure. By myself.

The greatest loneliness was past now, and I was learning to be Stefan, instead of "Francis's brother." Father had begun to teach me what I needed to know as a cooper; and I was already becoming more independent. When Francis came back from his voyage, I might even be ready to embark on an adventure of my own. I could dream.…

But I would wait for my brother. I would wait to hear his stories, the sights he had seen and the perils he had survived. Mother was already asking sailors from newly arrived ships if they had any news of the *Sea Wind* and when it would return. I could be patient and wait for Francis, though I would miss him.

The sun glared on the water, but I shaded my eyes to see a dark shape floating toward the beach, a piece of driftwood. I watched it bob along for a few moments and finally, when patience deserted me, I waded out to retrieve it.

I stood with warm water lapping about my waist, soaking into my coarse shirt. I looked at the wood.

It was a piece of wreckage, part of a ship, probably the splintered remnant of a rail. I turned it over, but in my heart I already knew.

Peeling gold paint … scratched and obscured by sailors' graffiti.

The ocean made soft rushing noises, and I stared at the rail for a long time. Many ships had the same design, many ships could have shed that piece of wood—but in my heart I had no doubt.

Mother would continue to wait, day after day, for some word, watching for the *Sea Wind* to return. How long will you wait, Mother?

I let the driftwood slip back into the water and I pushed it away from shore. I knew I wouldn't tell her. For all she knew, all any of us knew, the *Sea Wind* was still out sailing to marvelous unknown places.

I turned and walked back toward the beach, washing the flecks of gold paint from my hands.

My interest in the legends of the sea reached its apex in my giant epic fantasy trilogy, Terra Incognita, three doorstop novels and two crossover rock CDs. The sprawling story dealt with voyages of exploration, the monsters of the deep, and also religious fanaticism and intolerance.

Even though the Terra Incognita novels had dozens of main characters and multiple side stories, this was one tale that insisted on being a standalone, a close-minded "prester" (a priest) who is confronted with a mythical creature that his faith will not let him believe in.

MYTHICAL CREATURES

The prow of the *Compass* cut the rough gray waters like a knife carving a Landing Day roast. Prester Ormun closed his eyes and drove away all his pleasant memories of the traditional holiday ... or any other family memories, for that matter. Those were behind him now; only bleak settlements on the scattered Soeland Islands lay ahead. The prester had a difficult path to follow, even if he did not understand God's reasoning behind it.

The ship's damp sails creaked and sighed, and he felt the cold spray on his face, blown by the coming storm. Dobri, the bright-eyed cabin boy, came up beside him, leaning over the bow to peer down into the choppy waves. "Are you looking for *sylkas*, Prester? They say sometimes you can see them in the whitecaps just before a squall."

"I do not believe in *sylkas*. And neither should you." Prester Ormun knew that for a young man like this, the world was filled with mysteries and wonders, but also ignorance. It was his appointed task to enlighten the people of the islands.

The cabin boy squinted at the sea, which looked leaden under the thick sky. "They're real, Prester—beautiful women with golden hair or seaweed all over their bodies. Other sailors have seen them."

"I don't care what other sailors say. *Sylkas* do not exist. It is written in the Book of Aiden that God created the peoples of the land, but only fish, seals, whales, and sea serpents inhabit the sea—

no intelligent creatures. I can show you the Scriptures, if you like." Since Ormun knew the cabin boy couldn't read, the proof would be lost on him.

Dobri was both disappointed and skeptical to hear the prester's pronouncement. He had grown up in a small fishing village, and this was his first voyage away from home; he wanted to believe all the wondrous, imaginative stories, whether or not they were true. Now the boy gazed ahead, intent on spotting one of the imaginary *sylkas* so he could point out the creature to Ormun.

With a pang, the prester realized that his own son Aleo would have been about Dobri's age now....

A large wave gushed over the *Compass*'s bow, and the cabin boy scuttled away, but the prester did not try to avoid the splash; instead, he let it wash away his past again. His family was gone, and nothing remained for him in the city of Calay. That was why he'd been sent across the rough waters to the bleak Soeland Islands. A new chance ... a last chance.

The church's prester-marshall had sent Ormun to preach among the roughshod and hardy islanders; he would bring them the Book of Aiden to comfort the people in their storms and cold northerly winds. Ormun accepted his first mission with neither enthusiasm nor complaint. He was humble enough not to expect redemption, but he did hope to achieve something positive with whatever remained of his life. That he was all he asked God for....

Back in Calay, before he became a prester, Ormun was a shoemaker with a wife and two children, a home, friends—a lifetime ago, or a year ago, depending on whether he measured time by a calendar or the gulf in his heart.

The gray plague had swept through the Craftsmen's District, as it did every few years. Shops closed their doors and latched the window shutters. But Ormun had his family to feed: his son, his daughter, and his wife, a dark-haired, tan-skinned beauty named Risula. And so, he kept working, while others hid.

He never knew which customer exposed him to the plague. Ormun lay shivering in bed for days while his family tended him: Aleo, only twelve years old, acting as the man of the house, Risula giving him salty broth to drink; even little Essa brought him flowers that she'd picked outside.

Ormun gained strength day by day, then suffered a relapse, falling back into a deep fever, sleeping like the dead, drenched in cold sweat. His last murky memory was of Risula shushing their daughter and leading her away, telling her to let her father sleep. And then his wife had started coughing.…

When his fever broke, Ormun emerged from his coma, very weak, and he could barely open his crusted eyes. His throat was parched, and he called out for water, but heard nothing. The house seemed quiet, much too quiet. After he gained enough strength to crawl out of bed, he found his family huddled together, dead, victims of the fever that he had somehow survived.

Ormun had walked away from his home, wandering the streets in a daze, until he finally came upon the kirk. He stumbled inside, and the local prester cared for him, read to him from the Book of Aiden. It was then Ormun decided what his mission in life must be. The gray plague had left him with an empty heart, no laughter, and no love. He clutched onto his service to the church like an anchor of hope, read the Book several times through, and debated with great fervor. When the kindly local prester could no longer answer his questions, he sent the gaunt and intense Ormun to the main kirk in Calay, where he met with the prester-marshall himself.

Cast adrift in life, Ormun begged the church leader for a new course to set. The prester-marshall did not try to explain God's personal message for Ormun, didn't pretend to reveal the purpose behind all the pain he had suffered. "I know a place where you can be of service. The Soelanders need you, and I think you belong there." He anointed Ormun a prester and presented him with the Book and the fishhook pendant that was a symbol of their faith.

No one called Soeland a pleasant place to live, but that mattered not a whit to Ormun. He took his Book and his letters of passage, and begged a bunk on the *Compass*, which was ready to sail back for the islands.…

Now the sea grew rough, and waves rocked the vessel. Captain Endre Stillen came to join the prester, looking troubled. He was a red-bearded man with a muscular chest and potbelly as hard as a wine cask. "Your cabin would be more comfortable, Prester. No sense staying out here in the storm—the weather is going to get worse."

"Discomfort doesn't bother me, Captain," Ormun said.

Stillen shot an uncertain glance to the anxious cabin boy who hovered nearby. "Dobri says that you don't believe in the mysteries of the sea." He raised his bushy eyebrows.

"I do not."

"The ocean is vast and uncharted, and we've all seen things we can't explain. I'm as inclined to believe in *sylkas* as in anything else. If nothing else, it gives me hope to know that those dark waters might contain benevolent creatures, should anything happen to my ship."

"I don't need mythical creatures to give me hope, Captain. The Book of Aiden says that *sylkas* don't exist, so therefore they don't exist. It doesn't matter what tales you've heard or what you think you've seen."

The conversation reminded Ormun of a recent outspoken stargazer who had adapted a seaman's spyglass so he could stare at the stars and planets in the night sky. The astronomer convinced himself that he saw tiny satellites circling one of the planets—an impossible idea. To prove his assertion, the stargazer had asked the prester-marshall to observe for himself; but the church leader refused to raise the spyglass to his eye. "The Book of Aiden tells us that God made the world as the center of all things, so therefore other satellites *cannot* circle one of the tiny planets in the sky. I have no need to look, when I already know." He handed the telescope back to the baffled astronomer. Ormun thought it was an amazingly profound demonstration of the prester-marshall's unshakable faith. He only hoped he could be as worthy someday.

Seeing that the prester's mind was set, Captain Stillen chose not to pursue the argument. "Those legends are a vital part of Soelander life and folklore, Prester. You'll be in for some lively discussions when you get to the fishing towns, that's for certain."

"I'm not afraid of debate."

The captain ordered the sails trimmed against the squall. As the winds picked up, waves hammered the side of the ship. Most of the crew hurried belowdecks before the rain started to sheet down.

Dobri yelped, pointing off to starboard. "I saw one! Look, Prester—it's a *sylka*!"

Ormun froze, wanting not to look, *almost* strong enough to

refuse, but he couldn't help himself. He turned to where the boy pointed—and that was his weakness, his failure.

While he looked in the other direction, a rogue wave swamped the bow and gushed over the rails with enough force to knock him overboard. He reached out, grabbed for anything, and his fingers caught the slick wood, but couldn't get hold. Then the rush of curling foam bore him overboard into the wide gulf of the sea.

Prester Ormun sucked in a breath to shout for help, but he swallowed a mouthful of salt water instead. Flailing, sinking, he coughed and retched as the wave crest bore him upward, then plunged him under again. He clawed at the water with his hands, seeing grayish light above. His face burst from the waves again, and he drew in a deep breath. He rose and sank, completely lost, adrift. His heavy woolen shift pulled him down.

In the pouring rain he spotted Dobri and Captain Stillen struggling to their feet on the deck. He caught a glimpse of the cabin boy, his mouth open in dismay as he saw the prester in the water. Dobri waved and shouted.

Ormun raised his hands to signal, but the seas were too rough. Currents whisked him farther from the ship. The *Compass* could never send out a boat to rescue him.

He tried to stay afloat, but his arms and legs felt leaden. His shoes—good leather boots that he had made in his own cobbler shop long ago in that other life—filled with water. He was going to drown out here.

Oddly, he didn't view the thought with any particular terror, but he did feel a heavy confusion. God's course for him had been so clear—to spread the word out in the Soeland Islands. What was the purpose of saving Ormun from the gray plague only to let him be swept away by a capricious wave, drowning before he even had a chance to preach to his new charges?

He went under again, struggled to the surface, caught another breath. Letting go, he let himself be flung about by the waves. Barely able to think, he experienced a paradoxical sense of calm and peace.

Then clammy hands grasped him from below. A firm grip took his woolen shift, cradled his head, buoyed him up to where he could breathe. But Ormun didn't want to breathe. He struggled and fought against the strange figure below, but he was too weak.

In the end, he simply surrendered to the water and the mythical savior that his imagination had created in his last moments of life. Prester Ormun sank into the darkness, trying to remember a prayer.

WHEN PRESTER ORMUN AWOKE, he smelled fish in the dank and cold air around him. Dried saltwater plastered his hair to his head, and he had to pry open his crusted eyes. Before his vision adjusted, he rolled over onto his knees and retched, puking up foul-tasting saltwater.

He saw that he was in an empty cave at the waterline, which looked out upon the open sea. Outside, the waves sounded like drumbeats against the algae-encrusted rocks that he could see beyond the cave opening. With a start, the prester realized he was naked, his woolen shift spread on a rock nearby. The cloth was stiff and salt-encrusted, but reasonably dry. He shivered and pulled his clothes back on, hiding his nakedness.

He noticed four gutted fish on a flat rock next to him, along with a pile of oysters and clams, all of which had been pried open, ready for him to eat. Weak and starving, Ormun devoured the food without thinking, without tasting, and he felt reborn, as when he'd emerged from his fever after the gray plague. Now, however, questions clamored in his mind, and he looked around, trying to understand what had happened to him.

A figure swam in the sea outside the cave. It seemed human at first—until the creature hauled itself onto the rocks and climbed dripping into the cave. Covered with luxurious locks of golden fur, it was obviously female, with rounded breasts covered by matted weeds. The face was narrow and ethereal, with large brown eyes— soulful eyes, like those of a sea lion. She smelled of salt from the sea. Her lips curved in what was an unmistakable smile as she saw him awake and looking at her.

Ormun squeezed his eyes shut and felt for his fishhook pendant in a protective instinct, but the religious symbol was gone. Perhaps it had washed away when he'd been swept overboard, or perhaps this *thing*—this *sylka*?—had stolen it, fearing the sign of Aiden.

Ormun opened his eyes again, but the creature was still there; he had expected her to vanish like a mirage-shadow. She came forward to squat near him, briny water trickling from her fur, and he struggled away. The *sylka* picked up the empty oyster and clam shells and cast them out of the cave, then she turned back to scrutinize him, like a raven fascinated by a shiny object ... or a predator deciding how best to devour its prey. A thrumming sound echoed from her throat, a call that was at once mysterious, mournful, and hypnotic.

When the creature edged closer, Prester Ormun backed away until his shoulders struck the cave wall. "You're not real!"

The *sylka* trilled at him. Her eyes showed a yearning to communicate. She repeated the sound and chirruped with a higher note at the end, like a question.

"You're not real." Though he could see the *sylka*'s form as if she had been sketched from the logbook of a delusional sea captain, could smell her musky iodine odor, and hear the sound she made, Ormun clung to what the Book of Aiden taught: That God had blessed *mankind* with intelligence, giving only His *chosen children* the minds to understand and worship Him. All other creatures of the land and sea were lowly animals. In another verse, the Book specifically denounced mermaids and *sylkas* as distractions for a devout man, superstitions unworthy of a true follower of God.

But now Ormun found himself faced with the contradiction. The Book of Aiden stated plainly that this *sylka* could not be here. Ormun had read those words of scripture with his own eyes ... yet those same eyes showed him this impossible creature. Right here.

Back in Calay, the prester-marshall had instructed him in the use of rational thought. If this *sylka* truly existed, then the statement in the Book was in error. A small error, perhaps—and how could anyone know all the mysteries and all the creatures in the vast sea?

Yet one error in one verse was as bad as a thousand errors, for either way it proved that the Book of Aiden was flawed.

And because it was the word of God, the Book of Aiden could

not be flawed. Therefore, that one verse, and all verses, had to be correct. By definition.

Hence, the *sylka* could not exist, and she was not there. He stared hard at her, willing the illusion to go away.

The *sylka* hunkered down and continued to gaze at him with mournful eyes. She let out a series of complex musical trills, but Prester Ormun closed his eyes and covered his ears.

∼

THE *SYLKA* LEFT the cave several times throughout the day, diving into the sea and swimming away. She always returned with fresh fish, oysters, or abalones for him, all of which he ate suspiciously. Ormun used the empty abalone shells to capture dripping water that trickled from the moist rocks of the cave. It tasted gritty and dirty but soothed his parched throat.

Each time the mythical creature went away, Ormun tried to convince himself that she was only an illusion brought about by delirium, perhaps a relapse of the gray fever. Then the *sylka* returned, and they would stare at each other again....

He feared she might bring back others of her kind to show them the strange captive she had hauled from the stormy seas—but, again, the prester knew that couldn't happen, because *sylkas* did not exist. There were no others. Each time she came to him, she was alone ... and so was he.

When he felt strong enough, and desperate enough, Ormun made his plans and waited for the *sylka* to swim away again. The creature slipped out of the cave one afternoon, and Ormun decided it was time to escape—if he could. He ventured out of the opening and climbed up on the rocks, hoping to find some landmark that would tell him where he was.

If this was one of the Soeland Islands, Ormun could make his way inland, where he might find people—a fishing village, a shack, or a boat dock. But when he scrambled up the algae-covered boulders above the tide line, he saw that this island was merely a tiny patch of land, an elbow of reef that barely rose above the waterline —a few acres of forlorn boulders and tufts of misplaced grass. He could see the full swatch of land from end to end, side to side. The island was empty. He was alone.

Staring at the watery horizon with tears burning in his eyes, he discerned the gray hummocks of other islands in the distance, larger shores that might be inhabited ... but they were much too far away. He could never swim that far, and if he tried to escape, he was sure the *sylka* would come after him, grab his legs, and drag him beneath the water. He still didn't understand why she had saved him in the first place.

As he stood there in empty dismay, the *sylka* rose out of the surf and climbed onto dry land on the other side of the islet. Silhouetted in daylight, she looked like a seductress, her form voluptuous, the golden kelplike fur haloed by the sun. Ormun had looked at women once, had found Risula so lovely that she made him dizzy with desire ... but he had been a different man before the gray fever—someone without the same convictions, without the same priorities. He averted his eyes.

The *sylka* came toward him, clearly alarmed to see him out of the cave. On land, her movements were ungainly, like a seal's, although he had seen how sleek and lissome she was in the water. When the creature urged him back to the cave that was his prison, he recoiled at her touch, but could not resist. He saw no point to it; he had nowhere else to go.

Back in her lair, the *sylka* was intent on showing him something. She trilled, inducing him to come to a dank alcove in the rear of the small cave. Under a weed-covered overhang, she had piled rocks to create a protective barrier, a sort of nest. The *sylka* looked at him with great wonder in her eyes as she grasped the rocks with her webbed hands and lifted them away one by one.

Beneath the protective barrier rested a group of pulsating, grayish spheres, pearlescent objects, each one larger than a ripe melon. Ormun counted five of them grouped together with loving care, moist with a filmy membrane—a clutch of eggs! The creature's young. She was reproducing, about to unleash five more of her kind into the world!

Obviously the *sylka* wasn't entirely alone out there in the waters. Ormun imagined her out in the gray cold sea, at night, letting out her trilling song, calling a mate from across the waves.

Did she lay her eggs here in the cave and wait for a male to spray his milt on the clutch like a frog? The very idea made him shudder with disgust.

The *sylka* inhaled and exhaled wet burbling breaths, and she crouched closer, cooing. The creature extended a pale finger and stroked the nearest egg. Her touch activated something within, a sparkle in the air accompanied by the smell of ozone, and Prester Ormun felt an overwhelming sense of importance and hope—a magical, unnatural connection.

On the egg's shifting metallic surface, he saw distorted images, like memories seen through the fever fog. The *sylka* touched a second egg, and a third, and more images formed on their reflective shells ... the prester's hopes and possibilities from the lost part of his life, things she could not possibly know about him.

Ormun saw the blurry, uncertain features of his son Aleo, laughing, full of tales of fish he had caught or beetles he had collected. The second eggshell displayed sweet, doe-eyed Essa, who loved to pick the flowers that grew in meadows just outside the city. And exotic, beautiful Risula.

But the last time Ormun had seen his family, they were dead, plague-ridden, their bodies huddled on the floor of their home, while he shivered in a coma on the narrow bed. Now, he gasped a quick, perfunctory prayer, but he continued to look. He knew he should turn away, even though those faces made his heart ache.

Sensing his reaction, the *sylka* trilled with happiness.

Then Ormun realized these visions were not just memories, for he saw Aleo as a young man, standing with a thin and pretty red-haired woman. They held each other, kissed—Aleo's wife-to-be? Ormun saw another maiden with fresh-picked flowers in her hair, unmistakably Essa, just at the edge of growing up. He saw Risula cradling another baby—her own, or a grandchild?

The eggs held possibilities, a wellspring of the future.

"No," Ormun whispered, drawing away. "No, this never happened! This can't be." He covered his eyes. The *sylka* was distraught, not understanding his reaction, but Ormun clung to strength within.

The images that pooled on the shells of her eggs did not repre-sent the path that God had chosen for him. He had endured the pain. He had read the Book. He had fought for understanding and acceptance, like a pathfinder hacking through persistent under-brush, rather than taking a simple and easy trail that did not lead where he wanted to go. These elusive memories were not *his* memories, and that future did not belong to him.

"No," he said again.

With obvious disappointment, the *sylka* piled the rocks again over her eggs.

∾

EVEN THOUGH THE prester understood his mission now, he feared he wouldn't have the necessary strength. As he shivered through the cold, damp night while wrestling with his thoughts, Ormun once again told himself that none of this was *real*. Maybe he had actually drowned when the wave swept him overboard, and this was his test before God let him enter Heaven. The only thing that had kept him alive after the plague, the purpose that allowed him to get through one day, then the next, was the anchor of his faith, his dogged belief in what the prester-marshall had taught him. If he abandoned that, then he would be abandoning everything he had left.

The eerie, tempting images he'd seen in the *sylka*'s eggs—his family, his happiness, a bright future—none of that was true. How he longed for what he saw in those illusions, wanted that reality more than anything else he could ever imagine. But that, in itself, was what warned him. *His* wishes did not matter: It was about what God wanted. Ormun had to be strong, and his only strength was his faith.

On the fourth morning after being washed overboard, Ormun watched the *sylka* return to the cave, climbing out of the water. As the creature sloshed toward him, she looked excited, gesturing with a webbed hand. When the prester didn't follow, she hurried back to the cave opening and stared out to sea, then trilled a sharper sound, more urgent than her soothing music. Ormun felt compelled to look out upon the sunwashed waters.

In the channel between the islands, close enough that he could see the sails and rigging, a two-masted vessel cruised in from the north. He even recognized the lines, the look of the hull, the cut of the sails. It was the *Compass*! Maybe Captain Stillen had come back to look for him, or maybe this was just the ship's regular return route through the archipelago.

Thrumming, the *sylka* looked at him with her limpid eyes. Ormun's heart lurched, and he knew the time had come. This was the crux, and he clung to the truth like a man grasping a lifeline. He had not dared to pray for a chance at redemption, to demonstrate his devotion and his acceptance—and now the sailing ship had returned! The *Compass* would rescue him.

He lurched to his feet, uttering a prayer of thanksgiving. The *sylka* gestured for him to hurry, and by her demeanor and bright expression he guessed that she intended to swim out to the *Compass*, draw the attention of the sailors, and get Captain Stillen to change course to the islet. This creature had already rescued him from drowning, and now she would save him from being marooned on the small island. She turned away, looking out to sea.

Ormun picked up one of the melon-sized reef rocks, held it in both hands, and brought it down with all of his strength on the back of the *sylka's* head. He bashed as hard as he could, and her skull was much softer than the rock. The *sylka* collapsed, letting out a mournful hooting sound, and Ormun struck again.

He stood tall and dropped the rock on the floor of the cave. "You don't exist." If the captain, the cabin boy, and the rest of the crew saw her, they would not have the strength to cling to their faith. Ormun had no other choice but to save them from their own gullibility.

He went to the back alcove, pulled away the rocks piled over the clutch of eggs, and gazed down at the quicksilver pooling—the reflections that were mocking echoes of a past that was already gone and a future he would never have. Useless and dangerous, a mocking temptation. Prester Ormun was strong enough to avoid fantasies, no matter how attractive they might be. He knew his life's course.

Ormun picked up another rock and smashed the first *sylka* egg, obliterating the illusions of things that might have been. Then he destroyed the rest of the clutch, one by one, until he felt safe again.

When he was finished, he was surprised to discover that the

sylka's body still lay on the cave floor; the dripping slimy fragments of broken eggs remained strewn about their nest. Now that he had passed his test of faith, Ormun expected them to vanish instantly, but he didn't search for, or want, explanations. It was time for him to be rescued, to return to his role as a prester preaching the Book of Aiden. The Soelanders needed him.

Ormun carried one of the abalone shells as he scrambled out of the cave and onto the high point of the small islet. There, he jumped and waved, seesawing his hands in the air, trying to get the attention of the *Compass*. He caught the bright sunlight with the shiny interior of the shell, flashing a signal. He yelled until his throat was raw.

And finally—finally—he saw pennants raised on the mainmast, and the ship turned toward the rocky island. Someone had seen him.

When the *Compass* anchored at a safe distance from the islet, Prester Ormun watched the ship's boat lowered, saw men rowing toward him. Though he was not a good swimmer, he dove into the water and struck out to meet the boat partway. He recognized the boy Dobri at the front of the boat, and two sturdy Soeland sailors pulling at the oars. The prester flailed in the waves, swimming as far from the islet as he could.

He needed to be away from the persistent imaginary remnants of the *sylka* and her eggs. He didn't want any of these men from the *Compass* to see the evidence, otherwise they would be deceived by what they wanted to believe.

Gasping and exhausted, Ormun reached the boat, and his heart swelled with joy. Dobri leaned over to catch his hand. "Prester, we thought you were dead!"

"I thought I was, too," he said as they helped to haul him aboard. "But I survived, and now I know that God still has more work for me to do."

The cabin boy laughed, and the sailors rowed back toward the *Compass*. Ormun was too tired and shaken to tell his story, and he still had much to think about before he revealed anything.

When they tied up to the sailing ship, he climbed aboard to congratulations from Captain Stillen. "We couldn't believe it, Prester! No man ever survives out here. How did you make it to that small island? We were just continuing our passage among the islands, but Dobri spotted the flashing light."

"An abalone shell," the prester said.

The captain admired his cleverness, and Dobri added, "I was at the bow looking for *sylkas* when I saw it."

"*Sylkas* don't exist, boy," Prester Ormun said, more convinced now than he had ever been.

But while the crewmen took him to change into dry clothes, the prester watched Dobri hurry back to the bow with a spyglass in hand. Seeing the boy's eager willingness to believe, he felt only sadness and disappointment. He had to teach these people the truth, no matter how difficult it was.

Nevertheless, Dobri continued to scan the waves, always looking, always hopeful.

This was my first collaboration with Rebecca, right after we got married. She had been working on an eerie, atmospheric idea for a story, inspired by the Beatles' haunting song "Julia." When she got stuck, she asked me to work on it with her, and we hashed out a story unlike most of my other work. Around the same time, my friend Janet Berliner invited me to contribute to an anthology she was editing with Peter S. Beagle, The Immortal Unicorn, *stories not just about actual unicorns but the metaphor and symbology of unicorns. The character of Julia seemed to fit with the theme, and Janet and Peter included "Sea Dreams" among other more traditional unicorn stories.*

SEA DREAMS

(WRITTEN WITH REBECCA MOESTA)

Julia called me tonight as she has so many times before. Not on the telephone, but in that eerie, undeniable way she's used since we met as little girls, strangers and best friends at once. It usually meant she needed me, had something urgent or personal to say.

But this time I needed her, in a desperate, throw-common-sense-to-the-wind way … and she knew it. Julia always knew.

And she had something to tell me.

Alone in the tiny bedroom of my comfortably conservative Florida apartment, I felt it as surely as I felt the cool sheets beneath me, and the humid, moon-warm September air that flowed through my half-opened window. At such times, common sense goes completely to sleep, leaving imagination wide awake and open to possibilities. And she called out to me.

Julia had been gone for five years, gone to the sea. Others might have said "drowned," might have used "gone" as a euphemism for "dead." I never did. The only thing I knew—that anyone could know for certain—was this: Julia was gone.

IT HAD BEGUN when we were eleven. That year, my parents and I left our Wisconsin home behind to spend our vacation at my grandmother's oceanside cottage in Cocoa Beach, Florida.

I had grown up in the Midwest, familiar with green hills and sprawling fields, but nothing had prepared me for my first sight of the Atlantic: an infinite force of blue-green mystery, its churning waves a magnet for my sensibilities, a sleeping power I had never suspected might exist.

Excited by the journey and the strange place, I was unable to sleep that first night in grandmother's cottage. The rumble of the waves, the insistent shushing whisper of the surf muttering a white-noise of secrets, vibrated even through the glass … and grew louder still when I got up and nudged open the window to smell the salt air.

There, in the moonlight, a young girl stood on the beach— someone other than grandmother, her friends, and my parents, talking about grown-up things while I patiently played the role of well-behaved daughter. Another girl unable to sleep.

I put on a bikini (my first) and a pair of jeans, tiptoed down the stairs, and let myself out the sliding glass door onto the sand. As I walked toward the ocean, reprimanding myself for the foolhardiness of going out alone at night, I saw her still standing there, staring out into the waves.

She seemed statuesque in the moonlight, fragile, ethereal. She had waist-length hair the color of sun-washed sand, wide green eyes—I couldn't see them in the dark, but still I knew they were green—and a smile that matched the warmth and gentleness of the evening breeze.

"Thank you for coming," she said. She paused for a few moments, perhaps waiting for a response. As I carefully weighed the advisability of speaking to a stranger, even one who looked as delicate as a princess from a fairy tale, she added, "My name is Julia."

"I'm Elizabeth," I replied after another ten seconds of agonized deliberation. I shook her outstretched hand as gravely as she had extended it, thinking what an odd gesture this was for someone who had probably just completed the sixth grade. Which, I discovered once we started to talk, was exactly the case—as it was for me.

We spoke to each other as if I had been there all along and often came out for a chat, not like strangers who had just met on the beach after midnight. Within half an hour, we were sitting and talking like old friends, laughing at spontaneous jokes, sharing confidences, even finishing each other's sentences as though we somehow knew what the other meant to say.

"Do you like secrets? And stories?" Julia asked during a brief lull in our conversation. When I hastened to assure her that I did—though I had never given it much thought—she fell silent for a long moment and then began to weave me a tale as she looked out upon the waves, like an astronomer gazing toward a distant galaxy.

"I have seen the Princes of the Seven Seas," she said in a soft, dreamy voice, "and each of their kingdoms is filled with more magic and wonder than the next.... The two mightiest princes are the handsome twins, Ammeron and Ariston, who rule the kingdoms of the North."

She had found a large seashell on the beach and held it up to her ear, as if listening. "They tell me secrets. They tell me stories. Listen."

Julia half-closed her green eyes and talked in a whispery, hypnotic voice, as if reciting from memory—or repeating words she somehow heard in the convolutions of the seashell.

"They have exquisite underwater homes, soaring castles made of coral, whose spires reach so close to the surface that they can climb to the topmost turrets when the waves are calm and catch a glimpse of the sky...."

I giggled. Julia's voice was so earnest, so breathless. She frowned at me for my moment of disrespect, and I fell silent, listening with growing wonder as her story caught us both in a web of fantasy and carried us to a land of blues and greens, lights and shadows, beneath the shushing waves.

"Each kingdom is enchanted, filled with light and warmth, and the princes rarely stay long in their castles. They prefer instead to ride across the brilliant landscapes of the underwater world, watching over their realms.

"Their loyal steeds are sleek narwhals that carry Ammeron and Ariston to all—"

"What's a narwhal?" I asked, betraying my Midwestern ignorance of the sea and its mysteries.

Julia blinked at me. "They're a sort of whale—like unicorns of the sea—strong swimmers with a single horn. Ancient sailors used to think they were monsters capable of sinking ships...."

She cocked her head, listening to the shell. Her face fell into deep sadness for the next part of her story, and I wondered how she could make it all up so fast.

"The sea princes enjoy a charmed existence, full of adventure—they live forever, you know. One of their favorite quests is to hunt the kraken, hideous creatures that ruled the oceans in the time before the Seven Princes, but the defeated monsters hide now, brooding over their lost empires. They hate Ammeron and Ariston most of all, and lurk in dark sea caves, dreaming of their chance to murder the princes and take back what they believe is rightfully theirs.

"On one such hunt, when Ammeron and Ariston rode their beloved narwhal steeds into a deep cavern, armed with abalone-tipped spears, they flushed out the king of the kraken, an enormous tentacled beast twice the size of any monster the two brothers had fought before.

"Their battle churned the waves for days—we called it a hurricane here above the surface—until finally, in one terrible moment, the kraken managed to capture Ammeron with a tentacle and drew the prince toward its sharp beak, to slice him to pieces!"

I let out an unwilling gasp, but Julia didn't seem to notice.

"But at the last moment, Ammeron's brave narwhal—seeing his beloved prince about to die—charged in without regard for his own safety and gouged out the kraken's eye with his single long horn! In agony, the monster released Ammeron and, thrashing about in the throes of death, caught the faithful narwhal in its powerful tentacles and crushed the noble steed an instant before the kraken, too, died."

A single tear crept down Julia's cheek.

"And though the prince now rides a new steed, his loyal narwhal companion is lost forever. He realizes how lonely he is, despite the friendship of his brother. Very lonely. Ammeron longs for another companion to ease the pain, a princess he can love forever.

"Ariston also yearns for a mate—but the princes are wise and powerful. They will accept none other than the perfect partner … and they can wait. They live forever. They can wait."

We watched the moon disappear behind us and gradually the darkness over the ocean blossomed into petals of peach and pink and gold. I was awed by the swollen red sphere of the sun as it first bulged over the flat horizon, then rose higher, raining dawn across the waves like a firestorm. I had never seen a sunrise before, and I would never see one as beautiful again.

But with the dawn came the realization that I had been up all night, talking with Julia. My parents never got up early, especially not on vacation. Still, I was anxious to get back to my grandmother's house, partly to snatch an hour or two of sleep, but mostly to avoid any chance of being caught.

I knew exactly what my parents would say if they knew I had gone out alone, spent the quiet, dark hours of the night talking to a total stranger—and I wouldn't be able to argue with them. It did sound crazy, completely unlike anything I had ever done before. Irresponsible. Even thinking the terrible word brought a hot flush of embarrassment to my cheeks.

But I wouldn't have traded that night for anything. Though I resisted such silliness for most of my life, that was the first time I ever experienced magic.

~

THE VACATION to Cocoa Beach became an annual event. Even when I went back to Wisconsin, Julia and I were rarely out of touch. My parents taught me to be practical and realistic, to think of the future and set long-term goals. Julia, however, remained carefree and unconcerned, as comfortable with her fantasies as with her real life.

We wrote long letters filled with plans for the future, and the hopes and hurts of growing up. We weren't allowed to call each other often, but whenever something important happened to me, the phone would ring, and I would know it was Julia. She knew, somehow. Julia always knew.

During our summer weeks together, Julia spent endless hours telling me her daydreams about life in the enchanted realms beneath the sea. She had taught herself to sketch, and she drew marvelous, sweeping pictures of the undersea kingdoms. After listening to her for so long, I gradually learned to tell a passable story, though never with the ring of truth that she could give to her imaginings.

From Julia, I learned about the color of sunlight shining down from above, filtered through layers of rippling water. In my mind, I saw plankton blooms that made a stained-glass effect, especially at sunset. I learned how storms churned the surface of the sea, while the depths remained calm though with a "mistiness" caused by the foamy wavetops above.

I learned about hidden canyons filled with huge mollusks, shells as big and as old as the giant redwood trees, which patiently collected all the information brought to them by the fish.

Julia told me about secret meeting places in kelp forests, where Ammeron and Ariston went to spend carefree hours in their unending lives playing hide-and-seek with porpoises. But the lush green kelp groves now seemed empty to them, empty as the places in their hearts that waited for true love....

One day we found a short chain of round metal links at the water's edge. What its original purpose was or who had left it there, I could not fathom. Julia picked it up with a look that was even more unfathomable. She touched each of the loops again and again, moving them through her fingers as if saying some magical rosary. We kept walking, splashing up to our ankles in the low waves, until Julia gave a small cry. One of the links had come loose in her hand. She stared at it for a moment in consternation, then gave a delighted laugh. She slid the circlet from one finger to the next until it came to rest on the ring finger of her right hand, a perfect fit.

"There. I always knew he'd ask." Julia sent me a sidelong glance, a twinkle lurking in the green of her irises. She loosened another link and slipped it quickly onto my hand.

"All right," I sighed, feeling suddenly apprehensive, but knowing that it was no use trying to ignore her once she got started. "Who is 'he,' and what did he ask?"

"I am betrothed to Ammeron, heir to the Kingdom of the Seventh Sea," she said proudly.

"Sure, and I'm betrothed to his brother Ariston." I held up the cheap metal ring on my finger. "Aren't we a bit young to get engaged, Jule?"

Julia was unruffled. "Time means nothing in the Kingdoms beneath the sea. When a year passes here, it's no more than a day to them. Time is infinite there. Our princes will wait for us."

"You really think we're worth it? Besides, how do they know whether or not we accept?" I challenged, always adding a completely out-of-place practicality to Julia's fairy tales. But my sarcasm sailed as far over Julia's head as a shooting star.

"Wait," she said, grasping my arm as she swept the ocean with her intense gaze. Suddenly, she drew in a sharp breath. "Look!" Her eyes lit up as a dolphin leapt twice, not far from where we stood on the shore. "There," she sighed, "do we need any more proof than that?"

Even in the face of her excitement, I couldn't keep the slight edge out of my voice. "I'll admit that I've never seen dolphins leap so close to shore, but what does that have to do with—"

"Dolphins are the messengers of the royal families beneath the sea," she replied in her patient way. Always patient. "One leap is a greeting. Two leaps ask a question. Three leaps give an answer." She flashed a smile at me. There was certainty in her voice that sent a shiver down my back. "And now they're waiting for us to respond!"

I struggled for a moment with impatience but couldn't bring myself to answer with more of my cynicism. I tried my most soothing voice. "Well, I'm sure Ammeron will understand that you—"

But she wasn't listening. Before I could finish my thought, she was running at top speed along the damp, packed sand. I looked after her, and as I watched in amazement, she executed three of the most graceful leaps I had ever seen, strong and clean and confident. I knew I would look foolish if I even tried something like that. I'd probably fall flat on my face in the sand.

By the time I caught up to her, Julia was looking seaward, ankle-deep in waves, with tears sparkling on her lashes—or perhaps it was only the sea spray.

In her hand she held two more of the metal links from the chain she had found. Silently she handed me one of the links, then closed her eyes and threw the remaining one as far into the water as she could. I did the same, imitating her gesture but without the same conviction.

"Elizabeth," Julia said after a long moment, startling me with her quiet voice, "you are a very sensible person." It sounded like an accusation—and coming from Julia, it probably was.

We moved to dryer sand and sat for a long time watching the waves, letting the bright sun dazzle our eyes. Perhaps too long. But Julia's hand on my arm let me know that she saw it, too.

Far out in the water a dolphin leapt. Three times.

OUR LIVES WERE DIVIDED each year into reality and imagination, north and south, school and vacation, rationality and magic, until we finished high school.

I planned my life as carefully and sensibly as I could. My parents had taught me that a woman had to be practical—and I believed it. I chose my college courses with an eye toward the job market, avoiding "frivolous" art and history classes (no matter how much fun they sounded). After all, what good would they do me later in life?

My one concession to the lifelong pull the ocean had exerted on me, was that I chose to go to school at Florida State. Luckily, it was a perfectly acceptable school for the business management and accounting classes I intended to take, so I wasn't forced to define my reasons more precisely.

And it allowed me to see Julia more often.

Julia, on the other hand, always lived on the edge of reality. My parents disapproved of her, and I grew tired of defending her choices, so we came to the unspoken agreement that we would avoid the subject entirely … though even I couldn't help being a bit disappointed in my friend. To me, it seemed Julia was wasting her life at the seaside.

I tried to help her make some sensible choices as well. She wasn't interested in college, preferring to spend her days hanging out near the ocean, making sketches that she sold for a pittance in local gift shops, doing odd jobs.

I convinced her to learn scuba diving. With her love of the sea, I knew she would be a natural, and in less than a year she was a certified instructor with a small, steady business. I even took lessons from her, as did one of my boyfriends, though that ended in disaster.

As for romance, I occasionally went out on dates with men I met in classes, since I felt that our mutual interests should form a solid basis for long-term partnership, but my dating resulted only in passionless short-term relationships that usually ended with an agreement to be "just friends." I never let on how much these breakups really hurt me, except to Julia.

After each one, I would call Julia and she would meet me at the Original Fat Boy's Bar-B-Que, waiting patiently while I drowned my sorrows in beer and barbecued beef. Then we would drive to the beach, where I'd cry for a while, tell her the whole miserable tale, and vow never to make the same mistake again. Sometimes she drew tiny caricatures of my stories, forming them into comical melodramas as I spoke, until I was forced to acknowledge how silly or inconsequential each romance seemed as I dissolved into laughter and tears.

Julia dated often, drifting through each relationship with little thought for the future, until the inevitable stormy end—usually (I suspected) sparked by Julia's spur-of-the-moment nature and consequent unreliability that frequently frustrated men. Somehow on those nights, she would call to me and, no matter where I was, I would feel the need to go walking on our beach. And she would be there.

Once, particularly burned at the end of a tempestuous relationship, she asked what she was doing wrong—a rhetorical question, perhaps, but I answered her (as if I had had a better track record in love than she). "You're spending too much time in a fairy tale, Jule. I used to really love your stories about the princes and the sea kingdoms, but we're not kids any more. Be a little more practical."

The ocean breeze lifted her pale hair in waves about her face as her sea-green eyes widened. "Practical? I could say you're living in just as much of a fairy tale, Elizabeth. The American Dream …

following all the rules, taking the right classes, expecting to find treasure in your career and a prince in some accountant or lawyer or doctor. Doesn't sound any more realistic to me."

I felt stung, but she just sighed and looked out to sea, getting that lost expression on her face again. "I'm sorry. I didn't mean to dump on you like that. Don't worry. I guess I shouldn't be so upset either. It doesn't really matter, you know. After all, I'm betrothed to the Prince of the Seventh Sea."

And I managed to laugh, which made me feel better. But Julia had a disturbing ... certainty in her voice.

THE LAST TIME I ever saw Julia, her call was very strong. I was studying late on campus preparing for a final exam when for no apparent reason I felt an overpowering need to get away from my books, to talk to Julia. It had been months since I'd seen her.

No—she needed to talk to me.

Even though there was a storm warning in effect, I ran out the door without even stopping to pick up a jacket, got into my car, and sped all the way to Cocoa Beach. As I sprinted down to the beach behind Julia's house, I saw her standing on the sand. Dimly silhouetted against the cloudy sky, wearing nothing but a white bathing suit, her long hair blew wildly in the wind as she stared out to sea. It reminded me of the first time I had seen Julia as a little girl, standing in the moonlight.

When I came to stand beside her and saw her startled expression, I abruptly realized that something was very wrong: Julia hadn't expected me.

"You called me, Jule," I said. "What's going on?"

"I ... didn't mean to." She seemed to hesitate. "I'm going diving."

Then I noticed the pile of scuba gear close by, near the water. I understood Julia's subtle stubbornness enough to realize that she placed more weight on her feelings than on simple common sense, so I stifled the impulse to launch into an anxious safety lecture and kept my voice neutral. "I know you have plenty of night diving experience, but you shouldn't dive alone. Not tonight. The weather's not good. Look at the surf."

For a while, I thought she wouldn't answer. At last she said softly, "David's gone."

"The artist?" I asked, momentarily at a loss before successfully placing the name of the current man in her life.

She nodded. "It doesn't really matter, you know. He fell head-over-heels for a pharmacist. It hit him so hard, I almost felt sorry for him. Don't worry; I don't feel hurt. After all ..." Her voice trailed off. Her fingers toyed with the plain metal ring that hung from a silver chain around her neck. She had kept it all these years.

Her face was calm, but the storm in her sea-swept eyes rivaled the one brewing over the ocean. "After all," she finished with an enigmatic quirk of her lips, "I think tonight is my wedding night."

Uneasy, I tried for humor, hoping to stall her. "Don't you need a bridesmaid, then? I'll just go get my formal scuba tanks and my dress fins and meet you back here, okay?"

After a minute or so she looked straight at me, clear-eyed and smiling. "Thank you for coming. I really did need to see you again, but right now I think I need to be alone for a while."

"I'm not so sure I should leave," I said, stalling, reluctant to let her go, unable to force her to stay. "Friends don't let friends dive alone, you know?"

"Don't worry, Elizabeth," she said, barely above a whisper. "Remember, no matter what happens ... I'll call you." She put on her diving gear, letting me help her adjust the tanks, kissed me on the cheek, and waded into the turbulent water. "I'll call you in a week—probably less. I promise."

As I left the beach I looked back every few seconds to watch her until I saw her head disappear beneath the waves.

～

LATER, Julia's tanks and her buoyancy compensator vest were found in perfect condition on the shore a few miles away. And a plain silver neck chain. That was all.

～

THAT WAS FIVE YEARS AGO. And tonight, when I needed her the most, I heard her call again.

Now, sitting on the damp sands, I listen to the hushed purr of the waves and stare at the Atlantic Ocean under the moonlight.

At times like this, here on the beach where Julia and I used to sit together, I wonder if I really was the sensible one. Yes, I made all the "right" choices, earned my degree, found a suitable job, got a comfortable apartment—though no dashing prince (accountant, lawyer, or otherwise) seemed to notice. I had been supremely confident that it would only be a matter of time.

But then, with a simple blood test, I ran out of time. Next came more tests, then a biopsy and a brief stay in the hospital. And behind it all loomed the specter of more and more time spent among the other hopeless cancer patients, walking cadavers, with the ticking of the death watch growing louder and louder inside their heads.

I would rather listen to the ocean.

It wasn't fair!

I raged at the universe. Hadn't I done everything right? Then why had I fallen under a medical curse, with no prince to kiss my cold lips and dislodge the bit of poisoned apple from my throat?

I needed to hear Julia's stories again. I longed to know more about the princes and their sea-unicorns, the defeated kraken, the tall spires of coral castles, in that enchanted undersea world where everyone lived forever.

I found a seashell on the shore, washed up by the tide, as if deposited there for me alone. I picked it up, brushing loose grains of sand from the edge, held it to my ear … and listened.

Far out in the water, I saw a dolphin make a double jump, two graceful silver arcs under the bright light of the moon.

My heart leapt with it, and I stood, blinking for a moment in disbelief. Then, feeling surprisingly restless and full of energy. I decided to go for a run along the beach.

And if I happened to leap once, twice, or three times … who was there to know?

Kris Rusch has been one of my best friends for most of my life. I met her in an undergrad fiction workshop in college in 1981 and we've been close ever since, bootstrapping each other's careers, helping each other out through ups and downs. She served as Dungeon Master for years as our gang of college friends played D&D every Sunday night. She was my "best person" when Rebecca and I got married. She's been my mentor, and I've been hers. Our writing styles and writing techniques couldn't be farther apart, and yet it works.

We wrote two novels together, Afterimage *and* Aftershock, *dark fantasy thrillers that featured a race of shape-shifters that live in the redwood wilderness near Santa Cruz, California, who try to integrate among humanity. This story is loosely connected with that universe, a standalone piece that I still find gut-wrenching.*

CHANGE OF FACE

(WRITTEN WITH KRISTINE KATHRYN RUSCH)

I

I stand on the street below her apartment and watch as she rocks in the chair by the window. During the day, she leaves the shades up and the windows open. Sometimes she sings. Her voice quavers with a sadness I fear will never leave her.

She won't recognize me now, even if she looks out.

Early memories, they say, are the strongest. Ask all darklings, and they will tell you of their first solo change: the way the skin twists; the deep, arching, almost erotic pain; the creaks and groans as the bone structure shifts; and the sudden awkward sensation of wearing a rejuvenated, but different, body.

I, too, remember my first solo change. But I am only half darkling, and I remember something else:

The morning was cold in the forest. I sat at the edge of the group of darkling children, my feet buried in ferns. The teacher leaned on the burned-out stump of an old redwood, his personal scent evoking sand and old leaves. He was telling us all a story. But he kept glancing at me. He called me "human," although I was not. My father had rescued me from a human mother, bringing me back out into the forests. My father taught me little, except to repeat over and over that I was the child of his blood, the child of his heart.

"Humans are strange creatures," the teacher said. His body that season was angular, with dark hair and long fingers. "They wear the same shape their entire lives and identify each other by sight, not scent. They don't believe in other species like themselves, yet they have more stories of us than we have of them. Humans will imprison you, torture or kill you. Stay away from them."

Most of the children looked at me, and a few moved away. Only a very little girl stayed beside me to prove she had no fear. "But he's human," she said, pointing at me.

"He is half-human, and if he survives his first solo change then perhaps he has earned the right to call himself a darkling. But if he dies, that will be another lesson to you." The teacher's deep voice sent shivers down my back. He continued talking of other things, but I stopped listening. I hugged my knees to my chest, feeling fear settle at the base of my stomach. Around us, the green-scented forest intertwined with life. The human city seemed very far away.

Perhaps I wouldn't survive the first solo change.

When I brought that fear to my father, he leaned against a tree that formed part of our small shelter and smiled. "You've been through three changes with my help," he said. "You're more darkling than they think."

And he was right. The change came three days later as a deep fog settled in the mountains, obscuring the trees and making the river's gurgle echo throughout the forest.

I felt the tingle at the base of my spine and called out for my father, but either he didn't hear me, or he refused to come. The first rending ripped through my ribcage, tugged on my arms, and pulled at my legs. Each cell screamed as it renewed itself.

I was going to die. I was human and I would die, half-formed and broken, like newborn babies who went through a change without the help of a parent.

My skin pooled around itself and my hair twisted, blowing into my face. I felt the shift, seized it as my father had taught me, used it to bend myself into another form, a survivable form. The tingle grew into a buzzing around my head and the pain reached through me, grabbing each muscle, each ligament, each bone, pulling, pinching, and reforming until I thought I would explode. The explosion built, built, built—and stopped.

I staggered forward into the cool mist, tripping over a tree limb, wondering at my long legs and my short fingers. How rejuvenated I felt, reborn and made new again. An energy pulsed through me, and for a moment I thought I could survive anything.

"Father!" I shouted. "I'm a darkling now."

His nutmeg scent appeared out of the fog before he did. My father's new body—squat and large—strained at the seams of the coat he had put on that morning. "Not full darkling," he said. "Tomorrow I'll take you for a visit to the human city. When you grow, you'll have to choose between being a darkling and being human."

"I change, like all darklings."

"Yes. And you ask too many questions, and you cling like no darkling ever does." He had smiled, a secret smile that was his alone. "And you are strong."

But I am not strong at all. I still stand below my lover's window in the human city, gazing up at her in the rocking chair, torturing myself. I want just one glimpse of her face.

I hear my father's voice mixing with the teacher's of that cold childhood morning: *You are strong, human, more darkling than they think. Stay away from humans. They will imprison, torture, or kill you.* They will make you stand beneath open windows, because to go up the stairs is to confess that you made the wrong choice on the day you met Shelli, over one long year ago.

II

When I was sixteen, my first darkling lover left me for a boy who smelled of earthworms and tree rot. My father had his own concerns, and the rest of the darklings avoided me. I learned tree craft, oral history, and river fishing, I took other lovers and discarded them, according to the darkling way. I fathered two children in the forest, both of whom were raised by their mothers. Still I wasn't satisfied. Half human, half darkling, with urges that belonged to both or neither. I was never sure how to behave, or even what I wanted for myself. I had to choose.

I awakened one morning on a bed of leaves and dried redwood fronds, and I decided I would go to see the hustle and thrum of human contact. I had been to the city before, on several prolonged trips with my father, and he had showed me many of the things that are held important in human society. He taught me how to make a home, find a job, flit from class to class at night school, learning in snatches.

In the darkling community cache, I found old clothing that suited the tall, slender body I wore and took some of the money we stashed away for the times when we went to the city. Then I followed the river through the woods, veering off as the smells of the city became stronger: car exhaust mingling with wood smoke, human sweat and perfume, discarded garbage.

I wandered past the permanent-looking houses, the old Mission, and the clock tower, down to the Pacific Garden Mall. The strangeness swallowed me, and that day I became human, or pretended to be.

I sat on a bench and just watched for a while. People thronged among the caged trees and manicured bushes in the bright sun. Two cellists sat in front of the spaghetti restaurant and played. A woman walked by in heels and a navy skirt, intent, it seemed, on something far away. A flowery, alcohol-based perfume covered her real scent. A boy whose long hair smelled of sunshine rode a skateboard along the blocked-off streets. I had learned, in my previous visits, that every human, when asked, expressed a purpose, a reason for being. Darklings had no such purpose. Darklings simply were.

The cellists took a break, and I had a sudden craving for coffee that smelled thick and black and strong. I wanted some place simple, some place quiet. Few people sat in the coffee shop across the street, and even before I realized I had made a decision, I reached for the polished metal handle that smelled of the oil from a thousand hands.

I pulled open the door and felt the air conditioning kiss the sweat on my arms. The air tasted of metal, dish soap, and cinnamon. I crossed the worn linoleum floor and took a booth by the window, where I could see if the cellists returned. The seat was old and soft, the plastic scent buried beneath years of sweat, grease, and ammonia.

"Can I help you?" Her voice was quiet. I looked up.

She smelled of peppermint and moonlight. Her eyes had a downward cast, and I knew her skin would be like velvet to my touch. I felt a quick moment of desire, a darkling thought (*Take her now, or that body will escape you and become something else*), before I remembered that she was human. I smiled. "A cup of coffee. Black."

She tucked her notepad into her pocket and put her pen behind her ear. "That all? Coming right up."

She headed back to the counter with a light step. She poured coffee into a large mug and made a comment to one of the cooks. The sound of her laughter washed through me like the whisper of redwoods.

I gazed out the window. Three more boys on skateboards went past, followed by college students on bicycles. The cellists' chairs and music stands were gone. Perhaps I should have come earlier, given myself a chance to listen longer.

The rich aroma of coffee mixed with her peppermint and moonlight reached me. I turned as she set the mug down. "Do the musicians play here every day?" I asked.

She put a knee on the booth's other seat and gazed out. "I never notice anymore. They used to come in here."

"To play?"

"Oh, no." She smiled. "They would sit in this booth, drink coffee, and talk about music."

I recognized something in how her personal scent changed, something I had been feeling all day. A wistfulness, a desire to be someone else. "Are you a musician?"

Her laugh had a derisive edge. She took her knee off the seat and stood up, as if she were going to leave. "I'm just a waitress."

"No one is 'just a' anything," I said. "What do you do on the days you don't come here?"

"Put my feet up." She wiped a strand of hair from her face and frowned, as if she thought the remark had been too curt. "Or go to Woody Allen movies."

"Woody Allen movies?" We had reached the end of my cultural sophistication. I had watched some television, but I had never been to a movie. I couldn't understand why anyone would sit in a large room, watching images flicker on a screen for two long hours, smelling the popcorn, the candy, the soft drinks, and the gathered people together in the darkness, crammed close to each other.

"You've never seen a Woody Allen movie?"

A flush crept up my cheeks. "I haven't seen many movies at all."

She stared at me as if she couldn't believe what she had heard. Behind her, a bell rang. She waved without turning, then looked back at me. "Is it something political, religious, or what?"

"I just never had the opportunity." I wrapped my hands around the coffee mug. Its ceramic sides warmed my palms.

"You haven't been in California long, have you?"

I smiled. I hadn't been in her California long at all.

The bell rang again. "Gotta get an order," she said and hurried away from me.

I sipped the coffee. The rich aroma lingered in my nose. I hadn't smelled anything so good in a long time.

A flautist and a violinist replaced the cellists in front of the spaghetti restaurant. I could barely hear the strains of music rising above the background street sounds. I would get a hotel room for the night, then search for a job and an apartment. This was an interesting diversion, to play human for a while.

"Listen, I'm going to a movie tomorrow."

I looked up, startled. The coffee's rich taste had dampened my sense of smell. She stood next to me and I hadn't even noticed.

"Maybe you could meet me there. It's *Annie Hall.* If you're going to start seeing movies, you may as well start with the best."

I savored the moment, as I had that first sip of coffee. No human woman had ever asked me to go anywhere with her before. "I'd like that," I said. "Where do I meet you?"

"You got a car?"

I shook my head.

"Then why don't you meet me here at noon? The movie's on campus. I'll drive you."

"All right."

She grinned and sprinted away. We didn't talk again that day, except to murmur a goodbye as I walked out the door. I didn't even learn that her name was Shelli until the next day.

III

We made love for the first time a week later. Her apartment was a small one-bedroom on the second floor of an old Victorian house not far from the Pacific Garden Mall. The place smelled of peppermint, cat fur, ammonia, and musty paper. Shelli had more books than I had seen outside of the library.

She took me into her bedroom. I had no plans to seduce her, afraid, I think, that our bodies weren't compatible even though I knew they would be. My half-darkling existence had proven that humans could be darkling mates.

Shelli undressed me slowly, with a sort of reverence for the body I wore, exclaiming about its thinness and the softness of its hair. She felt heavier, more solid than any darkling lover, more permanent, as if her skin were welded to her bones and her entire body were attached to the earth. When I sank into her, it felt like plunging into the warmth of the river.

Later, I found a job at a garden store—the people there loved my affinity for plants, though I rarely knew the human names for them all. The store seemed like the forest to me, smelling of flowers and earth, of fresh air and growth. I belonged there more than I had belonged anywhere, except with Shelli.

She and I passed through each day, eager to be with each other, and soon after that I moved in with her.

For the first time, I felt safe inside a permanent structure. For the first time, I lost my urge to roam. Life became like a series of Woody Allen movies: Each small event seemed to have an overlying meaning that I couldn't quite grasp, but which seemed very clear to Shelli and the others around me.

She told me once that she loved my spontaneity.

I loved her certainty.

Every morning, I promised myself that I would tell her about me and who I was. And every night I clutched her tightly, bracing myself for the change that had to come.

IV

That afternoon in the garden store I found a pink African violet that reminded me of Shelli. I set it aside and smiled each time I thought of it. A tiny thing to celebrate our third month together. Marking anniversaries was a human practice I was beginning to enjoy. When I walked down the street, I finally felt I had a sense of purpose.

I clocked out at five, tied a pink bow around the pot, and went out the back of the store. The alley was empty, dark with early evening, and smelled of dying plants. Through the rows of buildings, I could hear my cellists playing something modern and atonal.

The tingle at the base of my spine didn't alert me. I was so intent on crossing through the darkness to Shelli that I ignored the sensation altogether.

I had made it three steps across the alley when the pain ripped through me, long and hard and full. I stopped walking, preferring to concentrate on molding myself. I felt as if I were being torn from the inside out, broken and reformed. My father used to love the change, love its randomness and unpredictability, but it brought up the fear in me, the fear of death.

The flowerpot slipped out of what had been my hand and shattered against the concrete. My skin jelled, liquefied, and ran like chocolate in the sunshine. I screamed—once—then felt the transformation run through me, coursing inside my skin like blood. The lengthening stopped, my body shrank into itself. And when the pain ended, I was short and fat, lost in the clothes that Shelli had bought for my old body.

The back door of the garden store opened, and Tom, one of my coworkers, peered outside, he glanced at me and looked away, a habit he used when approached by panhandlers on the street. He closed the door again.

I got up. With shaking hands, I brushed the dirt from my clothes, then rolled up my long pant legs. I had to get to Shelli. I had to tell her. I hurried down the Mall, pulled open the coffee shop door, and stopped as Shelli smiled at me. She grabbed a single menu and asked, "How many?" in her most polite, and distant, tone.

I backed out, and continued backing away until I could no longer see the shop. Then I ran, tripping as my pant legs fell and my shortened steps missed their marks.

V

I went back to the woods and found no solace. I dreamed of cello music and peppermint perfume and Woody Allen's nasal voice. I even told my father about Shelli. He smiled at me. "You remember your first human like you remember your first lover. The experience is so different, so exciting. But she never would have believed your story of change, and she wouldn't have believed who you were, no matter what you said."

Shelli's eyes came back to me, the blank stare of non-recognition, the flat, polite tone in her voice as she looked at me in the doorway of the coffee shop. Humans didn't understand change. I would have had to leave regardless of what I told her. I stayed in the woods and tried not to think of her, declaring my experimentation with being human a complete and total failure.

I became a darkling again. I helped my father gather roots, herbs, and berries. We made poultices, ground spices, and stored food for the lean months. I took darkling lovers, seeking something solid, a woman who felt as if she were made of earth and water instead of air and flame....

Almost a year later, I found myself sitting on the same brick planter in the Mall again, watching Shelli's coffee shop.

At first, I told myself that I only wanted to see if she was all right. But it was more than that. The darkling teacher, in one of his many lectures about humans, had said they mated for life. The children had laughed. Darklings were like cats, sharing a casual affection, but moving from lover to lover, sometimes within the same evening. Change versus consistency; certainty versus spontaneity.

I pulled open the door of the coffee shop and felt the kiss of air conditioning again. The air still smelled of metal, dish soap, and cinnamon. A strange woman stood behind the counter. She brushed a strand of dark hair from her face and asked, "Just yourself?" as she grabbed a single menu.

I couldn't smell peppermint or moonlight. "Is Shelli here?"

"Shelli?" The waitress squinted and clutched the menu to her chest. "Oh, Shelli. She quit months ago."

My stomach lurched. I knotted my fingers together. "Do you know where she is now?"

"No. I'd only been here a few weeks when she left."

I nodded and pushed my way out the door. She was gone. Maybe the job had gotten bad for her. Maybe she had decided to go back to school, study acting or something.

I hurried through the crowded streets, ignoring the human scents of sweat and suntan lotion. Other bodies pushed against mine, but the jostling didn't disturb me. I finally turned on a residential street and saw the familiar tall Victorian home where Shelli and I had lived for such a short time.

Her name was still on the mailbox. I felt a thread of relief run through me.

"Help you?" A man stopped in front of me, smelling of oil and gasoline. His large hands looked as if they had always been stained black.

"I was looking for Shelli," I said.

"She's at work. I'm her downstairs neighbor."

I didn't know what to say. "I checked at the coffee shop," I said. "She wasn't there."

His half-smile now seemed a bit suspicious. "You haven't seen her for a while."

"No," I said. "I was going to surprise her. She took me to my first Woody Allen movie."

"She does love Woody Allen." He studied me for a moment. "She works at the spaghetti place across the street from the coffee shop. Changed jobs half a year back. Needed the extra money, you know, with Danny and all. She should be there now."

I thanked him and was about to leave when I stopped myself. "Do you mind answering a nosy question? Who's Danny?"

To my surprise, the man only smiled. "Her baby. I took her to the hospital for the delivery."

A shiver ran down my back. "A child? When was he born?"

The neighbor put his big hands on the mailbox, his fingers leaving marks in the dirt. "Must be about a month ago now. That was some night, let me tell you."

"I bet it was," I said and moved back along the sidewalk. I had left her alone with a child. Our child. I hadn't even thought it a possibility.

Fortunately, we hadn't had a change since the baby left the

safety of her womb. I could help her and little Danny. I would have to.

VI

I walked through the city that night, trying to decide how to tell her, how to warn her about the change that was bound to come. The child was only one-quarter darkling, and perhaps he wouldn't change at all. I knew nothing of genetics—how thin can darkling blood become before the change refuses to come? But if little Danny would indeed change with all the other darklings, then he needed to be guided through the process until his mind developed enough to control a change alone.

I had to talk to Shelli. She wouldn't know what to do, how to hold Danny's body in her hands and mold him, even as she was molding herself.

I slept for a few hours on the bench at the bus stop across from her house. When her bedroom curtains opened—a sure sign she was awake—I straightened my clothes, combed my hair with my fingers, and let myself into the foyer of her big house.

The hallway was dark and smelled of fresh-brewed coffee. I took the stairs slowly, my heart pounding in my chest. My father had said she wouldn't believe me. The thought gave me pause. My mother had been human, and he said she still lived. Perhaps he had tried to convince her of what he was, and she hadn't believed him. No wonder he didn't say much when I ran back to the woods. He thought that I was saving myself some pain.

But I couldn't run away any longer.

I took a deep breath and pounded on Shelli's door. I heard footsteps; then the door eased open as far as the protective chain would reach. I smiled at the familiar scent of peppermint and moonlight, mixed with something else, something milky.

"Yes?" Shelli asked.

Words left me, the prepared speech, the carefully reasoned arguments that I had worked on all night. Shelli's face peered into mine, her downturned eyes and strong lips. I wanted to touch her skin. I wanted to hold her. "I'd like to talk to you," I said.

"Who are you?" She hadn't moved, but her tone had changed. Now she smelled of fear.

"I ..." I couldn't blurt out the words. I felt the ridiculous phrase hang between us. "I know Daniel."

She laughed once. The sound was short and bitter. "Then you know that he left me."

"There's something you need to know about Daniel. It'll affect the baby."

The fear scent grew stronger. She braced herself between the door and the frame. "Does he know about Danny?"

My heart pounded. The lies made this even more complex. "He didn't know about Danny until a very short time ago."

"And you're here to tell me that he wants the baby, right? Well, Danny is mine. All mine. I had him alone and I will take care of him alone, do you understand?" She slammed the door. The sound echoed in the small hallway. I grabbed the knob, but it was locked.

"No! You need to listen to me! Daniel had some health—problems—that he might have passed on to the baby. Please—"

"Danny is perfectly healthy. The doctor says so." Her voice sounded muffled through the door.

"It's not something that will show up in tests. It's hereditary—"

"Get out of here or I'll call the cops! Get out."

A door downstairs opened. In the dark light, I could see her neighbor's silhouette. "Need help, Shelli?"

She wouldn't listen to me, yet, anyway. "I was just leaving," I said and hurried down the stairs. I had to figure out another way.

VII

I tried to talk to Shelli several more times. I left her notes, talked to her neighbors, and the police threatened me. I waited near the apartment, hoping to be close if something should happen. I took sponge baths in public restrooms, ate cheap sandwiches to stay alive, slept on the bus bench across the street from Shelli's apartment. I had to do something. My own search—to be human or darkling—had caused this. If I hadn't run away, perhaps I would have stayed with Shelli when it counted, helped her raise my son.

My father must have gone through this. He finally decided to take me. If I took my son away, I would break Shelli's heart a second time. If the child died ...

A tingle at the base of my spine woke me from my sleep on the bus bench. I saw that it was early morning, just before all the commuters went to work. The tingle persisted, and I suddenly knew that I had to move.

I got up, but my legs had fallen numb from the position I had slept in. I stumbled against the bus stop. The tingle expanded into a ripping pain, and I heard a shriek from Shelli's house. I was too late. I lurched forward. Shelli was crying for help.

My legs wouldn't carry me across the street. I collapsed in front of a parked car, my skin melting and reshaping as I subconsciously guided my body through the process. I wasn't thinking about my own change; I wanted to get up the stairs to help Shelli. I barely made it onto the curb when the transformation finished, leaving me taller and gaunt. An energy coursed through me, and now I bounded up the stairs to find Shelli's door open. Her downstairs neighbor shouted into the phone, demanding an ambulance. Shelli screamed in the bedroom, one long continuous wail.

I saw the thing in her arms: the mass of gelatinous skin, the arm sticking into what had been the baby's stomach, the nose bulging prominently out of what remained of his head.

I took him, thinking perhaps some remnants of the change would allow me to mold his skin. I cradled my son for the first time, tugging at his malformed limbs, trying to shape him into a child again. Please, I prayed to unseen gods, one more change. One more change. But it wouldn't help him. My son.

He was dead.

Shelli had stopped screaming. She took Danny from me and cradled him against her chest. Her eyes were empty.

"He's mine," she said. "He's all I have left."

I touched him, my hand trembling. He had died the way I had always feared, but not because of his human side. He had died because his darkling father lacked courage.

"Shelli—"

A siren echoed nearby, growing closer.

"They can't save him, can they?" Her fingers stroked his misshapen skull, the fringe of his fine hair.

"No," I said.

The siren stopped. Voices rose amid some clanking outside. Shelli pushed past me and carried Danny down the steps to meet the attendants.

I remained behind.

VIII

And so here I stand, beneath her window, watching, as I have done every night since Danny's death. *Child of my heart,* my father used to call me, and I finally understood what he meant. I am waiting, waiting for the tingle at the base of my spine again.

Sometimes I think I will run up the stairs, command her to watch me change. And when it is over, I will explain everything, who I am and how I have never really left her. Then I wonder how much more pain that will cause her.

Sometimes I think I will just sit here, for change after change, until she heals enough to come out on her own, begin her life again, for Shelli is constant, and she is certain. She will heal. That much I know.

The darkling teacher was not so far wrong when he called me human. A darkling would have left long ago. Even my father left the child of his heart. Love has no place in a changing universe. And darklings suffer enough pain without adding the constant ache of a breaking heart.

All my life I have tried to be either darkling or human, being instead a strange hybrid of both. I want to be human, to be with Shelli, but my darkling side interferes. I have lied to her, tried to be one or the other. Perhaps if I had told her so long ago, we would have had a chance. Danny would have had a chance.

Shelli sits in the window and rocks, looking out at the people below. Her voice, plaintive and low, slides over the words to Brahms's *Lullaby.* I listen to her. I ache to comfort her grief, ache to share it—to feel her blame, her anger, and maybe, just maybe, her forgiveness.

A shiver runs down my back. I pause. Not a shiver, but a tingle. A tingle at the base of my spine.

I have only a moment to choose: change versus consistency,

certainty versus spontaneity, human versus darkling. My body begins to shift.

Before I even realize it, I am bounding up the stairs. I want to tell Shelli I choose both.

I choose both.

This is a very mythic story, dealing with powerful archetypes, the many aspects—and obligations—of Death. It was an experiment in structure for me, one of the more unusual and literary short stories I've written. And maybe even a little sympathy for the Grim Reaper himself.

DARK ANGEL, ARCHANGEL

The train thundered toward him, its sharp light pinning him like a spear. He stood in the center of the tracks facing it, not moving. Defiant. Impotent. The night seemed to laugh around him.

He opened his arms to greet the onrushing locomotive, waiting for its juggernaut embrace. In its glowing headlight he saw a glimmer of what humans called Heaven.

And then the train passed through, leaving him unharmed. He turned to watch the train rumble into the distance. It always happened the same:

He remembered leaping off a high rooftop to fly like a dark angel toward the pavement below. The wind was cold on his face, ruffling his hair as he soared down and down … then he landed with a ballerina's grace on the night sidewalk below. Unharmed. Even his hair dropped back into place.

And again: Pressing the pistol against his temple, he squeezed the trigger with genuine nonchalance. His ears rang with the explosive gunshot, and he turned to look at the bullet hole on the wall.

He wasn't going to die—that had never been an option. But he knew that if he kept trying, the new incarnation of Death would appear. She would want to taunt the predecessor who had failed in his duty. When commanded to make the human race extinct, he had refused. But the new Death had no such qualms.

Suddenly, she stood beside him on the moonlit tracks. A shroud of pearly mist hung from her beautiful shoulders. Her hair glinted like spun quicksilver. "Why do you torment yourself so much? You know I won't let you die." The White Lady's voice was a tangled mix of sarcasm and sincerity.

"Don't I have the right to be fascinated by Death, after half a million years of doling it out? Let me talk with you. You have to stop what you're doing."

He had been the Dark Angel, the Grim Reaper, flaunting his power in front of human beings until his masters, the aurorae who hung shimmering above the world, decreed another mass extinction, as had happened several times in the Earth's past. But the Grim Reaper had developed a fondness for humans over the millennia, and he would not wipe them out as ordered. So, the aurorae stripped him of his title.

He glanced into the clear night sky above the train tracks, but over the years he had purposefully made his way down to lower latitudes, where the aurorae rarely showed themselves. They hung in shimmering curtains from the Earth's poles, charged particles from the All-Father Sun that spiraled in the magnetic field-lines, auroral beings so alien that inquisitive human scientists regarded them merely as interesting electromagnetic phenomena. The aurorae doled out nourishing energy to their servants, such as himself and the White Lady.

She regarded him now with scorn. "You gave up your duty. This species is scheduled to end. How can you be sentimental after all this time?" She laughed like broken glass and threw her glowing garments back into an unfelt breeze. "*I* listen to the aurorae. I know what they expect of me."

He opened his mouth to speak, but she held up one nailless finger, showing no vestigial remnants of the claws of lower animals. "Because of the respect I used to have for you, I'll listen. Briefly. Come with me as we talk. I've got work to do tonight."

~

THE OLD WOMAN lay on sterile hospital sheets, waiting in silence as she felt the tumors growing, squirming, fighting inside her. Veins stood out on her neck with the effort as she kept her lungs rhythmically filling and emptying.

Her eyes remained open, and she watched the White Lady who sat in the shadows of her room. "If breathing is so difficult," the White Lady asked, "why not just stop?"

And the old woman did.

∾

AS SHE WALKED BESIDE HIM, the White Lady appeared genuinely concerned for him, but she didn't understand. "What happened to you? Why do you care anyway? You've done many routine extinctions. It's the order of the universe."

The order of the universe? That wasn't the reason at all. The aurorae could not survive in a static environment, and so they forced constant flux, constant change, and turmoil on the world. "The aurorae asked too much this time."

One of his predecessors had been Death when the aurorae ordered the obliteration of most dinosaur species to which he had expressed an attachment. That incarnation of Death had hurled an asteroid whistling and flaming through the atmosphere. He had summoned up volcanoes, earthquakes, and in the end, he had devastated the world, wiping out thousands upon thousands of species, out of defiance.

It had driven him insane, turned him into a gibbering mass of random energy. The aurorae were forced to imprison him under the ice of the polar caps where they could watch over him.

And now that the aurorae had decreed the extinction of human beings, he thought he understood how his predecessor must have felt.

The Lady laughed at him. "Mankind's been dominant for half a million years, and their time has come. The aurorae know." She shook her head with a flirtatious toss of her beautiful hair. "I don't see why you're making such a fuss."

"It's different. *They're* different. Humans are ... special, in a way. Listen to me." He dropped his voice and leaned closer to her. "I know something our masters overlooked."

~

THE RABBIT TWITCHED its nose in the cool night air, looking up into the darkness just in time to see the White Lady swoop down on owl's wings, talons extended to plunge into warm blood.

~

THE WHITE LADY REMAINED ALOOF. "And what is the redeeming virtue of humanity that *you* know but even the aurorae don't understand?"

He didn't want to fight her. He was weak now, and she was strong. And if she defeated him, all would be lost.

"Humans are *afraid* of Death, and this gives us power. That's why the aurorae need to get rid of them, so that you and I remain weak." He paused to let the idea sink in. "The lower animals have a self-preservation drive, but their fear of dying is just instinct. Humans, though, spend their lives obsessed with Death, worshiping it. I watched people die beside their hunting fires at the dawn of time. I listened to emperors, warlords, and slaves. I took each dying soldier away from his comrades."

He opened his hands to her. "Don't you see? Their constant preoccupation gave us form and substance. You choose to appear as beautiful Lady Death in her white garments to seduce the doomed with promises of Paradise. *I* always preferred to come as the Grim Reaper."

He waved his hands in front of himself, and his human form dissolved away. He stood cloaked in tattered black garments full of the mustiness of tombs; the skin peeled away from his face, leaving a leering skull with honeycombed eye sockets and rattling teeth. In his bony hand he clutched a scythe, razor-sharp and bloodstained in the moonlight. Its long wooden handle was slick and polished smooth from aeons of use.

The White Lady stood dumbfounded to see the transformation. "But you've been stripped of your position! How—?"

The Reaper's voice sounded like dry autumn leaves. "The aurorae don't know everything. I still hold much of my power, even after you thought I was banished. Humans gave me a shape, an idea to conform to. Before their race began to think, Death was nothing more than an abstract, lurking fear. Our predecessors had no names. They remained formless, weak, just a brooding force that came and went, taking lives with them. But human fear and superstition built *us* into something more powerful." He raised his scythe high and pointed a finger of ivory bamboo at her white shrouds. "Look at us now!"

She spoke in an exasperated voice, "What difference does it make if I appear as the White Lady or as some shadowy force? I am Death, and I am the most powerful force in the universe."

"You're only a tool. A pawn of the aurorae, to bow and scrape to them."

She crossed her arms over her chest, and the Reaper remembered how full and fresh the new power had once felt to him. He saw that the White Lady would not listen to him. She didn't care, and humankind was doomed.

He had to stop her. He threw back his black hood and turned to face her, holding his Deadly sickle in a combat stance. She laughed again, still not taking him seriously, but the Reaper gave her no time to prepare. He leaped forward and swung his scythe.

~

THE THREE TEENAGERS had managed to get themselves so drunk that, one of them claimed irreverently, they wouldn't need an undertaker to embalm them. The driver found it difficult enough to keep the car on the road, not to mention on his own side.

The two full-moons of dazzling truck headlights hurtled toward them, and it took the teenaged driver too long to recognize the threat. But somehow, he managed to swerve at the last instant, bouncing the car into the ditch and careening back up onto the road as the truck's horn bellowed back at them.

The teenagers giggled and drove on, thrilled but unconcerned at their close brush with Death.

~

THE WHITE LADY stumbled backward and looked up at him in awe. "You can't!"

He lunged again, but she dodged, focusing her strength. In her pallid hand appeared a dove with heavy claws and a cruel beak. She flung the bird at the Reaper, and it swooped at him with a fire in its holocaust eyes. The dove's claws skittered on his bony face, and its beak tried to crack the Reaper's skull.

~

SOMEONE ELSE WAS DYING. It couldn't be him.

He clutched his chest, but his heart refused to follow the clockwork commands of his brain. Shadows rushed through his bloodstream into his head. He fell.

His wife frantically rubbed his wrists, pounded on his chest, and tried to breathe in his mouth ... all the treatments that worked on TV. Finally, she had the sense to call an ambulance. The shrieking vehicle arrived after an eternity as his heart, duty-bound, still tried to perform.

Paramedics pushed the frantic wife away. They had arrived in time. It wasn't too late.

"No," said the White Lady, echoing in his ears, "it's not too late." His heart finally surrendered and stopped forever.

~

SHE CRAWLED BACK to her feet as the Reaper snatched at the attacking dove. With the swiftness of unexpected Death, he caught one of its wings in his skeletal grip and hurled it back at the Lady. Then he stormed after her down the railroad tracks, swinging his scythe. He could not let her recover, because she was much stronger than he was.

Overhead, the sky began to glow as the distant aurorae noticed the battle.

He slashed the White Lady's gossamer garments. Desperation and elation added strength to his swing.

~

HER LUNGS WERE ready to explode. Her starved blood had used all the oxygen, and now her eyes turned glassy under the murky water. The girl saw the White Lady swimming behind her eyes, urging her just to breathe deeply one more time.

Yet the girl refused, struggling against the tangle of old barbed wire on the bottom of the lake. Tears came out of her straining eyes to be washed away in the surrounding water. Darkness took chunks out of her sight.

As the last morsel of hope died inside her, years of underwater exposure took their toll on the rusted wire, and the girl broke free with only the inconsequential cost of torn skin.

The light of the All-Father Sun beckoned her to the surface. And she knew she would make it—by a miracle.

～

THE DOVE ATTACKED HIM, but the Reaper felt rejuvenated. He reached up and blasted the bird to a cinder.

The White Lady held her ground, raised her hands to the brightening auroral sky, and new power sang through her. When the Reaper struck again, the scythe glanced off her immortal flesh.

This time he staggered, tasting despair in his mummified throat. The White Lady moved toward him, glowing brighter. Even her garments seemed alive.

The Reaper swung his curved blade, channeling his remaining power into one final attempt. The scythe struck the granite flesh of her throat and almost, *almost* cut. The long wooden handle that had lasted five thousand centuries broke in two.

The White Lady leaped on him with a vampire's embrace.

～

EACH SLEEPING pill looked like a tombstone in her hand. She had stopped counting how many she'd swallowed, and still she swallowed more. The White Lady urged her on.

The nagging fear of Death, the persistent drive to stay alive—to live without David, without a future, without love—shouted in her conscious mind. No. Nothing mattered any more. Nothing. The Nothing of Death.

But doubts assailed her, begging her to give life one more chance. Her hand weighed a thousand pounds as she reached for the telephone. She managed to punch two numbers before the pills stopped her.

The White Lady laughed. And the telephone receiver dropped to the floor.

~

THE REAPER LAY CRUSHED on the railroad ties and looked up at her with his hollow eye sockets, trying to evoke sympathy. "Please don't," he whispered. "Think of what you're doing!"

The White Lady placed her hands on her hips, and her eyes held the inferno of mankind's future. He had made his stand, and failed, but he felt something final brooding inside him. There was one remaining thing he could do.

"Your victory isn't complete, Lady." He clasped the broken halves of his Deadly sickle to his own breast. "The humans gave us things even the aurorae don't know."

He summoned the shreds of his power, remnants he wasn't sure he possessed until now. No defeat for him, no imprisonment in the polar ice caps, no torment as the aurorae stretched his soul across the Earth's magnetic field-lines and flayed him as infinite punishment for his betrayal.

The mystery opened itself to him, and the Grim Reaper embraced his own Death.

~

THE WHITE LADY was taken by surprise as he crumbled into glittering dust. The spangles of the Reaper's soul—free now, even from the aurorae—spiraled like dust motes into the future.

She stared. He shouldn't have been able to do that! The aurorae claimed they had stripped him, and he should have been so weak....

Overhead, the sky brightened as the aurorae absorbed energy

that streamed from the All-Father Sun as the slumbering star awakened in the upswing of His eleven-year cycle.

She looked up at the sky, but the aurorae offered no answers. She began to wonder—how much did they hide from her?

The White Lady loved her new power as Death. If she did exterminate the human race, what would her existence be like without the fears that gave her form?

She thought of the Reaper and how he had somehow escaped his punishment. She thought of their dark formless predecessor; he had caused the mass extinctions at the end of the Cretaceous Period, and he now seethed in his prison under the ice caps.

The aurorae had promised her that eliminating the human race would be so easy. The White Lady had events to set in motion, antagonisms to build. Perhaps a new plague, perhaps a nuclear holocaust, perhaps another asteroid strike. Maybe she would wait and think about this.

For now, she would enjoy and ponder her power.

She was in no hurry.

I'm known for writing giant, complicated stories with intertwined story-lines and a large cast of characters, multi-volume epics that have cost the lives of many trees. But sometimes I like to stretch my creative muscles in the other direction, seeing just how short I can write. These efforts can turn out to be extreme, micro-fiction of only a few words, like:

"Cliché"

Once upon a time, they lived happily ever after …
 But then they woke up, and it was all a dream!

Or,

"Letter of Resignation"

Dear Mr. Escher,
 I quit. I just can't take it anymore.
 Your housecleaner

Or another one,

"Tea Time Before Perseus"

The lonely Medusa sat inside her ever-growing statue garden. She waited for more company to arrive, hoping that today there might be a chance for some conversation.

While clever, those don't comprise an entire story. The following piece was inspired by the memory of my parents frequently forgetting the two-hour time difference after I had moved away from home, leaving Wisconsin for a job in California. They would often call at odd times, not realizing it was still very early in the morning for me, for instance, or that I wasn't home from work yet. "Time Zone" uses that as a springboard for a Twilight Zone-style story.

TIME ZONE

I had just gotten home from work, ready to start dinner for myself, when the phone rang. It wasn't even 5:30 yet, but the dinner hour is exactly when phone solicitors like to prey on customers. I answered with a "Hello" that was more like a sigh.

"Ronnie! Are you all right? We're so worried!" Not a salesman, then—my parents, back in Wisconsin.

I had moved to California only a month ago, and my parents seemed as lonely as I was. They often called just to hear my voice.

Right after college I had taken a job for a large company in the San Francisco area. I was a young man living on my own for the first time, far from home. My fiancée would follow me in six months, but for now I was solo, except for babysitting her dog, a fat and snorting pug named Beau that she loved for reasons more unfathomable than the reasons why she loved me. Beau greeted me now with far more exuberance than I wanted, demanding attention while I concentrated on the phone.

"Of course, I'm all right. I just walked in the door from work. Did you forget about the time change again? I'm not usually home this early." My parents lived in rural Wisconsin, had never traveled farther than the adjacent states, and certainly never left the country. Their business was local, never had to worry about calling New York or Los Angeles. "You're two hours earlier, remember?"

"No, the earthquake!" my mom said. "It's been on the news non-stop."

My dad broke in, talking on the extension. "A major quake. San Francisco is leveled. We couldn't get through—the phone lines have been jammed for more than an hour, but we tried and tried."

I looked around my intact townhouse. "Everything's normal. No earthquake."

Beau snorted and farted, wagged his tail so forcefully that his entire body wobbled. I bent over to pat him on the head, hard.

"We're watching the report on Fox right now," my dad said. "Total devastation. We thought you were hurt. We couldn't get through."

I thought about fake news. My parents have often been duped. "No quake, honest. Not even a little devastation."

My mom was crying. My dad was tense. "I'm reading the crawl right now! Magnitude 6.0 earthquake hit the East Bay at 5:35 PM."

I looked at the clock on the wall. "It's not even 5:35 yet. You're forgetting the time change again. You're two hours ahead."

At my feet, Beau whined and then began barking, much more agitated than his usual excitement about my lukewarm affections. Then he began to howl.

"I'm so glad." Mom's voice still sounded strangled with disbelief. "I don't know how to explain it."

I tried to shush the dog, but Beau was going crazy.

"Nothing to worry about, Mom." I wondered what other crackpot conspiracy theory would set them off next.

The clock hit 5:35.

The ground started to shake beneath my feet.

For a more traditional fantasy short short, I wrote this story for a flash-fiction class in my recent coursework to get my MFA. I always wondered about those virgin sacrifices ...

THE SACRIFICE

The foul-smelling mist exhaled from the cave opening, a swirl of brimstone and smoke. A soft reptilian growl echoed, low and steady. The dragon was still sleeping, but when he awakened, he would be hungry.

The young woman, the virgin sacrifice, struggled against the ropes that bound her to the stake. Her wrists were already raw, but she couldn't get away. She waited for the monster to emerge, to devour her.

The charred bones strewn about the lair—crushed skulls, cracked femurs drained of marrow, curved rib cages—gave evidence of previous meals that had not satisfied the beast.

She tried to be strong, straining and grasping against the bonds, but she didn't dare twist too hard, because that might make her wrists bleed, and blood would certainly draw the dragon. A tear stole aimlessly down her cheek, but she forced herself not to whimper. The fear, too, would bring him out.

Months ago, the dragon had awakened from its ancient slumber and terrorized the countryside. With broad razor wings, it swooped down on the shepherds' flocks, roasting sheep and leaving charred fields. It attacked the villages next, setting thatched roofs on fire, burning cottages to the ground, feasting on any victims it could seize.

When the priests consulted their holy texts, they knew there could be only one solution to appease the dragon: a virgin sacrifice, a pure young woman offered to keep the beast at bay. And the townspeople, her own people, had turned on her. They chose her because she was the least important, an orphan with no one to speak on her behalf. Though she was pretty, kind, and well loved, she had no dowry and was not likely to find a husband anyway. She had no say in the matter.

Now she was tied to the stake before the lair, waiting, doomed, sure the dragon would soon emerge, a nightmare of scales and fangs and deadly fire. And it would see her there, a sacrifice.

But all she could think of was the brave knight and his kisses, his reassurances ... how he had held her the night before. It was their secret. None of the villagers suspected.

But she wondered if the dragon would know ...

Again diving into myths and legends, I was intrigued by the numerous stories of great kings who hadn't really fallen in battle, but who were hidden away, caught up in some kind of magical sleep, waiting to return someday when the world needed them.

"Heroes Never Die" is another story inspired by my neighbor, the kindly old farmer, Mr. Reindahl, who lived all alone in his big white farmhouse. He wouldn't tell anyone his past, if he'd ever been married (though I did see a framed black-and-white portrait of a pretty woman on his desk once). Though I went over to his house often, he wouldn't let me anywhere in his house beyond the kitchen.

A curious kid had to wonder what secrets a man like that might have in his past.

HEROES NEVER DIE

He awoke after seven centuries of God's Slumber, with the vision still burning inside him. He remembered leading his army across Europe, fighting against the Infidels and sending great sacrifices of blood to the Divine Creator; he remembered trying to cross the swollen and churning river ... and he remembered drowning. It had been cold and mysterious.

Now he lay in a hidden cave, motionless on a stone table, placed there by some elder race. His heavy red beard had indeed grown completely around the table, just as the Legend had decreed; and as he sat upright, with painful slowness, he clearly recalled the geas, the relentless mission the Angel had placed on him. He was destined to save the world, to unite the Holy Roman Empire into the grand Christian kingdom. He was a legend come back to life, he was a hero who could never die.

After nearly 700 years, Frederick Barbarossa returned to the world.

~

DANNY SAT COMFORTABLY against the cardboard box which contained books, knick-knacks, and an old pair of shoes. With her usual amount of consideration, his mother decided she needed to unpack that box next, even though dozens of them still cluttered the new house. He tried to ignore her by intently watching super-hero cartoons on the portable black and white television. Static and fuzz-balls of light danced across the screen: the reception out here wasn't nearly as good as it had been in the city, and Mom said they would never be able to get cable again.

"Come on, Danny—move!" she snapped, and he absently scooted out of the way. Danny had helped her with the unpacking —the new house had so much more room than the old apartment— but he had quickly lost interest. The superheroes rescued him from boredom every afternoon; he still didn't know how to tell time, but some inner clock always told him when cartoons would be on.

"Who do you think the next one will be about, Mom?" He didn't take his eyes from the TV, didn't really notice when his mother paid no attention to him. "I hope it's Spiderman he's my favorite!"

Mom picked up the box with a tired sigh. Danny waited impatiently for A Word From Our Sponsor to be over.

"Danny, come and open the door for Mom." She stood by the door, ladling the box in her arms, balancing it against her left thigh.

"Just a minute."

"Danny—now!" she snapped.

He got up and listlessly opened the door for her, with his full attention still fixed on the television. "Aww, it's only Captain America anyway."

A few moments later she reentered the room with a box containing encyclopedias, volumes A through J-K, which his dad had purchased "for when Danny goes to college."

"Why don't you go play outside?" she said, throwing some of her frustration at him. Dad would have watched superheroes with him ... Dad sometimes even bought him comic books to look at.

"Outside, Daniel!"

"But, Mom, don't you want me to help you?"

She pushed a sweat-curled strand of hair out of her eyes and managed a small smile. "No, Danny. Mom can do it by herself. Why don't you go and explore our big back yard?"

"Okay ..." he said, after a long pause.

He let the screen door slam behind him even though he knew he wasn't supposed to. (Dad said the previous owners had purchased a piece of land bordering a patched and bumpy country road and had erected an out-of-place tri-level house, with beautiful landscaping and young trees standing in small islands of flower beds.) Behind the house, rows of corn stretched to infinity like green corduroy on the hills. But rusty barbed wire fences set up a barricade behind and to one side of the yard—farmers were like wild animals, marking off their territory. Off to the other side a narrow alfalfa field separated them from the run-down farm of Mr. Rossa, their closest neighbor.

Danny's new yard had still not been sufficiently explored, but the mere fact that it was his own yard made it a great deal less interesting than the neighboring farm. He began to run across the alfalfa field.

He knew the old farmer lived alone, renting out his remaining fields to younger, more ambitious farmers who called themselves "agricultural engineers." Mr. Rossa's drab house was old and peeling white; the yard was infested with clover and dandelions, and the weeded-over driveway was almost indistinguishable from the rest of the yard. In front of the house lay the carcass of an ancient tractor, decaying into rust as if it had collapsed there and died, with the weeds growing up to surround it, looking for new footholds among the crumbling gears and sprockets.

This was the way old farms were supposed to be.

~

PRISMATIC LIGHT REFLECTED from the crystalline stalactites, making even the air seem to sparkle. He saw with some amazement that time and dampness had turned his armor into a thin coating of reddish soot on his body. Alongside the stone table, the Angel had provided him with a heavy white robe and sandals.

He looked for his sword, his one true friend through a thousand battles. The blade still gleamed, unnotched and razor sharp, untouched by the centuries, protected by the Angel. The waters of the Calycadnus River had washed away the bloodstains and had brought eternal life to the jewels on the hilt. Seeing his sword, his companion, he felt happy again.

He used the blade to chop off all but a span of his red beard, leaving the rest to lie in long coils on the cave floor. He washed himself in the hot spring at the back of the grotto, donned the robe and sandals, and lovingly picked up his sword. The Angel would not help him again, would never so much as contact him whether he succeeded or failed. He went bravely to the mouth of the cave and prepared himself to go out into the world at last.

∼

THE GIANT OLD trees fascinated Danny. The thin saplings in his own yard were too small even for him to climb ... but these! They had to be at least a hundred years old. Huge, gnarled, and chapped trunks with a circumference larger then he could embrace, oaks and box elders with abundant knobs and sucker branches for footholds. Danny had seen trees this big in parks, of course, but his parents had never let him climb them. Only once, with one of his babysitters, had he been able to. He had told his mother how much fun it had been, looking down from so high. They had never had that babysitter again.

Danny stood in front of the challenge of the first tree, looking up into the sea of leafy branches, the hidden world high above the ground. He circled the trunk slowly, contemplating, and then grabbed a clump of small branches, hoisting himself upward. He jammed his left sneaker against a bald lump on the trunk and fought with his fingers in the wide cracks in the bark, trying to find another handhold.

He reached up to grab a real branch, not a twig, and climbed again, wedging his foot into the first handhold. The tree seemed to cooperate now, offering many branches to assist him. His fingers were sore and raw, and his arms were tired, but this was wonderful! The air was still, and he could hear birds somewhere higher in the tree. He went up to the next branch and looked down to see how far he had climbed. This was triumph! This was scary! He felt like Spiderman.

Above him, one branch jutted out, tantalizingly out of his reach. He shimmied out farther on the branch, reached up, stretching, feeling like he would fall at any moment, and then grabbed the branch. Danny inched himself forward, then stopped, panting, as high as he could go.

And that's when he knew he would never be able to get down.

He felt his heart stop cold; he had thought only grown-ups knew how to sweat. He moved his eyes slowly down to where his sneaker balanced on a small bulge, and he couldn't move it. Danny felt like crying, and somehow knew he was going to.

"There's a little branch below your left foot. If you rest your weight on that, you can come down—no trouble at all."

Danny was so startled he almost fell from the tree. Below him, with hands on his hips and peering up into the tree, stood a large, old man with a huge, bushy beard, scowling and squinting as if the sun were in his eyes. Danny knew it must be Mr. Rossa and tried not to look at the farmer's fierce expression as he searched for the small branch. He found it, but it was too small, and too far away for Danny to even consider reaching.

"It's too far!"

Mr. Rossa hemmed and bit on his lip, running his fingers through the thick mass of his beard. "Just a minute—I'll get you down. Just you wait right there!"

The old farmer jogged out of sight. Danny waited, and waited, and felt like he was going to cry again. What if Mr. Rossa had called the police? He shivered and wished he were back home watching cartoons.

Mr. Rossa reappeared, puffing and carrying a weathered gray ladder. Danny held his breath and waited as the farmer tried to maneuver the end of the ladder up into the mass of branches. He heard the thump as the ladder banged against a branch and came to rest, just a little below him.

"Now can you climb down?" Mr. Rossa looked up at him expectantly.

Danny saw the ladder, just below him, but his fingers were cramping and wouldn't let him release his hold. He knew he could easily reach the ladder, but his body didn't.

"No." His voice sounded thin and small.

"All right then ..." Mr. Rossa grunted. Danny heard the ladder creak as the old man began to climb up. The farmer made puffing sounds as he ascended, rung by rung, muttering to himself probably out of habit rather than in anger at Danny.

"Come on, now, can you reach? That's a good boy. Come on." Danny saw that Mr. Rossa was just below him, reaching up with a hand that was strong and calloused, not the least bit arthritic and frail as his grandmother's had once been. Danny looked down into the old man's eyes—deep, ancient eyes, older than he could imagine, filled with more knowledge and more memories than Danny could ever hope to know, or want to know. He felt that the distance to the bottoms of those pupils was far greater than the distance to the ground.

"All right then." Mr. Rossa broke the trance and climbed two rungs higher until he could easily pluck the boy from his perch. Danny shivered until Mr. Rossa stood firmly on the ground again after a long and toiling descent from the rickety ladder. And then the fear piled up on him, expressing itself in long sobs. He bawled and clung to the old man's neck, burying his face deep in the bushy, streaked beard. It was a tangled brownish-gray color now, but all the rampant red hairs dotted throughout testified that it had been a flaming scarlet color once.

He didn't notice the old man stiffen. Mr. Rossa stood for a long time, holding the boy, and then finally pulled Danny away from him and set him back on the ground. "Come on now—it's not all that bad. Come on, stop your crying."

Danny sniffled, but the sobs had already begun to fade. The old farmer looked at him intently, frowning, and suddenly Danny realized Mr. Rossa wasn't going to yell at him for climbing his tree. "Now, young man, you'd better introduce yourself. I don't think I've seen you before."

"I'm Danny ... I—" His voice convulsed with a leftover sob, and he managed to point across the alfalfa field. "You live next to us."

Mr. Rossa smiled, and the crow's-feet around his eyes folded together. "Ah! And does your mother know you're here?"

Danny wiped his eyes, nodding his head in a diagonal way, not knowing if the old man would interpret it as a yes or a no.

Mr. Rossa stood for a long time, inspecting Danny but also looking slightly uncomfortable. The old man opened his mouth several times as if to say something, but he seemed reluctant. "Would you like to stay here a while?" The farmer ran a finger slowly down his bearded chin, pursing his lips, as if trying to think of something that might interest a five-year-old boy. "I was just going to look at some old books in my attic."

Danny looked up at the old man, then past him at the farmhouse standing ancient and spooky even in the bright afternoon.

All the tears vanished, evaporated and forgotten, as his eyes lit up. "Yeah!"

"Come on, then." Mr. Rossa strode toward his porch door with a strange mixture of firmness and pride in his steps, seeming to show that he was more than just an old farmer.

~

HE CAME down out of the desolate mountains, protected from the cold by his own immortality, carrying only his beloved sword as a support. The path was winding and complex, the beginning of the long road his mission would require him to travel.

All those centuries ago, he had united the squabbling German principalities, fused them into an empire like Rome, and called it Holy. He crusaded against the Turks and sacrificed to his God. He would have won, but the Angel and the rushing waters of the river had taken him too soon.

And even after seven centuries of slumber, it never occurred to Barbarossa that he might have been forgotten.

~

GRAY PATCHES OF NAKED, weathered wood stood out where the old white paint had chipped from the porch door and fallen to the grass. The door squeaked as Mr. Rossa pulled it open, gesturing for Danny to enter. The boy's eyes were wide as he entered the farmhouse, I breathed deeply and smelling the fuel oil, the dark and musty shadows....

And up in the attic, the trapdoor groaned loudly, to Danny's delight, as Mr. Rossa grunted and heaved it up, letting it crash backward to the attic floor. It seemed perfectly right to Danny that the old man had brought a candle with him, instead of a flashlight, to light their way.

"Come on, now—be careful there!" Mr. Rossa warned as the boy squeezed past him up the ladder.

In fascination, Danny stared at the old, mysterious objects in the attic: broken chairs, a dusty lamp, boxes filled with yellowed paper paraphernalia. Thick cobwebs gilded everything—Danny wondered how the spiders ever found enough to survive up there; did they eat each other?

Mr. Rossa made his way over to a box of books in the corner, dribbling globs of melted wax on the floorboards. He bent over the books, spilling his globe of candlelight into the box. He squinted and ran his fingers over the cover of an old, hand-bound sheaf of parchments.

"What's that, Mister Rossa?" The old man looked up quickly, as if Danny had stopped him from entering a reverie. "Gosh, those books sure look old!"

The farmer smiled a little. "Do you know how to read, Danny?"

"I know my ABCs—and I know how to spell 'Danny.' But I can't read until I go to first grade, next year."

"Ah." Mr. Rossa looked back down at the books, paging through one so brittle that his gentle fingers plunged through a page with a puff of dust. The handwriting was old and faded, and illuminated with many stylized letters and illustrations, as if someone had painstakingly taken the time to make the documents beautiful for someone who could not read. "These are in Latin anyway." His voice was almost a sigh, and he dropped to his knees in front of the box, carefully shuffling among the parchments. The old man seemed to be sweating a little.

Danny fidgeted for a moment, losing interest in the books. He saw a painting hidden behind some piled, discarded clothes.

"Do you have a hero, Danny?" Mr. Rossa asked, slowly turning to look up from the books. His eyes were strange again, but Danny took sudden interest.

"Yeah! I like the Hulk—he's the best. And Spiderman." Danny began to sing quickly, "Spiderman, Spiderman, does whatever a spider can! Is he strong? Listen, Bud—He's got radioactive blood!"

Mr. Rossa frowned, releasing a long mouthful of air which rustled the strands of his once scarlet, now gray, beard. Danny stopped, and wondered what he had done wrong. "Do you have a hero, Mister Rossa?"

For a moment, he thought the old man was going to chuckle, but then the farmer forced his mouth into a wry smile, as if he knew something Danny did not. "Do you know who Frederick Barbarossa is, Danny?"

"Bobba Rossa? I know who Boba Fett is. He's from Star Wars."

Mr. Rossa sighed again. "Barbarossa was the king of a vast land, called the Holy Roman Empire ... oh, eight hundred years ago. He had flaming red hair, and a long scarlet beard. And the people loved him very much, for he was a strong emperor who had united the entire land. But the Empire had its enemies—the Infidels. So, Barbarossa gathered his army together and marched out on great wars, called the Crusades. He led his own armies to many great victories, farther than any other Crusade had gone—all the way to the land of the Infidels, in Asia Minor. Barbarossa would have destroyed the Infidels once and for all." The farmer smiled, and Danny listened carefully.

"But then, one day Barbarossa led the vanguard of his troops to a river, the Calycadnus River. It had been raining for days on end, and many of the men had died from fevers caused by the dark and cruel gods of the Infidels. The bank of the river was muck, and the water itself was gray and thick, swollen with mud. The current was vicious."

Mr. Rossa seemed to be looking through Danny.

"It was early afternoon. The troops had just eaten a meal, partly of dry rations and partly of fresh food we had taken from villages along the way. The ford of the river didn't look passable, but Barbarossa was brave, and knew he needed to get his men across. They could never hope to take prisoners, so they killed them and threw the bodies into the current. The sky was heavy, as if the rains were going to come again—the army had to cross now.

"The Emperor, the red-haired giant, urged his horse forward, trusting in God to protect him. He would cross first, to show his men that it was safe, and then they would follow. The horse entered the river, trembling, afraid of the roaring water. The current sucked at the horse's legs, but Barbarossa—all dressed in his war armor and strutting in his imperial glory—urged his horse on. The water rose higher, until, near the center of the river, the animal was dancing on the slippery rocks of the channel, half swimming and half walking." The old farmer seemed almost breathless, but he continued to talk quickly, in a low voice.

"Some of the other soldiers entered the river, following their Emperor, struggling to keep control of the frightened horses.

Others waited on the bank, watching and praying. Barbarossa drew his shining and deadly sword and raised it high so that the others could see him.

"Barbarossa's horse stumbled, became wild as it tried to regain its footing. The Emperor was flung from his mount as he grabbed for the reins. The horse thrashed and struggled, panicking, and was quickly drawn under, vanishing with the flow of mud and melted snow rushing down from the frozen mountaintops. Barbarossa knew how to swim, but his heavy armor dragged him down under the powerful current. He managed to keep a desperate grip on the hilt of his jeweled sword, as if that lifeline might save him. And then he vanished under the water, never to be seen again."

"Wow!" Danny let the word slither from his mouth.

"Now, a history book will say Barbarossa drowned that day. But the people, the soldiers, they all said that no, maybe he didn't die. Maybe the Emperor is still alive, sleeping in a cave somewhere up in the tall mountains of Asia Minor near the source of the Calycadnus River. He was a hero, so they built a legend around him … and nobody ever lets legends die. They said Frederick Barbarossa lies sleeping beside a huge stone table somewhere deep within a holy cave; and one day, when his red beard has grown all the way around that table, he will wake up and save the Holy Roman Empire from all its enemies."

"Gosh!" Danny looked into the old man's eyes. "And your hero is Bobba Rossa?"

The farmer let a wry grin settle onto his face. "No, Danny—I *am* Barbarossa."

Danny's eyes widened as he drew a breath in astonishment, but then he narrowed his gaze; he tried to imitate the look Dad had given him when Danny said an invisible monster had broken Mom's lamp. "Aww, you're just kidding me!"

"Am I?" Mr. Rossa looked at him, but Danny couldn't tell if the farmer's grin was sly or smug. The old man raised his eyebrows, as if waiting for Danny to challenge him further.

"Oh, yeah? Well how come you didn't die in that river, then?"

"I was a hero, Danny. Heroes never die." It was almost a sigh. "We're not allowed."

Danny continued to look at the old man, not wanting to disbelieve the story because that would make the world less interesting, not even really caring if it were not true. Mr. Rossa kept staring at his own fingers, as if amazed they had suddenly gotten so old.

"How come you're not still sleeping in that cave? By the table? And how did you get here?"

"You can't sleep forever, Danny. Who's to say that I didn't wake up a century ago, and I've been around ever since? Nobody noticed me, and nobody believed anyway."

"And did you save the Holy Roman Empire from all its enemies?"

Mr. Rossa lowered his eyes. "It was already dead when I woke up again. The boundaries were all different ... the people were all changed—"

"Did you even try?"

"No." He searched for understanding in the boy's eyes, but Danny felt only disappointment. "I was just an ignorant king from the end of the Dark Ages. My solution to a problem was to gather up an army and charge with swords flashing. People don't do things that way anymore. How could I do a better job than the modern leaders, the very least of whom is more educated—and with an extra eight hundred years of experience to draw upon—than the most brilliant people I ever knew in my day? I decided it would be better to leave the people with their legend, and their hope, rather than destroying both."

Danny frowned, condemningly. "Well, do you at least go out and fight crooks and bad guys, like Spiderman does? Like all the Superheroes do?"

"Danny ..." The boy should have been impressed by Mr. Rossa's patience, but he was not. "The only reason we are heroes is because people make us into them. I'm still just a man inside—I can't wave my hands and make all the evil go away."

Danny stood up abruptly, looking uncomfortable. "I gotta go. My Mom'll yell at me for being gone so long."

Mr. Rossa frowned, as if trying to preserve the threads of his own confession. He picked up the candle, following Danny down the ladder. The porch door squeaked as the farmer held it open for Danny. "Come back again—anytime!"

Danny plunged into the alfalfa field, wading and running at the same time. He didn't answer immediately, until he could rationalize something in his mind. "Okay, I will." He started to go faster, calling into the wind ahead of him and hoping the words would drift back to the old man. "Promise!"

He wandered across the mountains of Asia Minor, got passage on a creaking ship up the coast of the Black Sea and then down the Danube. Many questioned him, but none believed his story. The Holy Roman Empire had been swallowed by history, as were the Crusades, as were the Infidels, as was Barbarossa.

Hoping to find something, he went across Eastern Europe, scavenged for some memories in his beloved Prague, and then moved southward to Rome. He read voraciously, discovered what had happened during his long slumber, and fell into despair. His beautiful Empire had turned cannibal and had fallen prey to itself. Even an Angel-gifted hero could not battle such an enemy.

For Danny, the summer was forever condensed into a day. The heart of the season struck when he had forgotten completely about his previous year in kindergarten, and first grade seemed infinitely far away. Danny's skin was blotched with freckles that hadn't been there a few weeks before. The alfalfa field had been cut and baled once already by the men who rented Mr. Rossa's land, and it had grown high enough to await its second cutting.

"I'm going to Mister Rossa's!" he called back at his mother as he let the door slam behind him. By now, he no longer really needed to tell her.

"You never watch cartoons anymore!" he heard her say, but he was already sprinting across the field....

Under the big boxelder tree in the farmyard, the two of them sat in the shade of the afternoon, watching the world, seeing nothing and everything at the same time. Mr. Rossa reached down to expertly remove a tall grass blade and stuck it in his mouth. Danny tried to imitate him, pulling up the grass by its roots and then slowly extracting the right part. The old man had once shown him how to whistle through a grass blade, but Danny had succeeded only in cutting his lips.

"Mister Rossa?"

The answer was a long time in coming. "Hmmm?"

"What's it like? Fighting in a big battle? I bet it's exciting."

The old farmer looked lost for a moment, and then let a smile spread slowly under his beard. "The first time I went out on a battlefield was the most terrifying experience ever. Even worse than the time I drowned. Just to look at the enemy army, and to see all those sharp swords—each one of them waiting to stick into your chest or chop your head off.

"I'll bet you didn't know I had my side cut open once, slashed right down the ribs all the way to my belly. Imagine looking down at your own innards, steaming up at you because it's a chilly morning. And then sitting there brave like a king, trying not to grunt as a healer sews your wound back together. Mind you, we had none of the anesthetics you have now. Here—I've still got the scar."

Mr. Rossa fumbled with the buttons on his shirt, exposing the thermal undershirt and part of his hairy chest. Danny saw a long white line, very straight and lumped together with scar tissue which looked centuries old. Just like the downstroke of a sword would leave.

"Your sword becomes the best friend you have in the entire world. After a while you forget that you might be ten seconds away from your own death, and you concentrate only on fighting. A red haze hovers around the edges of your eyes, slowly closing in, and pretty soon all you see is red. You're completely blind, but your arm knows what it's doing and you trust to your fighting instinct. And then, an instant later, sight floods back to you and you see all the trophies you've collected, all the heads in a pile. You go to your own soldiers, look at the comrades who didn't survive, the mangled ones with their mouths and their eyes and their wounds gaping open—and they seem to be angry at you because you survived, and they didn't."

Mr. Rossa paused for a minute and spat out his grass blade, breaking the spell. He looked at his hands, flexing them, and then ran his fingers through the once-red beard. "Ah, Danny, with you here I am older than I ever was before."

～

HE TRAVELED FOR YEARS, north into France, then to England and Wales. An unwelcomed savior, he did various jobs, strenuous work even a battle-conditioned medieval king could barely endure. He married once, almost twice, but after several decades he had begun to realize the curse placed upon him by the Angel—he aged at only a sliver of mankind's rate. He had learned to keep his identity to himself, and he moved on as he grew restless with one place, as people noticed he had spent too many years looking the same age.

To Ireland, to a crowded, stinking steamer which carried him with a festering mass of other immigrants across the Atlantic to America, beyond the edge of the 12th Century's known world. He endured the abuse, traveled west from New York to try to start a farm for himself. He found this demeaning, for in his memories only peasants did such work. The horrors of the Dust Bowl nearly ruined him, and he moved back east, to the rolling hills of Wisconsin, on the outskirts of a small town where the people asked poignant questions. Lonesome, deserted by history, Frederick Barbarossa had decided to die here. After nearly a century of second life. And without a single friend to retell his story or remember him.

～

DANNY TURNED the pages of the encyclopedia slowly, deliberately. He clutched the scrap of paper on which Mr. Rossa had printed "Frederick, Barbarossa."

"I want to look this up in the 'cyclopedia, Mister Rossa." he had insisted.

"Come on, do you think I'd be in there?"

"Of course! Everything's in the 'cyclopedia!"

Danny remembered the order of the alphabet, and he hoped to find a picture of Mr. Rossa. He had found the F volume and paged through it with the patience only a determined child could have, insisting on doing it himself, without asking for help from his mother or father who both sat in the kitchen finishing their lunch.

Danny crossed his legs in a lotus position. He finally found F-R and quickly proceeded through France, then Benjamin Franklin, and finally found Frederick I. And he saw the picture.

It was a crude drawing, a sketch simpler even than Danny imagined he could do—the Emperor Barbarossa riding like a superhero on a cartoon horse. Without a doubt, it was indeed Mr. Rossa. He stared at the picture, wishing he could read, and slowly realized that his parents' conversation had risen to the proportions of an argument.

"He's over there every day, all afternoon!" His mother shouted. "You aren't home often enough to hear him come up with words and ... and comparisons he has no way of knowing! That old farmer is telling him stories! It was almost better when he watched those crazy superhero cartoons—at least he only half-believed them!"

"Now wait a minute." His father's voice was calm, almost forcedly so. Dad always had a way of understanding the boy's point of view; Danny almost wondered if his father had been a boy once, too. "You're the one who wanted to move out here to the country. There's no one Danny's age within miles, no one who's even interested in the things he likes to talk about. Except for Mr. Rossa. They're keeping each other company. Besides, that old man is probably even lonelier than Danny is—"

"That old man is filling Danny's head with crazy stories! Do you know he's been telling Danny he's some German king who's been dead for centuries?"

"It is not a story!" Danny exploded into the dining room, still carrying the encyclopedia. He slammed it down on the table among the lunch debris. "His picture's right here, in the 'cyclopedia!"

"Daniel John!" his mother snapped, but Danny was angry enough to overcome his fear and awe of her.

"And he's not dead 'cause he's a hero, and heroes never die! Mister Rossa knows!"

His mother started to shout something else, but Danny turned and ran toward the front door where the screen let in the summer heat, but no breeze.

"Daniel John, you come back here this instant."

But Danny didn't listen, throwing the screen door shut behind him. "And besides, he's not a German king—he's a Holy Roman Emperor!" He began to run, charging through the alfalfa field which had been mown and raked, leaving the hay to dry in the sun before baling.

And he didn't stop running until he had reached the old farmer's peeling white door. "Mister Rossa! Mister Rossa!" He burst into the farmhouse.

Something was different. The house was quieter than the sound of soft breathing, and the sun seemed reluctant to penetrate the cream-colored shades over the windows. "Mister Rossa?"

The kitchen, the sitting room with its old wooden radio, the bathroom, and the bedroom were all together on the first floor, near the door, so that Mr. Rossa needed to take fewer steps. Now the bedroom was dim ... but Mr. Rossa always opened his shades early each morning.

"Mister Rossa?"

The old man lay on his bed, breathing slowly but not sleeping. The bed had been made, but the farmer was only half-dressed, as if he had realized he would never finish. Danny went close to him, saw that his hands were trembling, both his own and Mr. Rossa's. The old man's eyes were open, but glazed, exhausted—the fires within them which had always frightened Danny were now so dull that it terrified him even more.

"Mister Rossa ... what's wrong?"

The old man's breathing picked up, as if he had just noticed Danny, and he inhaled several times before answering. "I am very old, Danny ... even older than I had thought. I was frozen in what I had been ... you made me realize that I may be a hero ... but I am still very human inside. And that made me vulnerable. Thank you."

Danny gasped as he suddenly realized what was taking place. "Are you dying, Mister Rossa?" His eyes stood wide in the dimness, in his disbelief.

Mr. Rossa closed his eyes gently, wearily, and breathed deeply, with difficulty. "You can bet I'm going to tell that Angel a few things ... when I see him again."

"But you can't die! Heroes never die! 'Member? Remember! You said!"

He waited, and waited, but received no answer. He watched the old man's labored breathing. The eyes remained closed, but a thin, tired whisper flickered through his lips. "I think I need to sleep ... again."

"You promised!" Danny's ragged voice convulsed with spasms of sobs he wasn't supposed to express in front of a legendary king. Tears seemed to be streaming down his face. "You can't go to sleep! I don't want to wait a thousand years to see you again. You can't!"

Mr. Rossa opened his eyes again, looking at Danny from within himself, at some far-off place. "Remember, Danny."

The boy heard the words, although they had been barely spoken. He grabbed the old farmer's hand and buried his face in the wrinkled and musty shirt. "I love you, Mister Rossa."

The old man seemed to become completely lucid for a moment. Danny could see a reflection of the young Emperor, with fiery red hair and a fiery red beard, the leader of men, holding his sword high in the air.

"Danny ... my friend ... in my dresser ... bottom drawer ... it's yours." Strength in his voice seemed to drain into the air, leaving him no energy at all.

"What is it?" Danny whispered, but grief masked his curiosity.

The farmer didn't seem to hear him. He gripped Danny's hand so tightly it hurt, looking into the boy's eyes, "... best friend ..."

"You're my hero, Mister Rossa."

The old man was stricken with a spasm through his entire body. His loud gasping breaths were almost convulsions in themselves, keeping a different rhythm.

Danny wanted to cry out, but his vocal cords froze. This wasn't the way it was supposed to happen. He had seen people die on TV before. They said goodbye, or whatever they needed to say ... they closed their eyes and then breathed their last. Mr. Rossa's eyes were so tightly clenched that tears streamed between them. His teeth ground together, and a continual force of shudders rippled through his body.

But Mr. Rossa was already dead. The spirit had left his mind, and his body hadn't yet accepted the fact. Danny slid to the floor, beside the old man's bed, and cried and cried until Mr. Rossa's body settled into a peace. And Danny continued to sit, staring at the farmer who told so many stories, until his tears had dried by themselves.

Finally, he got to his feet, sniffled a few times, and wondered what to do. He went slowly to Mr. Rossa's dresser, almost afraid. The old chest of drawers sat dusty in the shadows, cluttered on top with odds-and-ends, treasures of a sort. The handle of one of the drawers was broken off.

He bent to the bottom drawer and pulled it open, surprised to find it lined with plush red velvet in imperial splendor. And inside the drawer, nestled among the velvet ... it had been lovingly polished and oiled over the years, more than a memory, more than a story. Danny trembled with his own awe and reached down to lift up Barbarossa's sword, his own sword, the Emperor's sword. He smiled broadly and silently vowed to care for it.

I've been friends with Sherrilyn Kenyon for at least fifteen years. Sherri has written stories for my Blood Lite *anthologies and we've often discussed collaborating. When Christopher Golden was tasked with bringing together big-name collaborators for his* Dark Duets *anthology for HarperCollins, he asked who I might have in mind. The answer was obvious to me, and Sherri readily agreed.*

I had the start of an idea. I asked her, "What lives under bridges?" She said, "Homeless people." I said, "And what else lives under bridges." She thought for a moment. "Oh!"

This story began as a true horror story, but then became much more mythic and far different from what either of us expected.

TRIP TRAP

(WRITTEN WITH SHERRILYN KENYON)

He huddled under the bridge and hid from the world outside, as he had done for as long as he could remember … No, he could *remember* a time before that, but he didn't like those thoughts, and he buried them away whenever they appeared.

The bridge was old and unimpressive, long ago marred by spray-painted graffiti, mostly faded now. The county road extended from an Alabama state highway and crossed over a creek that was more of a drainage ditch, overrun with weeds and populated with garbage tossed out from the occasional passing car. Brambles, dogwoods, and tall milkweed grew high enough to provide some shelter for his lair.

Skari lurked in the shadows next to piled cans, mud-encrusted debris he had hauled out of the noisome drainage ditch, a bent and discarded child's bicycle (struck by a car). A stained blanket provided very little warmth and no softness, but he clung to it nevertheless. It was *his*. All the comforts of home.

He had a shopping cart with a broken wheel, piled high with the few possessions he had bothered to keep over … over a long time. He hunched his back against the rough concrete abutment, shifting position. The dirt and gravel beneath him was a far cry from a grassy, flower-strewn meadow he sometimes saw in his dreams. He didn't belong in meadows anymore—just here in the shadows, standing watch at the nightmare gate. He had to guard it. Skari wouldn't leave his post.

The tall milkweed rustled aside, and he looked up at the freckled face of a skinny little girl. "I see you there," she said. "Are you a troll?"

Skari tensed, half-rose from his crouch. Many layers of tattered and filthy clothing covered his skin, masked his monstrous features. The girl just blinked at him.

"What are you doing here?" When he inhaled a quick breath, through the humidity and the odors of the drainage ditch, he could smell the little girl. The tender little girl.

"My brother says you're a troll, 'cause trolls live under bridges. You're living under a bridge," the girl said. "So, are you a troll?"

Yes, he was, but she didn't know that. In fact, no one was allowed to know that. "No. Not a troll," he lied.

She smelled tender, savory, juicy.

"Come closer."

The girl was intrigued by him, but she hesitated. She was smart enough for that at least.

Skari squeezed his eyes shut and drove his head back against the concrete abutment of the bridge. Again. The pain was like a gunshot through his skull, but at least it drove away the dark thoughts. Sometimes it just got so lonely, and he got so hungry here. He'd been thinking about eating children, tasty children … thinking about it altogether too much.

With a crash through the underbrush, a boy came down the embankment. Her brother. He looked about nine, a year or two older than the girl. Both were scrawny, their clothes hand-me-downs but still in much better condition than Skari's. The children did have a raggedness about them, though, a touch of loss that had not yet grown into desperation. That would come in time, Skari knew … unless he ate them first.

Next to his sister, the boy made a grimace and said with a taunting bravery that only fools and children could manage, "I think you're a troll. You smell like a troll!"

Skari leaned forward, lurched closer to the edge of the shadow, and the children drew back, but remained close, staring. "Methinks you smell yourself, boy."

Rather than hearing the threat, the boy giggled. *"Methinks?* What kind of word is *methinks?"* He added in a singsong voice, "Methinks 'methinks' is a stupid word."

Skari grumbled, ground his teeth together. His gums were sore. He picked at them with a yellowed fingernail. No wonder witches ate children. His stomach rumbled. It was sounding like a better and better idea to him.

He wanted to lunge out from the gloom, but he knew the night-mare gate was there somewhere behind him, just waiting for him to let down his guard. Skari had been assigned here to stand watch, *sentenced* to stay here.

For many centuries, evil had bubbled up from the depths of the world, and the nightmare gates through which demons traveled always appeared underneath bridges. Skari couldn't leave his post, had to stay here and protect against anything that might come out. It made no sense to him why a vulnerable spot might appear under this small county-road bridge in northern Alabama, but it was not for Skari to understand. He hadn't felt the evil gate in some time, although there was plenty of evil in *him.*

"How long have you been there, Mister?" asked the girl.

"Longer than you've been alive."

A car peeled off the highway and drove along the county road. Its engine was loud and dyspeptic, one tire mostly flat so that as the car crossed the bridge overhead, it made a staccato *trip-trap-trip-trap-trip-trap.*

"What's your name?" the boy asked, as if it were his turn to dare.

His name. Yes, he had a name. Other people had called him by name, laughed with him, even a beautiful maiden who had once whispered it in his ear. But not anymore. He had no friends, no home, just what he clung to under this bridge where he stood guard.

But he did have a name. "Skari."

"Scarey Skari!" the boy shouted, and the girl laughed with him.

"Come closer!" He was so hungry for those children, so anxious to emerge into the sunlight again, even though it would cause him pain, make him twist and writhe. Skari grew ill from the very thought. It might be worth the pain, though, just for a bit of free-dom … or maybe just for a taste of fresh meat.

"Billy! Kenna! Leave the poor man alone."

The two children whirled, startled. They looked as if they'd been caught at something.

Their mother came up, a woman on the edge of thirty, her brown hair pulled back into a ponytail. She wore no makeup, but her face was washed clean. Her clothes also had that worn look to them.

"He's a troll, Ma—he lives under a bridge," said the girl, Kenna.

"He smells," said Billy.

The mother looked mortally embarrassed, rounded up the two as she peered under the bridge where Skari huddled with all his possessions. "I am so incredibly sorry they disturbed you. What can I say?" She hauled the children out of the weeds, maybe to keep them safe from him. "They both flunked home training, but it wasn't from lack of effort on my part."

She sounded conversational, a forced friendliness, as if she felt they had something in common.

"Why does he live under a bridge, Ma?" Kenna asked.

Skari was startled to see the woman hesitate. A bright sheen of tears suddenly appeared in her eyes. "Just be thankful we don't live there."

He heard the unspoken *Yet* in her voice.

"It's all right," Skari said. "They weren't bothering me." His stomach growled, but not loudly enough for anyone else to hear. "I've been called worse than smelly … and that by my own family."

"Well, I appreciate your understanding. I'm Johanna. It was nice meeting you."

She seemed uncomfortable, backing down the embankment, protecting her children—and good thing. She didn't want them talking to strangers, especially ones who hid under bridges. Especially trolls.

The air was full of the whine of insects, laden with ozone. Overhead, dark thunderheads clotted. If a downpour came, it would make the humidity more tolerable for a while.

"We need to get back to the car, kids," Johanna said. "It's the only shelter we've got."

"I don't want to go back and sit in the car, Ma! It's hot."

"Been there for days. There's nothing to do," Billy added. "When are we gonna keep driving?"

"As soon as we get gas money. Somebody'll come by."

Whenever Skari saw people, they were from the cars that stopped at the rest area on the highway next to the bridge. It had beige metal picnic tables, trash cans, running water, restrooms, and not much else. Not even traffic. Skari had seen vehicles come and go, and most of them didn't stay long, but now he remembered a rusted station wagon piled with belongings. It had been there a while. He thought he'd heard a loud muffler, a struggling engine, tires crunching gravel, doors slamming—two nights ago? Johanna and her children probably had a hand-written sign on a scrap of cardboard asking for help with gas money or food.

Skari tried to remember how to make conversation. Some part of him didn't want the family to go away ... not yet. "Are you having trouble, ma'am?"

"No ... yes ... maybe."

"Which is it?"

"All of the above. But it's my problem. Don't trouble yourself."

Skari glanced behind him, sensed the nightmare gate. But the barrier was strong, stable—as it had been for many years. Nothing was trying to get through right now. He ambled closer to her, taking comfort in the thunderclouds that muted the afternoon sunlight.

"We don't got a home no more," Kenna said. "The mean man made us leave."

"What mean man?"

Their mother let out a heavy sigh. "We were evicted. I lost my job a year ago and haven't been able to find another one. I used up my savings, and we're trying to make it to Michigan where my cousin lives."

"Michigan?" He didn't have much familiarity with maps anymore, but he did understand that Michigan was a long way from northern Alabama.

"We'll manage somehow," the mother said. Fat raindrops started to strike the ground. "We just need a little to get by, step by step. If we make it to Michigan, we can have a fresh start." Her expression tightened, as if she had forgotten about him entirely. "We'll find a way to survive."

Before he could stop himself, Skari blurted out, "It's not so bad. You and the girl could live off the fat of the boy for at least three days."

Johanna's eyes widened, and she drew back, startled. Billy thought it was a joke and he nudged his sister. "They wouldn't want me anyway. Girls are the ones made out of sugar and spice and everything nice."

Skari's stomach rumbled. "Don't believe too many fairy tales."

The rain began falling in earnest, thick drops pattering and hissing all around them like whispered laughter. Johanna grabbed the two children. "Come on, back to the car!" She flashed a glance over her shoulder, then ran with a squealing Kenna and Billy off to the rest area.

Skari went back under his bridge, took up his post at the long-sealed nightmare gate, and watched the world as the rain washed the scent of children from the air.

WATER RAN down the side of the bridge, trickles turning his dank and gloomy lair into a soupy mess. Skari just huddled there. The bugs seemed to enjoy it, though. Even after the storm stopped, leaving only leftover droplets wrung out from the sky, he heard frogs wake up in the creek. Something splashed in a puddle farther downstream. It wasn't yet full dark, but the clouds hadn't cleared.

All the burbling background noise masked the sound of stealthy footsteps, and the fresh rain covered the girl's scent until she appeared. "Mister Skari, are you hungry?"

He was startled. The appetite became ravenous within him. Was she taunting him? He could lunge out right now, grab her before she could run, use his dagger to break her up into delectable pieces, roast her meat over a fire and have a feast. But after the rain, he'd never be able to build a fire. No matter, he was hungry enough to eat her raw.

Skari slammed his head against the abutment again to drive away the thoughts. No, *no!* The hungers, the dark desires had always been gnawing in him, but he could fight them back. He could ... he *could!*

Kenna extended a rumpled white paper sack. "I brought hamburgers. Do you like fast food?"

No, I don't like fast food. I want something slow enough I can catch!

"Hamburgers?" he asked, his voice a croak.

"Somebody gave them to us at the rest area. They're leftovers. Mostly good, but the fries are cold and soggy. I wanted to offer you the last one. Ma doesn't know I'm here." She extended the sack closer, and with a quick movement he might have been able to snatch her wrist. "It's still fine. Only a bite taken out of it."

With a sense of wonder, Skari took the sack and pulled it open. An explosion of wondrous smells struck him in the face. His mouth watered. He was so hungry!

He stuffed the burger into his mouth, fished around with his paws in the bottom of the bag to grab every small, withered French fry. "Thank you," he said, his words muffled around the food. Tears stung his eyes.

He remembered feasting with some of the other warriors, a delicious banquet thrown by the victorious lord after a particularly long and bloody battle. They had slain countless scaly demons that day, driven them back through the nightmare gate and barricaded it under a stone bridge. Skari remembered how much blood there was in the air on the battlefield, how the smoking black demon blood had a sour acid smell, unlike the vibrant freshness of the roasted boar in the lord's firepit, unseasoned meat shimmering with grease. He and his fellow foot soldiers had eaten the celebratory feast, drinking the lord's best wine and his cheapest ale. It was all so delicious!

That was before Skari had failed, before he had been cursed ... before he'd been given this sacred duty.

He finished the food now, licked his crusted lips, and straightened, searching for his scraps of pride and memory as desperately as he looked for more fries.

"Is this your stuff?" Kenna was rummaging in his shopping cart, moving aside the piled possessions he had gathered over the years, decades ... centuries.

He sucked in his breath. He didn't dare let her find his weapons, the spell-sealed dagger. "Get away from there!" The girl jerked back. "You shouldn't be here. Go back to your mother, your family." He raised himself up, and Kenna looked awed and terrified as Skari grew and swelled, an ominous lurching shape under the bridge. She backed away, stumbling in the weeds. Skari lowered his voice, speaking more to himself than to her. "You have a family. Don't forget that."

She ran back to their forlorn station wagon, and he heard her crying, which made his heart heavy. Another stone of guilt, another failure, another thing to atone for. But Kenna had her brother, her mother … a mother who actually cared for her children.

Skari's mother hadn't been like that. When he'd run away to fight in the demon wars, he'd been cocky, full of false bravado, sure that no nightmare monster breaking out of hell could be worse than the shrewish woman who had beaten him, starved him at home.

He'd been so wrong about that.

For a while, his comrades had become his family. The clerics had blessed them all, the noblemen had armed them, the wizards provided magical talismans with blades dipped in bloodsilver that could strike down demons.

In the first two engagements, Skari had been out of the fray, far from where the monsters boiled out from beneath the bridge. Warlords and armed warriors had fought the slavering demons, while clerics and wizards struggled to seal and barricade the night-mare gate. Skari was terrified, but uninjured—and the war went on.

In the third battle, though, when the fanged and clawed monsters turned, charging into the pathetic group of Skari and his friends, he watched his best comrade Torin die. He was a baker's boy from the same village … they'd run off together—and Skari saw the demons tear him apart, twisting Torin's arms and legs from his torso like the bones from a well-roasted quail carcass. Another demon had bitten off Hurn's head. The long-haired tanner's apprentice had feminine features and a cocky smile, and the fanged monster had opened its hinged jaws, engulfed the boy's entire head, bit down, then spat it out amidst a gout of foul breath. Hurn's head had struck Skari right in the chest.

He didn't remember dropping his sword or running screaming

past all the other soldiers. Many hundreds of human soldiers had died that day, but the demons were driven back at an incredible cost of brave blood. Skari, though, was captured by the lord's men, found to be a coward, sentenced to be executed by a headsman's axe. But he was given a choice—a choice that he hadn't known was so terrible. The wizards offered him the opportunity to become the guardian of a sealed gate, to be made immortal, to stand watch in case the nightmare hordes ever tried to break free again.

Babbling, Skari had agreed. He dropped to his knees weeping, begging them to make him a guardian. He had not known that choice would be worse than simply dying.

Skari had lost his family, his friends, everyone and everything. He had been alone for centuries, moved from bridge to bridge when it was deemed necessary, when a new vulnerable spot appeared anywhere in the world.

"Your job is to protect mankind," the wizard had said.

The lord who stood before him had a grim, heartless face. He had lost a hand in the last battle. He had seen Skari run in terror from the monsters, and Skari knew he had earned his isolated eternity. His crime was not so great that he deserved hell itself, but bad enough for him to be sentenced to this purgatory. His fate, his *job*, was to protect humans against evil ... even though his close proximity to the nightmare gates had twisted him, too.

He could never let the evil escape again. He couldn't let it get to Johanna and her two children.

He turned to the bridge wall behind him where he could sense the simmering gate. It had been quiet, silent, but he dare not let his guard down. Dare not leave ... dare not have hope. He clenched his filthy, scabbed fist and hammered against the hard wall. "I hate you!" Nothing was worse than to be trapped alone where you didn't want to be.

While he kept the nightmare gate guarded, he thought of Kenna and Billy, homeless, penniless, cast out by a "mean man," vulnerable to human predators and unkind fate. Even if the demon wars were over, the darkness of human society was heartless, too. At least the demons were obvious enemies, and they could be defeated.

His thoughts kept going to the woman and her children. How could he defend against the troubles Johanna faced? The family was like the one he'd never had. Maybe that was another part of his punishment: to feel such helplessness after he'd begun to sense a connection. But what could he do?

We just need a little to get by, step by step, Johanna had said. *If we make it to Michigan, we can have a fresh start.*

As he thought of them, he sighed. They were the ones he fought for. But if he simply ignored their very real, though not supernatural, plight, he might as well let the evil behind the nightmare gate eat them. It would be like running away from the battlefield, a coward again.

He went to his cart and dug through his cluttered possessions, the detritus and treasures piled and packed there ... until he found the last two things he had from his original life in another time, another world: a thick gold medallion, one small ring, and a handful of silver coins, spoils from his first battlefields. The trinkets had amounted to a fortune even then, an even greater one today.

For centuries, he'd kept them safe. Now, they would help a young mother and her children reach safety.

It was full night now, and the nightmare gate seemed strong, stable. He sensed no whispers of evil back there, only emptiness. But he did feel the pain and the need of Johanna and her children.

Halfhearted rain began to fall as he trudged to the parking lot of the rest area. The station wagon was dark, closed up for the night as the family huddled there for shelter, safer and warmer than under a bridge. It was the only vehicle there. A single, white mercury light shed a pool of illumination over the picnic tables. A metal sign peppered with divots from shotgun pellets said NO OVERNIGHT PARKING—STRICTLY ENFORCED. But no one had bothered to enforce it for days.

Shambling forward, a looming shadow surrounded by deeper shadows, Skari approached the driver's side window and thumped on it. He heard a startled gasp from behind the glass, the children stirring. He saw a glint of the mother's eyes; she was concerned, ready to fight. In the darkness, they would be able to discern his gargantuan size, but unable to see his ugly twisted features, his scabrous skin.

He held up the pouch. "Didn't mean to scare you, ma'am. I just thought this would help you get on your way."

Johanna rolled down the window just enough for him to push the pouch through. She took it, and he turned, not wanting to speak with her, not waiting for her to see what he had given them.

Skari ambled back into the night, hurrying before any demons could discover the unguarded nightmare gate, before he would have to endure the mother telling him "Thank You."

~

No more than an hour later, as he sat in the damp gloom of his lair, Johanna, Billy, and Kenna appeared under the bridge, walking closer. They weren't afraid of him. The mother held the sack with the medallion, the ring, the old coins. "I can't take this."

"Yes, you can. Those things do me no good, but for you they can make the difference. Buy yourself a new chance." He tried to remember how to soften his words with humor. "It should keep you from having to eat the boy for at least a week."

She laughed, and her brow furrowed. "It'll keep us from living under a bridge." The boy and girl gathered closer, and they all looked at Skari. Johanna's face was tight, and he saw tears in her eyes. "This is the nicest thing anyone's ever done for us. Thank you."

The little girl burst forward, threw herself against him, and hugged him tight. "You're not a monster."

Billy nodded and said strangely, "You're saved. I'm glad we didn't have to kill you."

No sooner had the boy spoken than pain shot into Skari's body. He hissed as it burned through him, screaming through his muscle fibers. His skin began to boil and turn color. Underneath his layers of old, encrusted clothing, his body twisted in a spasm. He bent over, threw himself against the bridge abutment, and his mind rang with terror.

Were these people escaped demons? Had they come here to attack him? He staggered into his shopping cart, grabbed it. He had to get the bloodsilver dagger, defend himself, defend the world—but the cart crashed to one side.

Unable to stand the pain, Skari doubled over, dropped to the muddy, garbage-strewn ground—

And shrank in size. Confused, Skari looked at his hands that were no longer gnarled ugly paws. They were hands again. Human hands. He flexed his arms, pushed himself to his feet.

The mother and children stood before him, watching, but their eyes didn't look evil. In fact, they seemed glad … relieved.

"The demon wars were over long ago," said Johanna. "The nightmare gates are permanently sealed, but after all this time, the *guardians* themselves have become dangerous."

Billy added, "Not only were you immortal, you became inhuman, too—so close to the darkness that it found a home in you."

"We've been sent to find the last few remaining trolls, to test them," Kenna said in a voice that did not belong to a little girl. "To see if they need to be destroyed, or if they have learned human decency and compassion. You, Skari, are one of the last. We were afraid for you."

Instead of the eyes of a little boy, Billy's eyes were hard and ancient. "But you convinced even me."

"You are free now," Johanna said. "The world is safe from demons … and it is safe from you."

Kenna grinned, and her eyes sparkled. "We release you from your post."

Returning to the weird Wisconsin town of Tucker's Grove, I did this story of two quirky characters, a pair of warm-hearted circus freaks from a traveling carnival, people who want to fit in and they see the homey small town as a place that might accept them.

There's a bittersweet tone to this tale, because while I grew up in a welcoming small town myself, I also experienced how unwelcoming and narrow-minded they can be to anyone who doesn't fit into their neat mold, such as a nerdy kid who liked monsters and comic books and wanted to be a writer, for instance ...

JUST LIKE NORMAL PEOPLE

Pestilence had spread across the acreage adjacent to the road, through the hilly cornfields half a mile back, and all along the barbed wire fence lines. It looked as if the Grim Reaper had flown over at midnight and shaken the bad blood off his scythe blade, letting droplets poison the ground.

After years of producing nothing but horrors as crops, the farmer and his family had split up and fled Wisconsin in their separate directions, abandoning the land to seek a normal farm and a normal life.

For a pittance, Collier & Black's Traveling Circus and Sideshows had rented one of the vacant fields.

As the sun thought about setting and the muggy air hoarded its heat, the roustabouts set up tents and rides and midway games and concessions. The sideshow wagons pulled into their slots. The birds and bugs had quieted down for the afternoon; mosquitoes would soon be coming out in full force.

A few people from Tucker's Grove had driven by in old pickups on the county trunk road, slowing down to take a glance, then speeding up as they saw the surly looking strangers pitching the tents and stringing the lights—not the type of people normal folks wanted to be seen with. Some farmhands might finish their chores and creep over to get a preview after dark, but most would wait until crowds and daylight made it safe to look around....

Two of the sideshow freaks hiked away from the main activity with their own peculiar gaits, heading toward the blighted cornfields, as if drawn there. The two had been together a long time, and they knew how to walk side by side, adjusting to each other's pace. Scarecrow remained silent, while his companion jabbered, as always.

"Something ain't right around here," said the Raven, indicating the sick and stunted trees along the fence line with his stubby arm. He scampered ahead with a birdlike gait, jerking his elbows behind him and up in the air. Cocking his head, he added, *"Rawwwkk!"* for good measure.

The Raven's grotesquely outthrust face made him look like a surly bird. During shows he wore a costume adorned with black feathers, but even without the plumage his dark skin, his mannerisms, and his raucous voice kept him in character. In cut-off trousers for the humid heat, the Raven's short legs looked like drumsticks. His large eyes glinted black as he jerked his attention from one sight to another. "You know where we're going?"

Beside him, Scarecrow sighed. "No. I just want to be away from the sideshow for a while. I'm tired of getting stared at everyplace we go."

He looked into the rows of weirdly rotten corn: freakish corn, as misshapen as he and the Raven. Purple-gray blobs of smut oozed from the cornstalks. One of the ripe ears had split open, showing sharp kernels like the yellowed teeth from an old skull.

Scarecrow shambled along, flopping his many-jointed arms and legs in the choreographed jittery walk he had learned to master. Tall and gangly, he wore patchwork clothes, mussed his blond hair, and seesawed too much as he moved, like his namesake from *The Wizard of Oz*. But his sunken skull-face and dead-man's skin made no one look at him as a lovable buffoon.

All summer long as the circus worked its way across the Midwest, both he and the Raven would wander around the midway before and after their scheduled appearances in the sideshow tent, handing out leaflets, fascinating the towners, and steering them toward particular shows. The two freaks were comic relief, horrid enough to titillate the customers into wondering what *else* might be lurking inside the sideshow tent.

Today though, with the roustabouts doing all the setup, Scarecrow and the Raven took the opportunity to blow the show for an evening. But Scarecrow wasn't certain if he wanted to come back. What, after all, would they really be leaving behind?

They passed a dead chokecherry tree so gnarled that it looked as if a huge hand had crumpled it. The bark writhed in the heat, contorting into silent screaming faces. The tall crabgrass hissed like a pit full of snakes. Virginia creepers had twisted into the rusty barbed wire fence, snapping the posts with slow violence.

Keeping his voice neutral, Scarecrow gestured into the cornfields, toward the low hills. "Let's go straight that way. The farmhouse should be over there."

He plunged into the rows of sharp, drooping cornstalks. When his arm brushed one of the ripe ears, the kernels burst like a line of boils, splattering yellow pus onto his patchwork clothing. A very odd place indeed.

The Raven leaped into the field, knocking down stalks and flapping his stubby arms. "Look! I'm doing your job for you, Scarecrow!"

He startled several crows, which flew toward the sanctuary of trees along the fence line. Through the fluttered blur of black wings, one of the crows appeared to have two heads.

Scarecrow watched but said nothing.

～

THE DIRT LANE ended at a cleared yard where the nameless farmer had once lived. An old, dilapidated barn stood near the toppled carcass of a windmill, but only a foundation with burned timbers, broken glass, and scorched ground marked the former location of the farmhouse. The floor had caved in, showing the cellar to be an empty pit.

Scarecrow stared. The air was silent. He heard no birds. The sky bled orange with sunset, and the breeze died down.

"Over here!" the Raven said, hopping up and down beside the hulk of a tractor. One giant wheel had slumped off its axle and fallen to the ground. Black oil oozed from the crankcase into the dust. The rest of the body sagged under its coating of rust.

Flopping his arms and popping his knee joints, Scarecrow ambled over to the tractor. Behind it, a wide rake had been attached, the kind with hundreds of detachable tines used to roll new-mown hay into a long swath that a baler could scoop up. The rake was blood-rust brown, with globs of dust-clotted grease cementing it to the hitch of the tractor.

"Here, here!" The Raven cocked his head and jerked his protruding chin to indicate the rake's claws.

Though dead weeds and clumps of crabgrass covered the farmyard, every scrap of vegetation had been erased in a circular swath extending outward from the rear of the tractor, as if the plants had pulled up their roots and fled.

Scarecrow could not bend down the way other people did. Instead, he marshaled all of his joints and *folded* himself down closer to the ground, wrapping his body into a tighter package so that he could see.

One of the detachable tines was strikingly different, oozing a rainbow-colored light like an oil slick on a dirty parking lot. It was a smooth metal claw, a talon of steel designed to rip into the dirt and tear the soil free for the crops—but this one *felt* different from all the seemingly identical tines on the tractor rake. He touched the cold, weirdly slick metal, the center of the whirlpool of strangeness here. The curved tine seemed to pop off in his hand, jumping into his grasp as if it wanted to be free of its attachment. Scarecrow held it up to the failing light of sunset.

"What is it, Scarecrow? What did we find?"

Scarecrow could feel the fundamental oddness of the piece of metal. Was it a freak of nature? Had it been fashioned from a meteorite fallen from the sky? Or had it been dipped in human blood? Or forged by a blacksmith with murderous thoughts in his heart?

"Something that doesn't belong here," he said, caressing its edge with an extra-long finger. "I wonder if the farmer even knew about it."

Scarecrow held it as he stood up, unfolding and straightening himself, snapping joints into place until he was reasonably sure his body would hold him upright. Scarecrow could not understand it himself, but he felt a kind of affinity for the anomaly, the out-of-place metal. Something that normal people would never understand. "I think I'll take it with us."

The Raven looked toward the darkening sky, at the burned-out ruins of the farmhouse, at the distant field where the traveling circus had set up. "Shouldn't we ... get back?" he said. He cocked his eye at the dead spot on the ground, performing none of his antics now.

Scarecrow had no interest in returning just yet. "No." He nodded toward the barn. "Let's spend the night here."

Oil-stained rags had been tossed next to rusty coffee cans filled with equally rusty nails. Three empty bottles of Southern Comfort lay label-up in a corner. The upper loft held a dozen old bales of hay, their fresh green-tan turned gray with age.

The Raven scrambled up to the rafters and tucked himself into a V-brace, brushing fat spiders out of the way and wrapping one stubby arm around the beam. He stuck his distended face into his armpit and fell fast asleep.

Scarecrow lay down on the hard-packed dirt floor. He tossed and turned, finding little comfort, but enjoying himself nonetheless just to be spending a night away from the circus tents, the freaks' trailers, and the curious towners.

He clasped the prong-shaped piece of odd metal to his chest, as if it were a treasure, rubbing his many-jointed fingers along the slick surface, like Aladdin rubbing his lamp.

Scarecrow couldn't doze off: his mind crackled with images of the small Midwestern towns the circus had pulled through on its summer circuit, the homey, isolated villages so pleasant and so peaceful, the elm-lined main streets with white Victorian homes, the tire swings in the front yards, the town square with the hardware store and the drugstore and the independent grocer.

Scarecrow remembered in particular the churches, from the high-steepled Presbyterian or Lutheran buildings to the Catholic churches with long purple-prosy names. In Tucker's Grove, as the circus trucks and wagons passed down Main Street, the signboard in front of the Methodist church had caught Scarecrow's eye. "Sunday Service—All welcome." The phrase in quotes denoting that week's sermon read, "We are all God's children!" It struck him with the force of a hammer blow.

All welcome. He wondered if he could believe it. *We are all God's children!*

Scarecrow knew about the towners who came to gawk at the sideshows, laughing and pointing their fingers, saying the same crude comments—he and the Raven had to endure, continue to look freakish because that's what the towners paid to see. But after diverting themselves with the circus, the normal people could go to their normal homes, play their normal card games, listen to their normal radio programs, go to their normal churches.

He drifted on the surface of sleep, with vivid images sprouting in his mind like a bumper crop, and he saw *himself* without his freakish exterior, clothed instead in a normal body. He could have been a steadfast farmer, tall and blond like many of the Nordic settlers of the area, hardworking. He would have suntanned skin, and dirt under his fingernails, and a huge appetite for a home-cooked meal after a day working out in the fields or in the barn. He could have been a pillar of the community, not a leader but just a wholesome, honest worker like these other good folk.

Into his dreams came the Raven, too, but without the defective body-costume his genes had forced him to wear—Raven might have been an eccentric but friendly shopkeeper, maybe running the drugstore or the hardware store, a good-humored stout man who took in strays, fed birds, let kids build a treehouse in the big elm in his front yard....

As dawn brightened the sky, he felt his heart ready to burst with genuine longing and envy. Scarecrow knew he had seen what he and the Raven were really like inside, their true worth—and he was certain the townspeople would see it, too.

Scarecrow picked up a rock and hurled it toward the rafters. It clattered and bounced around the thick beams. The Raven awoke with a squawk and fell to the ground. Some instinct made him flap his stubby arms, as if he had forgotten that he couldn't fly. He landed with a thud and turned a somersault, opening and closing his mouth in silent gapes like a blind chick. "Whaaaaat?!"

Scarecrow tucked the wondrous metal tine into his patched pocket as if it were some sort of treasure; he was sure it had something to do with his vision, a funhouse mirror that brought reality into a clearer focus.

"Come on," he said. "It's Sunday. We're going to church."

～

THEY ENTERED Tucker's Grove amid stares of horror, fear, and amazement—but Scarecrow and the Raven were used to stares. They had spent over an hour walking along the country roads, shuffling in the dandelion-choked gravel by the shoulder. A pickup truck roared by, and the driver hurled an empty beer can at them, which banged and clattered on the pavement.

Tucker's Grove Welcomes You! read the sign at the town limits, adorned with emblems of the various civic clubs, the Lions, the Rotarians, the Optimists.

The two companions passed along streets of quiet houses, then up Main Street, where the shops were all closed for Sunday morning. Above their heads, squirrels chattered in the branches of the elm trees. The center of the town drew Scarecrow like a magnet. The curved metal piece in his pocket pulled him along.

Finally, they stood on the well-maintained sidewalk of the white-washed Methodist church. Scarecrow imagined monthly church get-togethers, families spending a Saturday afternoon weeding, mowing the church lawn, trimming the bushes. A true sense of community and home, the way Scarecrow *should* have felt back at the circus and among the other sideshow people.

He touched the curved tine in his patched pocket. It felt slippery and cold even through the fabric, strange, unusual, wonderful.... Maybe he would offer it as an unexpected gift to the kind pastor in charge of this church, set it gleaming in the middle of the offering plate as it was passed from hand to hand. Scarecrow and the Raven could settle down, become part of Tucker's Grove, fit in like real members of the community.

The early church service had already begun. The congregation sang an opening hymn in a group voice that blurred the melody and the words. The organist lifted the singers along with the force of the music.

Scarecrow opened the door just as the congregation fell silent for the opening prayer. Most of the people did not turn around, focused on the service, thinking that perhaps some oversleeping member had arrived a few minutes late.

But children dressed in stiff, uncomfortable clothes squirmed to look at the freaks, eyes widening to the size of plates. The rest of the congregation did not notice until the pastor himself raised his head from the beginnings of a prayer. His jaw dropped, and he stopped in the middle of a word.

Scarecrow unfolded his long arm and then unfolded his index finger, indicating the outside. "All welcome," he said. His voice cracked.

This startled the pastor, and his expression changed, as if he found himself trapped by his duty. "Please find a seat," one of the ushers whispered. Scarecrow felt no warmth or welcome from the words.

The pastor raised his hands to the rest of the congregation. "Shall we continue our prayer?"

The people in the pews mumbled along, reading the words of a preprinted prayer in their bulletins. Scarecrow and the Raven went to the empty back pew closest to the door. The ushers stood at attention, perhaps hoping the two would go away. Tentatively, showing some fear, one usher handed Scarecrow a mimeographed bulletin that listed the order of hymns and prayers, a program for the sermon and offertory and benediction.

The pastor was a gray-haired man, clean-shaven, with wire-rimmed glasses that looked sharp on his face. Deep lines around his mouth made him appear to be pursing his lips like a chimpanzee. He finished his prayer and called out the next hymn just after the two newcomers sat down. Scarecrow sighed and went through the process of unfolding himself again to stand up. His many joints ached after having spent the night on the hard dirt floor.

Using his long fingers to shuffle through the pages of the hymnal from the pew pocket in front of him, Scarecrow located the proper hymn before the end of the first verse. Beside him, the Raven jostled and fidgeted, making harsh singing noises without paying much attention to the words.

The congregation members surreptitiously found excuses to turn around and glance at the two. A fat little boy picked his nose and flicked a booger toward the Raven, who lunged forward to catch it in his distended mouth. In the pew in front of them, a prim family shuffled toward the aisle, moving one row up and squeezing in with the already-crowded people there. The pew ahead of Scarecrow and the Raven stood empty, like a barrier between them and the others.

Scarecrow felt a stab of disappointment. They had both joined the circus because the normal world would not accept them, but the small Wisconsin towns had seemed so different, so welcoming, like a place from a fairy tale. An illusion.

The pastor began to read a passage from the Old Testament. It had something to do with demons and the devil walking among men, but Scarecrow found himself staring dreamily at the walls adorned with paper butterflies that had been cut out and finger-painted by Sunday School children. A bright poster said JESUS LOVES ME!

The pastor began his sermon, but his thoughts rambled, and Scarecrow could determine no point to the lecture. The pastor stuttered and lost his place several times, frequently glancing back toward the two newcomers. A sheen of sweat stood out on the man's forehead. Scarecrow felt a heavy ache in the pit of his stomach. Apparently, not everyone was welcome after all.

Raven fidgeted against the hard, wooden pew that was not conformed to his lumpy back. As he squirmed, he made cheeping noises that sounded too loud in the sanctuary.

The sermon ended, and the ushers marched up the aisles to take two offering plates from the pastor's extended hands.

Scarecrow fidgeted, realizing that neither of them had any money—but he took out the wondrous, otherworldly tine from his pocket. It would be a strange offering, but it would be magical. Something these people had never seen before. Maybe that would make everything better.

As soon as the Raven realized what the offering plates were for, he hopped to his feet, jerking his elbows up in the air. "Whaaat? They want us to pay?" He looked down at Scarecrow with his black-lacquer eyes. "It ain't even much of a show!" His voice was raucous and loud enough for everyone to hear. "Cheat! Cheat!"

A man stood up three rows in front of them. His face was livid below his greased hair. His suit had gone out of style a decade before. "I've had just about enough of this ... this sacrilege!" He seemed pleased to have an opportunity to use the portentous word. Several others spoke their agreement.

The ushers stopped their offertory and uncertainly marched toward the back, glancing at each other as if they had never dreamed they might have to act as bouncers. Soon most of the congregation was shouting.

The pastor banged his hands on the lectern for quiet and turned his attention to the freaks. "I think it would be best for you two to leave now," he said. His voice was low and menacing. "You've caused enough trouble in my church."

As he gripped the slick tine with his overlong fingers, Scarecrow heard an echo in his head, shadows of words, as if he could see into what the self-controlled pastor was actually thinking, the phrases the man really wanted to shout.

We hate you! You're too ugly, too strange! You are not wanted here. Go back where you belong, despicable freaks! You're loathsome. You're not NORMAL like we are.

Scarecrow stood, slowly unfolding himself from the hard pew. His long legs made him appear to be rising, rising, like a cobra from a snake charmers basket. The Raven hopped onto the pew seat, standing up and glaring at the congregation with his vulture-like face. Saying nothing to the pastor or the people, Scarecrow nodded to his companion, unable to express his disappointment. "Come on," he said, "let's go."

The Raven gave an excited caw and leaped over the back of the pew to the rear aisle. As they walked toward the church door, adjusting to each other's gait again, Scarecrow expected the people in the sanctuary to cheer. The larger usher followed them to the door, but the other merely stared in silence.

All welcome! If any sideshow in Collier & Black's tried such blatant false advertising, Scarecrow thought, the owner would be locked up for fraud.

∾

THE MORNING WAS fresh and full of sunshine as he and the Raven stepped outside. Behind them, the door closed, and Scarecrow heard the click of the lock. Muffled through the walls, the organist threw herself into playing a hymn so that the whole congregation could heave a joyous sigh of relief.

With the church barred behind them, Scarecrow and the Raven stared out at the masked town of Tucker's Grove. Few other man-made sounds came to them: an occasional car driving by, some people working outside, three children playing. Several blocks away, the Presbyterian and the Lutheran church would be having their services; Catholics would be at Mass. He and the Raven would have received a similar reception no matter where they had gone. *All* normal people *welcome.*

Slowly, feeling it cling to his fingers as if it had been coated with drying slime, Scarecrow pulled the metal tine out of his pocket. The curved shape gleamed like a claw in the humid air. The idea came into his mind, but he couldn't tell if it came from himself or ... something else.

The Raven hopped a step back. "Whatcha gonna do? Whaaaat?"

"I'm giving them a gift," he said. "A glimpse of something—a show like they've never seen before."

Scarecrow bent at the knees, extended his long body forward, and stretched his arm down to the ground. He thrust the sharp metal end into the manicured lawn with a sound like an ice pick going into meat.

He hesitated as other, innocent images came to him: church socials with kids and their parents, old people, teenagers laughing and working together, children squealing as they jumped into piles of leaves, bankers and dentists pulling up weeds, housewives serving up orange drink and almond windmill cookies to everyone. He thought of the congregation praying for each other when they grew sick, helping out when times were hard, laughing together at church craft fairs or bake sales or ice-cream socials.

Scarecrow dug the tine into the ground again, as if stabbing a sacrificial knife into the chest of a victim. He pulled the curved piece along as he took a step backward. The lawn and the dirt parted like flesh in a rotten fruit.

With his strangely sharpened vision he saw the tine open a bloody furrow in the earth, splitting the grass and leaving a pulsing red-purple wound that glittered with shadows. Heat and a lava-light rose from the gash with an odor like the breath from a furnace cooking spoiled meat.

"Follow me," he said, listening to his instincts, to what the unearthly artifact *wanted* him to do. He wondered at the destruction at the old farmstead, what sort of poisoned life the farmer had had and how he had been unable to bear seeing the veils slashed away.

With the Raven keeping his distance, Scarecrow worked his way backward across the lawn, ripping the gash open wider. He turned the corner and passed under the stained-glass windows, pulling the furrow along with him. Inside, he heard the pastor reading a passage from the New Testament.

One step at a time, Scarecrow scribed a bloody ring around the church, where all were *not* welcome. When he had dragged the scarlet tip across the clean cement of the sidewalk to meet the beginning of his circle, he thrust the tine into the dirt like a nail holding the ring together. That would be his offering to this congregation.

When he let go of the tine and stood all the way up to survey the raw furrow he had made, he saw nothing other than a scratched line in the dirt.

Inside, the pastor raised his voice in benediction, and the organist played the postlude as the churchgoers buzzed with conversation, no doubt tittering over the excitement they had experienced that morning.

Scarecrow and the Raven stood out near the street under a tall oak tree. "Watch," Scarecrow said.

The doors flew open, and four rowdy—but well-dressed—children burst out, crossing the invisible boundary, and brought themselves to a standstill. Other congregation members strolled out looking smug and self-important as they chatted about their business, the crops, the weather.

A broad-shouldered and jowly man caught sight of the two freaks standing on the sidewalk in front of the church. His face turned florid, and he pointed at them while grumbling to another deacon beside him. Like bouncers in a roughneck bar, they strode forward as the other people emerged from the church.

"Uh, we should go!" the Raven said, flapping his arms in alarm.

"Go!"

But Scarecrow remained where he was, rigid and watching. His vision sharpened, darkened—and as the people crossed the line he had drawn in the soil, he watched their masks peel away. He snapped up his awkward head and stared at details he had not seen before.

—The little bald pharmacist, with the twinkle in his eye and sugar-free candy for little kids, who added a little "extra" to some of his prescriptions for people he didn't like, giving them an attack of diarrhea.

—The tallest boy in the choir, desperately clean-cut, out in the darkness of the milking barn with three of his friends, whispering "Hold her steady! Hold her steady!" as he thrust his erection inside the confused cow. The others would each have their turn, after the first had "loosened her up." They had made a pact among themselves never to tell anybody....

The crowd stopped in their tracks, milling about. Some people screamed at what they saw in the faces of those they had known all their lives. Some were appalled by their neighbors, while others were repulsed by *them* in turn. It was a regular freak show.

—The old woman who fed stray dogs hamburger laced with ground glass to "teach them a lesson for pooping on her yard."

—The Sunday School teacher who had been planning how to invite several of the young boys over to his house, where he could have some "fun," the details of which he himself had not yet decided.

—The unmarried bank teller who took a vacation each year to visit mythical relatives in Milwaukee, though her primary objective was to hang out in pool halls and pick up as many city men as possible, preferably two or three a day. Last time she had come back home to Tucker's Grove with syphilis....

As Scarecrow watched, he felt more than vindictiveness or revulsion—he sensed an eerie fascination at these flaws and shames of others. He realized with a start that this must be what the spectators experienced when they came to look and point and titter at the freaks in the circus. He pitied them.

Hearing the babble of frightened commotion, the pastor himself strode out of his church. He looked around, saw the freaks on the outer sidewalk, and then he marched forward, taking charge, intending to throw them off the church property. And then he crossed the line.

—The pastor added false backs to the drawers in his dresser, where he kept bras and panty hose, negligees, and other items of women's clothing he liked to try on and model for himself in front of a tall, bordello-style mirror. Even this morning, as the pastor gripped the lectern, flecks of bright whore-red nail polish clung to his cuticles.

The congregation members turned on him like a wolf pack, shrieking in horror at yet another exposed small-town secret.

As Scarecrow and the Raven turned to leave the screams and commotion behind them, he could still see the shadows of the real people here, the fat women and the ugly men, the pimple-faced teenagers, scarred and retarded people who had no other place in the world. They had turned their scorn upon Scarecrow and the Raven—misfits even worse than they—upon whom they could dump their own shame and revulsion.

"It's only right for them to know just how normal they really are," Scarecrow said.

He also realized that the previous night's rose-tinted dream—him steadfast and hardworking, Raven good-natured though eccentric—was not how things *might* have been without their freakish exteriors ... but how the two truly appeared in their hearts.

As they walked away, Scarecrow hesitated once, looking back toward the church. He had left the wondrous tine behind, thrust into the dirt. The artifact pierced the masks all people wore, and he could imagine its incredible power.

If he took it with him back to the circus, he would be able to see Collier and Black for who they really were—harried businessmen full of bluster but caring deeply for their show—or the big-hearted fat lady, or the game hucksters who sometimes gave the most wonder-filled kids an extra chance at the games, or the cook who always did his best to help them get by....

No, Scarecrow decided he didn't need the tine after all. He might not be a perfect judge of character, but he knew his friends well enough. He felt the empty pocket of his shirt. The skin on his chest tingled where it had touched the tainted metal.

Scarecrow and the Raven walked without shame down the main street of Tucker's Grove as the day grew brighter and warmer. "If we hurry, maybe we can catch the show before they pack up and leave," Scarecrow said. "I don't think there's any particular need for us to part company with them."

"Nope," said the Raven, who hopped ahead, excited. "Nevermore!"

As I continued writing stories about Tucker's Grove, I eventually fleshed out the history of the town, from its founding in the 1800s to the modern day. This story bridges the two time periods. It's influenced by the wonderful Richard Matheson novel (and equally wonderful film) Somewhere in Time.

Even across history, sometimes lovers get to have happy endings. Sometimes they don't.

MIRROR, MIRROR ON THE WALL

C louds congealed in the sky like a smoke pudding. The weather report on the TV news talked about severe storms, heavy rains on the way.

Thunderstorms fascinated Peter D. the way a rattlesnake fascinates a mouse, and he stood in the shelter of the old house's front porch watching the clouds, smelling the ozone in the air, waiting for the crack of lightning and the roar of thunder. He could sense a raw, elemental power just waiting to be unleashed on the thirsty cropland.

If piddling Kansas twisters could transport little girls to the Land of Oz, he thought, what could the whim of a big-blast Wisconsin thunderstorm do?

The first raindrops smelled like metal as they came down. When a stray horizontal gust splattered him with raindrops, Peter D. pulled open the screen door and darted back inside the farmhouse. Within moments, heavy rain began to rattle the rippled windowpanes.

As the storm built, the ancient Waltercroft house creaked and groaned. At least the tornado siren from nearby Tucker's Grove hadn't sounded—not yet. Peter D. empathized with the people who had lived in this same house a century before. He tried to transport himself mentally into the past, smelling the dampness in the air, the wood of the old house. How could he write about history, even a piddling history of Rutherford County, if he didn't *feel* it? It sounded like some creative-writing class exercise.

In the hallway Kathy tugged his arm. "Come on, Peter D.—we're alone at last. Better make the best of it." She used her playful voice. She was 23, half a year older than himself, both of them fresh out of college with liberal arts degrees, neither having the slightest clue what they wanted to do with their lives.

Only an hour ago, his eccentric aunt Lillian had driven away on her Florida vacation as what she called a "doozer" of a storm built overhead. While Lillian was gone, he and Kathy would house-sit and work on their local history book that his dear old aunt had convinced her women's club to sponsor.

Now he turned to Kathy, stroked her short brown hair. "Why, what did you have in mind, ma'am?" he drawled in what he considered to be a passable Rhett Butler imitation. They had been together for two years, yet still found opportunities to act like high-school sweethearts. "This is a respectable old house. We should act appropriately."

Kathy arched her eyebrows. "Appropriately? The original owners must have fooled around sometimes."

He slipped his arms around her waist and glanced up at their reflection in the antique hall mirror. Aunt Lillian once told him the mirror had been hanging in that hallway undisturbed, open and glazed as a dead man's eye, for more than a century (and she should know, he thought, since she was almost that old). "Look at us, the perfect couple."

The thunderclap sounded like the eruption of a Midwestern Mount Vesuvius. A jolt ran through the walls, threatening to knock the entire Waltercroft house off its foundations. The lightning flash, simultaneous with the thunder, was blinding, disorienting, powerful.

Peter D. found himself sprawled on the hardwood floor, knocked flat as much by the sound as by the blast itself. He rubbed at the blotches of color that danced in front of his eyes. Kathy lay next to him, trying to focus her eyes. He grabbed her shoulders. "You all right, Kath?"

"Just rattled." She sounded confused. "Listen. Did you hear something?"

"My ears are ringing louder than an out-of-control stereo." Peter D. shook his head to knock his brain back in place.

"—struck by lightning," a young man's voice said.

"What if the roof is on fire?" A woman's voice this time, frightened, followed by a sudden gasp. "Will! How are we ever going to explain you being here?"

Peter D. got to his feet and helped Kathy up. The voices were coming from the hall mirror. "What the hell?"

The decor shown in the reflection did not match the actual things in Lillian's home. The furniture looked old-fashioned, but the pieces themselves were new. Peter D. turned around to see Aunt Lillian's TV on its imitation-wood stand, the paperback historical romances strewn on the coffee table, curio shelves on the walls filled with ridiculous knick-knacks from the old bat's world travels. None of those things showed up in the mirror.

The young couple talking in the reflected parlor were definitely not Peter D. and Kathy.

"She looks like Jane Seymour in *Somewhere in Time,*" Kathy whispered.

"Somebody better start playing the *Twilight Zone* theme."

"It's raining too hard for the house to catch fire," said the young man in the mirror. Will? He looked about twenty years old, with blond hair and a few wisps of beard. "It'll be all right, Audrey. I promise." He placed his hands on her shoulders, projecting calm confidence.

The young woman was seventeen or so, quite pretty, with big eyes and long brown hair wrapped up in an intricate bun, leaving a few curls to hang at the sides of her face. She gazed at Will for a moment, then slid into his arms for a hug.

Peter D. raised his voice to the mirror. "Hey, can you two hear us?" The figures in the reflection did not react, even when he repeated the question in a loud shout. "I guess not."

With her face pressed against Will's faded work shirt, Audrey's voice became muffled. "You should get going now—Nels will be home soon."

"He doesn't even care about you."

Audrey drew back in alarm. "He *owns* me! You'd be a thief stealing one of his possessions—and he has the right to shoot any thief he catches in his own house."

"He doesn't have the right to ruin your life."

Audrey kissed his continuing scowl away. "He saved my life, remember? Please don't make things worse by getting yourself killed."

As Audrey hurried the young man toward the front door, Will glanced at his reflection in the hall mirror. He seemed to stare directly through Peter D. "Something's wrong with your mirror. I can't see my reflection."

Audrey was concerned only with getting him out of the house. "Nels will know how to fix it. Now you have to go."

Before the door swung shut, the young man called, "See you next Wednesday!" and Peter D. could hear a horse and wagon departing. Audrey didn't even look at the mirror on her way to the parlor, where she sat in silence, trying to compose herself.

"From their clothes, I'd place those two in the mid-to-late 1800s." Kathy headed to where boxes of old records and local books sat on an enormous dining room table in front of seven potted geraniums. "We've got three names—Audrey, Nels, and Will —connected to this house. With all the research material your Aunt Lillian left here, we should be able to find out something." She was always the "hard facts" person, while Peter D. considered himself the "creative genius in training." For a project like this, they were a perfect team.

Not long afterward, another voice came out of the mirror. "Damn storm hit me half an hour before I got to Tucker's Grove."

Nels was a tall, sturdy man of about forty, his light brown hair just on the verge of turning gray, with rugged features that showed no hint of softness. His blue eyes glimmered with a common-sense intelligence. His flannel shirt and overalls were faded and worn to the point of being comfortable. By the careful way Nels wiped his boots on the front rug and looked around the foyer of his house, Peter D. imagined him to be a hard-working man.

Soaking wet, he carried a brown paper package, which he had

shielded with his body in an effort to keep it dry from the downpour.

Audrey stopped several steps away from him, well out of reach —trying to hide her fear? discomfort? Peter D. couldn't tell. "You'd better change your clothes. You're getting the floor all messy." Her voice held nothing more than the required emotion as she said the required comment.

"I still need to do some chores outside. I just … stopped in to see you."

A long silence.

"How was Bartonville?" She was obviously forcing herself to talk to him, but the chill in her voice was obvious.

Nels extended the package to her. "I got you some sewing material. You can make a new dress."

She stepped forward to take it from him, tugged on the strings and brown paper to reveal a pale, flower-print material. "Thank you, Nels," she said with no warmth or genuine thanks. She retreated toward the parlor with her package.

"Who was here?" he said quickly.

She froze, her back to him. "Who said anybody was here?"

"I can see the cart tracks out front, Audrey. Who was here?"

Audrey finally faced him. "Mrs. Litch came, from church. Just after the storm." Peter D. thought he saw defiance in her eyes as she told her bold lie. "She wants every family from around town to make one square for a community quilt they're going to auction off at the church. That's why she was here."

"She couldn't have come *after* the storm." Nels kept his voice carefully even, though he seemed charged with more static electricity than any thunderstorm. "There's only one set of wheel tracks in the mud, leading out from here. And a dry patch where a wagon sat during the storm."

Fear sparkled in Audrey's eyes. "Maybe she came before the storm, then. I can't remember. We were talking." Then, with a hint of exasperation, she added, "Shouldn't you be out doing your chores?"

Peter D. noticed Nels clenching his fists as he turned and pushed his way back through the front door.

~

DURING THE NEXT THREE DAYS, Kathy buried herself in the names and dates of Rutherford County, poring over the data and waiting for her mental junction-boxes to throw the proper information into the proper places.

Before leaving for Florida, Lillian had gathered all the local historical documents she could find: birth records, death records, tax records, court records, even a boxful of yellowed letters, diaries, and postcards gathering dust in the attics of those "nursing home fixtures" Aunt Lillian resented so much. Everything was grist for Kathy's data-crunching mill, raw material to be digested into a detailed story that Peter D. would tell with all the verve he could muster. Kathy chewed the pink erasers off pencil after pencil—it helped her concentrate, she said.

"Want to hear a rundown of everything we can get from names and dates?" She tapped her pencil on the legal notepad where she had jotted her thoughts. "Nels Waltercroft, born March third, 1854; married Leilah Miller in 1880—he was twenty-six. He built this house, and the two of them lived in it for ten years until Leilah died. Seven years later he married young Audrey Bailey. She was seventeen, he was forty-three. Audrey died on August 25, 1897— less than a year later. Nels never married again and died in 1901."

Peter D. paced the room, tapping his fingertips together as he painted a picture in his mind. "How did any of them die?"

"These death records aren't very explicit."

He looked over her shoulder to scan the notes on the yellow pad. "What about that Will guy?"

"No way of knowing. No last name, no other concrete information. I can't work miracles."

"I beg to differ." He gave her a peck on the cheek.

Peter D. stationed himself in a folding chair where he could watch the mirror. Restless, he waited for something important to happen. He toyed with Aunt Lillian's enormous collection of knick-knacks, even tried to read one of her romance novels, and kept Kathy supplied with fresh pencils.

"This really gives me insight into how boring life was in those days." Peter D. said. "No TV, no video games, no stereo, no internet, nothing to keep you occupied at all. Get up with the sunrise, go to bed shortly after sunset, unless you feel inclined to light a lamp. Just listen to how quiet the house is! It's enough to drive you up a wall."

At the moment, in the mirror, Audrey was alone in the house, writing in some sort of diary. "No wonder so many people kept journals … although why anyone would want to relive an uneventful day is beyond me." He stopped as an idea occurred to him, then looked closer at what Audrey was doing. "Wait a minute! I've seen that book before."

He hurried to the boxes of records, shuffling through them until he held up a faded brown book and flipped to the front page. "Audrey Waltercroft's diary."

Thrilled, Kathy took the book from him, flipped pages, looked for dates. "She didn't write in it every day, so the entries are sporadic. They start a little before she married Nels." She thumbed through the journal to where the writing ended, leaving half a book of blank paper. "And the last entry—an interrupted one—is dated Saturday, August 21, 1897."

Peter D. did the math. "That's only four days before she died."

Her eyes darted along the neatly written words on the first several pages. "Listen to this—the Bailey family home burned down when she was seventeen. Nels came to help put out the fire and rescued Audrey from the burning house. Later, when the Methodist church took the family under its wing, Nels asked Mr. Bailey for his daughter's hand in marriage, in gratitude for rescuing her."

Peter D. snorted. "As if she *owed* it to him!"

Kathy could not take her eyes from the pages. "Well, it makes a lot of sense, given the time. Audrey was old enough to be married, and Nels Waltercroft could certainly support her. Remember, her family had lost everything in the fire, and Audrey was one more mouth to feed. Nels offered to take her away from all that, so her parents consented. Good deal for everyone."

"If you say so."

Kathy bent closer to the faded handwriting. "I'm reading from Audrey's diary now: 'Nels is a good husband, in his own way. He provides for me, but he doesn't love me, or at least he never shows it. I want the man that I marry to love me with all his heart—like Will does. I have always loved Will. He's such a kind and loving person. Even the animals love him! Will is going to be a horse doctor. He finds hurt animals and tends them. We were going to get married, but we'd decided not to tell our parents until he saved up some money. That was before the business with Nels.

"'Will and I still see each other every Wednesday, when Nels goes to Bartonville to pick up supplies. It's our only chance to be together, but better that than nothing.

"'I know that what Will and I are doing is wrong—but what Nels did to me was wrong, too. I don't have to feel guilty! I love Will, and that's all the reason I need.'" Kathy frowned, turned several pages, then closed the book. "The entry just stops there … and it's the last one."

"A little anticlimactic," Peter D. said. "But it sure explains the frostbite I got when Audrey and Nels were talking."

In the hallway, Audrey's voice came from the mirror. "What are you doing here? It's Saturday!"

Will laughed. "Nels is in town, so I figured he wouldn't be here."

"But he could be back any minute—"

In the mirror, the young man had a definite swagger. "Nope. He's getting the horses shod at the blacksmith's, and he's having a wheel fixed on the wagon. He'll be gone all afternoon—and *I'll* be right here. Come on, it's a beautiful day. Let's go for a walk down the lane."

After they went out through the front door, Peter D. saw that Audrey had left her diary open on the table.

When Nels returned home later that afternoon, Audrey did not come to greet him, merely acknowledged him from the kitchen. As the man strode into the parlor, his pale blue eyes were drawn to the open diary on the table like iron filings to a magnet. He moved silently over to pick up the book, his forehead furrowed with curiosity. He began reading the latest entry.

"Uh-oh," Peter D. called from his chair by the mirror. "Nels just found the diary."

Kathy hurried over. *"Everything's in there."*

Nels's eyes went wide as he continued to read. First his expression registered shock, disbelief, then horror. His big hands trembled and clenched as if he were trying to rip the book in half, then he squeezed his eyelids shut so tightly that he squeezed out tears. But he kept silent all the while. Nels stood rigid for a full minute until he managed to compose himself. He closed the book with an awkward gentleness and placed it under some papers at the bottom drawer of his writing desk. With calm deliberation, he locked the drawer.

"I guess everybody can't be the perfect couple, like we are," Peter D. said.

Nels gripped the back of a chair as if he needed support, then cleared his throat. When he spoke, his voice was surprisingly firm, loud enough for Audrey to hear him in the kitchen. "I saw Mrs. Litch in town today."

Silence hung in the air for a moment before Audrey's reply came from the other room. "Oh? What did she have to say?"

A long pause, and Peter D. waited for the man to throw his accusations, to expose his young wife's lies. Nels took several long breaths and said instead, "She said she looks forward to seeing your quilt square completed."

Suddenly, the pieces fit together in Peter D.'s mind. "Hey, Kath— you said the last entry in Audrey's diary was on a Saturday, right? And it was an interrupted one? In the mirror, *this* is Saturday. And Will interrupted her this afternoon while she was writing … and now Nels has locked the diary away. I get the feeling Audrey isn't going to be writing in it again."

"The plot thickens." Kathy snapped her fingers as an idea occurred to her, and she shuffled through a pile of papers until she found the one she wanted. "I should have thought of this before. On August 25, 1877—the same date as Audrey's death—a William Jacobsen, age twenty, also died. August 25, by Audrey's diary, was a *Wednesday.*"

"They always met on Wednesdays," Peter D. said.

Kathy looked at him with wide eyes. "Aww, no—Nels? This Wednesday?"

"They're going to be murdered in four days. And all we can do is wait, and watch."

~

THE FOLLOWING DAY he and Kathy observed as poor Audrey searched frantically through the parlor for her diary but did not find it. Peter D. paced the front hall, angry, sad, and helpless. He tried shouting to the young woman, pounding on the mirror glass, but could not get her attention. Audrey moved unsuspecting, one day at a time, toward the date of her death.

"Hey, mirror, mirror, on the wall! How can we stop this from happening?" Peter D. said. He received no answer, and he got the feeling there would be no fairy-tale ending for Will and Audrey.

He saw Nels's mood steadily darken. The man's eyes were puffy and red, bloodshot, as if he passed his restless nights plotting instead of sleeping. He and his young wife barely spoke to each other. Audrey must have sensed that something had changed, but she refused to broach the subject.

Now that they knew the exact dates, Kathy found an entry in the Rutherford County court records: "Nels Waltercroft acquitted of the murder of his wife Audrey and her adulterous lover William Jacobsen." During the brief trial, Nels had offered the diary as evidence of their affair, which was all the straight-laced judge needed to see. The book had survived locked away in a court vault until Aunt Lillian resurrected it for their historical project.

On Wednesday morning Peter D. watched the mirror with growing horror when Nels left, as he always did, supposedly off to distant Bartonville. Not long afterward, Will appeared, taking Audrey in his arms and leading her into the parlor. The young woman needed his comfort and his love with a level of desperation she had not showed before. Will dismissed her worries, but Audrey seemed more fearful than ever. She told him what Nels had said about Mrs. Litch, how he should have caught her in the lie, and how her diary had now gone missing.

But Will erased the fear from her eyes as if she were a bird with a broken wing that needed mending. He brushed away her tears, stroked her cheeks to calm her. They began to kiss on the sofa, steadily becoming more caught up with each other.

These two reminded him very much of himself and Kathy, a couple meant to be together, and he admired Will's strength and confidence, his ability to show his love. Peter D. would have made wisecracks instead, trying to get Kathy to laugh.

The young couple in the mirror were already doomed. They had been murdered more than a century ago.

And it was going to happen again in only a few minutes.

Peter D.'s stomach churned, and his pores wept tears of sweat. "I hate feeling so helpless!" He clutched one of Aunt Lillian's inane knick-knacks—a cheerfully painted vase that said "Greetings from Puerto Rico." He should have taken Kathy off on a sunny vacation somewhere rather than staying here in this house with dreary historical records and old tragedies.

Standing close to him, squeezing his other hand, Kathy stood engrossed in the mirror. She choked back a muffled cry as the door opened silently and Nels entered the front hallway, cradling a shotgun in his arms. Tears streamed down his weathered cheeks, and his whole body trembled. His skin had a grayish tinge, as though he were about to be sick.

Peter D. nearly crushed the Puerto Rico vase in his sweaty hand.

Nels strode forward like a thunderstorm and loomed in the hallway, staring at the two kissing in the parlor. His face twisted into an anguished expression, and he let out a bestial cry.

Audrey looked up and screamed. Will tried to turn in his shock.

Nels raised the shotgun and pressed his eyes shut as he squeezed the trigger.

Peter D. hurled the knick-knack at the mirror. "No!" It was the only thing he could think to do.

The roar of the gunshot sounded simultaneously with the crash of breaking silvered glass as the vase struck the mirror.

Another violent jolt went through the Waltercroft house, and a roar of thunder detonated in the air. When the mirror shattered, the whole house writhed on its foundations. Splintered glass reflected random timelines in different directions, bouncing possibilities into alternate futures, leaving the future to change the past.

And *Now* changed instead.

❦

LILLIAN HESITATED, then decided to hang up the phone, leaving her nephew's number undialed. Writing a history of Rutherford County would have given Peter D. a chance to showcase his writing talent, but she was sure he'd make some derisive joke about the project. Better if he never even knew of her silly idea.

Here in Rutherford County, local historical landmarks were few and far between, now that the subdivision builders had torn down the old Waltercroft house. Even the locals had little interest in forgotten people from an unremarkable past.

In the cramped kitchen of her "senior" apartment, Lillian went to the coffee maker and poured the untouched pot of old coffee down the drain before starting a fresh batch. Lillian never drank coffee, but she loved the warm, roasty smell of a brewing pot. It helped ease the annoyance of being trapped in an old timers' complex—"Prep School for the Nursing Home," she called it. But she had nowhere else to go.

Lillian had uncovered many fascinating Tucker's Grove stories to share with Peter D., excellent fodder for a historical book, in her opinion. As his aunt, Lillian had always felt free to give him ideas for novels, hoping he would take up writing again. Given Peter D.'s creative streak, he must be bored in his dead-end job as a bartender. She wanted to be supportive of the poor boy, but her goof-off nephew had been moody and withdrawn since he'd broken up with Kathy. She had always thought the two made a wonderful couple.

Lillian kept waiting for him to snap out of his funk. "Here's a wonderful romantic story about the old owners of the Waltercroft house," she wanted to suggest to him on the telephone. "A young girl was torn from her true love and forced to marry a cruel old farmer, but the girl never stopped loving her young beau. Corny, right? When the farmer found out about the affair, he took up his shotgun and went to confront them. But—surprise!—he was struck by lightning on his way to kill the two. Struck dead by a bolt out of the clear blue sky. Not a cloud in sight. Can you believe that?"

Of course, Peter D. would have groaned and rolled his eyes,

dismissing the tale. "Yes, I know it's a true story, but people just won't believe it. Too much of a coincidence for fiction. There has to be some *reason* for things like that to happen."

Oh well, she supposed he was right. Lillian wished Peter D. could be happy. He and Kathy had been so captivated by each other, so in love, just like the young couple in the story. She sighed. Things change, and sometimes there's no explanation.

The bitter smell of coffee began to fill the kitchen.

When I learned that Shakespeare's famous Globe Theater had burned down during the initial performance of his play, Henry VIII, *I began to sense the possibility for a story. When I discovered that the theater itself had been torn down and rebuilt using the same wood, and that some players may or may not have been murdered there ... well, I decided it just had to be a ghost story.*

After having my fiction appear for years in numerous small press magazines, "Final Performance" was my very first professional sale, to The Magazine of Fantasy and Science Fiction.

FINAL PERFORMANCE

Scene I.

"London, this last day of June, 1613. No longer since than yesterday, while Burbages' Company were acting at the Globe the play of Henry VIII, *and there shooting off certain (cannons) in way of triumph, the fire catched and fastened upon the thatch of the house, and there burned so furiously as it consumed the whole house, all in less than two hours, the people having enough to do to save themselves."*

—Thomas Lorkins, eyewitness to the burning of the Globe Theatre.

Setting—London. Night. *The charred ruins of the Globe Theatre. Little remains of Shakespeare's playhouse: skeletal, blackened beams, the stone foundations. It is late November, 1613—a light dusting of snow covers the ground.*

Enter Cuthbert Burbage, *half-owner of the Globe, brother of Richard Burbage, who is the famous actor of the Lord Chamberlain's Men, Shakespeare's company.*

Strange how silent London was so late at night. The houses surrounding him were dark, all candles extinguished for the night as sleeping townspeople huddled under deep piles of blankets. It was a cold November.

His breath congealed into thick plumes of steam as he walked, looking upward at the stars—intensely bright in the cold, crisp air. His left hand was kept warm from the rising heat of the lantern he carried, spilling out a small pool of dirty, orange light on the snow ahead of him. The numb fingers of his right hand groped among the folds of his coat pocket, searching for warmth.

Burbage's cheeks were flushed, and his ears hummed in the silence; his belly felt warm and full from the several tankards of beer he had drunk at the inn. The loud voices and forced laughter still rang in his ears. But everything else was silent now, the night air with barely a breeze, the thin covering of snow which seemed to muffle his footsteps. He had so little to do now—and it would remain the same all winter—with only his trips to the inn, until spring. In spring he and Richard were going to rebuild.

His footsteps impressed black marks on the new snow in Maiden Lane, and he stood before the ruins of the Globe. Only a few charred beams stood upright, painted white with a thin coating of snow—like the skeletal remains of some mythical beast. It was dark, and he could see little by the light of his feeble lantern: a pile of burned timbers and blackened foundation stone blocked his view of the stage.

A sadness filled him—perhaps the beer made him more susceptible—but it was an eerie, powerful, almost tangible emotion. This, the greatest theatre in London, which once had seated fifteen hundred people, now stood a pile of cinders and lonely ash.

No one had died in the fire, even though they had had a full house that last day. Well, one *had* died ... but not from the flames. Burbage had carefully covered that up: the brothers planned to rebuild the Globe, and superstition would drive people away from a playhouse where it was known a murder had been committed.

The external feeling of sadness strengthened, and waves of despair and pain buffeted him, seeming to emanate from the ruins, like the cries of a mortally wounded animal in its death throes. Burbage frowned: he hadn't realized how much beer he had drunk. Now, perhaps, he understood the way Richard felt every time he came near this place.

But then Richard had always been the sensitive one, the one so filled with passion. At times, Burbage envied his brother, who was so sure of himself always, totally devoted to his profession as an actor. Richard's one desire was to perform on stage, and he did such a tremendous job. He lived for the Globe—Shakespeare himself had written many parts specifically for him to portray. Cuthbert Burbage had also acted on stage, only occasionally; but to him it was nothing more than repeating the lines he had memorized, picturing himself as a tool to move the play along. For Richard the characters were *real*.

It was not a hating envy he had for his brother, but a gentle one. Richard had no doubt as to his calling in life. The other Burbage was still waiting for his own calling. He had acted at times, when it was necessary; and he also managed the Globe Theatre, because his father had bequeathed it to Richard and him—and because he did a good job at it. His brother was a superb actor, and he himself was a shrewd businessman. The combination worked well, the previous success of the Globe had proved that.

But he wasn't sure that the loss of the Globe was the only reason for Richard's recent moody behavior, his anxiety. Being as popular as he was, Richard had little trouble acting in some of the other theatres in London. But Richard had seen something that night, when the Globe had burned, something that had shaken him badly. Burbage had waited for his brother to tell him, waited; but it had been five months, time enough for Richard's wound to heal … or fester.

Perhaps things would be better come spring, when they could rebuild the theatre. Smiling vaguely, he remembered when they had first built the Globe, fifteen years before. Their father had built his own playhouse, the Theatre, in 1576—the first playhouse in all of London—in all of Europe, Burbage had heard (but who could possibly know all of Europe?). And on their father's death over twenty years later, the Theatre had passed on to Richard and Cuthbert Burbage—just as its lease ran out.

The landlord, one Giles Allen, was a singularly uncooperative man, despite Richard's impassioned speeches about an actor's need to have a playhouse in which to dissipate his creative energy, despite Cuthbert's tedious, patient negotiations. Allen had it in his mind to tear down the original playhouse because of "the greate and greevous abuses that grewe by the Theatre."

But the Burbages had turned the tables on him, tearing down the Theatre themselves and using the old wood, taking it to the south side of the Thames where they had erected the new Globe Theatre. Burbage chuckled aloud as he remembered Giles Allen, his face splotchy, almost exploding with anger, cheated out of destroying the playhouse himself.

His low chuckle seemed alarmingly loud in the deep silence. Around him, the snow seemed to muffle all other sound; even the wind had stopped. He tensed as his ears, numb from the cold, picked up a low sound, a strange sound. The thin blanket of snow had been left undisturbed since the last snowfall early the previous morning—only his own footprints left a trail to the ruins. He was the only one around—he had to be. The effects of the beer buzzed in his ears—perhaps they were playing tricks on him. He took another step into the ruins, stopping beside a blackened beam fallen at an odd angle. He rested his hand on the charred wood; melted snow ran along his fingers, carrying black particles of soot. He listened again, and he was sure. He looked at the snow around him—no one had entered the ruins in the past day.

Yet inside, unmistakably, he heard voices.

Scene II.

On December 28, 1598, Richard and Cuthbert Burbage "and divers other persons, to the number of twelve ... armed themselves ... and throwing down the sayd Theatre in verye outrageous, violent and riotous sort ... did then also in most forcible and ryotous manner take and carry away from thence all the wood and timber thereof unto the Banckside ... and there erected a newe plahhowse with the sayd timber and woode."

—Giles Allen, in a lawsuit against the Burbages in Middlesex Court.

Setting—London. *The Globe Theatre, intact, before the burning. Morning. In the basement under the stage is Thomas Radclyffe, a young actor, rehearsing his lines, making sure he is satisfied with their delivery. He has been cast as Henry VIII in Shakespeare's new play, All is True, which will be performed for the first time at the Globe this afternoon.*

The basement is dim and shadowy, lit only by the light shining through the open trapdoor of the stage. It is cluttered with old props, a discarded mask of a ghost from an old play, costumes hang from sharp garment hooks on the wall beams.

Radclyffe closed his eyes tightly. He *was* Henry VIII. He filled his chest, thrusting it forward in a kinglike manner; he propped one hand on his hip. He imagined himself to be dressed in the garments King Henry wore in the portraits he had seen. His personality was putty, changing, fitting into a new mold, as an actor was required to do. He was almost ready.

His master, Havermont, had shown him this technique to *know* his characters, to *be* the people he was to portray. Radclyffe had been attached to Master Havermont almost seven years, lodging and boarding with the experienced actor since he had been ten years old. Thomas Radclyffe had been an extremely apt pupil—a bit impulsive, a bit impatient, his master had said, but Radclyffe wasn't sure now if the impressions he had given hadn't also been mostly an act.

After sending him through the typical women's roles—the bane of all apprentices before they started to sprout whiskers—Havermont had prepared him for the veteran actor's own particular types of parts so that Radclyffe could take his place at the time of his master's death.

And now Radclyffe had had the role of Henry VIII pressed upon him. Havermont had died suddenly; Radclyffe was not yet quite prepared, and perhaps he had let it go to his head a bit—his first salaried role, and it was *almost* the leading man. Radclyffe took it seriously—he always took his acting seriously—spending much of his free time down here, in the musty peacefulness of the basement of the Globe, where he could be totally alone, and let his dialogue fall into the quiet psyche of the theatre.

The lines came into his head—he was ready for them. He took up where he had left off the day before, trying to set his mind in the same mood. King Henry has just been informed that the people are outraged over a new tax, levied by the evil Cardinal Wolsey—no, not "evil," not yet, the King still considers him a trusted friend— Wolsey, played by Richard Burbage, the *real* star of the play, the part written by Shakespeare especially for Burbage. But the audience would go from the play remembering *him*, Thomas Radclyffe, Henry VIII.

He lowered his voice, taking on a forgiving, almost condescending tone, placing himself into the reality of the play. He is a king, he told himself, about to remove a tax he considers unjust, a tax which he has known nothing about, which Wolsey has placed upon the people but has just denied doing so. The King holds Wolsey as friend and believes him.

"'Things done well and with a care exempt themselves from fear; things done without example, in their issue are to be fear'd.'"

"Louder." Radclyffe reacted instinctively, raising his voice.

"'Have you a precedent of this commission? I believe, not any.'"

"More regal—more pride! With rising anger!"

"'We must not—'" He paused, looking around the shadows of the basement, frowning. "Who is there? Who has spoken?"

"With rising anger! What is the next line? 'We must not rend our subjects from their laws, and stick them in our will.' This must be spoken angrily—not in a condescending tone."

Radclyffe became distressed, looking around the cluttered, cobwebbed shadows of the Globe's basement, but saw no one. He listened to the voice, trying to pinpoint it—but it was a whisper, an echoing mélange of voices.

"Where are you?" Then his eyes centered on something, propped up against the wall, a mask of a ghost, used once for the part of the ghost of Hamlet's father. He felt an eerie chill crawling in the skin of his back. "*What* are you?"

Radclyffe moved toward the mask slowly, afraid, but intrigued. *"A part of your profession. A muse? No, not quite so ... quaint. We ARE the Globe Theatre."*

Radclyffe picked up the mask, his fingers trembling. He looked to see if anything hid behind it—nothing. The frozen, empty mouth of the mask continued to pour forth its words.

"Thirty-seven years ago, James Burbage built the Theatre—the first playhouse in all of Europe. And then his sons Richard and Cuthbert

Burbage tore it down and used the same wood to build this, the Globe Theatre. Can you think that all those performances, year after year, all those actors pouring their souls into these walls, could have no effect on the wood of this place? A part of it remains here. We are the soul of this playhouse—and you shall perform as we direct you when you perform on our stage, in our walls."

"No!" Radclyffe cast the mask back to the ground. The eye holes continued to stare back at him. Anger and pride sprang from his years of training. "I would be *no* actor if I did only as you tell me. My Master Havermont has taught me to be a great performer. He has shown me that I am to interpret the characters as *I* choose; I am to say the lines as *I* decide. The acting must come wholly from *me*, or else I am just repeating words. Master Havermont is right, and I cannot listen to you."

He had never doubted the existence of ghosts—nobody in London did. But he knew that ghosts were probably evil—and probably dangerous.

The voice paused, taking on a more sinister tone. *"You hold your dead master in high esteem, then?"*

"'The gentleman is learned, and a most rare speaker; to nature none more bound; his training such that he may furnish and instruct great teachers, and never seek for aid out of himself.' Indeed, I hold him in esteem."

"Then do you not think a part of him abides with us?" The voice was different now, familiar ... Havermont's voice.

"Be silent! I will believe that part of him abides with you—if you are truly the leavings of great actors—but it is a *bad* part, much like the scum on top of a beautiful pond. My master would never counsel me to listen to every whim of a spectator! I will speak *my* lines, with *my* voice, and *my* mind!"

Radclyffe turned, anger on his face, perhaps to cover his fear, and stormed toward the basement steps. Suddenly he was slammed against the wall by unseen hands and held there by a force he could not define. His eyes began to show fear. The voice came at him from every beam, every shadow.

"We have more power here than you think! You would be safer if you did not resist!"

Radclyffe used his anger again to push off the paralyzing fear.

"'Be advis'd; heat not a furnace for your foe so hot that it do singe yourself!'"

Radclyffe flailed his hands in the air as if to fend off the unseen enemy, and he broke away, running quickly up the stairs.

Scene III.

"Yea, truly for I am persuaded that Satan hath not a more speedy way and fitter school to work and teach his desire to bring men and women into his snare than these ... plays and theatres are, and therefore necessary that these places and plays should be forbidden and dissolved and put down by authority."

—John Northbroke, a clergyman, *A Treatise against Dicing, Dancing and Interludes with other idle pastimes* (1577)

Setting—The uppermost floor of the Globe Theatre, just under the thatched roof. Raw beams cast odd shadows. Cuthbert Burbage is loading gunpowder into one of three cannons, props, which he is preparing as a stage effect for the afternoon's first performance of All is True.

Enter Thomas Radclyffe, *moving tentatively, looking nervous, a little shaken.*

Burbage kept his eye on the stream of black powder, pouring slowly so as to spill none of it. He heard the young actor approach. "One moment, Thomas ..." he said aloud, and thought he saw Radclyffe jump, startled, from the corner of his eye. Burbage inspected his work and looked at the other two cannons for a moment, then turned to face Thomas Radclyffe.

The young actor fumbled with his words for a moment, and found it easiest to say, "What are those for?"

"They are cannons, Thomas! Stage effects! You know, in the first act, when you, King Henry, and your party enter Cardinal Wolsey's palace all cloaked and hidden? Well, when the King enters, we shall fire these cannons—armed with only paper wadding, of course—to let the *audience* know that the royal presence has just arrived—and also to give them a little start!"

Burbage smiled, rubbing his hands together, then looked at

Radclyffe, dissolving his expression into a frown. The young actor was pale and gaunt, obviously frightened. "And where is the bold, proud young actor who drives us all nearly mad with his outbursts of eagerness?"

Radclyffe seemed to fumble for words; he found different ways for his fingers to interlock with each other. "Well, Mister Burbage, sir, it is difficult to—"

"Speak!" Burbage snapped, not angrily, but with a tone of get-down-to-business that stopped all further stuttering from the young actor.

"Down in the basement—this theatre—Mister Burbage, there are *ghosts*!"

"*Hissst!*" Burbage turned him away, then looked worriedly down to the stage where some of the other actors were rehearsing. None of them seemed to be paying any attention. "King's deathbed, man! Hush when you speak of such things! Ghosts? If that rumor were to be unleashed, it would ruin us as surely as if we were to burn the place down ourselves!"

Burbage shook his head, concerned, then looked hard at Radclyffe. "Now, these ghosts—you have seen them? Where?"

"In the basement—I didn't *see* them, but rather heard them."

Burbage let out an audible sigh of relief. "The basement! Thomas, any man can get the jitters when he's alone down there among all the old props and shadows. The wood creaks a little, a few rats rustle about here and there. And your imagination makes the rest—"

"No! It wasn't like that, Mister Burbage! Not just odd sounds, but *words*! I had a conversation with the ghosts!"

"And what did these ghosts have to say?"

"They tried to force me to say my lines in different ways, making me act in their manner, and not my own. They tried to twist my talent, taking the … the *life* out of my portrayal."

Burbage almost laughed but contained himself. "Most ghosts try to murder people, Thomas—but your ghosts want to be your acting coaches!" He saw the expression on Radclyffe's face, became serious. "Maybe it's Havermont come back to help you?"

"No!" Radclyffe looked angry, upset, downcast. "You don't

understand! They are *evil*! They try to twist my acting talent to their own ends! I cannot perform that way!"

The young actor stopped and changed his emotions abruptly, saddened, almost accusing. "You can't understand—you're not an actor. You don't know what it means to me." He drew in a deep breath. "You don't believe me."

Burbage didn't. But he had enough tact to pause a moment, considering the best way to handle the young actor. He reached up to put a hand on Radclyffe's shoulder. "I know you, Thomas. I know that your temper is a little short, and that you are inclined to act without thinking sometimes. But I have never known you to have a wild imagination, and I have never known you to lie. Seeing this change in your mood, now, it is obvious to me that *you* believe what you say. But I ask you this, Thomas—say no word of this matter to anyone. If you must speak further on it, come to me, and only me. Surely you realize how this could ruin us if handled improperly. Any demon a man might find at the bottom of a bottle of ale would be seen as a ghost of the Globe—and people would flock away from this 'haunted theatre' as if it were a plague house! No, we must keep silent about this."

"But the ghosts will still be here!"

Burbage sighed. "Thomas, what would you have me do? I cannot get two strongmen and have them evicted as we would any other troublemakers!"

"Bring a bishop! Someone, anyone from the Church! To exorcise the ghosts!"

Burbage widened his eyes almost in shock. "A priest? King's deathbed, Thomas! Do you spend no time out in the city, or are you always sheltered here in the theatre? Have you not heard the Puritans' outcry against all places of amusement, theatres in particular? Did you not know that my father was forced to build the original Theatre outside the city of London because of the public outcry? And even then, he was brought before the London Lord Mayor in the Middlesex Court more times than you can count on your hands. No priest would come near the Globe unless he wanted to burn it down. The Puritans would like nothing more than to hear that Satan has haunted our playhouse."

Radclyffe seemed to hear, but not believe. He lowered his voice, almost glaring at Burbage. "You and your brother should never have used the old wood from the Theatre." Radclyffe's face was angry, and he turned to walk away.

"Thomas!" Burbage called, worried. The young actor didn't turn. "Don't do anything rash!"

Radclyffe didn't answer as he disappeared down the ladder leading from the loft. Burbage looked after him for a long moment, folding his lips into a troubled frown, then he began to load gunpowder into the other two cannons.

Scene IV.

"Things done well and with a care exempt themselves from fear."
—William Shakespeare, *Henry VIII*, first performed at the Globe Theatre, June 29, 1613

Setting—the basement of the Globe Theatre. It is mid-afternoon on the day of the first performance of All is True. *Upstairs, offstage, noises can be heard as people file in to fill the theatre. The play will begin soon.*

Enter Thomas Radclyffe, *afraid, but moving with determination. He carries a torch he has made, naked fire pouring light into the darkness.*

He paused, swallowing hard, forcing his mouth into a grim, determined line, holding the torch in front of him like a weapon. He filled his mind with anger and obsession. Martyr—like Buckingham in the play. If need be.

"Hear me, ghosts!" Radclyffe's voice trembled, then gained in strength. "You are evil! You are oppressive! You stifle the creative expression of all actors—I must destroy you to save my profession. 'Ye blew the fire that burns ye!'"

He picked up the mask from the floor. "What? Are you silent? Have you fled?"

Radclyffe dropped the mask and crushed it under his feet, finding a small, inadequate outlet for his anger and fear. He heard the people above, waiting for the play to begin. Someone would probably be looking for him.

"You are brave, young actor—are you not afraid?"

"'Things done well and with a care exempt themselves from fear.'"

Radclyffe looked up to find the source of the voice—and saw another mask, a new one he hadn't seen before, propped in the corner of one of the beams, finely painted and detailed enough to look lifelike. Almost lifelike. It was Henry VIII, but subtly, hauntingly, familiar, with definite traces of Radclyffe's own face embedded within the features.

The young actor shuddered briefly, then steeled himself. "I will burn this theatre down and destroy the cursed wood which you inhabit. You will not harm me—I have chosen this time with care—for if you do, you will expose yourselves to all of London!"

He waited for a reply, hearing only the crackle of his torch in the silence, until the voice spoke again.

"Ah, but you forget, young actor, that we ARE this theatre ... and when we are filled with an audience—" Radclyffe's torch was suddenly snuffed out, plunging him into darkness. *"We are strongest of all!"*

And he felt a cold, icy grip, not quite like hands, around his throat.…

Scene V.

Will not a filthy play with a blast of trumpet sooner call thither a thousand than an hour's tolling of the bell bring to a sermon a hundred?
—A preacher, Stockton, in a sermon against the Theatre, 1578

Setting—the ground level of the Globe Theatre; the yard is filled with people, trying to get a clear view of the stage, which is raised above the crowd. At the entrance stands a placard announcing the day's play. Similar leaflets are scattered throughout London, tacked onto wooden posts, competing with many other announcements.

As people file through the single, narrow entrance, a man stands with a small box in hand, collecting one penny from all who enter. Those who are content to stand continue into the yard; those who wish a seat or a private box are required to pay an extra sum.

Cuthbert Burbage *sits among others in a Twelvepenny Room, one of the best seats in the playhouse, with his guest, Lady Dalton. She is older than he, dressed in gaudy finery, decked with jewels. Burbage looks at the activity around him; he is impatient.*

"If they don't start soon, we won't finish the play before sunset," he muttered to himself. "Can't have a performance without daylight, you know."

"Cuthbert, this is so exciting!" Lady Dalton peered excitedly into the crowd, as if to find out which of her social acquaintances had failed to attend the play, and how many had failed to get seats as exquisite as her own.

Burbage looked at her, scowling slightly. The Lady Dalton was rather rich ... and rather old, and rather dim. Damn his business sense.

"Is Shakespeare *himself* here today, Cuthbert?"

"Of course, he is—" Burbage snapped, "You don't think he'd miss the first performance of his new play?" He caught himself, placing some sweetness into his voice. "There he is, just across the yard from us ... see, in one of the other Twelvepenny Rooms."

"Sooo!" she cooed.

Burbage looked around uncomfortably: he wondered if Radclyffe had been found yet. The play had to start soon—he was afraid the young actor was going to ruin his first important role by chasing after ghosts in his imagination. Radclyffe—don't be a fool!

The noises of the audience waned like a dying fire after one of the Lord Chamberlain's Men stepped out onto the stage, speaking the Prologue. People smothered their random sounds, focusing on the words being spoken, waiting to be taken away to another reality.

And the play began.

Burbage leaned back in his seat, relaxing slightly, or at least seeming to. They wouldn't have started the play without Radclyffe, even though he didn't make an appearance until the second scene.

Lady Dalton seemed to be more interested in the audience than in the play. Burbage watched his brother Richard perform, strutting around as Cardinal Wolsey in all his evil glory—Richard enjoyed the villain parts at times, but then Burbage could never tell what his brother really enjoyed and what was just an act.

(Wolsey accuses the innocent Buckingham, the martyr, of treason, and has him arrested, to be brought before the King's court.)

The first scene ended, and Burbage grew tense again. He sat up, waiting the unbearable few moments. Why was he uneasy? The performance was of prime importance—Radclyffe knew that—he imagined himself to be a devoted actor, and he would never miss his first important role.

The audience background noise rose up quickly for a few moments but was dampened again as Scene II began. King Henry entered with pomp and glory—and Burbage finally felt at ease. After all, he should never have been worried. He knew Thomas Radclyffe—the young actor had been so proud of himself after receiving this part that he wouldn't have forfeited this performance for anything.

Yet Burbage squinted—and thought he saw something strange about Radclyffe's face. Of course, the makeup would have changed it somewhat—but he thought he saw sharp edges, shadows, almost as if Radclyffe were wearing a very detailed mask ... but no, he could see the mouth move.

Still, he felt uneasy again. Lady Dalton probably couldn't even see that far.

"What's happening, Cuthbert?" she whispered.

Burbage almost imperceptibly rolled his eyes heavenward. "This is the trial of Buckingham at the King's court. Queen Katherine has just entered to beg the King to withdraw a tax which takes one sixth of every man's possessions—"

Lady Dalton seemed to be barely listening. "Who's Buckingham?"

Burbage sighed.

The scene progressed. Radclyffe's voice was the same, but Burbage seemed to notice some special quality, a lilt, an intonation, which made the young actor's voice stand out. Burbage had never considered himself a theatrical critic—he heard the lines, saw which ones were delivered more masterfully than others. And people paid to see the performances—he drew his livelihood from that. But he hadn't felt any special drive, any special presence about acting. Until now, in Radclyffe's voice, he felt the very embodiment of a performance, the life, the calling—yet he couldn't pin it down.

He couldn't say why, but he was somehow aware that Radclyffe was giving the best performance he had ever seen.

Richard, though, seemed to be acting strangely. There—he had just stumbled over a line. Richard had never stumbled over a line before, not in all Burbage's recollection. Was it jealousy? No, it was almost as if he were … scared of something. But what would Richard ever be so afraid of that he couldn't successfully cover it up?

The scene continued, and Burbage felt a low buzz in the audience as the people remarked on how outstanding, how superb, the young actor was. What would have seemed an almost interminably long scene any other time, now held them enthralled.

And at last the scene was over.

He felt a tap on his shoulder. Burbage was startled and turned to find the man next to him pointing out into the corridor where stood a young boy, one of the apprentice actors of the Lord Chamberlain's Men. The boy looked agitated, pale, and sweating. He seemed unable to speak but gestured desperately for Burbage to come to him.

"Excuse me, Lady Dalton," he whispered in her ear. She smiled. "One of my actors wishes to speak with me."

"Oh, of course, Cuthbert—please hurry back."

Burbage went to the boy as the third scene began. They spoke in quiet voices. "What is it?"

The boy was trembling. "I've found him, Mister Burbage!"

"What? Who?"

"Come! Quickly!" The boy took his arm and drew him down the corridor through the curtains behind the tiring room, backstage, and to the narrow basement steps.

"What could possibly be down here, boy?"

"He is dead, sir! *Murdered!* Thomas Radclyffe, sir! He's hung up on the wall, by his neck—on one of the clothes hooks!"

"You're *mad*, boy! He's just been—"

They entered the dimness of the basement, surrounded by the muffled echoes of the performance overhead. Burbage didn't need to look very closely to see a burned-out torch on the floor, and a shadowy figure hung on the wall with its feet dangling off the floor. And the face was that of Thomas Radclyffe.

"King's deathbed!" Burbage gaped a moment, realized what he was doing, then composed himself almost immediately, thinking fast. The boy stood next to him. Burbage made his face firm and expressionless, but he felt cold.

"This … could ruin us. A murder! At the Globe Theatre!" He looked quickly at the boy. "You have told no one?"

"No, sir! I thought it wisest to speak only to you!"

"Good! You are intelligent, boy. I have a gold piece for you if you tell no one. Not one word. If you *do* speak of this, I will find it very easy to destroy your acting career for the rest of your life."

"Oh, not one word, sir. Please don't feel you need to use threats, Mister Burbage."

"No … no. I know. I have to think of what to do. Keep quiet and be *sure* no one else comes down here. Calm. I must be calm. *We* must remain calm." He sighed. "I'd best be back to the Lady Dalton before she says anything. Until I can talk to Richard." He heaved a long breath, then muttered, "Oh, deathbeds for the entire royal family! How are we ever going to patch *this* up?"

They walked up the stairs. "But, Mister Burbage—if Thomas Radclyffe is dead down here … then *who* is on the stage?"

Burbage paused, gripping the rail. "I don't know … and I am afraid to know."

He walked slowly back and seated himself beside Lady Dalton as Scene IV was just beginning. He gripped the arms of the chair to stop his hands from trembling. Burbage was surprised to find her watching the play.

She pointed to the action on the stage. "What are they having a party for, Cuthbert?"

Burbage tried to get his mind back on the play, to focus on something other than his cold fear. "Uh … the Cardinal Wolsey, my brother Richard, is having a great dinner at his palace, with many lords and ladies. See … they're all sitting around having idle dinner conversation, until—" He waited: it would have been glee and childlike anticipation in other circumstances. Trumpets sounded; drums rolled; and the cannons blasted, thundering in his ears.

And as his ears rung, Burbage thought he heard Thomas Radclyffe's voice, somehow—the real voice, not the false acting voice on the stage, this was different, a whisper running through his head, though not intended for his own ears.

"Now, we fight on equal terms."

Unseen, some of the burning paper wadding settled on the thatched roof, smoldering, kindling itself, setting fire to the roof.

The Lady Dalton squealed in terror at the cannon sound, then in delight. The audience, half-deafened, murmured in confusion.

On the stage, a company of cloaked and hooded strangers entered, hiding their faces. Burbage continued to explain. "The Cardinal's guests think these are some foreign ambassadors—but they are really the King and his party in disguise. There ... that one is the King." Or is it something that I will never understand?—he thought to himself. There are more things in heaven and earth, Cuthbert Burbage, than are dreamt of in your philosophy.

"How do you know that's the King?" Lady Dalton asked.

"From the *cannons*—we wouldn't blast cannons for anyone but the royal presence, now would we?"

"Oh."

They watched as the hooded company made its slow procession across the stage.

"There, now Cardinal Wolsey suspects that one of the masquers is the King ... he says as much ... and he decides to unmask him...."

Burbage watched his brother walk on the stage toward one of the hooded figures, reaching up tentatively—more tentative than he actually should have been. He gripped the folds of the hood and began to draw it back.

"FIRE!" someone shouted.

Suddenly all hands were pointed toward the thatched roof which was in flames. Others took up the cry; tumult erupted. People fled toward the single narrow entrance.

On the stage, Richard Burbage cried out wildly; his face was white as a sculpture. The hooded figure was gone, the false Thomas Radclyffe, vanished; unnoticed in the uproar.

And flames began to devour the Globe.

Scene VI.

"... some of the Paper or other stuff wherewith (the cannons) were stopped,

did light on the Thatch, where being thought at first but an idle smoak, and their eyes more attentive to the show, it kindled inwardly and ran round like a train, consuming within less than an hour the whole House to the very ground ... yet nothing did perish but Wood and straw and a few forsaken cloakes. Only one man had his breeches set on fire, that would perhaps have broyled him if he had not by the benefit of provident will put it out with bottle ale."

—Sir Henry Wotton, eyewitness to the burning of the Globe Theatre

"*... while Burbages' Company were acting at the Globe the play of* Henry VIII, *and there shooting off certain (cannons) in way of triumph, the fire catched and fastened upon the thatch of the house, and there burned so furiously, as it consumed the whole house, all in less than two hours. the people having enough to do to save themselves.*"

—Thomas Lorkins, eyewitness to the burning of the Globe Theatre

Cuthbert Burbage found his brother Richard, much more shaken than he should have been from the fire, standing in the churning crowd around the flaming wreckage. Night was falling. A heavy beam collapsed in a shower of sparks.

Silently, together, they watched their Globe Theatre burn....

Epilogue.

Setting—London. *Darkness. Cuthbert Burbage has entered the cold, snow-covered wreckage. Voices.*

He listened, creeping closer—the voices were strange and scattered, speaking a pastiche of lines from old Shakespeare plays. They didn't sound like children's' voices: in fact, they seemed to carry a great deal of emotion, sadness, loss.

He stepped around some fallen timbers and came in view of the burned-out remnants of the stage. In the shadows he saw strange figures, masked and costumed.

"What are you doing there? Who are you?" Burbage shouted, his anger rising before he had time to think. He expected them to scatter and run like frightened children, but instead the figures turned to look at him.

Burbage stepped out from behind the wreckage and moved toward them. "Where did you get those masks?" he demanded, trying to place a tone of angry command in his voice.

The central figure turned toward him; he wore an old mask of the ghost of Hamlet's father, smashed-in but painstakingly repaired, blackened a little in the fire. He spoke in a deep, eerie voice, like many voices all in one.

"We are the Globe Theatre, and we are almost dead. Do not disturb our final performance."

Burbage halted a moment, then stepped forward. "You are trespassing," he said coldly, standing directly before the figure, glaring at the mask. He saw nothing behind the eyeholes. Nothing.

They confronted each other in silence; and, unexpectedly, Burbage reached up to pull the mask off. And beheld the face of a leering skull, desiccated and fire-blackened.

Before Burbage could cry out, the mask was snatched away from his numb fingers and placed back on the figure's head.

Burbage felt cold, and his eyes misted over with terror and confusion. *"What* are you?" The words slid through his clenched teeth like a cold wind.

"A truly talented actor leaves a part of himself, part of his soul, within the theatre in which he performs. This wood, these timbers, are from the very first playhouse in all of Europe, which has absorbed countless performances.... We are what is left."

Burbage first began to tremble. *"You!* Ghosts! You are what Richard saw! You killed Thomas Radclyffe! Murdered him!"

"We acted only to protect ourselves. In vain."

Burbage stood motionless, only his thoughts whirling—fear, anger, confusion—and he could not function until he accepted his inability to accept. "I do not understand ... I cannot believe this."

"You are not an actor. You will not understand." The central figure continued to stare at him with the frozen expression of the mask. *"Tell your brother Richard—he will understand. It will comfort him. He knows us, but he does not realize it. Tell him not to fear us."*

Burbage found he had taken one step backward, and another.

The masked figure raised his voice. *"Leave us! To complete our performance!"*

Burbage felt his fear taking precedence over all his other emotions, and he took another step backward, staring at the troupe of spectral figures one final time. Then he turned to flee from the ruins of the Globe Theatre.

The wreckage of the Globe lay in Maiden Lane, covered with snow, until the winter of 1614 passed.

"And the next spring it was new builded in a far finer manner than before."
—Master John Stow, *General Chronicle of England.*

When we were first dating, Rebecca diligently read most of my stories. After she'd finished quite a few, she gave me a near-impossible challenge: "I want you to write a story that has a happy ending. Something romantic for a change."

This was her Valentine's Day present.

FROG KISS

He had gotten used to it by now. The frog tasted cold and slimy against his lips, with a taste like brackish water, mud, and old compost. But Keric gave it a dutiful smack on its mouth, hoping that it wouldn't suddenly turn into the fat old king, who had also been enchanted, along with several more desirable members of the royal family.

But the frog just looked at him, squirmed, and then urinated on Keric's palm. Nothing. Again. He took a dab of red pigment from his pouch, smeared it on the frog's head, and then tossed the creature through the trees and marsh grass. He listened to it plop in another pool. Another one tried and failed.

Around him, the sounds of thousands of frogs croaked in the dense swamp, loud enough to drown out the whine of mosquitoes, the constant dripping of water, and the occasional belch of a crocodile.

Sweat and dirty water ran in streaks from his brown hair, down his cheeks, and avoided the frog slime around his mouth. He had caught and tested more than three dozen frogs already, but it would be years before he could find them all—and that was only if any members of the frog-cursed royal family remained alive in the deep swamps. A crocodile splashed somewhere out in the network of cypress roots and branches. Somehow Keric couldn't imagine the brittle old Queen Mother deigning to eat flies, not even if they were served to her by someone else.

When the evil wizard Cosimor had taken over the kingdom less than a year before, he had followed the traditional path of sorcerous usurpers by capturing the entire royal family and transforming them into frogs and then turning them loose in the sprawling, infected swamps of Dermith.

Cosimor had intended to tax the kingdom to its death, drive the subjects into slavery, and generally keep himself amused. But less than three weeks later the wizard had died choking on a fish bone —no vengeful curse, that; simply poor cooking. Now the kingdom had been left without any rulers, not even the incompetent but somehow endearing royal family.

Keric, who lived in a hut on the fringes of the Dermith swamps, trapping muskrats and selling the fur in the noisy walled town, had decided to try to find the royal family in its exile, free at least one of them with a kiss, and then count on his reward. A palace of his own, perhaps? Gold coins stacked as high as an oak tree? Fine clothes. He pulled at his dripping, mud-soaked rags. Yes, fine clothes first. And then perhaps the hand of one of the princesses in marriage?

He spat drying slime away from his lips. But first he had to catch the right frog—and they all looked alike!

He slumped down on a rotting log covered with Spanish moss, then looked across at the piled undergrowth to see a bloated old bullfrog sitting under a drooping fern. Plainly visible on the frog's back were three equally spaced dark blotches, just like the supposed birthmark carried by every member of the royal family! Was this the old king, then? The fat duchess, the king's sister? It didn't matter to Keric—the frog sat right in front of his eyes. It had always taken him too long to see what was right in front of his face.

He didn't want to hesitate too long. Keric shifted his body forward and then lunged, splaying out his mud-caked fingers. He skidded through a spiderweb, needle-thin fronds, and dead leaves, but the bullfrog squirted away from him. He scrambled and grabbed again.

He didn't see the girl until she leapt out from the bushes in front of the bullfrog, opened up the mouth of a large squirming sack, and swept the frog inside. The bullfrog made a croak of alarm, but then the girl spun the sack shut. "Got him!" she said, giggling. Then she sprinted away through the underbrush, leaving only disturbed willow branches dangling behind her.

"Hey!" Keric shouted and jumped to his feet. He ran after her, flinging branches out of the way. He splashed through puddles of standing water, squished on sodden grass islands, and ducked his head in buzzing clouds of mosquitoes. All around, the other frogs continued their songs. "That one was mine!"

"Not anymore!" He heard her voice from the side, in a different direction from where she had disappeared. He looked in time to see her running barefoot down a path only she could see. Barefoot!

Keric ran after her. He found himself panting and sweating. He had grown up in and around these swamps. He considered himself an exceptional woodsman in even the deepest parts of the morass. He could outrun and out-hunt anyone he had ever known. But this girl kept going at a pace he could not hope to match. He stumbled, he missed solid footing, he splashed scummy water all over himself.

"Wait!" he shouted. He heard only the crocodiles growling.

"If you'd look over here, you'd have a better chance of seeing me!" She laughed again.

He whirled to see her across a mucky pool, not twenty feet from him. Without thinking—since he was wet and filthy anyway—he left the path and charged across the way. "Give me my frog!"

Keric tried to run with both feet, but each step became more difficult as the ooze sucked at his boots. He had to get the bullfrog with the three spots. He *knew* it was somebody from the royal family. The girl probably didn't know what she had. Maybe she wanted to eat it!

He sloshed onward, but before he had gone halfway across the pool, he felt the muck dragging him down. He sank to his waist and found he could not take another step. He continued to submerge in the ooze. "Oh no!"

From the spreading cypress tree over his head, he heard the girl's voice. "You should be more careful out here in the swamps. Plenty of dangerous things out here. Crocodiles, water moccasin snakes, milt spiders bigger than your hand, poison plants." Keric looked up to see her sitting on one of the branches, holding onto the frog sack with one hand and munching on a dripping fruit in the other. "But you really have to watch out for that quicksand. That's especially bad."

"Would you help me out of this?" He looked at her. He had sunk up to his armpits and felt the cold muck seeping into his pores. The mud crept to the tops of his shoulders. Keric had to lift his head to keep his chin out of the ooze. "Um, please?"

"I don't know. You were chasing me." She finished her fruit and tossed the pit down. It splashed beside him.

"I'll tell you what you've got in that sack of yours."

"It's frogs."

"No, if you'll just let me kiss one of them I'll show you something magic!" He had to talk rapidly now. The quicksand had reached his lips.

"Oh, you mean *that*! Sure, I've got the whole royal family here." She reached in and pulled out another frog, this one sleek and small. It also had the three identical splotches. "You don't think you were the only one to get the idea for finding the frogs in the swamp, do you?"

Actually, Keric *had* thought he was the only one to think of that. Once again, the obvious was staring him in the face.

"But you were going about it all wrong," the girl continued. "You kept trying to kiss them out here in the swamp. Now tell me, just what would you have done if the frail and arthritic Queen Mother had appeared? Or one of the dainty princesses who would squeal at the sight of a beetle? How would you get them back? Makes more sense to me just to carry the frogs in a sack, go back to town, and then change them all back. Reward would still be the same, maybe more for saving them the journey."

Keric had to lean his head back to keep his nose and mouth above the surface. "Will you please help me now and give me advice later!"

She shrugged. "You haven't asked me the right question yet."

"What is the question?"

"Ask me what my name is! I'm not going to risk my life to rescue a total stranger."

"What's your name? Tell me quick!"

"I am Raffin. Pleased to meet you." She paused. "And what's your name?"

"I'm Keric! Help!"

She tossed a vine down that struck near his face. Keric grabbed at it, clawing at the slick surface of the vine with his mucky hands. But he managed to haul himself forward, toward the near edge of the pool of quicksand. He heaved himself out onto the soggy ground and shivered. He had lost his left boot, but he had no intention of going back to get it.

When he looked up at the tree, Raffin was gone.

～

AFTER DARK, when Keric remained cold and clammy but unable to light a fire, he saw an orange light flickering through the tangled branches. He followed it to Raffin's fire, then crept close to where he could see.

She sat humming to herself and holding four sticks splayed in the flames. Little strips of meat had been skewered on the wood and sizzled in the light. The bound bundle of royal frogs sat beside her. "Come closer and sit down, Keric. You're making enough noise at being quiet."

Angry, Keric came out of his hiding place and strode with confidence into her firelight. Finally, he sighed and shook his head. "I thought I was good in the swamps, moving silently, always knowing my way. I can't believe I am being so clumsy around you."

Raffin shrugged. "You *are* good. The best I've seen. But I'm better."

Her long pale hair must once have been blond but now had taken on the color of fallen leaves and dry grass. Her eyes looked startlingly blue within the camouflage of her appearance. Raffin had washed most of the grime from her face, arms, and hands before preparing her food.

Keric didn't want to imagine what he looked like himself.

Raffin took one of the sticks out of the fire and blew on the sizzling strips of meat. "Frog legs, filleted." At his shocked expression, she laughed. "No, just normal frogs. Don't worry. Would you like some?"

Keric swallowed. "I haven't eaten anything all day."

"Say please."

"Please. Uh, I mean, Raffin, may I please have some?"

"Of course. You're my guest. I saved your life. Do you think I'd refuse a simple request like that?"

He took the stick she offered and ate the crispy meat right off the bark so he wouldn't have to touch it with his dirty fingers. "What are you doing out here all alone in the swamps?"

"I live out here. Don't worry, I can take care of myself."

Keric could believe that. He guessed she was only a couple years older than himself.

"But I don't mind company once in a while." Suddenly, Raffin appeared shy to him. "Just listen to those night sounds, the frogs and the humming insects. Why would anyone want to live in the town?"

Keric frowned and ate the last piece of meat. "Then why are you trying so hard to get the royal frogs?"

"Because you are. I've been watching you for days. It's been fun. Besides, I have dreams of getting a prince of my own."

They talked for much longer after that, but Keric could get no better explanation from her. He felt the weariness from the day sapping his strength, making him drowsy. He interrupted what she was saying. "Raffin, I am going to sleep."

He saw her smile as he let his eyes drift shut. "Make yourself at home."

When Keric cracked his eyes open again an hour later, his body screamed at him just to keep sleeping. But he couldn't. He had something much more important to do.

Raffin had stayed beside the fire, which now burned low and smoky, still driving the mosquitoes away. She lay curled up on the ground, her cheek pillowed on her scrawny arms. She looked very peaceful and vulnerable. Keric frowned, but then thought of palaces and princesses and fine clothes.

The fire popped as two logs sagged, and Keric used the noise to cover his own movements as he crept to his feet. She had left the sack containing the royal family sitting unguarded on the other side of the camp. He shook his head, wondering why she had made it so easy for him.

He picked up the sack and slipped out of the firelight, starting to run as soon as he got out under the moonlit trees.

"Keric!" she shouted behind him.

He stopped trying to be silent. The marsh grass whipped around him as he picked up speed. Willow branches snapped at his eyes. He kept splashing in puddles or flailing his hands at large, flapping night insects.

"Keric, come back!"

He didn't answer her but started to chuckle. He could make it out of the swamp to his hut. He would go immediately into the walled town and kiss all the frogs, even the old Queen Mother, and bring them back before Raffin could find him.

He used all his forest skills to weave his path. He couldn't hear her following, but then he doubted if he would. She was too good for that.

Keric looked behind him as he ran, seeking some sign. Raffin did impress him with her knowledge of the swamps. She could teach him many things. He decided he would share his treasure with her anyway, once he got it, but for now he wanted to succeed on his own, to impress her that his own survival abilities weren't so trivial either.

He tripped on the tail of the first crocodile and could not stop himself until he had stumbled into a cluster of the beasts. Once again, he had been looking in the wrong place and missed what was right in front of him.

The crocodiles hissed and belched at him. Keric cried out. He could count at least seven of them, startled out of their torpor and suddenly confronted with something worth eating. An old bull scuttled toward him, looking as large as a warship. It opened its mouth so wide that Keric felt he could have walked inside without ducking his head.

He turned and searched for a way out. Hissing and snapping their enormous jaws, the crocodiles moved in. The old bull lunged. Keric leaped back, caught his heel on the long body of one of the smaller reptiles, and sprawled backward. Even the smaller crocodile chomped at him. Keric dropped his sack of royal frogs.

He scrambled to his hands and knees, looking for an escape. The moonlight made everything dim and confusing. He thought he saw a flashing orange light behind a sketchy web of cypress roots, but he concentrated only on the nightmare of wide, fang-filled jaws.

Raffin appeared and struck the snout of the nearest crocodile with her roaring torch. "Get away from him!" The beast hissed and grunted as it lurched backward. Keric blinked in amazement. In her other hand, Raffin held a pointed stick that she jabbed at the remaining crocodiles.

The beasts backed away. The enormous bull stood his ground and let out a deep growl from somewhere at the bottom of his abdomen.

Keric crawled to his feet, too stunned and frightened to be much help.

Raffin faced the bull's charge and shoved her torch at her attacker. The crocodile hissed and snapped at her, but she was quick with the end of her torch, touching the burning end to the soft tissue inside the reptilian mouth. Keric heard the sizzle of burning meat.

With a defeated roar, the bull backed away and then, in a final gesture of frustration and spite, he lashed out with his long snout and snapped up the tied sack of royal frogs. The frogs made a combined sound like someone stepping on a goose. The giant crocodile crunched down with his jaws, chomped again, then swallowed. After a satisfied grunt, the crocodile crawled out of the clearing and splashed into the water.

"I told you to be careful out in the swamps," Raffin scolded Keric. "Do I have to watch out for you all the time?"

Keric sat stunned. "They're all gone! In one gulp, the whole royal family!" He shook his head. "I never meant for that to happen."

Raffin took hold of his hand and pulled him to his feet. "The kingdom will do fine without them. They weren't particularly worth rescuing." She stared at him, but he continued to sulk. "Hey, it was fun while it lasted."

"No, I meant my reward. The gold, the fine clothes, the palace—"

"And what would you do with all that stuff?" She looked at him, then tugged at his old, mud-caked tunic. "Fine clothes? Are you seeking what you really want, or just what you think you're *supposed* to want? What other people tell you to want isn't always right for you."

Keric lowered his head, sighed deeply. He looked at himself and realized she was right. "If I had a palace, I suppose I'd just track mud in it all the time."

Raffin giggled. "It's not so bad out here, you know."

"But what about my princess?"

Raffin flicked her hair behind her shoulders and looked angry for a moment, then spoke in a very shy voice. "You could stay in the swamps." She paused. "With me."

Keric looked up at her and listened to the frogs and the night insects. One of these days he was going to learn to notice the things right in front of him.

Clockwork Lives, *written with Neil Peart—the legendary drummer and lyricist for Rush—is probably my favorite of all my books. Set in the same universe as our steampunk fantasy novel* Clockwork Angels *(based on the Rush concept album of the same name),* Clockwork Lives *is even more ambitious, I think, a sort of steampunk* Canterbury Tales *all connected by a frame story. It is one of those times when, as a writer, I felt that everything just worked right. When Neil read the final manuscript, he wrote me to say, "I think this is the best thing you've ever written."*

Because I love all the stories in Clockwork Lives *so much, and because they are all interconnected, it's difficult to choose just one representative tale. But this one, "The Sea Captain's Tale," is one of my favorites—yes, again it shows my fascination with maritime legends. How does someone who grew up in the farmlands of Wisconsin and has spent more than two decades living in the heart of the Rocky Mountains get so interested in the sea? Maybe because it's so far away and mysterious.*

Attentive Rush fans will find a dozen or more Easter eggs in this story (no, I didn't count them all).

CYGNUS: THE SEA CAPTAIN'S TALE

(WRITTEN WITH NEIL PEART)

On my first sea voyage, a man jumped overboard in the middle of the night. He was laughing the whole time until the waves swallowed him. That was how I knew something else was out there.

By the time the other sailors threw ropes and life preservers into the water, it was much too late. They shone coldfire lanterns down on the placid waves, but the man did not call out for help—not once—and we saw no sign of him in the dark and moonless night.

Captain Macallan looked disgusted. He let the other sailors take out boats to perform a perfunctory search, calling out their comrade's name, but they received no response. Finally, the steamer sailed on.

"He didn't fall overboard, Captain," I said, jarring the man out of his disturbed thoughts. "He jumped on purpose."

The captain narrowed his eyes, measured me. "The angels got him," he said. "The angels of the sea."

Then he went back to his stateroom and locked himself inside.

I GREW UP IN HEARTSHORE, a small fishing village south of Poseidon City. My father was a fisherman, and I learned to walk on a deck before I walked on land. I fell asleep each night with the sound of the waves as comforting as my mother's breathing. The sea called to me, and when my father saw me gaze out at the waves, he clapped me on the back. "You're a born fisherman!"

But that wasn't enough for me. The fishing boats from Heartshore rarely lost sight of the coast, and my gaze stretched farther—beyond the horizon. Heartshore was a warm and lovely place, but I wanted adventure!

I set off to find my fortune when I was old enough to sign aboard a cargo steamer—which is not very old at all. I ran away from home and went to Poseidon City, where I loitered around the port until I found a steamer looking for a crew. I would receive almost no pay, but the captain promised "a wealth of experience." Only two days after I arrived in Poseidon, I was crossing the sea in a ship full of metals, minerals, and alchemical powders for export to Albion.

Sailors whispered about the angels beneath the sea, beautiful women who could play a man's heartstrings like a musical instrument. I suspected they were just stories meant to tantalize or alarm a gullible new shipmate. I had grown up with fishermen, after all, and I knew about stories that were never meant to be believed, no matter how well told. But the undersea angels didn't sound like the usual tall tales; in the sailors' voices I heard as much fear as wonder.

And then that man jumped overboard in the middle of the night. Maybe he had seen the angels for himself, or believed so with a fervor that verged upon insanity.

For the rest of that first voyage, I stared over the edge of the steamer, looking in vain. I would go out at night and listen, trying to hear their mysterious song. But the sea kept its secrets, and I heard no ethereal voices beautiful enough to drive a man mad.

Not that time at least.

THE STEAMER ARRIVED in Albion to dock in Crown City. I was wide-eyed with wonder, the only one aboard who hadn't been there before. The other crew laughed and joked, telling me about sights I could see or incredible items I could purchase (many of which I didn't even understand, but I nodded sagely anyway, pretending to be mature beyond my years).

Standing on the deck, I jabbered about how I wanted to see the Alchemy College, Chronos Square, the Mainspring Hub where all the steamliners came and went, the majestic Watchtower that was said to be a mile high if it was an inch—and most of all, the Clockwork Angels.

But the captain put his hand on my shoulder, more like a vice grip than a paternal pat. "To a gullible boy like you, Crown City is more dangerous than a hundred undersea angels. Be careful. We set off at high tide on Wednesday. With all those clocks in Crown City, you'll have no excuse to be late. Better you stay close to the ship. You can always see more next time—if you come back for a second voyage." He gave me a sad smile that suggested just how unlikely it was that a young and unproven deckhand would be back.

I listened, though. I saw wonders, exactly as I expected, but I remained cautious, kept much of my money, and I kept my head about me. Leaving the Albion coast behind when we sailed back home that Wednesday, I counted my blessings as I looked at the hung-over misery of my fellow sailors: the swollen eyes, chipped teeth, and bruised faces from dockside brawls, the empty purses that had been full with their entire pay for the trip.

I didn't have to see or do everything the first time, because I knew I was meant to be a sailor, and I would be back.

After an uneventful voyage, we returned to Poseidon City eight days later. As I walked down the gangplank and into the city, I could tell from the look in Captain Macallan's eyes that he expected me to run home to Heartshore, settle into a typical life as a fisherman, and tell stories about the great adventure I'd had when I was young. I had no intention of doing so.

I had seen almost nothing of Poseidon City the first time, however, since I'd straightaway joined the steamer's crew. Now, I sampled restaurants; I got into trouble, and I got out of it; I was robbed, but not before I had spent most of my pay anyway, so the cost was more to my pride than to my financial situation.

And when it was time, I made my way back to the steamer and walked aboard with my head held high. Much to the surprise and approval of Captain Macallan, I signed my name in the crew book for the next voyage to Albion.

~

AFTER FOUR DAYS AT SEA, I did hear the music—more urgent, more beautiful, and more compelling than anything I had ever imagined.

I was asleep in my hammock belowdecks, off duty, and I sensed the presence dancing on the edge of my dreams. I woke in the darkness to the decidedly unmusical snores of my shipmates. The only light came from a half-shuttered lantern in the corner near the piss pot. The songs I heard came from the other side of the hull, at the waterline—and I knew I had to see for myself.

I swung out of the creaking hammock, careful not to wake anyone. With the voices of angels ringing in my head, I crept out on deck. Something told me I needed to keep this a secret. The undersea angels were calling to me and me alone. They had chosen *me*—none of the other sailors. I needed to hear their music for myself. It was an experience that could be cherished but not shared.

The night was black, without a moon, and I saw a pearlescent glow on the waves, rippling at the stern of the ship. The music came louder inside my head, an aria sung by voices that could never have come from human throats. Leaning on the rail, I stared down into the water, where I saw swimming figures—beautiful sleek forms with feminine curves and pearlescent skin.

Seeing that I had answered their call, the figures bobbed just beneath the surface. I could make out one angel, her face crystal clear, her features achingly beautiful. Her wings were made of iridescent scales, and they flapped like fins and drove her along. The angel easily kept pace with the steamer's engines.

My heart felt as if it would burst out of my chest. My throat went dry. I *ached* for her.

She looked up at me, her eyes wide and bright, her smile longing. She spread her gem-like wings as if to fly beneath the waves. She opened her arms to reach out for me. She wanted me! She *needed* me. She called to me to join her.

I felt a rush of hope, a sense of self-worth greater than I had ever experienced. It would be so easy just to swing over the side of the steamer and drop down into the sea. She silently promised me a kiss ... and an infinity more. Tears were pouring down my face. I *needed* this!

"Hey, you! Lad, what're you doing? Get away from there."

My life was shattered, the hypnotic manacles broken. The song jangled in my head as if a trapdoor had opened beneath an entire orchestra. When I felt strong hands grab my arm, I thrashed and struggled like a wild beast.

By the time I managed to look overboard again, the glow had vanished from the water, as had the angels beneath the sea. They were gone. They no longer wanted me—at least not tonight.

I had missed my chance.

～

THE OCEAN REMAINED silent for the rest of the voyage, and when I explored Crown City, even the wonders of that fabled place seemed flat. The Clockwork Angels were just inferior artificial contraptions, not remotely as beautiful as the angels I had seen in the sea....

In time, I became a true sailor instead of just a boy who wanted to run off to sea. I crossed the ocean over and over and again, growing wise in the ways of the tides and the weather. In a few years, with his appreciation and a heartfelt recommendation, Captain Macallan allowed me to transfer to another ship, where I would be groomed as first mate.

I kept longing for that elusive music, searching the sea and the wind for the songs of the angels. Though I sometimes heard it, the marvelous women never came close. They must have been haunting other ships and other sailors less prone to disappoint them. I yearned for them, but they did not answer me.

Eventually, though, I found another way to break that elusive call: The only thing stronger than the unrealistic longing of a fantasy love is a *real* love and a family, and ties that bound me to solid ground instead of the sea.

Each time my ship returned to Poseidon City, I frequented the dockside taverns, but I felt most at home at a particular inn with a flying swan on its signboard, the Cygnus Tavern. The common room was no different from other inns; the food and the ale no more special; but a young woman named Selise caught my eye, and I caught hers.

Selise and her brother Rickard ran the Cygnus Tavern together because their rotund old father had a heart condition that prevented him from doing heavy work. Selise was smart and beautiful, quick with a joke or just as quick with a barbed insult when a rude customer deserved it. Something about the set of her eyes, the curve of her cheekbones, made me think of angels beneath the sea —and when I realized that fact, I went from being smitten to being in love.

While I sat in the Cygnus Tavern like a mooncalf, Selise would find a way to brush my shoulder or stroke my arm when she thought no one was looking. Each time my ship steamed away to Albion, I held my memories of her like a jeweler polishing and repolishing a precious gem, and on each trip back to Poseidon City, I spent the days thinking about when I would see Selise again. That proved to be a cure from the seductive call of the angels.

Finally, at the start of a long storm season, which the weather diviners claimed would be the most severe in decades, I decided to stay behind and give up the sea. I had saved up my pay, because with dreams of Selise to occupy me, I had little need to spend my wages on carousing, though I did occasionally buy exotic treasures that I brought back to Selise.

In Crown City, I had bought a ring of the Watchmaker's gold, and when I returned to Atlantis, I purchased the most beautiful fire opal from the quarries of Endoline. It seemed a perfect balance—a gem from Atlantis, a gold ring from Albion, since the two continents pulled me back and forth, with the ocean in between. I intended to give that ring to Selise as a memory of my life as a sailor, the life I would be giving up for her.

Before the hearth in the Cygnus Tavern, I went on bended knee and asked Selise if she would marry me. The late-night crowd of drunken sailors fell into a hush as they realized what I was doing, then let out a roaring cheer when Selise accepted my proposal. From behind the bar, her brother gave me an approving nod, since he had measured me a long time ago.

When the rough storm season came, I was settled in my new home, landbound, a happy newlywed working in the tavern along with Selise and her brother. I felt no regrets; in fact, I barely thought of my former shipmates at all until they came back into the Cygnus Tavern when they returned to port.

A year later Selise's father died, not unexpectedly, but in Nature's odd sense of balance, she discovered she was pregnant soon afterward. Selise eventually gave birth to a healthy, red-faced boy who could squall with hurricane force. We named him Aiden. Selise was a good mother, and I thought I was a good father. The baby grounded me and anchored me. I learned the joys and the exhaustions of being a parent.

My shipmates came and went all year long, telling their adventures, which I knew were mostly lies, but I listened with an increasing wistfulness. Those days seemed so far away. Before long, my baby boy and my wife, both of whom I loved so much, who anchored me, began to feel like genuine anchors dragging me down.

The sea called to me.

I fought it for a long time, strengthening my resolve when Aiden took his first steps, or said his first words, but each time I left the tavern to go out on errands, I took detours to the docks and just stared at the ships, the names painted on the bow, counting which ones I knew.

I watched the brotherhood of sailors as they laughed and joked, singing chanties while they hauled crates, then went out to carouse in the town. They were alive and energetic, full of the moment instead of long-term plans. Back at the Cygnus Tavern, I saw only a horizon composed of everyday days.

Oh, how the sea called to me.

Rickard saw the different look in my eyes, the glances I gave the sailors in the tavern. "You are going to hurt her," he said to me in a low voice, and I was startled at what he had realized—what I, myself, had been unwilling to admit.

I held on as long as I could, but Selise already knew long before I found the courage to talk to her. "It will be just one more voyage," I promised her, a promise that I fully intended to keep. But Selise knew I wouldn't.

"Come back to me," she said. I could tell Selise was heartbroken, but she wouldn't surrender to tears. "As long as I know that, I can stay here. I have a home and a good business, my brother and his family to keep me company. I won't be the only sailor's wife in Poseidon City. That's how it is. Just don't make me a sailor's widow."

Several captains offered to take me aboard as part of the crew, and I chose my ship carefully. I kissed my wife and held her so tightly and for so long that I almost changed my mind. Almost. I hugged my three-year-old boy and swung him around so that his memory of me would be laughter and smiles.

Then we sailed off for Albion.

THE SEA WAS a calming influence on me. I had satisfied my hunger, and now I could relax, like sipping a glass of fine brandy after a delicious meal. The ocean was calm, and the passage both ways was uneventful—so uneventful, in fact, that when I brought my pay back to the tavern, I suggested that I make just one more voyage. I hadn't been gone that long—only a month—and I had barely gotten the taste of a sailor's life again. Selise was resigned but not surprised.

Then it became a third voyage, a fourth, and a fifth. I would stay home for a week in port, help as needed around the tavern, spend time with Aiden and Selise. The Cygnus Tavern prospered, and my family wanted for nothing.

On my seventh voyage, though, the angels beneath the sea called to me again, sang to me, and set their hook in my heart. That irresistible pull dragged me out onto the deck at midnight, stumbling, like a fish being reeled in. The songs swelled inside me, the voices like diamonds and honeydew. They sang to me of wishes that could indeed come true and of the tyranny of unfulfilled dreams. They moved me. How they moved me!

I tried to be silent as I went out on deck, for I wanted no interruptions, no sailor on the night watch to stop me as had happened before, but I felt as if I'd lost my sea legs. My knees were wobbly— though it didn't matter to me because when I joined the undersea angels I could fly with them beneath the water, maybe even sprout my own pair of iridescent wings.

I saw them swimming beside the ship, goddesses of light beneath the waves—wings spread, arms outstretched, mouths open and filled with promises. It would have been so easy to slip overboard and be with them. So easy ...

Although the temptation was like a storm front, I chose to resist. I thought of my anchor, my Selise, my Aiden, my family, my home, the Cygnus Tavern. Under the onslaught of the angels, my lifeline felt as thin and fragile as spider silk, yet I clung to it nevertheless. I cherished Selise's face, remembered running my fingertips along her cheek, kissing her lips.

Yet the angels still called me.

I remembered my laughing boy, swinging him around in my arms to make sure he remembered me when I was gone. Was that how he would remember me forever, if I went with the undersea angels now?

No!

I tried. I fought. I felt drunk with desire as the song resonated in my head, in my heart, and in my soul. The angels in the water spread their arms. They sang. My lifeline stretched and frayed, and I knew I was lost. I could not resist.

Suddenly, another sailor was beside me, grinning like a madman. His eyes were wide, delirious. Laughing, he leaped over the rail into the sea.

In that moment the spell was broken. I watched the man disappear beneath the waves. The angels enfolded him, and for a moment their iridescent wings looked sharp and dark, like shark fins.

I came to my senses, yelling, "Man overboard! Man overboard!" But it would be no use. The angels had wanted me—or they had wanted *someone*, and they were satisfied with the companion, or the victim, they had received. I was shaken, heartsick, and terrified because I knew that if they ever made that call again—and oh how I wanted them to!—I would not escape.

~

AFTER THAT ORDEAL, I hurried back to the safety of home. *Home*—the word meant something more to me again.

Those dark and tantalizing fears out in the sea had burned me, changed me, and when my steamer finally returned to the Poseidon City harbor, I could not get off the ship fast enough. I raced to the Cygnus Tavern, found my beautiful Selise and my laughing boy Aiden, swept them both up in a hug, and promised I would stay with them from that point on.

For months, I took solace in the daily routine of the inn— working the bar, sweeping the floor, dealing with customers, performing chores. At night I held my wife and slept soundly, though occasionally I was haunted by nightmares—and sometimes seductive dreams—of the angels beneath the sea. But *Selise* was my angel, and the call of family was far stronger than the call of the sea.

I managed to keep that promise for more than two years.

I would carry Aiden on my shoulders, but as he grew older he insisted on walking beside me. We spent days at the docks watching the steamers, seeing the cargoes they brought in from distant Albion, watching the crates of exotic gemstones and alchemical minerals delivered from the mines inland.

I told the boy of my seafaring adventures, and Aiden was enthralled, just as I had been as a boy in long-forgotten Heartshore. I described Crown City and the Clockwork Angels, careful not to mention those far more dangerous angels in the sea.

But as my life's pendulum swung back the other direction and the balance shifted again, the terrors of those feminine voices disappeared into memory. I never doubted what had happened to me that night, but the call of the sea tugged in the opposite direction, pulling me away from my home and out to that compelling expanse of ocean.

Selise saw the yearning in my eyes and in my heart, and she knew what I was thinking. She had never understood the pull on a sailor's heart, but she understood *me*, and she knew that I would be miserable if she didn't let me go. "I would rather have you part of the time than lose you forever," she said. "Find a ship, do a voyage or two until you get it out of your system, then come back to me and stay for a time."

Selise made me promise to stay home during the dangerous storm season, and I agreed to the condition, but I understood there were greater dangers out in the sea than mere storms. I knew what lay beneath.

Before I set off again, I prepared myself. When I signed aboard another steamer, I knew how to protect myself.

I had paid a blacksmith to craft me a pair of manacles.

I DID NOT HEAR the singing of the angels again for two more years, by which time I was captain of my own small ship. And the next time the ethereal music throbbed in my head and in my soul, I locked the manacles around the rail and around my wrist. To keep me safe. The keys were in my cabin, and my first mate had his instructions.

In the pale moonlight, I gazed down at the painfully beautiful women with their iridescent wings, their beckoning arms, their beseeching expressions. They insisted that I join them—and more than anything else in my life, I wanted to do just that. I longed to jump overboard.

But the manacles held me back. I fought and struggled, unable to think straight, and when I reached out for memories of Selise and Aiden and the cozy Cygnus Tavern, the angels' tone changed. They became angry, *jealous*. They did not like to be defeated. I had failed them, betrayed them, tricked them—and I thought I had betrayed myself.

I thrashed against the manacle, bemoaning my helplessness, wondering why I had been so foolish. Then other sailors ran down the deck toward me, grabbed me and held me even as I struggled. My wrists were raw and bloodied.

But the singing fell silent. The frustrated angels vanished, leaving me alone.

When I came to my senses again, I embraced the memory with great satisfaction, reveling in the experience. The angels were like a dangerous drug, but my resolve and my love for my family was stronger than the pull of that addiction. The manacles had bit into my wrists, but I was alive.

Though many sailors talked about the angels beneath the sea, and some claimed to have seen or heard the calling, no one had escaped them unscathed as I had.

~

AFTER TIME AND TRIBULATIONS, I found a satisfactory balance, a stable point between the pull of the sea and the pull of my family back at the Cygnus Tavern. It seemed appropriate when I learned that in ancient times Cygnus the swan was also a god of *balance*. What could be more fitting?

I would sail during the trading season, stay home during the storm season. I was reliable and competent, and eventually I became captain of a larger ship.

My son grew to be a sturdy lad who helped his mother and uncle at the tavern, but he also sneaked off to the docks to watch the sailors. Selise and I eventually gave Aiden a little sister, an adorable copper-haired girl we named Cythia—all blue eyes, sparkles, and freckles, as much of a joy to our family as our son had been.

When I sailed back and forth across the sea, the crew indulged my peculiar habit of staying out on certain nights manacled to the rail, so I could stare at the water with my head cocked just so, listening hard into the whooshing silence. Some thought I was eccentric; others thought me mad.

Five more times over the years, the angels came to me, calling with more and more urgency, and though I wrestled with the manacles, I could not detach them. I endured, and I adored, and I recovered from the pain of bruised wrists with the euphoria of the music I had heard and the beauty I had seen.

I became the captain of the *Rocinante*, a majestic ship with a thick hull and a wide beam that could ride through any storms. Our fighters could fend off the Wreckers if need be. I had the respect of my fellow captains, and I had my quiet, perfect home at the Cygnus Tavern. The best of both worlds.

Cythia grew into a spunky girl who stopped clinging to her mother's skirts and learned how to get into trouble all on her own. Aiden became a headstrong young man with dreams of his own, so

I was not surprised when, coming home from a voyage, I found Selise in tears and a shadow over the tavern.

"It's those stories you put in his head! You and the other men in the tavern." She clenched her fists and pounded my shoulders. "Aiden ran off to sea! He signed aboard a steamer to work as a cabin boy. He's gone!"

With a heavy heart, I held Selise as she let her anger rush out like the retreating tide. I had seen the look in our son's eyes, and I knew the call of the sea was strong in him. "He'll be all right," I reassured her. "Just as I was. It's in his blood. If you understand me, then you understand Aiden."

She was weak and shaken, and I knew she had been crying for days. "All that we can do is wish him well. It's what he wants." I made her a promise that I knew I truly would keep. "When he comes home, I'll take him aboard the *Rocinante*. He could work as a ship's mate with me. There's no need for him to be on a strange ship. We'll be together, and we'll both come home to see you."

She brightened, as if that thought had not occurred to her. I continued to hold her. "He'll be safe with me," I lied.

~

I LEARNED the name of the steamer Aiden had joined—a good vessel and a good captain, so I knew my boy was in satisfactory company. It would probably take a voyage or two before I could find him, work out an agreement with the captain, and bring my son aboard the *Rocinante*, but it would happen.

As my ship headed back out for Albion, the air took on a sour smell as of something dead. A red tide—a poisonous bloom of algae that sucked all life from the water like a spreading bloodstain on the waves.

A pall settled over the crew, and I gave orders for the *Rocinante* to keep going at full steam, anxious to make our way through the ocean sickness as swiftly as possible. But the red tide went on and on, and we hadn't found the end of it even by sunset.

Late that night with a full moon overhead, I couldn't sleep. I felt an uneasiness in my mind as if the angels were singing to me again, but this time in an off-key dirge. I ventured out onto the deck, heading to the bow where I could be alone. The stars looked down as I fastened my manacle to the rail, just in case.

Before long, the sea took on a luminous character, the phosphorescence that preceded the appearance of the undersea angels, but this time it was a sickly red glow, filtered through the algae and the belly-up fish bobbing in its path.

The angels began singing, and I heard them in my heart. I tugged on the manacle chain and looked over the side of the steamer. The beautiful forms appeared, oblivious to the death around them, spreading their iridescent wings as they looked up at me with unearthly eyes. Their song was as powerful as always, but compelling in a different way—not as seductive, not as jealous. Not as angry. This felt ... *victorious*, as if the angels were somehow satisfied at last.

I strained against the manacle, and the metal cuff bit into my wrist, but the pain didn't jar me out of the hypnotic trance.

The angels swam together at the waterline, glorious, yet also terrible. When they saw me gazing at them, they *laughed*, and the music broke off inside my head. Two of the angels swam away with a flash of their undersea wings, leaving only one behind.

I was baffled. I had withstood their advances for so many times, and they would no longer try to tempt me. The last angel looked up at me. *We don't want you.* Her voice was an insidious whisper within my brain. *We don't need you.*

She began to stroke away from the *Rocinante* before she laughed again.

We have your son.

Then the angel dove beneath the water, leaving me there, chained to the rail and unable to escape the heartbreaking news. I sobbed until dawn.

⁓

I STILL HAVE THE MANACLES, but the angels have stopped calling to me, singing to me. They are satisfied with what they took, and now the sea, for all its mysteries, is just an empty book.

Early in my career as a writer, my annual tradition was to spend the holidays with a group of writer friends, most of whom were clustered around Eugene, Oregon. I lived in the San Francisco Bay Area where I worked as a technical writer for a large research laboratory—in other words, I had a "real job"—but I very much wanted to be a full-time writer and worked at my stories and novels, gradually seeing some success.

Each year I would make the drive up Interstate 5 along the spine of California to Oregon, and in questionable mid-December weather, but I didn't want to miss my holiday gathering. One year I even took my fiancée Rebecca Moesta with me (and she and I just celebrated our 26th wedding anniversary).

One of the Eugene locals would act as the host, and we'd get together the day before Christmas for conversation and cooking. Some people baked cookies or other desserts; I always made my famous lasagna, a masterpiece of a recipe that has been in my family for five generations. (Yes, turkey or ham might be more traditional, but we were a group who broke with traditions—we were writers, after all—and formed our own.)

After the late afternoon feast, we passed out gifts. In keeping with being starving writers, no gift could cost more than a dollar, which forced us to do some imaginative shopping.

After the gift giving, we sat around for the highlight of the evening— the real sharing of gifts among writers, usually by a fireplace, usually with mulled cider. We would take out printed manuscripts, stories that we each had written specially for the occasion, which had never been read before. We went around in a circle, reading aloud one story after another. Some were heartwarming, some were scary, some magical, some imaginative, some haunting. Each of us had our own particular spin on the holiday season.

We were all new writers, learning our craft and learning the business. We poured our hearts and our energies into these stories.

In the years since, members of our group have become international bestselling authors, New York Times *bestselling authors, winners or nominees of almost every award in numerous genres, from the Writers of the Future Award, to the Hugo, Nebula, World Fantasy, Philip K. Dick, Bram Stoker, Shamus, Edgar, Pushcart, Endeavor, Sidewise, Scribe, Locus, Mythopoeic Society, Romantic Times Reviewers' Choice, and Theodore Sturgeon Awards (and probably many others). Some have become publishers themselves, or movie producers, record producers, game designers.*

Maybe there was magic in those Christmas Eves after all.

This was a novelette I wrote for that gathering, one of my most heart-felt stories that goes beyond the Christmas spirit to the core of what it means to be a writer.

THE GHOST OF CHRISTMAS ALWAYS

"After she died I dreamed of her every night for many months, sometimes as a spirit, sometimes as a living creature, never with any of the bitterness of my real sorrow, but always with a kind of quiet happiness, which became so pleasant to me that I never lay down at night without a hope of the vision coming back ... And so it did."

—Charles Dickens, in a letter to the mother of Mary Hogarth, 1842

STAVE ONE

Mary was dead, to begin with. And yet each Christmas Eve her ghost came to haunt Charles Dickens. He waited the year round for the one night he could see her again, if only for a brief time.

Dickens gripped the arms of his chair, then let his eyes fall half-closed. Across from him, aromatic smoke came from a fire in the sitting room hearth. On the mantelpiece sat a scrolled ivory-and-gold clock with slim hands reaching toward midnight, when Mary would come. Wind rattled the window panes, pushing winter cold into the great house on Devonshire Terrace. The Dickenses had added mahogany doors, marble mantels, and carpets to their new home—such extravagance was expected from the author of *Nicholas Nickleby*, *Oliver Twist*, and, of course, *The Pickwick Papers*.

But on the silent night before Christmas, the house felt like a deserted stage in the theater, filled with props and costumes but no actors. Mary had never lived here with them. His young sister-in-law had died before the unparalleled success swept over Dickens's life.

He stood up from the chair, brushed at his robe, and walked to the mantel. Dickens had urged the four children, his wife Kate, and the maid to retire early this night. None of them would suspect why he wanted them fast asleep. Beside the clock stood Mary's portrait, painted by Phiz, the artist who illustrated so many of Dickens's installments. After Mary's death had devastated him, Dickens begged Phiz to do the portrait from memory, as a special favor. Now Dickens touched the lines of her face, the soft eyes gazing at something unseen but wondrous, the curves of her dark hair. Sweet Mary Hogarth, the delightful sister of his moody and shallow-minded wife. Kate would be snoring upstairs, grossly pregnant with their fifth child. She would carry out the same chores on Christmas day as she did every day. She had no broader imagination, doing only what she felt her wifely obligations demanded. Not like young Mary, who was always so bright, so fascinated.... "Can't you gaze at that portrait any time, Charles Dickens? I have only a short while here with you."

Dickens turned, smiling. He felt a rush of happiness. Mary Hogarth stood there, spectral and unchanged since her death six years before. She wore a shimmering white gown that reflected a light not from the fireplace and blew in a breeze that Dickens himself could not feel. "I was waiting for you," he said.

"Just as I wait for this one night when I'm allowed to see you again." She took a step forward but did not touch him. She made no sound as she moved. "This year I have a present for you, Charles, a gift I hope you will treasure as much as I treasure giving it to you."

He could not think of what to say. He, Charles Dickens, who spoke in front of great audiences, who played in the theater, who read his own sketches aloud to crowds from the streets, found himself unable to utter a simple sentence to the wavering image of a sixteen-year-old girl. He finally said, "Merely seeing you again is enough to make me glad for the next twelve months." Mary smiled and, keeping her gaze on his, reached forward to touch the clock. "But this is better. I give you Time."

"Time?" he asked, not comprehending but feeling his heart filled with wonder. "I do need more of it, with all my commitments."

"No," she said with a lilt in her voice that reminded him of the times that they laughed, Charles and Kate and Mary, when they went on outings to the theater. "I give you *your* time, Charles. Your past, your present, and what is yet to come."

Before he could say more, Mary turned the hour hand backward from midnight in a full circle until it reached eleven o'clock. As the hand touched the top of the dial, the chimes rang out. Mary extended her fingers to him. "Take my hand, Charles. Let me show you."

Eagerly he wrapped his fingers around her cold flesh, insubstantial but as strong and insistent as the wind. Mary led him to the window and drew back the curtains. The distant lights of London sprawled out below, making him think of the crowded streets, tall buildings leaning out over alleys, small fires, and candlelit windows.

"Step with me into the past," she said.

Fighting back the tremors of fear in his voice, Dickens asked, "Long past?"

"No. Your past." And she stepped partway through the window, through the sash as if it were no more than a bit of fog.

"Wait!" he cried, "I am mortal! I cannot pass through brick and stone and glass."

"Bear but a touch of my hand, Charles." As Mary said this, she gave a tug.

Dickens walked forward clad only in slippers and dressing gown, blinking as he stepped through and out into a clear winter night. But he felt no cold, no wind, only astonishment, for he found himself many miles from his home on Devonshire Terrace.

STAVE TWO

Though it was dark, Dickens could make out the three-storey house before him, with glowing orange lights in several of the windows. By day he would be able to see the nearby Kentish countryside, Chatham, and the Medway Valley.

"Good Heaven!" Dickens cried, "I was a boy here! My father worked in the naval dockyard."

Mary just smiled at him and raised her hand. Dickens found that they floated off the ground, rising along the terraces and shingles, to one of the upstairs windows where a single light still burned.

"That was my room!" Dickens said, keeping his voice to a whisper.

"And here is someone you'll like to see, no doubt."

They pressed their faces close to the window, and Dickens noted that, though the winter air must be very cold, neither his breath nor Mary's left any frost upon the window.

Inside the room he saw a plump woman with grayish-brown hair tied neatly behind her head. She sat in a chair pulled near to a pair of beds in which lay a boy and a girl. Both children had eyes wide and mouths slack with rapt fascination and terror. The woman leaned forward to talk; her eyes squinted, and her face contorted as she spoke, waving her hands.

"Why it's old Mary Weller, our maid! Bless her heart—Mary Weller alive again!"

The maid lurched out in the middle of her story, splaying her fingers like claws.

Both children squirmed backward in their beds, defending themselves with nervous giggling.

Dickens, delighted, turned to the spirit beside him. "She used to tell us horrible stories about Captain Murderer! And how he'd indulge his taste in wives by killing them off and baking them into pies! Ugh—my sister Fanny and I used to lie awake shivering in terror every time she told us one of those stories. But I loved them. I used to make up my own."

Mary patted him with her cold hand. "You've been a writer since the time you were a little boy. Come with me, around the corner." They descended to the ground again, but when they turned the corner, Dickens found that they had reached an alley far distant from the old house. The light had changed to a gray wintry afternoon. People crowded the street, women wrapped in dark clothes tugging children alongside them on the frozen mud. Thawed patches of slush surrounded steaming piles of fresh horse manure. Dogs ran about, harrying burly men who carried packages and crates. Off to one side a man hauled a narrow pauper's coffin on his back, passing unnoticed through the streets. Signboards protruded out over doors proclaiming lodging houses, barbers, poulterers, a tripe shop, a sausage-maker.

"This is the Strand!" Dickens said, nearly letting go of Mary's hand in his excitement. "I got lost here one day when I was a boy."

"In fact, there you are right now." Mary indicated a small child gawking at the crowds, stumbling along with wonder-filled eyes. The boy looked as if he had been crying, but the tears dried to streaks in the cold air. "I had a shilling and fourpence in my pocket," Dickens said. "My godfather gave it to me. I knew I would be rescued somehow. And I was very hungry." They followed the boy, observing yet unseen by the pedestrians. Little Charles Dickens walked along, dressed in a warm jacket, bumping into unshaven men who ignored him. He stared from window to window in food shops, shuffling his feet, looking around. He kept walking. Finally, he stopped in front of a pile of cooked sausages in a window. A paper sign in front read "Small Germans, a Penny." The boy stared at the sausages, shivering. He licked his lips. He took a deep breath, mustering courage, and strode in. The shopkeeper squinted at him with an amused grin, but the boy seemed confident now that he knew what to ask for.

"If you please, would you sell me one of those sausages?" His voice sounded tiny as Dickens listened. The boy reached into his pocket and took out a single penny. The shopkeeper used his fingers to pick up one of the sausages from the back of the pile and plucked the penny from the boy's hand at the exact moment he surrendered the sausage. Charles Dickens felt his cheeks flushing with the delight of the memory. "The sausage wasn't very warm," he told Mary, "but it was one of the most delicious things ever to pass my lips. Of course, part of it was that I had bought it myself."

The boy wandered the streets again, in and out of yards and little squares, chased off by cooks he gawked at, bullied by a gang of young toughs who wanted the rest of the money in his pockets. The boy broke into a run, pushing through the crowds, splashing in the slush, until he lost the boys in a dark alley lined with dim counting houses where misers changed their gold.

The boy stood in the growing dark, looking unspeakably forlorn.

"Can we not help him?" Dickens said.

Mary shook her head. "No, Charles, we are here only to observe. You pity this boy now, but would you have traded that single day in your life for anything you can imagine?"

"No, never. It astonishes me even now to think of how much I used from that day in *Oliver Twist*, and in *Nicholas Nickleby*, and in half a dozen of my sketches for the periodicals."

"And you will continue to find ways to use it. You're a writer, Charles, heart and soul. Everything you experience is fodder for the tales that delight so many people."

As Mary spoke, Dickens heard a loud cough and saw a middle-aged man come up to the wretched boy and ask what was wrong. The man's clothes were drab and worn, but the brass buttons on his coat had been polished with care.

"That watchman took me home," Dickens said in a whisper. "I remember his cough, how he wheezed all the way. I was afraid I was going to catch the plague from him."

Mary strolled ahead, turning her back on the departing boy and the coughing watchman. "Why don't you come around the corner with me? We'll pass another decade."

Still astounded, Dickens followed her as the scene once again changed. He found himself in a dark court, narrow but clean. Clouds the color of ice on a deep pond covered the sky. In front of a dark office, a young man strode by with a polished walking stick. He looked like a twenty-year-old dandy, with gleaming shoes, black waistcoat, and jacket. His gray felt trousers were new and unwrinkled, his green cravat impeccably tied. The brim of a brushed top hat shaded his face. The young man moved with a nervous manner as he stopped in front of the dark office—and then Dickens recognized the mail slot and the stenciled letters above it that read EDITOR'S BOX.

"This is Fleet Street! That's me, posting my very first contribution for the *Monthly Magazine*." The young man pulled out a long envelope and, trying to appear nonchalant, slipped it into the black hole of the mail slot before striding away. He rapped his walking stick on the cobblestones, swaggering but hurrying, as if afraid to be caught at what he had done.

"I paid half a crown for the next issue of that magazine, and there it was in print! One of my sketches, 'A Dinner at Poplar Walk,' I think it was. I remember how it felt to see my words in print for the very first time."

Mary's voice took on a tone of chiding. "And you didn't even receive payment for the piece."

Dickens laughed. "What did it matter then? I was speaking to a whole world of readers! People were reading what I had written. I walked up and down Westminster Hall for half an hour. My eyes could hardly see, I was so excited!"

"Yet now you grow angry at anyone who prints even a bit of your correspondence without offering you royalties."

Dickens stiffened. "They make enormous amounts of money off me just by placing my name on their masthead! Pirates have made me lose thousands of pounds by flaunting the copyright law."

She had touched a sore spot, but he did not want to ruin their short time together by arguing. He softened his voice to change the subject. "These memories are delightful, Mary. Show me more!"

Her expression remained solemn. "Do not thank me until you have seen them all. Some of them may not be so precious, though they are as important."

Dickens felt a chill from inside. "What do you mean?" His tone spoke plainly that he did not want to hear the answer.

"Our time grows short," she said. "Quick! You must see one last memory of your past."

As she led him down the street, the sky darkened into night, growing blacker with each step they took. Greenish-white glows from gas street lights made the scene shift with a harsh mixture of glares and shadows. As Mary hurried him along, Dickens saw the buildings again, recognizing the brick facade, the wrought iron fence, the decorative lintels and arches of Mecklenburgh Square.

As they approached, Dickens saw a tall man open the wrought iron gate in front of a three-storey brick home. He was accompanied by two women, one larger and hanging on the man's arm, the other thin and delicate with dark hair pinned up under a bonnet. The man gestured for them both to precede him through the gate, then caught up with them under the rounded arch of the doorway. They all seemed to be laughing and enjoying themselves.

Dickens stood trembling, refusing to go another step. Mary pulled at him, but he closed his eyes. "No, Mary! Oh no, no!"

But she was insistent and drew him stumbling toward the door. "Was I not always a good friend to you, Charles? Without this visit, you cannot hope to receive everything I bring to you."

She led him through the half-open door into the rented home where young Charles Dickens lived with his new wife Kate and her sixteen-year-old sister Mary.

"We had just gone to the theater, do you remember?" Mary said in a distant voice, as if she barely remembered herself. "It was late when we got home, about one o'clock in the morning. I had gone up to bed—"

"Stop!" he said. He had spent years with every detail of that evening pounding in his head, haunting his nightmares. There, in front of him, in the old house he and Kate and the children had left only a short time ago, he watched a younger, carefree version of himself removing his coat and handing it to the maid. He set his walking stick against the rail of the stairs, tossed his top hat behind him in a cocky gesture to hit the hat rack, but of course he missed and was just bending over to pick it up when he heard a choking cry from upstairs. Mary's voice.

It echoed in his ears, in his memory.

Sweating and shivering at the same time, Dickens watched himself, running up the steep staircase, grabbing the rail and launching himself upward with every step. "Mary!" his younger self cried in concerned surprise.

Watching the scene unfold again, the elder Dickens could not stop himself from shouting the same as he dashed up to the second-floor bedrooms. His footfalls made no sound on the steps.

Just inside the door of her room, Mary lay on the floor gasping, begging for help. Young Dickens sent for a doctor. His face was drawn and horrified. As he watched from his invisible vantage, the elder Dickens shook his head. "The doctor will not be able to do anything. They said you had a diseased heart, Mary. And now I have a broken one, all over again."

He turned to the spectral form of Mary, who watched without emotion the image of herself writhing on the floor. Young Dickens and Kate helped her onto the bed. She would die there the following day.

"This scene has haunted me more than any other," Dickens said. "Every letter I wrote for a year bore a black border in remembrance of you." He sighed, but it came out more like a moan. "When I was writing *The Old Curiosity Shop* and the time came when Little Nell had to die, I trembled for days beforehand, recalling your death. It cast the most horrible shadow upon me, and it was all I could do to keep moving at all."

Mary sighed, and he felt her spectral hand squeeze his. "Sometimes you are too sentimental, Charles."

Dickens saw that time had changed again. Mary Hogarth lay on her bed, but sunlight streamed through the windows, and the younger Charles Dickens held her in his arms, pulling the bedclothes over to keep her warm. He stroked her tangled hair … and felt her die in his arms.

Dickens watched himself take her cooling hand between his palms and slip one of the rings off her finger. "I will wear this ring of yours until the day I might join you," he said.

Dickens the observer stared at the ring on his own finger, still there after six years. To crush away the tears he rubbed his knuckles against his eyes. His head rang from the memory. Then the ringing sound became the chiming of the clock, and he and Mary's ghost returned to the warm sitting room in Devonshire Terrace. After all this time and all the years observed, the hour of midnight was just striking.

STAVE THREE

Dickens drew a deep breath to drive back all the memories he had thought tucked away safe and sound. He warmed his hands over the fire in the sitting room, but his heart seemed to regulate its own warmth and chill. Exhausted, he shuffled back to his chair, but before he could turn round and sink into the cushions, before the clock finished striking the hour of twelve, Mary stopped him.

"We have no time to rest, Charles. This is a busy night for both of us."

He blinked at her, but now the delight of his reunion with Mary had been blunted by watching her death all over again. "I can't bear anymore of my memories just now. I'm afraid of what else you might dredge from the mud of my past."

He squeezed his eyes shut and tried not to think of all the things he did not want to see again, all the black shadows of his younger life. But Mary's voice grew lighter.

"Not your past, Charles. Now we will go and see who you are right now. Until the clock strikes one, let us observe your present."

This baffled him, and he made sure to let her see it on his face. "What do you mean? I know who I am."

"Are you quite certain?"

"How can I not?"

In answer, Mary narrowed her eyes and looked at him with a penetrating gaze that made her seem centuries older than her sixteen-year-old form suggested.

"All right then, Spirit," he said submissively. "Conduct me where you will."

Mary went to the door of the sitting room and beckoned him. "Shall we go upstairs, then."

The hall was dim and orange, lit by candles Kate had left burning for him after she went to bed. The flickering light seemed to set off sparks from Mary's flowing white dress.

As they went up the stairs, Dickens felt light on his feet, and he wondered if he was really moving himself. When the fourth stair failed to creak under his step, he knew that this would be another shadow-show of visions, a theater performance Mary had staged for him.

She turned down the upstairs hall and opened the door to the wide Master Bedroom. By the sunlight in the window Dickens saw it was morning again, that very morning. Kate sat back in a rocking chair, working on another embroidered pillowcase; their maid Anne had drawn the pattern for it, as usual. Draped along the scrolled arm of the rocker hung limp bundles of bright threads. Kate shifted and tried to be comfortable, but her pregnancy made her look awkward no matter what she did. Her eyes, her cheeks, everything about her looked bloated, especially in contrast to the shining spirit of her sister. Kate's face looked like a poor reproduction of Mary's carved out of a potato.

Three of the four children sat in the room with her, little Katey and Mamie peered at a book showing sketches of knights in shining armor; baby Walter lay on the bed making sounds like the water draining out of a wash basin.

"Kate sits here all day and does nothing," Dickens said. "Not at all like you, Mary. She takes no interest in my activities—"

Mary cut him off abruptly. "What would you have her do? The baby is due in less than a month. She watches the children, makes certain they refrain from bothering you, though many times they bother her to no end. Do you even notice?"

Interrupting her, the door burst open and five-year-old Charley ran in with tears brimming in his eyes. The boy made hiccupping noises and brushed past Dickens, missing him by no more than an inch, but he did not even see his father. In his small hand he held a little white note and a pincushion.

Kate looked up from her embroidery, saw the note, and allowed a brief and surprising expression of anger to flicker behind her eyes. Dickens remembered writing the note himself and placing it on Charley's bed, after he had completed his daily inspection of the household.

"What is it, Charley?" Kate asked. Her voice sounded soothing. Mamie and Katie turned the pages of their book, studiously ignoring their brother's anguish, while the baby kept gurgling.

The boy had to snuffle twice before he could hand her the note. His mother had no chance to read it before he burst out, "I only forgot to put my brown shoes in their box. I left 'em by my bed. I was going to." He drew a shaking breath and tried to fend off his tears long enough to speak what disturbed him the most. "And tomorrow's Christmas!"

Kate shook her head. "Don't expect mere Christmas to make your father an easier man. What reason has he to be merry?" She smiled at the boy. "We'll have to make twice as merry ourselves!"

Dickens remained at the door, stung, as Kate heaved herself out of the rocking chair. She set her embroidery aside, fumbling but unable to catch a packet of bright green thread that unraveled and spilled onto the floor. She paid it no heed and gave the boy a gentle hug.

"Look at this, Charles," Mary's spirit said from across the room. She ran her translucent fingers over the frame of a small water-color portrait showing the four children at play. "Do you remember it?"

Indeed, he did—it was the going-away gift from a painter friend when he and Kate had departed for six months to see America. Dickens insisted on leaving the four children behind, claiming that the stress of travel and the inconvenience of having them along would be detrimental to his own activities.

Kate had mourned the thought of being separated from her children for half a year and begged not to go, but Dickens went ahead with the plans, the arrangements, the packing. Finally, Dickens sent his ebullient actor friend William Macready to speak to Kate and, as instructed, Macready gruffly told Mrs. Dickens that a wife's duty was to accompany her husband wherever he wished to go, and to be happy doing it. Kate took only the watercolor portrait of the children to keep her company; she propped it up in their room every night during the journey.

"You dragged my sister against her will to a foreign land she had no wish to see. The sea trip was the roughest passage for years. You never asked her if perhaps she would like to include something in your plans. But instead you took her to see you speak, to see you read aloud and give performances on the stage. You travelled to visit Washington Irving and Edgar Allan Poe and Henry Longfellow, and what did she profit from it all? The chance to hear you quietly insult your hosts and America in general, to complain about conditions there?"

Dickens took a step back out to the hall, and Mary's spirit whisked across the floor, passing through Katie and Mamie by their picture book. The anger in her eyes frightened him. This was not the type of visitation he had expected at all.

"Can we not see something else, Mary? I beg you!"

"Of course," she said, passing him, and flowing back down the stairs. "Let's go watch the great Charles Dickens at work."

Still light on his feet, he dashed after her as Mary went down the hall to his writing study. Inside, he saw the new fire licking at fresh logs in the large fireplace. It was the first blaze of the morning, and he had added enough logs to keep it burning for a long time; he knew he was bound to be distracted by his writing and pay it no attention.

Dickens saw himself sitting at the desk, bent over a sheet of paper with pen in hand and inkwell nearby. A jumbled stack of papers lay at his left elbow, with one page nearly falling to the floor. A smudged thumbprint from a spilled drop of ink obscured a word in the margin. The only sounds in the room were the scratching of pen against paper, a rapid clink into the inkwell, the sizzling sound of the fire, and his own rapid breathing.

But as Dickens stood and watched the scene, he heard a rustle and saw little Mamie bundled in a blanket on the sofa. Her face had the rubbed-raw blush of one recovering from a fever. She propped a book on her bent knees. Keeping both eyes on her father at his desk, Mamie very carefully turned the page, as if terrified she might make a sound.

"I remember this day! A week ago—Mamie was sick, and I told her it would be all right if she wanted to rest in my study while I worked." He turned and looked to Mary for reassurance.

"You don't appear to be paying much attention to your daughter." Mary's voice remained cold.

The Dickens at the desk sprang to his feet and ran to a small mirror on the wall. He pushed his face to the reflection, opened his mouth, made bizarre contortions of his lips and eyebrows, then ran back to the desk. Picking up his pen, he scribbled down an entire paragraph without stopping, tilting the pen at an extreme angle to keep the words flowing without interrupting the sentence to dip into the ink again.

A moment later he stood up, went to the mirror once more, and proceeded to have a stop-and-start conversation with himself.

"It's nothing unusual," Dickens said to Mary. "Sometimes I get rather involved with my characters." But he felt his cheeks burning at this intrusion into a private moment as he worked. "It helps me stage some of my scenes."

But Mary seemed not at all concerned about that, looking instead at the girl on the sofa. Mamie watched her father's actions, bewildered and frightened, but she made not a sound.

"Your children are afraid of you, Charles. They see you as a whirlwind, always busy, never to be disturbed. You're a great mystery to them."

"Nonsense, they love me. I am their father!"

"You are a stranger."

Upset and impatient, Dickens stepped back out to the hall, turning his back on the scene in the study. "I presume you have some design with these pantomimes, Mary. Get on with it."

She took his hand, and this time it felt colder than ever. "Follow me, then. We'll take a walk outside." She threw open the front door to a sunny winter's afternoon, and they set foot on a street deep in the heart of London. The great house on Devonshire Terrace vanished behind them as they stepped into the bustle of activity. Dickens saw that they left no footprints in the snow.

They moved unhindered by the constant stream of passersby, the businessmen, the beggars. Coming from behind, Dickens recognized the man stumping along at a furious, distracted pace. He was dressed in a fur greatcoat over a brown frock coat, then a waistcoat in red from which a gold watch chain dangled. Two linked diamond pins fastened an extravagant cravat poking up around his Adam's apple. Mary hurried up beside the man, dragging her companion along.

"What are you trying to show me here, Mary? I know I like to walk, sometimes as much as thirty miles in a single day. It helps me to plan my stories, to converse with my characters. And I know very well what I look like."

"Do you know what you look like?" Mary asked, pulling him around to face the image of himself. The man kept walking ahead, eyes cast down, with steam from the cold air spurting out of his nose. "Look closely. See yourself not posing for the mirror."

Dickens inspected the familiar clean-shaven boyish-faced man, with wide nose and thick lips, long brown hair curling around his ears. But then he saw the shadows under the eyes, the sagging weariness in his defiant stride, the hunch of the shoulders, the tight frown heavy on his lips.

"I thought you said this would be visions of the present," Dickens said. "Surely this must be me some years in the future."

Mary shook her head. "No, that is how you appear to others even now. You appear harried, overworked, with never enough time. Constantly pushing yourself beyond goals no man could meet."

"With good reason!" he said, turning defensively toward her. "Is it so quiet in the grave that you can't hear them shouting how Charles Dickens has lost his popularity? The last installments of *The Old Curiosity Shop* were selling a hundred thousand copies a week, but now *Barnaby Rudge* barely sells a third of that, even at its best!"

His eyes blazed at her, and he stopped walking. Mary faced him, as the other image of Dickens continued his lonely walk along the streets, muttering to himself.

"I took a year away from writing to travel in America, and when I returned I thought the public would be hungry for my work, waiting to snap up anything I might do. But my American Notes received nothing but a cool reception from my readers. They used to snap up every tidbit so eagerly—are they all tired of it now? This week's installment of *Martin Chuzzlewit* is selling only twenty thousand copies, no matter what I do."

Mary's face grew stern, an alien expression on the girl he had cherished for so long in his dreams and nightmares. "And how much time do you waste giving speeches, attending gaudy social events? And that's only when you're not losing your temper with your friends or shouting at your publisher or carrying on your endless fight for a reformed copyright law."

"The pirates are stealing me blind with bastard copies of my stories!"

"You don't seem to be doing much good work with the money you already possess. What good would you do with more of it?"

Dickens made no answer, but Mary had not finished taunting him. "You write weekly sketches, you work on two novels at a time, you write one-act farces and you star in them as well. No wonder your children don't know their father; no wonder dear Kate ignores you in simple defense against how you ignore her."

"But writing is my business!" Dickens said, crossing his arms over the gaps in his robe.

"Business!" cried Mary, "Mankind is your business. Don't you realize that a single story from you could do more good work than the House of Commons can manage in a year? In your constant challenge to produce more and more, you've forgotten what stories mean. Don't you remember your passion for a story that demands to be told? Or are you more interested in instant projects to increase your fame—if only for the moment?"

He stammered, "But, but that is not how I think of it at all."

Mary turned and pointed to the figure of Charles Dickens still striding away. "Look at him, walking as fast as he can but with his eyes to the ground. He'll reach his destination and go right past it without even knowing. You are a writer, Charles, surely you can appreciate such a metaphor?"

Dickens, feeling a heavy weight inside his chest, turned away. "I want to go back inside now."

Mary stopped in front of a leatherworker's shop and grasped the handle of the door. Behind the glass, Dickens could see only shadows of the proprietor and customers moving about. Before she opened the door, Mary softened her expression into gentle girl-ishness.

"Think of your children," she said, "and the story that Kate tells them of the three little pigs. Is it better to build a hundred huts of straw, or one or two fortresses of stone?"

She opened the door. "Stop writing books of straw."

He followed her inside, into his own sitting room again. The single chime rang out into the room as the clock struck one.

STAVE FOUR

"I have only one more thing to show you, Charles," Mary said to him. "A glimpse of things yet to come."

Dickens wanted to go nearer the fire but found he could not move. "I think I fear that more than the other images." He realized his voice sounded thin.

"But I know you must have good intentions in your heart." Mary's eyes twinkled, and she flashed a smile at him. Once again, she looked the playful sixteen-year-old, and his heart began to ache. "Stop your worrying. You may even enjoy this."

With a lilt in her step, Mary crossed the sitting room to a door Dickens had never seen before. It looked dark and narrow, perhaps a place where Captain Murderer would keep his blades for trimming wives into bite-sized pieces. Mary drew the door open without a creak. The firelight sparkled on the brass work of the knob, which was different from any of the ornate latches Dickens had installed on the other mahogany doors.

Inside, he could see a shadowy passage, lit by a white glow along the ceilings, as harsh as gaslight but not the same. Mary snatched his hand and drew him inside. He tried to resist, but his feet felt like leaden weights hooked to puppet strings.

The warm light of the sitting room hearth dwindled into nothing and vanished as they stepped forward. The air felt cool and smelled musty. The room was too dark to be observed with any accuracy, but Dickens glanced around, anxious to know what kind of room it was.

As his eyes adjusted he saw that the narrow walls were not walls at all, but shelves. Bookshelves, filled with row upon row of bound volumes. "What is this place, Mary? A library perhaps?"

She stopped in front of a long shelf and raised her hand. Around them the light grew brighter, and he could distinguish all the books of different heights and sizes, with cloth or leather bindings of black, blue, brown. "Have a look at this one, Charles." With a crook of her finger, she tugged the first volume on the shelf a little way out. He squinted down at the gold-stamped letters on the spine.

"Why, that's my *Pickwick*! In an edition I have never seen." He made a small groan. "Someone else has pirated it then!"

Mary's gentle laughter sounded like a bird in the forest. "Have you forgotten that we stepped into your future? Things yet to come."

Dickens ran his fingers over the spines. "And here's *Oliver Twist*, and *The Old Curiosity Shop*!" But as he continued down the line he stopped. "*Hard Times? A Tale of Two Cities? Great Expectations? Bleak House? The Mystery of Edwin Drood? David Copperfield?*" He looked at her, dazed. "Who are all these people? Where are these places? Did I write so many books?"

Mary seemed entranced by the delight she saw on his face. "Of course." He reached out to pull one of the books from the shelves, but Mary stopped him. Sliding the volume back into place, she shook her head. "That is forbidden. If you'd like to learn these characters and know these stories, then you must write them yourself. Only that way can you, and the world, have these books."

He continued to stare at his own name engraved on the spines as if on a monument, CHARLES DICKENS. The thought of all those novels whirled in his imagination; he felt his fingers itching to get back to his pen and paper. Then he remembered the other things Mary had showed him that evening.

"Here is something you will enjoy even more," Mary said as she turned to the opposite shelf, and he saw more books, so many that they were stacked on top of each other, piled up out of sight, causing the shelves to bow in the middle. His name appeared on many of those spines, often in the titles. "Biographies of you, critical treatises, textbooks. The scholars have had as much enjoyment chronicling your life as studying your novels."

Dickens could only gape in astonishment. He felt his vision going dim with euphoria. He had never imagined this, not even in his most pretentious fantasies.

Mary took down one of the tomes and flipped to a page, then began to read in the flickering light. "'Charles Dickens was a great English novelist and one of the most popular writers of all time. A keen observer of life, Dickens had a great understanding of people. He showed sympathy for the poor and helpless, and mocked and criticized the selfish, the greedy, the cruel.'"

She closed the book with a slam and a smile. "What you will find even more remarkable, I think, is that the passage I just read will be written *more than a century after your death*. Your own fame will outshine that of Walter Scott, and Poe and Irving and Longfellow, all those you so admire."

Dickens had to grasp at one of the shelves to keep from falling backward. By the stiffness he felt on his face, he knew he must be grinning like an idiot. But then a suspicion of her own words cast a cloud across his thoughts. "Answer me one question, Mary—are these the images of things that *will* be, or are they the images of things that *may* be only?"

Mary began to walk back down the long corridor of shelves toward the sitting room.

"Mary! Tell me!" His slippers made skittering noises on the hard floor as he ran to catch up with her.

She stood at the door out into the firelit room. "Perhaps. But you must remember that your writing is not about *writing*, but about people. As is your life. It won't matter how clever you are, how many projects you can juggle at once, how many instances your name appears in the newspapers. You have a power to move the world if you choose to do so. But will you make the effort?"

Dickens pushed back into the sitting room. "Yes, I will! I won't forget the lessons you taught me."

He felt like dancing. The hands on the clock had somehow returned to midnight, and as he looked the hour began to chime once more.

Mary stood alone in the center of the room, and her white gown took on a grayish tinge, as if shadows seeped into the fabric. Her skin seemed paler than before, with a shimmering quality like cheap candlewax running into puddles.

"Now I must leave you, Charles. My time here is finished. Look to see me no more. And look that, for your own sake, you remember what has passed between us!" She stepped backward toward the window, fading as she went. Dickens reached for her, but the euphoria made him numb to the thought of never seeing her ghost again.

"Wait!" he called. "You've given me a gift beyond measure. Isn't there something I can do for you? Some way I can repay you?"

Mary continued to dissolve into the air, but at the last moment she turned her gaze full on him. "Write me a Christmas story," she said.

And when the last stroke of twelve had chimed, her ghost vanished completely.

Charles Dickens remained before the glowing hearth for a full hour, watching the logs slump into embers, before he finally turned and left the sitting room, going to the stairs that led to his bed. Kate would be long asleep, but he would do his best not to disturb her.

As his foot fell on the fourth step, the creaking wood reminded him that he was whole and substantial, and alive. As were his family and his friends.

A Christmas story? he thought. His head pounded with the dizzying memories of the evening, and he knew sleep would be a long time coming.

He wondered if he would get any ideas.

ABOUT THE AUTHOR

Kevin J. Anderson has published 150 books, 56 of which have been national or international bestsellers. In 2012 he launched his humorous horror series of mysteries featuring Dan Shamble, Zombie P.I., who has starred in five novels and numerous short stories, even a graphic novel. Anderson has written numerous novels in the Star Wars, X-Files, Dune, and DC Comics universes, as well as unique steampunk fantasy novels *Clockwork Angels* and *Clockwork Lives*, written with legendary rock drummer Neil Peart, based on the concept album by the band Rush. His original works include the Saga of Seven Suns series, the Terra Incognita fantasy trilogy, and the Saga of Shadows trilogy. He has edited numerous anthologies, written comics and games, and the lyrics to two rock CDs. Anderson and his wife Rebecca Moesta are the publishers of WordFire Press.

IF YOU LIKED ...

SELECTED STORIES: FANTASY, YOU
MIGHT ALSO ENJOY BY KEVIN J.
ANDERSON:

The Gamearth Trilogy
Clockwork Angels
Clockwork Lives
Selected Stories: Science Fiction, Volume 1

Printed in Great Britain
by Amazon